TOUCHED BY
FIRE

Catherine Spangler

BERKLEY SENSATION, NEW YORK

THE BERKLEY PUBLISHING GROUP
Published by the Penguin Group
Penguin Group (USA) Inc.
375 Hudson Street, New York, New York 10014, USA

Penguin Group (Canada), 90 Eglinton Avenue East, Suite 700, Toronto, Ontario M4P 2Y3, Canada
(a division of Pearson Penguin Canada Inc.)
Penguin Books Ltd., 80 Strand, London WC2R 0RL, England
Penguin Group Ireland, 25 St. Stephen's Green, Dublin 2, Ireland (a division of Penguin Books Ltd.)
Penguin Group (Australia), 250 Camberwell Road, Camberwell, Victoria 3124, Australia
(a division of Pearson Australia Group Pty. Ltd.)
Penguin Books India Pvt. Ltd., 11 Community Centre, Panchsheel Park, New Delhi—110 017, India
Penguin Group (NZ), 67 Apollo Drive, Rosedale, North Shore 0632, New Zealand
(a division of Pearson New Zealand Ltd.)
Penguin Books (South Africa) (Pty.) Ltd., 24 Sturdee Avenue, Rosebank, Johannesburg 2196,
South Africa

Penguin Books Ltd., Registered Offices: 80 Strand, London WC2R 0RL, England

This is a work of fiction. Names, characters, places, and incidents either are the product of the author's imagination or are used fictitiously, and any resemblance to actual persons, living or dead, business establishments, events, or locales is entirely coincidental. The publisher does not have any control over and does not assume any responsibility for author or third-party websites or their content.

TOUCHED BY FIRE

A Berkley Sensation Book / published by arrangement with the author

PRINTING HISTORY
Berkley Sensation mass-market edition / October 2007

Edgar Cayce Readings © 1971, 1993–2006 by the Edgar Cayce Foundation. Quoted by permission. All rights reserved.

ISBN: 978-0-425-21795-5

BERKLEY® SENSATION
Berkley Sensation Books are published by The Berkley Publishing Group,
a division of Penguin Group (USA) Inc.,
375 Hudson Street, New York, New York 10014.
BERKLEY SENSATION and the "B" design are trademarks belonging to Penguin Group (USA) Inc.

PRINTED IN THE UNITED STATES OF AMERICA

10 9 8 7 6 5 4 3 2 1

In memory of my mother-in-law,
Bonnie Spangler.
She enjoyed my stories,
and she loved her family
and had a heart as big as Texas.
We love you, Mom, and we miss you.

Acknowledgments

Writing may be a solitary endeavor, but the creation of a book for publication requires the efforts of many people. As always, I had to turn to others for accurate, expert information, as well as feedback and encouragement. I couldn't possibly have pulled off the creation of *Touched by Fire* without the help of these people who gave so generously of their time:

Sergeant Frank McElligott, who always directs me to the people I need.

Officer Mike Letzelter, for his general and technical information on bombs (without giving me *too* much information!).

My friend Henry, for his military knowledge and expertise.

The staff of the Houston Police Department public information office, who made sure I got the details right.

Janet Underwood, for her medical expertise.

Angelica Blocker, Robyn Delozier, Beth Gonzales, and Carole Turner for reading and kibitzing and keeping me sane (sort of).

James, Deborah, Jim, Linda, and Jennifer, for their ongoing support and love.

Roberta Brown, for being . . . Roberta.

Cindy Hwang, editor extraordinaire, and Leis Pederson, editorial assistant extraordinaire. You two are the best!

Thank you all. Walk in Light.

Glossary of Terms

Atlantis—A mystical, magical culture that some believe actually existed in the North Atlantic Ocean, bordering parts of what is now the eastern U.S. coast. It is also believed that Atlantis had an extremely advanced culture, and destroyed itself through civil war and the misuse of its great Tuaoi stone.

Belial—The cunning, evil leader of a rebel Atlantian faction, Belial advocated human slavery, human sacrifices, and the dark side of magic. His group gained control of the Tuaoi stone and orchestrated the destruction of Atlantis.

Belian—A follower of Belial (also known as the Sons of Belial). Adhering to their leader's original dark practices, Belians are now reincarnating in human form on Earth, and wreaking violence and havoc on its inhabitants. They thrive on chaos and terror and blood offerings to Belial. Although they occupy mortal bodies, they have superhuman abilities. They operate from the four lower spiritual chakras, and can shield their presence from Sentinels.

Belian Crime Scene (BCS)—The scene of a Belian crime. A Sentinel investigates the scene, absorbing the psychic energies left behind by the Belian, in order to track it down.

Belian Expulsion (BE)—A forced exile of a Belian soul to Saturn for spiritual rehabilitation. It requires the joint efforts of a Sentinel and the High Sanctioned.

Chakras—The seven spiritual centers of the human body, starting in the lower abdomen and moving upward. Each corresponds to a physical part of the body, and also to a specific color. The first four are the lower chakras and are grounded to the Earth. The last three are the higher chakras and are linked to the Creator and the spiritual realm.

Conduction—The process in which a Sentinel and a conductor link spiritually through the seven chakras; most specifically, the sixth chakra and third eye. This amplifies the psychic energy the Sentinel has absorbed from a Belian crime scene and helps to identify the Belian. The process also raises powerful sexual energies and has a physical component—sexual intercourse—which further enhances the psychic energies. Often several conductions are required before the Belian's shields are breached.

Conductor—A regular human who is psychically wired to link with some Sentinels, and to magnify and enhance the Sentinel's psychic tracking abilities. Conductors are relatively rare, and a good conductor/Sentinel match is even rarer. A matched conductor is always the opposite sex of the Sentinel, and there's a powerful sexual attraction between them.

Crystal Pendant—A pink quartz crystal edged in silver, it's worn by many Sentinels. Attuned to the great Tuaoi stone, and to the Sentinel's personal energy, it helps to focus and magnify psychic energies, and helps with shielding.

High Sanctioned—Those entities (souls) that were the high priests of the temple of The One on Atlantis. Generally, they don't occupy physical bodies, but act more as spirit guides for Sentinels. They assist with Belian expulsions.

Initiate—A fledgling, a young Sentinel who is still learning how to shield energies and use the Sentinel powers.

Law of One—The spiritual law and belief followed by most Atlantians, it acknowledged a higher Supreme Being and placed the focus on the Light and positive energies.

Psychic Signature (PS)—The energy patterns left behind by a Belian, more pronounced if a violent crime has occurred. A Sentinel collects and absorbs these energies, and pieces together clues and mental pictures to help identify the Belian.

Sanctioned—Spiritually advanced Atlantian entities who served the high priests in the temple of The One. They occupy human bodies and are the overseers and the decision makers in the day-to-day Sentinel operations on Earth.

Saturn (Burning/Experience)—Saturn, the "grim reaper," rules the moral and karmic lessons souls must experience and overcome. Also called the "karmic initiator," Saturn is where Belian souls are sent until they learn their spiritual lessons. It is not a pleasant experience— more like purgatory.

Sentinel—An Atlantian soul reincarnating into a human body to track down Belians and dispense karmic justice. Like Belians, Sentinels are mortal, but possess superhuman powers. They operate out of the three higher chakras, making it difficult for Belians to sense their presence. They often use conductors to help them identify Belians.

Sexual Surge—The raw, powerful surge of sexual energy that occurs at the beginning of a conduction, when the lower chakras open and pull in Earth-based energies— which most resemble the vibratory levels of Belians. This surge helps the Sentinel get a better fix on the Belian.

Shielding—Using psychic energies to create a spiritual shield that blocks the presence of either a Sentinel or a Belian.

The One—The Atlantian term for God/Supreme Being.

Third Eye—A spiritual center which is linked to the sixth chakra and the pineal gland, and represented by the color indigo, the third eye enhances "seeing" and "hearing" on an ethereal level. A Sentinel, often with the aid of a conductor, works through the third eye to track Belians.

Tuaoi Stone (The Great Crystal)—A huge spear of solid, multifaceted quartz crystal, the Tuaoi stone was housed in a special temple on Atlantis. It provided all power, as well as a means of communicating with The One, and was ultimately used to destroy Atlantis. It now lies at the bottom of the Atlantic Ocean, its power undiminished.

White Brotherhood—(Does not refer to race or gender.) This was the Atlantian priesthood established for the perpetuation of the Law of One. They had the ability to transport themselves in thought or body wherever desired. Many of them have incarnated as Sentinels, the Sanctioned, and the High Sanctioned.

PRELUDE, BOOK 2

Atlantis, 10,014 B.C.E.
Final chronicle of the High Priest Menax

THE end is near. Even as I write, violent tremors shake my chamber. Very soon, Atlantis will be no more. Our beautiful cities—Amaki, Achaei, Poseidia—all will be lost. Already, the Temple of the Sun, and with it, the great Tuaoi stone, have plunged into the depths of the sea.

Nothing can halt this destruction set in motion by the Sons of Belial. The Belians display no remorse for their sins, no repentance for their misuse of the Tuaoi stone, which has caused this great catastrophe. Even now they refuse to turn from their evil ways and their blood sacrifices, and continue to worship their gods of darkness, forsaking The One.

I have foreseen that these souls will one day return to Earth, given another chance at redemption, but I fear they will not veer from the dark path. There is hope, however. The souls of the Children of One will also return as Sentinels of the Earth, the balance of Light against darkness. The eternal battle of good versus evil will resume.

May the Light prevail.

Corpus Christi, Texas, Current Day
From the private journal of Sanctioned Adam Masters

There was another Belian incident today, and twenty-three innocent lives—all of them but one were children—were lost from Earth. The implement of destruction was a bomb; my meditative vision showed it was a sophisticated device.

The Belians reincarnating on Earth are coming in stronger, smarter, and more malevolent than even those during the prohibition of the last century and World War II. They're playing larger roles in the darkness rising from the Middle East, in the increasing violence in our cities.

They're also coming in at a faster rate. Perhaps it's because the technology now rivals what they knew on Atlantis; or perhaps it's the prejudice and hatred escalating in every society, or the waning faith of all religions, that's drawing them. Whatever it is, Earth is in crisis.

The Sentinels are not coming in as rapidly. Our numbers are dwindling, as some are killed, and others lead a life of solitude, choosing not to take mates and have families. The battle against the Belians has become more arduous and more dangerous. Yet the Light is bright, the Sentinel souls pure and dedicated.

My visions have shown changes coming, many in my region. More conductors will be discovered and will provide aid for the tracking. More Sentinels will take mates, Damien Morgan being the most recent. I've also seen new Sentinel souls awaiting a channel to be born into the Earth. There is hope.

I don't know the specific details; I've only been shown the Universe facilitating the energies to create the potential reality. I can only wait for further guidance.

Every meditation, I visualize the Earth being touched by the fire of divine love. I believe that one day, all will walk in Light.

Those who worship Belial will not win.

The Sentinels will prevail.

ONE

For ever, day by day, is there a choice to be made by each soul. One may lead to happiness, joy; the other to confusion, to disturbing forces, to evil . . .

(Edgar Cayce Reading 1538-1)

SEX. Desire, fueled by lust and pheromones. They coiled through the atmosphere of the Red Lion Pub, edged by forced gaiety, quiet desperation, drunkenness, and cigarette smoke. It was relatively early in the evening—six o'clock—but happy hour was in full swing, and the bar was packed with business professionals eager to celebrate the arrival of Friday night.

Some simply wanted to unwind from the week; some—the extroverts—to recharge their psyches. But many, like Marla's friend Rebecca, wanted to roll the dice on the possibility of finding someone to scratch a sensual itch, to stave off the loneliness, and maybe extend that companionship through the weekend, or even longer.

Marla was: D) *None of the above*, but she was also Rebecca's ride home, and had been unable to refuse her request for a happy hour stop. Rebecca was lonely and searching for a masculine fix, and it wasn't Marla's place to point out that no one could make you happy; that particular commodity had to come from within.

Like Marla was the poster girl for good mental health.

She had her own personal demons, but at least she understood the source and was working on it. She should be able to pick up men in bars in, say . . . ten years or so.

With a sigh, she surveyed the smoky room. She wasn't surprised that Rebecca, a Brit, had chosen a pub for her trolling. The Red Lion had beautiful, classy décor—dark wood and red leather upholstery on booths and bar stools, and even a fireplace. The television discreetly placed in one corner was turned off, thank God.

If Marla saw one more news report on the tragic school bus explosion and ensuing fire that had taken the lives of twenty-two children, she was going to be sick. She'd already grieved her heart out for those children and their families. A good reason, in her opinion, why it was a bad idea to watch the news—too damned depressing. In lieu of television, there was background music playing in the pub, but it was low enough that it didn't hinder conversation.

Rebecca was already across the crowded room, sliding into a booth with three guys, plying them with her British charm and knockout body. Resigned to the fact that it might be awhile, Marla made her way to the bar. No one gave her a second glance, which wasn't surprising. She knew she was dowdy, slightly plump, with unruly hair and eyeglasses—although they were Vera Wang designer frames—and in her conservative cocoa-hued suit. Like the rest of the country, Houston business dress leaned toward a more casual look, but Marla had had a meeting with her company's CFO earlier in the day, and had wanted to look professional.

She hitched herself onto a bar stool at the very end, sliding her purse into her lap. A burst of energy, like electricity, shot through her, and she jerked her hand from the counter. Strange . . . must have been static electricity, but the surface appeared to be laminated wood. And the electricity was still tingling through her. Baffled, she looked at the man to her left, just as he glanced at her.

He gave a brief, polite nod, looked away, then stiffened and snapped back around. His eyes widened, fixed on her face. He appeared to be studying her. "Well," he said in a deep, rich voice. "Hello."

She twisted to look behind her and see who he was talking to in such a sensual come-on tone. No one was there. She turned back around, saw he was still staring at her. "Are you talking to *me*?"

He arched dark blond brows. "To the best of my knowledge." He extended his hand. "I'm Luke Paxton." It could have been just a friendly introduction, but the intense, predatory look in his deep-sea eyes warned her otherwise.

Disbelief and confusion rolled through her. This striking male specimen couldn't possibly be coming on to *her*. He had a strong, interesting face with sensual lips that practically moaned *I'm a great kisser*, those incredible eyes, and thick sun-streaked hair that swept back past his shoulders—very broad shoulders attached to a large, well-muscled body. He wore a black long-sleeved pullover, jeans, and boots; a black leather jacket was slung over the back of his chair. Everything about him screamed *sexy*—and *dangerous*. No way was he interested in her. She was obviously delusional.

"Uh . . ." Ingrained southern manners insisted she respond civilly. She placed her hand in his. "I'm Marla Rey—" She didn't get any further, because another jolt of electricity shot up her arm. She instinctively jerked back, but he wrapped his long fingers around her hand.

"Oh. Sorry I shocked you." She stared at her trapped hand, wondering how to retrieve it gracefully. Unfortunately, her skills at verbally sparring with sophisticated, gorgeous men were abysmal. "I seem to have a buildup of static electricity."

A smile teased his sensuous mouth. "I like being shocked. Especially by an attractive woman."

Now she *knew* he was giving her a line. Great. Why not pick on any number of females in the Red Lion—women who were not only willing, but *really* were attractive?

She wormed her hand free. "That's very nice of you to say, Mr. Paxton, but—"

"Luke. Mr. Paxton sounds old and decrepit, and hopefully, I'm not over the hill yet."

Oh, man, he was anything but. Suddenly warm, Marla wished someone would turn up the air-conditioning a few notches. There were too many bodies in here. And way too many pheromones, because her own body was tingling with energy, and there was an ache between her legs.

For the past eleven years, she'd been unusually sensitive to the emotions of people around her. Apparently the combined barrage of the guys with wet-dream mentalities and the women with desperate sexual appetites was strongly affecting her tonight. She wasn't sure she could handle much more of it.

"Luke," she conceded, grasping her purse. "Very nice talking to you, but I've got to go."

"Meeting someone?"

"Not exactly, but—"

"Stay. Have a drink with me." When she just sat there, too surprised to react, he added, "Please."

His steady gaze was as alluring as his dark magic voice. Disconcerted, she felt as if she were falling into those Caribbean eyes. "Well, I don't know."

"Just one drink. You sat at the bar, and you're not meeting anyone, so I have to assume you were planning to have . . . something."

The way he said *something* sent the words, *hot sex, tangled sheets*, ricocheting through her mind. *Whoa! Down, girl.* What was the matter with her? She hadn't been interested in men since . . . that night. She shoved back the memories before they could surface and ruin the evening, and possibly the weekend. Obviously, it was time to get new batteries for her trusty bedside companion.

"What do you want?" he asked.

That was a loaded question. She struggled to force her thoughts back to something—anything—away from disturbing memories. "What do I want?" she parroted, still trying to get her brain back in gear.

Humor and sensual knowledge gleamed in his eyes. "To drink. What do you want to drink?"

"Oh, I—" *Am an idiot.* She realized the bartender was standing there expectantly, a knowing smirk on her twenty-something face. "A glass of merlot, please," she told the young woman.

Luke tapped his mug. "Another beer."

The woman nodded and left. Marla drew a deep breath, still feeling the strange energy in the air, despite her attempts to ignore it. "Well," she said lamely.

"You didn't finish telling me your name," he prompted.

"I didn't, did I?" She managed a shaky smile. "Maybe we should try this without the handshake. I think one shock is enough, don't you?"

"I don't know." He rested one arm indolently on the bar, turning his body toward her. His full, charismatic attention was focused on her. "Some shocks are very . . . stimulating."

This guy was definitely out of her league. Where the hell was Rebecca? Marla cast a quick glance to the corner, and saw Rebecca practically wrapped around the man next to her, laughing at something he was saying. Maybe she'd decide to go home with him, and then Marla could leave. The sooner, the better.

Luke's gaze followed hers to the corner booth. "Someone you know?"

"The blonde in the red. Her car's in the shop—again—and she's riding with me."

"So you're only here because of her." He said it as a statement rather than a question.

"Well . . . yes."

"Then her mechanical misfortune is my gain." He was giving her that look again—pure, masculine appreciation.

She didn't understand it. But then his gaze swept down her legs. Her awkward position on the stool had forced her skirt to ride up, and a generous expanse of thigh was exposed. Ah. He was a leg man, which might explain some of the attraction. Her legs were her best physical feature.

All the Reynolds women had great legs, which was a good thing, since they tended to be plain and brainy otherwise. Plus Marla had on her bronze Prada pumps, which she'd gotten in a great closeout deal because they were from last season. They extended the leg line nicely.

With apparent reluctance, Luke returned his gaze to her face. "Nice shoes."

Yeah, right. "Thank you."

The bartender returned with their drinks, and she fumbled in her purse for money to pay for her wine.

"I've got it." Luke handed the young woman a credit card and she whisked it away.

"Thank you again." Bemused, Marla picked up her wine and took a healthy sip. She wished this damned energy buzzing around and setting her nerves on edge would ease off. If this was the usual ethereal pattern at the Red Lion Pub, she wasn't coming back, no matter how much Rebecca tried to strong arm her into it.

"So back to your name," Luke said.

"Oh, I guess I never got to that."

"No, you didn't."

"I'm Marla Reynolds." She felt foolish, as if she were introducing herself at a self-help conference.

"Pleased to meet you, Marla Reynolds." His hand slid over to cover hers, sending another jolt through her.

"What is it with this place?" she muttered. "They need to invest in some serious antistatic measures."

He murmured something, but she barely heard him. Her attention was on the acute awareness of the fact he was touching her, and the incredible warmth of his hand over hers. Not to mention the sexual energy that swirled between them, causing her nipples to pucker and the ensuing dampness between her legs. Pure, raw chemistry. She'd heard of it happening, but had never experienced it. This guy was potent, especially since he appeared capable of stirring to life her sexual desires, which up until now, had been nonexistent around men.

She gently extricated her hand, pretended she needed it

to straighten her napkin beneath her wineglass. "What do you do for a living, Luke?"

Those blue eyes watched her with an intensity that was both flattering and unnerving. "I'm a private investigator. How about you?"

That explained the aura of power and danger he exuded. She'd be willing to bet he was ex-military or ex-police. "Nothing even remotely exciting. I'm the head accountant for a large manufacturing firm. Very ordinary."

He actually looked interested. "What does your company manufacture?"

"Building tools and equipment. Hydraulic shearing machines for metal roofing and siding, power saws, that sort of thing."

"Accounting, huh?" He smiled, and she felt the force of his charm all the way down to her toes.

She willed her racing heart to slow. "Guilty."

"I like smart women. Especially when they're also pretty."

She resisted the urge to look over her shoulder again. Maybe he just needed eyeglasses. Or maybe he was desperate, but she simply couldn't imagine a man who looked like he did having difficulty getting any woman he wanted. She took another sip of wine. "How do you like being a private investigator?"

He shrugged, turning toward the bar to drink his beer. Muscles rippled beneath his shirt, and she inwardly sighed. He was definitely built. "I like the independence and flexibility, being able to pick and choose my jobs, set my own hours. But man, I see some nasty stuff. People can be so . . ." He paused, shook his head.

"Inhuman?" she supplied. A chill went through her, as the nightmare memories that were rarely far away finally succeeded in sliding into her mind.

She must have shivered outwardly, because he leaned close, putting his arm around her. "Hey, you okay?"

His scent drifted to her, woodsy, like sandalwood, and clean, primal male. Another jolt of electricity went through her. His hand rested lightly over the nape of her neck, a possessive gesture dating back to prehistoric man. She couldn't find the strength to protest. Her senses seemed heightened, excruciatingly aware of this man on a visceral level; every look, every touch, every nuance.

"You okay?" he repeated, concern in his voice.

She gave herself a mental shake, managed a smile. "Oh, I'm fine," she lied. "I just drank my wine too fast. I'm a lightweight when it comes to alcohol. A really cheap date." *What on earth had possessed her to say that?*

He laughed, the sound low and sexy. "Really? In that case, how about having dinner with me tomorrow night?" He massaged her neck gently, persuasively, and tingling sparks jumped down her spine.

This whole thing was surreal, and his touch, not to mention the uncomfortable energy throbbing through the pub, was making it hard for her to think straight. Even so, she was certain there could be no legitimate reason for this Chippendales candidate to be interested in *her*. It just didn't make any sense. Unless, of course, he was one of those men who thrived on challenge, and was able to ferret out the women who just weren't interested. How insulting that would be.

Regardless of his motives, Marla didn't date *anyone*, gorgeous stud or otherwise. She hitched her shoulder, trying to shrug his arm away without being rude. "Thank you, but no."

He took the hint and dropped his arm, but his gaze remained locked with hers. "Why not?" He sounded disappointed, which was very strange.

Even stranger, she felt a . . . link, almost, with him. She told herself it was just the stunning chemistry between them—and she wasn't biting. "I'm sorry," she said with real regret. "But I don't know you."

"I don't know you either. I'd like to learn more about you. What harm could there be in us having dinner together?"

He certainly was persistent. She drew a deep breath, decided to be blunt. "You're not my type."

His brows rose again. "And what is your type?"

No man was her type. None, nada. Damn. If she had more experience, maybe she could better deal with this. But she'd never had to deflect regular men, much less one with the looks and stature of an Adonis. "I don't make it a habit of picking up men in bars," she said. "Nor do I go out with strangers."

"I'm glad to hear it." He leaned toward her, his hand trapping hers again. More energy buzzed through her. This pub had a serious static problem.

"So we're basically strangers," he said. "And you're cautious about going anywhere with a man you don't know. That's understandable, and smart. But if we let it go at that, we won't get a chance to learn more about each other. Let's do this: Let's meet somewhere tomorrow night—any restaurant you want. You don't have to give me your phone number or address. We'll just meet, have dinner, and see where it goes from there."

His touch had her distracted again. His thumb stroking over her skin was sending little waves of sensation up her arm. Yet at the same time, she was starting to feel comfortable, very relaxed, almost light-headed, as if she'd had several drinks. "Well . . ."

"Where do you want to meet?" His voice was low, hypnotic.

Wow. That wine must have been extra strong. She was actually considering having dinner with this guy. *What harm could it do?* she asked herself. Maybe this was a good sign. Maybe she was finally ready to put what had happened to Julia behind her, to let go of the terror and the guilt. God only knew she had normal biological urges, which for some reason, hadn't yet fizzled out with Luke, as they had with others.

"Just name the place and time," he said in that deep bedroom voice.

Her body tightened, and she felt a renewed rush of dampness between her legs. *Maybe it is time.* Surely it couldn't hurt to meet him in a public place, to do a little socializing. She was so damn tired of being wounded. Here was a chance to test the waters. Although why he wanted to have dinner with her remained utterly mystifying. Still, she found the opportunity intriguing, even . . . exciting.

"Marla." His voice rolled over her in a warm rush. "Say yes."

"I—oh . . . yes." She let out her breath, felt as if she'd just reached the top of Mt. Everest.

He smiled again, and she almost melted then and there. "That's great. Where do you want to meet?

"Um, what do you like to eat?"

His eyes gleamed. "Oh, I eat *everything*."

Code red, code red, there's a fire here. Marla resisted the urge to fan herself, instead focused on a restaurant choice. "Do you like Italian?"

"One of my favorites."

"How about Damian's Cucina Italiana? It's on Smith Street, not too far from here. They have wonderful food."

"Damian's. Smith Street." He turned, extracted a heavy gold pen from his inside jacket pocket, and wrote the information on a cocktail napkin. His writing was bold and sure, like him. "I'll find it. What time?"

Tomorrow was Saturday, and they'd have a long wait if they got there too late. "How about seven?"

"Great." He wrote that down. "Do they take reservations?"

"I think so."

"Then I'll reserve us the best table available. How does that sound?"

Terrifying. Exhilarating. Stomach twisting. *Go for it*, she told herself. *It's time to get on with your life.* She knew Julia would approve. "Sounds good." She looked up as Rebecca strode toward them, managing to look both elegant and efficient at the same time.

"There you are." Rebecca's gaze was as sharp as her British accent was crisp. She took in Luke, couldn't possibly miss how he was turned toward Marla, or his body language proclaiming—amazingly—his interest. "Hello." She extended a perfectly manicured hand. "I'm Rebecca Smithson. I work with Marla. And you are?"

"Luke Paxton." He shook her hand.

"Watch out for static," Marla muttered.

Rebecca shifted her blue eyed stare to Marla. "What?"

"Didn't you feel anything?" At Rebecca's confused look, Marla said, "Never mind."

"Right, then. Stephen over there has offered to take me to my flat, so I'm heading out with him. Thanks for the transport today."

Relieved that she could also go home, Marla said, "Will you have your car in time for your trip next week?"

Rebecca had resumed staring at Luke; with apparent reluctance, she turned her attention Marla. "Don't know yet. I'll ring the garage tomorrow and see if my roadster is ready. And I'd like to pay you for petrol."

"We can settle up later." Marla slid off the bar stool. "Good night, Luke."

His gaze locked with hers, intense, hot. "Don't forget. Tomorrow at seven."

As if he was remotely forgettable. She managed a smile. "I won't. Thanks for the drink." She walked away, acutely aware of him watching her.

Rebecca followed. "You're actually going out with him?"

Marla paused just inside the entry. The strange energy wasn't present here, and her head felt clearer. A twinge of doubt snaked through her. "I was planning on it. Why? Did you sense anything wrong with him?"

"Oh, no. He's bloody gorgeous. Probably incredible when he's starkers." Rebecca sneaked another peek his way. "Makes me wonder if I even want to bother with Stephen. Poor comparison, and all that."

More doubt crowded in. "I'm wondering now if I should do it," Marla murmured.

"Oh, don't be barmy. I haven't seen you with a single bloke the whole time I've known you, and that's—" Rebecca considered a moment. "Over three years. I was beginning to wonder if you might be a homosexual—mind, not that you acted like one."

Marla suspected many people thought something was wrong with her, and they were right, since post-traumatic stress disorder was a definite problem. But it was something she didn't want to share. "I just haven't found the right man," she hedged.

"You'd be barking mad not to go for *him*."

"I guess." But away from the strange electrical charges and the sexual energy inundating the pub, Marla had more clarity; common sense told her this might not be a good idea.

Rebecca glanced toward the corner booth. "Oh, Stephen is signaling. Listen, I want to hear all about this hot date. I don't leave for Mexico until Monday—assuming my roadster is ready—so we'll chat before then. Cheerio." She was gone with a flash of red and a whiff of the Burberry perfume she favored.

And Marla was left with growing doubts. Digging out her keys, she stepped into the night air. It was early April and already warm, which, along with the ever-present humidity, was normal for Houston. Looking around, Marla walked quickly to her car, beeping it unlocked as she approached. Since that night, she'd taken self-defense classes, learned all she could about staying safe—even if it was belated.

She was about to slide into her car, lock the doors, and drive away without delay, when a movement caught her attention. She looked over to see Luke striding through the parking lot. He had on the black leather coat, which made him look even more dangerous. He glanced her way and she took an involuntary step backward, but he didn't appear to see her.

He strode on to a huge black and chrome motorcycle—a Harley, if she wasn't mistaken. She watched as he straddled the large bike with surprising grace. The motor started with a deep, smooth rumble, and he wheeled the bike out of the parking lot and down the street, accelerating rapidly.

Marla stood there, her heart pounding, until the sound of the motorcycle faded away. *Are you crazy?* she asked herself.

What the hell was she doing, agreeing to go out with a man who was drop-dead handsome, unbelievably sexy, and wore black leather and rode a Harley? He was definitely not the ideal "starter" date for a woman who'd avoided all nonplatonic encounters with men since she was nineteen.

She was playing with fire—the gasoline and blowtorch kind of inferno—with this one. And she knew then—knew with absolute certainty and considerable disappointment— that she wouldn't be meeting this man at the restaurant tomorrow night.

Her instinct for survival was too great for her to take such a high-stakes risk with a guy like Luke Paxton.

TWO

"SHE had absolutely no idea what I am. She thought the energy reaction was static electricity." Luke leaned back in his chair and drummed his fingers restlessly on the cheap Formica table. "So it's probably safe to say she doesn't realize what she is, either."

"You know that's not uncommon," Adam Masters responded in his gravelly voice. "Conductors can be born into any family. There are no cultural, racial, or socioeconomic barriers. And no instruction manual explaining their purpose on Earth. When the time is right, they are guided where they need to be."

Luke had never much concerned himself with the process of locating conductors. He left that up to the Sanctioned. His job was to track unimaginable evil and administer karmic justice. But he had to admit Marla's crossing his path could only be divine intervention. "No doubt she was guided to me."

"Is she a good match? Responsive to your energy?"

Oh, yeah. Luke thought about how Marla's breasts had tightened beneath her silk blouse; of the sweet scent of arousal she'd exuded. "She responded to me, all right. She just had no idea why. It's a very precise match—maybe the best I've ever experienced."

"Excellent." Adam released a raspy breath. "We'll have to educate her, give her time to adjust and accept."

"There's not much time for niceties. This Belian just blew up a bus full of *children*, damn it." Luke gritted his teeth against the surge of pure fury. "May its black soul burn on Saturn for eternity."

"Those children's souls have departed the Earth plane," Adam said with the unwavering calmness of a Sanctioned. "You can't bring them back. A matched conductor is a rare find, and Ms. Reynolds must be treated with great care, until she fully understands and gives her consent to work with you. Do you think she'll be receptive to your overtures?"

Luke thought about how reluctant Marla had been to go out with him. "Maybe not at first. She was pretty skittish."

"Then you will have to handle her very carefully. I again remind you that she must willingly agree." Steel edged Adam's quiet voice.

As always, it came down to the Sentinel bottom line, to which Luke was honor bound. Yet sometimes those lines had to be blurred; there were ways to accelerate reaching a goal. "You know I've never forced a conductor's cooperation, Adam. I can convince the lady to help me."

"I'm sure you'll be your usual persuasive and captivating self," Adam said dryly.

Luke had no trouble charming women. Even when he was trying to keep a low profile, he had plenty of ladies willing to scratch any itch he might have. He wasn't in the habit of notching bedposts when he was between Belian trackings, but he wasn't celibate, either. He had a healthy libido that didn't require conductor inducement to kick into high gear.

He could handle Marla Reynolds. "I'll take good care of her," he told Adam.

"See that you do. And keep me updated on every development."

"You know I will."

"Walk in Light." Adam disconnected.

Luke snapped his cell phone shut, tossed it onto the table. He studied the information on his laptop screen. Thanks to modern technology and portable satellite service, he had access to the Internet, even in this rural area. And thanks to the skills he'd cultivated as a private investigator, he knew how to find all kinds of information.

While it was true most women responded readily to him, Marla had not fit that mold. She had been wary and reluctant, despite his best efforts to charm her, and despite the sizzling Sentinel/conductor chemistry between them. It had taken mild mental inducement for her to capitulate on having dinner with him, and his intuition told him she wasn't a sure thing.

Fortunately he had her name and her license tag number. When he left the Red Lion Pub, he'd spotted her getting into her car and had memorized the tag with a quick glance. She probably didn't even realize he'd seen her.

So now, he had her home address. If she decided to brush him off, he knew where to find her. If he couldn't woo her over dinner, couldn't convince her to help him via conventional ways, then he would have to resort to his alternate plan.

He hoped it wouldn't come down to that.

"I'M tired of Tom Cruise movies," Ashley said. "They're all the same—action and adventure with no real human interaction. But I'd really like to see the new Johnny Depp movie that hit the theaters last weekend."

Marla sat on the couch, sipping wine and trying to focus on the conversation. She was at the home of her good friends, Ashley and Scott Anderson, and they were discussing whether or not to go out to a movie or watch a DVD there at the house.

"Not Johnny Depp." Scott made a dismissive gesture. "He's an offbeat character actor, and you just like him because he's supposedly so sexy."

"He *is* hot," Ashley shot back. "But he's a good actor, too."

They bantered on, but Marla hardly heard the discussion, because she couldn't stop thinking about Luke Paxton. She knew she'd done the right thing when she'd called the restaurant and left a polite *sorry but I can't meet you tonight* message for him—even though she felt awful about it.

So when Ashley called to see if she had plans for the evening, Marla jumped at the chance to spend some time with her friends and put Luke behind her. Since she'd decided to indulge in a few drinks—or maybe a lot, given her current state of mind—Scott had offered to pick her up and drive her home later.

Forgetting about Luke wasn't working very well. She told herself again that canceling the date had been the right thing. It wasn't cowardly, it was smart. He was way out of her league, and she was too damaged to deal with a man like him—maybe *any* man, for that matter. She knew all that on an intellectual level, and yet emotionally, there was a gnawing sense of loss, like she'd given up something very special.

Partly because she knew the odds of a man like him ever again showing interest in her were pretty much nil. And because, for a few moments, she'd actually had a surge of feminine interest in a man. Oh, who was she kidding? She'd felt pure, raw lust; experienced the primal urge to get down and dirty between the sheets.

Even more amazing, she'd felt almost *normal*, as if that terrible night had never happened.

"Agreed," Ashley said. "Marla, is that all right with you?"

She dragged her thoughts back to the here and now. "What?"

"The movie. Is that one okay with you?"

She shrugged, feeling foolish. "I'm sorry. I wasn't paying attention. What did you decide?"

Ashley shook her head. "You goof. Scott and I compromised, and agreed on the last *Pirates of the Caribbean* movie. It has enough action and adventure that maybe he won't whine too much, and you and I can drool over Johnny. It just came out on DVD, and I bought it yesterday. Okay with you if we hang out here tonight?"

"Sure. Go ahead and start it. I'll be right back." Marla went to the kitchen and refilled her wine while Scott got the DVD going. Feeling the need for emotional numbness, she took a few gulps and added more wine to the glass.

Returning to the family room, she sat back and tried to focus on the movie. But every time she looked at Depp's enigmatic brown eyes, instead she saw mesmerizing, sea blue eyes. Kept remembering the stunning chemistry that had sizzled between her and Luke.

A strange, restless energy clawed through her, and her body hummed to life in response. Something was very wrong. And it was triggering memories from that night. Maybe she needed some sessions with Dr. Jackson— although she hadn't seen the psychologist in over three years. If not therapy, then what? She'd struggled for years to overcome the memories of the trauma and get on with her life. Yet one chance meeting with a handsome stranger had sent her into a tailspin.

What the hell is happening to me?

MARLA Reynolds lived in an older suburb on the southeast side of Houston. The homes were circa 1960s, small, but well kept. Luke knew a fair number of astronauts lived in the area, which was fairly close to the NASA Johnson Space Center.

Marla's house was a neat, beige brick structure with a small front porch that was well lit by a brass light fixture. A sign in the flower bed warned the home was protected by a security company. Luke parked a little way up the street, swung off the bike, and walked up the sidewalk.

The porch light illuminated a solid wood door with a small fan of glass at the top and large terra-cotta pots of azaleas. The woven doormat had a cheerful ivy border and the word Welcome in large block letters. The porch was neat and orderly, just as he suspected Marla was.

He rang the doorbell, heard frantic, high-pitched barking on the other side of the door. But he didn't hear any other sounds, or sense human movement. He rang again and got another frenzied round of barking. He knocked. Nothing. He'd not only been stood up—a first for him—but apparently she'd gone elsewhere for the evening. Either that or she simply wasn't coming to the door.

"Trying to avoid me, Marla?" he murmured. "Or maybe you don't like the way the energy makes you feel." He knew how disconcerting the Sentinel/conductor energy link could be, especially for an uninitiated conductor. He was a seasoned Sentinel, and he couldn't always control his reactions to the physical surge.

Marla was a good case in point. Last night, her close proximity had sent a knockout punch of sexual energy through him. Hell of a deal to get a massive hard-on in a public place, with a woman you didn't even know. Fortunately for him, she'd been too disoriented by the energies to pay much attention to his lap. But he hadn't missed her strong reaction. She'd been turned on, her body responding to his, which would make what he now had to do easier.

He knocked again, and then used his mental powers to slide back the dead bolt. He opened the door, stepped inside, closing it quietly behind him. A table lamp in the living area was on, giving him a visual of the room.

"Hello!" he called out. "Marla, are you here?" He sensed she wasn't in the house, nor were there any other humans, although he was rushed by a "killer" apricot toy poodle with the aggression and bloodlust of a third-world dictator.

Damn. What was it about small dogs that made them so warlike? And that high, incessant yapping was incredibly annoying. He sent a quick flash of power; with a little whine, "Fifi" stopped barking. Tail tucked under, the fluffy peach-colored mass masquerading as a real dog circled warily behind Luke, with intermittent, low growls.

"Keep that up, and I'll knock you out completely," he told the fur ball. It scuttled beneath the sofa, where it regarded him with hate-filled eyes. No love lost there. Wondering why a seemingly down-to-earth woman like Marla would have such a froufrou pet, Luke tracked the warning beep down the hallway, found a state of the art alarm system in a small closet and disarmed it.

He returned to the front room and looked around. It was comfortable and homey. The contemporary beige sofa, with brightly colored pillows on top and psycho dog beneath, took up one wall. Two matching upholstered armchairs, done in a deep green, with a dark oak table between them, were situated away from the wall, closing in the area and making it cozier. An oak entertainment cabinet held a modest television and stereo equipment. The pale carpeting was lush and immaculate.

Closing his eyes, Luke inhaled deeply, sent his senses flaring out. It felt good here, serene and welcoming. He wondered if this was Marla's haven from the world, again wondered why she'd been so nervous around him.

Sudden barking and a sharp tug at his leg jolted him from his reverie. He looked down to see psycho dog clamped on his leg, jerking at the chaps he wore over his slacks. Fortunately the leather was thick and durable; a must for driving a motorcycle on the frenetic Houston freeways, and the dog's teeth weren't even penetrating.

"That's it," he said, pointing at Fifi. "Don't say I didn't warn you. You're out of here." He directed a power flow and the dog slumped, unconscious, its mouth still gripping Luke's ankle. Shaking his head, he bent down and gently pried the jaws open before moving away. It should be out for about an hour.

He did a quick sweep of the house, confirming no one was there. Then he went to the kitchen and through to the door leading into the garage. There was a car parked inside, a sporty red Solara convertible, the one he'd seen last night. Sweet. Luke took a moment to admire the classy lines of the car before returning to the kitchen.

What now? Most single people didn't own more than one vehicle, so Marla had either walked somewhere or gone with someone—a date? That would be a pisser, but maybe she'd been so damned skittish around him last night because she was seeing someone. Yet Luke didn't think that was the case. There'd been something about her—a vulnerability and wariness that told him she was a loner.

Regardless, he planned to wait for her. To try to explain what he was, and convince her to help him. He didn't have time for a civilized dance of getting acquainted. But what if she didn't come home tonight? Blowing out his breath, he considered his options.

If she didn't return soon, he'd have to track her down.

HE watched the blood oozing from the self-inflicted cut on his lower arm. His arm throbbed where he'd slid the knife through skin and muscle, slowly, so slowly. Pain was good. Pain made him feel real. Alive. He liked pain.

But he liked blood even better. Liked the red color, liked the smell and the feel of it between his fingers.

Blood was life. Blood was power.

He rubbed his forehead, listened for the Voice that came to him sometimes. The Voice could be annoying as hell, ordering him to do things when he was already taking care of it. He knew what to do and how to do it. He didn't need the Voice to tell him what he already knew. Sometimes he wanted to scream at the Voice, tell it to leave him the fuck alone.

But he didn't do that, because the Voice had chosen *him*. The Voice had acknowledged *his* importance and ability. He knew the Voice wasn't God, because God didn't exist. But the Voice . . . ah, it resonated with force and with darkness and blood. It whispered that it was far more powerful than any other being in existence. That it was known as Belial.

And *he* was the only one brilliant enough, deserving enough, to do Belial's bidding.

Belial liked the blood. Belial wanted the blood. Praised *him* whenever *he* made a blood offering of sinners. Especially a really big offering . . . like an entire busload of children.

The children were tainted, just like their parents. No one

was listening to Belial, or giving him the homage he deserved. They all had to die. Belial had been very pleased that justice had been dispensed.

And because *he* was so clever and industrious, so intelligent, he would be administering many more punishments.

He drew the knife across his arm again, far too self-controlled to flinch. Ah . . . The pain . . . The blood . . .

UNLOCKING her door, Marla turned and waved to Scott. He waved back and drove off. She went inside, closing the door and using her key to relock the double-sided dead bolt. She put her keys in the top drawer of the small antique chest by the door, and turned, feeling a twinge of dizziness.

Maybe the third glass of wine had been overkill, especially since she'd used one of Ashley's largest wine goblets. She didn't drink that much very often. And damn if she still hadn't been able to focus on the movie, or put Luke Paxton out of her mind. Johnny Depp deserved better than that.

Bryony trotted slowly into the small foyer area, looking listless and tired. "What's the matter, baby?" Marla cooed, leaning down to pick up the poodle. "Were you asleep?"

Bending over was a mistake. The vertigo rush sent her staggering as she came up, tightly clutching Bryony to keep from dropping her. The dog let out a squeak.

"I'm sorry, baby. Definitely too much wine."

She started down the hallway to reset the alarm. But her peripheral vision picked up something odd. She turned back, starting violently when she saw the man sitting on her sofa.

"Hello, Marla."

She stared as he rose, noticing first how large he was, how threatening. Like that night . . .

"I've been waiting for you, Julia." The man stepped from the kitchen of their home in Kingwood.

Both Julia and Marla gasped, startled and shocked to see him there. He moved toward them, an ordinary looking man with a monster's soul. "You've been going out again,

Julia," he said in a soft voice. "Even though I told you not to. I was watching. I saw you flirting with those men. Why did you disobey me, Julia?" . . .

"Why did you stand me up, Marla?"

The deep masculine voice jerked her from the nightmare memory. Marla stared at the man coming toward her. With an adrenaline avalanche and pounding heart obliterating clarity, it took a moment to recognize him.

"You," she gasped. "What are you doing here?"

"Waiting for you."

Bryony started growling, and Marla skittered backward toward the front door. *Think, think, think!*

Luke Paxton stopped, held out his hand in a placating gesture. "I'm just here to talk."

How had he found her? Gotten into her house? Oh God, oh God, oh God! He was stalking her! Just like—

"I can't have you talking to other men, Julia. I'm going to have to teach you a lesson so it won't happen again." The man grabbed Julia. She screamed. Marla rushed forward, but he hit her in the head. She stumbled, fell . . .

The memory sent panic exploding through Marla. She whirled and jerked open the chest drawer, grabbing for the keys.

"Wait! Let me explain." A strong hand clamped down on her arm, pulled her around. "I just want to—"

She shot her knee up and out. "Whoa!" He sidestepped and swung her against the front door. He pressed against her lower body, pinning her. "No fighting dirty."

Why hadn't the alarm gone off? *Think!* She'd taken defense courses since that night. But the wine made her fuzzy, and the fear sucked the air from her lungs. "Let me go!" she screamed.

"Calm down. I'm not going to hurt you."

But she was beyond reason. She remembered far too clearly every detail of that other night eleven years ago. She struggled against Luke's hold, to no avail. Panicked, she leaned forward and bit his upper arm. It was rock solid, but she dug in hard, ripping at his shirt.

"Shit! That hurts!" He wrenched his arm away. "Stop this. *Now.*"

A sudden, soothing warmth curled through her chest, and she could breathe again. More warmth spiraled to her head. She could actually feel her heart slowing, feel the fear dissipating. She felt surreal, like this was all a dream. She heard Bryony barking frantically, but it seemed far away.

"Shut up, Fifi, or I'll knock you out again," Luke said.

Marla shook her head, trying to clear it. This was wrong. She needed to fight, defend herself, to get the hell out of here. She turned back toward the chest, but she was uncoordinated, sluggish. She was never drinking that much wine again.

"Oh, no you don't." Luke grabbed her arm, pulled her into the living room and pushed her down on the couch. "Stay there."

Only until her head cleared and she could figure out what to do. Her alarm system had apparently malfunctioned, so it appeared she was on her own. Luke went into the kitchen, but before she could push herself up, he was back with some paper towels. He sat on the other end of the couch and her heart rate kicked up.

He turned his startlingly blue gaze on her. "Just calm down. I swear I'm not going to hurt you."

Was the man a mind reader? And did he really expect her to believe him? He'd stalked her and broken into her house, for God's sake. Yet her fear was dull, distant, and she couldn't seem to react. Still hazy, she watched him fold the paper towels and press them over his arm. He lifted them a moment later, and she saw red stains. She'd nailed him. Good. She had more defense moves—if she could just think straight, and get close enough.

Luke sat back with a disgusted sound. "This is going really well." He lifted the towels again, looked at his arm. "What's with the biting? First the dog, then you."

"I'll fight you to my dying breath," Marla assured him.

"I don't think that will be necessary." He sighed, shook

his head. "Look, I'm sorry. I handled this all wrong. It's just that—" His eyes narrowed. "What are you doing?"

Marla tightened her hand around the gun in her purse. She'd just realized it was still slung over her shoulder, had subtly slipped her hand inside. "Nothing."

"Give me the purse."

"Sure." She jerked her hand out, aimed the gun at him, and flicked off the safety. "Don't move."

He didn't appear too concerned. "Do you know how to use that thing?"

"Try me." She attempted to shift toward the opposite end of the couch, but her body wouldn't move. What the—?

He slid over, grabbed her arm, and pried the gun out of it, and she couldn't do a damned thing. It was like she was frozen in place. "I'll take that as well," he said, leaning across her to slide the strap off her arm and confiscate her purse. For the life of her, she couldn't move. But she could sure feel the surge of electricity that arced between them.

This couldn't be real. But as quickly as her body had locked up, it relaxed and she was mobile again. "I'm going crazy," she muttered. "Oh, wait. Too late."

"You're not crazy, Marla." His face was inches from hers. She stared into his mesmerizing eyes before her gaze shifted helplessly to his sensual lips. He leaned closer and her body tingled in anticipation. He was going to kiss her. And she wanted him to. The man was probably about to dismember her—after raping and torturing her—and she wanted him to kiss her!

Instead, he inhaled a deep breath. "How much have you had to drink?"

"Not much," she said defensively. Then it occurred to her that maybe he'd let his guard down if he thought her faculties were impaired. "Okay, a lot."

"You don't appear drunk, but you're not completely sober, either. Ah, hell!" He sat back, ran his hand through his hair.

She watched the silky blond mane of hair fall back into place. She knew she should be afraid—no, make that terrified—yet a strange lethargy settled over her. If she didn't know better, she'd think she'd been drugged, but that wasn't possible.

He turned toward her again, and she tried to decide what defensive move she could use from this position. Assuming she could get her body to cooperate.

"Look," he said. "I know you don't understand any of this, and I know you're frightened. I mishandled this. I planned on explaining it to you, but I want you completely sober when I do. You're going to have to come with me. I need you at the house as soon as possible. I'll just have to explain things after we get there."

She stared at him. Either the alcohol was still kicking her senseless, or he was crazier than she was. "What the hell are you talking about?"

Ignoring her question, he stood and offered his hand. "Come on. I know you're shaky, but I figured that was the best way to keep you from hurting yourself—and me."

She refused to give him her hand, so he took it and pulled her up. Her legs tried to buckle, but he steadied her.

"Something's wrong with me," she said, concerned by her weakness. *"What's wrong with me?"* Her voice rose, as the panic resurged. Immediately, she felt that rush of warmth, felt herself calming.

"Easy now. You're fine." Luke turned her toward the hallway. "We're going to pack a few things for you, and then you're coming with me. I'll tell you everything after we get there."

He was kidnapping her. A new fist of fear punched through the calm. That was the worst possible scenario. In every course she'd taken, the instructors had stressed to never get in a car or go anywhere with an assailant. It was a death sentence.

Oh, God, she was going to die, and she was too weak to fight. She didn't want to die, or relive what Julia had endured. "No! I'm not going anywhere with you." She tried to jerk free. When that didn't work, she kicked his leg as hard as she could.

"Ow!" Luke hopped to one side, gave her a little shake. "*Cut it out*. Damn! Dealing with you is going to maim me for life."

"Why?" she gasped, trying to twist free. "Why are you doing this?"

"Oh man," he muttered. "This is definitely not working. I don't like doing this, but . . ."

There is was again—that odd warmth flowing through her body, and the ensuing haziness, only far more potent this time. Marla felt as if she were floating, euphoric. Her legs tried to give out, but his grip on her arms kept her upright.

"Look," he said. "I'm afraid we don't have any choice here. You have to come with me." He started her walking—stumbling—toward her bedroom again.

"Fine," she said, feeling giddy. That was some *great* wine Ashley and Scott had. She'd definitely be buying some.

"The situation is getting desperate," he continued, steering her into her bedroom.

"Sorry to hear that." Thank goodness she'd finally realized she was dreaming.

"Sit here, and I'll try to round up some stuff for you." He perched her on the edge of her bed and started away, but had to make a grab for her when she began sliding off. "Oops. Maybe I overdid the relaxing energy a little."

He lifted her fully onto the bed, propping up the pillows for her back. "Think you can maintain?"

"Sure," she said with a bright smile. "I'm controlling this—or my subconscious is."

He gave her a funny look and started opening her dresser drawers. Yep, this was an interesting dream, all right. She must be having it because Luke had made such an impression on her, and because the memories had been resurrected.

Only she refused to think about them for the rest of this dream. Much more interesting to study how well Luke's leather chaps framed his very fine butt. What was it about men and leather?

"So tell me again, what are you doing?" she asked, although she didn't really care. For her part, he could come over here and demonstrate how well he could use that sensual mouth.

"I'm packing some of your stuff, and you're coming with me to my house. Then I'll explain everything when you're a little more—" He glanced at her. "Grounded."

Whatever. She was game; a dream trip to his house sounded like some quality time with this man. She felt her hand nudged, looked down to see Bryony curled on the bed next to her, shivering. "Oh, baby, what's wrong?" She picked up the poodle, cuddled her close. "You don't like this dream?"

A thought drifted through her mind, but it took a moment to corral it. "Hey, how long are we going to be gone?"

"There's no telling." He stepped into her bathroom, started taking things. "At least several days, maybe more."

"Then we have to take Bryony with us."

He leaned out of the bathroom. "Who, or what, is Bryony?"

He butchered the name, like everyone did. "It's pronounced 'Brigh-oh-nee'." She held up the poodle, who growled low in her throat. "Bryony is this precious baby."

"Oh, no. No way is psycho dog going with us."

"She can't stay by herself for more than a day." Marla dug in, lifted her chin rebelliously. This was her dream, and by God, she would have her way. "She goes with us, or I'm staying here. You'll have to drag me out kicking and screaming if you leave her behind."

He ran his hand through his hair again, obviously a nervous—but sexy—habit. "Ah, shit," he muttered.

Marla smiled. This was really a cool dream.

THREE

THE first thing she saw when she opened her eyes was a wall that might have been white once, but was now dingy and grimy and sported a fist-sized hole in the plaster. Confused, Marla blinked against the strong sunlight streaming into the room, shifting and wincing when her head protested the movement. That's when she realized she was in a rumpled double bed with navy sheets. What the—?

She pushed upright, looking for her glasses. They were on the scarred imitation pine fiberboard nightstand by the bed, neatly closed. She grabbed them up and put them on, and looked around a room she'd never seen in her life. It was so weird, she couldn't process it. Unless she was dreaming . . . Bits and pieces of another dream drifted to her. Luke had been in it, and Bryony, and they'd taken a wild ride on a Harley motorcycle, roaring down the highway into the night.

But that had been vastly different from this—surreal and fuzzy, like most dreams. She ran her hand along the sheets, pressed it against the mattress. She didn't think she was dreaming now. This appeared too real. She didn't feel drunk or disoriented. She felt fairly normal, except or the throbbing headache. She stared around the small room, taking in the threadbare indoor/outdoor carpeting, the casement window with no curtains, and the general rundown condition.

She still couldn't process, except for the crazy thought that she'd entered *The Twilight Zone*. She tried to think, and more of last night's dream came back to her. Luke in her house, disarming her, telling her she had to go with him. . . .

"You're in a rental house in Needville."

Marla gasped and whirled toward the voice. Luke Paxton stood in the doorway. Her heart started pounding. "What are *you* doing here?"

He stepped inside the room, looking large and dangerous in jeans and a plain white T-shirt. "I'm renting this place. I brought you here last night."

She tried to digest that, tried to make sense of the situation. *Uh-oh.* "Last night wasn't a dream, was it?" she asked. Fear slithered through her even before he answered.

"Afraid not."

Adrenaline punched her heart rate off the charts. Oh, God. Not a dream. He really had kidnapped her! She reacted blindly, rolling to run from the bed. Luke was there in an instant. In one smooth move, he had her flat on the mattress. Sitting on the edge of the bed, he captured her hands and pinned her by leaning his upper body across hers. She was basically helpless, despite her frantic heaving and twisting. He managed to stay out of the reach of her head and teeth.

She screamed at the top of her lungs.

"Stop it! No one can hear you."

She voted in favor of him lying and kept screaming. Until her throat locked up and all she could do was make a rasping sound. A fresh wave of terror roared through her and she made a choking noise as she struggled to get air.

"You can breathe, Marla. Be calm and relax," Luke said quietly. A soothing warmth flooded her throat and chest, and she gasped in a lungful of air.

Sinking back against the bed, she stared up at him. "I want you to listen to me," he told her. "Take another breath, and *listen*. Okay?"

The next breath came easier, and some of the tension left her body. She managed to nod, but her mind was whirling with horrendous possibilities.

"We've been together since eleven thirty last night, and I haven't made any move to hurt you. Right?"

She nodded again, trying to push away the utter panic that was making it difficult to think clearly.

Regret filled his gaze. "I mishandled this. I wish I could go back and do this differently. Obviously, I can't." He eased his weight back a little. "You're completely safe with me. I'm not going to harm you. I give you my word of honor. But I really need your help."

"Help with what?" she asked, now distracted by the powerful chemistry between them. Despite the circumstances, her breasts were tingling; heat was spreading downward between her legs. How could she react this way to a stalker/kidnapper/possible rapist-murderer?

"I think it would be easier for you to concentrate with a little distance between us." Luke released her and stood. "But don't try anything. I hate to keep zapping you."

Marla had no idea what he was talking about, but she was pretty sure she didn't want it either. As she slipped out of the opposite side of the bed, she suddenly remembered Bryony. "Where's my dog?"

Luke grimaced. "Psycho dog is tied up outside. I got tired of it trying to amputate my foot." As if on cue, a high-pitched barking started up in the yard. "Terrorizing birds and squirrels," he muttered. He gestured toward the doorway. "The bathroom is off the hallway, if you need it."

She walked toward the door, keeping a wary eye on him.

He followed behind her until she reached the bathroom. "Like I said, don't try anything. Unless you want me monitoring your bathroom visits."

She nodded her understanding and shut the warped door as far as it would go. The bathroom was ancient, with a battered linoleum floor and a stained sink. Luke had obviously hedged his bets, as there was nothing but a toothbrush, toothpaste, a plastic cup, a bar of soap sitting on the sink, and a stack of towels in a plastic storage tub.

There was a rusted medicine cabinet—empty—with a mirror over the sink, but no way for her to break the glass to use as a weapon. She was shaking, from fear and adrenaline overload. But she knew she had to stay calm and focus on a plan to escape. For now, she resigned herself to taking care of necessities.

When she came out of the bathroom, Luke was waiting in the entryway to the kitchen. "In here," he said.

She walked past him into a kitchen with battered white metal cabinets and stained torn linoleum. The back door was open, a screen door with peeling paint offering unlikely protection from the Texas-sized mosquitoes. Beyond the tiny concrete stoop, Bryony was sniffing along the ground, a rope dragging behind her. The smells of fresh coffee and humid, warm outdoors permeated the room.

In the center was a cheap Formica table that had her purse sitting on it. There was a laptop on the other side, next to a stack of newspapers and what appeared to be handwritten notes. "Have a seat," Luke said.

She took the chair in front of her purse, but didn't scoot it in, allowing room to make a run for it. The open door and Bryony within reach were two points in her favor.

"You can have your purse," he said. "I took your gun, pepper spray, army knife, cell phone, and nail clippers. Their eventual return could be negotiable."

Too bad, she thought, pulling the purse to her.

"You might want to take a couple of the ibuprofen in there," he suggested. "To help with that headache."

She looked up at him, not liking his astuteness. "How would you know about that?"

"First off, I can sense it. Second, you'd had a fair amount to drink when you got home last night. And the energy bursts I was forced to use can also cause a residual headache."

"Energy bursts?" What was this guy, an alien?

"Yeah. I'm sorry I had to do that to you."

"I don't understand."

"I know. But I'll explain. Coffee?" When she nodded, he took a travel mug, poured from the coffeemaker on the counter. "Milk or sugar?"

"Black is fine." She couldn't believe she was sitting here, calmly talking to her kidnapper. But then, she didn't have any good way to escape at the moment.

Luke screwed on a spill-proof lid, tightened it with a flex of his muscular arms. He set it before her with a warning look. "Do *not* remove that top, or you will lose coffee privileges."

Damn. She'd hoped to hurl the hot coffee in his face and make a run for it. He obviously knew many of the self-defense moves taught to women. "You can't keep me here," she said. "People will know something is wrong and start looking for me."

Luke leaned negligently against the counter, a coffee mug in one hand. "That's not likely. The manufacturing company you work for is closed next week. Your coworkers won't miss you."

Shock jolted through her. He couldn't possibly know that for a fact. "You're wrong," she lied.

"While I was waiting for you last night, I checked your e-mail. I saw your discussion with Rebecca about your plans for next week, with the plant being closed."

"You read my e-mail?"

He shrugged. "I did it only as a contingency in case you didn't come home."

His every action was that of a stalker. She knew the moves they made, having gone through it with Julia. Clenching her hands in her lap to keep them from shaking, Marla glared at Luke. "My family will certainly be looking for me."

He set his mug on the counter. "I also sent an e-mail to your sister Julia, telling her you had decided to take off for a few days, and were heading to Mexico. I'm sorry, but it was necessary. I meant it when I said I was desperate."

She felt like she'd been gut punched. Fear and anger intermingled, burning in her chest. "You bastard," she hissed.

"Yeah, probably true." He pulled his wallet from a back pocket. He opened it and took out a white square of paper, which he pushed toward her. "I really am a private investigator."

She picked it up, saw it was a private investigator license for the state of Texas, embossed with the official seal. That didn't mean he couldn't be a monster. The man who'd stalked and almost killed Julia had been a well-respected business owner. Luke's actions up until now were not positive indicators.

"I know." Marla pushed it back. "I checked you out." Luke Paxton was indeed listed as a PI license holder on the State of Texas Private Security Bureau website.

He slid his wallet into his back pocket and refilled his coffee before taking the chair across from her. He had his hair pulled back today, and his face was even more striking, with the well-defined bone structure, the strong jawline, and those startlingly blue eyes. She wondered if he wore colored contacts.

"If you checked on me, maybe you went a little further and saw the requirements for PI licensing in Texas. Then you'd know my fingerprints were run in the national databases, and that I underwent a background check. I'm also a licensed PI in Louisiana, Mississippi, Alabama, Georgia, and Tennessee. That means I've been investigated from six ways to Sunday, and it's now public knowledge that my favorite foods are green fried tomatoes, lasagna, and pineapple upside down cake—not necessarily in that order."

He took a sip of coffee, sat back. "Before that, I served four years in the Air Force Security Forces. You wouldn't want to cross my path if you were a criminal, but I'm sworn to protect the innocent."

She fervently hoped he was telling the truth. But if he was, why had he kidnapped her? "Then what am I doing here?"

"That's a tough one to explain." He rubbed the bridge of

his nose. "No good way but to come right out and say it. Just hear me out before you react. And try to keep an open mind."

She waited, apprehension skidding through her.

"I don't do the usual private investigations," he began. "I use my training and skills to track down special criminals. I also use unique abilities. Sentinel abilities."

She wasn't comprehending. "Sentinel?"

He raised his hand in a "wait" gesture. "Let me finish. I am a Sentinel." He leaned forward, pinning her with his gaze. "I'm not completely human, Marla. I'm a being with superhuman powers. More specifically, I'm a reincarnated Atlantian."

She stared back, aghast. *Superhuman? Atlantian?* Delusional was more like it.

"My job on Earth," Luke continued, "is to track Belians, which are also reincarnated Atlantians, but very evil. They thrive on terror and chaos, on pain and bloodshed. They come into human bodies and they take on the roles of serial killers, mobsters, gang members, dictators—anything that allows them to do their dark work. They cause of a lot of destruction and suffering on Earth, and the Sentinels are sworn to find them and dispense karmic justice."

He was more than delusional. He was probably a paranoid schizophrenic psychopath. She inched her chair back a little. They were both equal distance from the back door, but she had the element of surprise and speed.

"There's more," he said. "Sentinels track Belians using psychic powers. We can pick up the energies they leave at crime scenes and where they hole up. We then take those energies and filter them through a our 'third eye,' which is a special spiritual center everyone has."

Yeah, and there were little green men from Mars, too.

"And," he continued, "there are a small number of humans who are psychically wired to enhance the Sentinel tracking abilities. They're called conductors, and they can be very crucial in some investigations."

Before she could fully absorb this, he leaned closer,

placing his hand over hers. "You're one of those humans, Marla. You're a conductor."

She jerked her hand free and bolted to her feet. Time to check out of Hotel California. She raced toward the back door. It swung shut before she reached it. *On its own.* With a yelp, she whirled and ran for the front of the house. A chair skidded to the entryway. She tried to go around it, but it moved with her. She feinted right, then sprinted to the left, bouncing off the chair, which moved with lightning speed to block her.

She hit the floor hard, but juiced on adrenaline, she leaped to her feet. Freaked, she whirled to see Luke still sitting at the table, his expression impassive. "I asked you to hear me out."

Chest heaving, mind in a tumult, she could only gape at him. He looked at the chair she'd knocked over; it levitated and floated to the table. "Sit down, and allow me to finish."

Her gaze went to the chair and then back to him. She was still dreaming, that had to be it. Only it sure felt *real.*

"Sit down," Luke said again, steel edging his words.

Feeling a strong urge to obey, she went reluctantly to the chair, perched on the edge. Now what? She looked around the kitchen for a weapon, anything she could use against this . . . *What the hell was he?*

"Give me your hands," he ordered, holding his own large hands out.

She balled her hands into fists in her lap, wincing at the pain. Then she felt that strange urge again—the compulsion to follow his order. Of their own volition, her trembling hands came off her lap, and placed themselves, palms up, on the table. She saw they were scraped from her fall on the floor, but her fear at her inability to control them obliterated the pain.

Luke placed his hands over them, and a heated tingling immediately shot up her arms. It was like she'd placed her finger in a light socket, only it wasn't painful. She tried to pull back, but he tightened his fingers.

"Easy now," he soothed. "Part of what you're feeling is

the natural Sentinel/conductor energy. Part of it is energy I'm sending to your wounds. That was me closing the door and moving the chair, by the way."

And that's me, either being murdered by a space alien, or being taken away to the psych ward at Harris County Hospital.

"Better?" Luke asked, and she realized her palms weren't stinging anymore.

She nodded, and he released her. She stared at her hands. They weren't healed, but they weren't as red.

"Our abilities are somewhat limited," he said, watching her closely. "I can't totally heal wounds or cure diseases, but I can send a calming energy to an injury. It helps reduce the inflammation that causes the pain."

She looked at her palms again. "I'm hallucinating."

"No, you're not."

"I must be drugged." Her gaze shifted to her coffee. "You put something in my coffee!"

"No." He picked up her mug, took several swallows, set it back down. "See? It's not drugged. You're not dreaming. You're not hallucinating. This is real, Marla."

Her practical accountant's mind simply couldn't accept that. There were nice orderly laws that kept the universe running smoothly, laws like gravity, aerodynamics, and thermodynamics. She'd had a double major in college—accounting and science—so she was familiar with these laws. Doors closing on their own, chairs levitating, spontaneous healing were *not* the natural order of the universe.

"Sometimes you just have to step outside the box," Luke said quietly. "Do you believe in God, Marla? That's something that can't be seen or touched, yet it's a reality to many."

God's existence was a questionable subject since the night of the attack. Yet she'd never quite relinquished her hold on something she'd believed as far back as she could remember. "Maybe. I don't know."

"Here's something you can't deny." He pushed back his chair and rose. He came around the table, very large, very intimidating.

With a little squeak, she leaped up, intending to flee, but he was there. He gripped her upper arms, drew her closer, until only a few inches separated them. The assault on her senses was instant, the electricity, the powerful current flowing between their bodies, heating her blood like molten lava. She could only stare up at him, caught in the snare of those glowing blue eyes.

"There's no denying this," he told her. "No denying the power of the chemistry between us, of the sexual surge just beneath the surface, waiting to be triggered by chakra energies. When we met at the bar Friday night, that wasn't static electricity you felt. That was the Sentinel/conductor energy. You can't tell me you're not affected."

She didn't understand any of it, but her body did, responding to his like a spark to lighter fluid. *Mind over matter,* she told herself. She damn well would deny it. She shook her head. "No. There's nothing between us."

Dark blond brows raised "No? Then how do you explain the fact that your nipples are hard? That you're also aroused elsewhere? What would you call it?"

She didn't have to look down at her swollen breasts to know what he saw, although she didn't have a clue how he could know about the wetness between her legs. She struggled to find some logical explanation in this insanity. Thought of the stories of women who'd been kidnapped and, oddly, bonded with their abductors. "Stockholm syndrome."

He had the nerve to laugh. Shaking his head, he gave her that sexy, devastating smile. "I don't think so."

Her body didn't think so, either. She shivered, and he shifted, pulling her against him. "Hey, it's okay. Really. This attraction between us is a *good* thing, Marla. It means you're a natural conductor, and you can help me."

She rested against him, mentally exhausted. It was surprisingly comforting, in a totally insane/Stockholm syndrome/raging lust kind of way. His body was hard, yet that only reinforced the sense of solidness and security surrounding her. She wasn't a small woman, but he dwarfed her. Her face was pressed against a very impressive chest. She drew a deep breath. He smelled great.

It was crazy—this whole thing was whacked—but somehow, she actually was starting to believe him. Maybe it was all that warmth flowing through her, the whisper of safety and protection she so desperately sought. Or maybe it was the way he was holding her, with infinite gentleness. No man had ever held her that way.

Or maybe it was the pheromones zinging around them. He was right about one thing—there was no denying the incredible chemistry between them.

And that, more than anything, was starting to convince her. Ever since that night eleven years ago, when she'd helplessly watched her sister being brutally beaten and raped, she'd had no sexual desire, at least not with a partner.

She definitely had normal, biological urges, but whenever she attempted to date someone or act on those urges, she went dead inside. Since she felt absolutely nothing sexual for women, either, she knew it wasn't a gender preference issue. Watching Julia being raped had so traumatized her, her body simply wasn't able to respond to sexual situations.

Until she'd met Luke. Then her body's reaction had been instantaneous—and explosive. It responded that way every time she got into close proximity to him, subsided when she was away from him. Her reaction was specifically to him. What were the odds of that?

What if he is really telling the truth? Like *The Twilight Zone*, only in real life.

She just didn't know. Nor did she have much choice in the matter—for now. So she'd hear him out, and see where it went from there.

She pushed against him, and he let her go. Backing away, she shoved her glasses back up her nose and tried to finger comb her wild mass of hair out of her face.

"All right," she said. "I want something for this headache and some more coffee. Then I'm ready to listen."

* * *

JULIA Reynolds lived her life by discipline and order. Both work and personal endeavors were planned out in a detailed schedule, performed methodically and flawlessly. It was the best way to avoid chaos, which to her way of thinking, clouded the mind with unnecessary clutter and emotions.

Being in control of her life and her emotions was crucial to her well being.

So she got up at nine o'clock Sunday morning (the one day she allowed herself to sleep that late), had her customary egg white omelet, whole wheat toast, cup of blueberries, and coffee. Not that her sensible diet seemed to have any effect on her voluptuous figure, she thought wryly. Reynolds women just had nonskinny genes.

Like it really mattered what she looked like.

She cleared the breakfast dishes and then enjoyed her second—and last—cup of coffee as she read the newspaper. Her leisurely Sunday mornings were a luxury she savored, and she read until noon sharp. She didn't care that sitting so long left her stiff; reading the paper was worth it.

She pushed up from the chair and reached for her cane. Eleven years ago, they'd thought she wouldn't walk again. But Reynolds women were made of sturdy stuff. Julia's determination had been as strong as the plates and pins holding her shattered leg together.

She laboriously made her way to her study and settled at her desk to grade test papers from the differential equations mathematics course she taught at the University of Houston. She found a deep satisfaction working with numbers. They were so precise, so predictable, so stable. Unlike a lot of things in life, you always knew what to expect when dealing with numbers.

She was well aware why she felt that way, why she lived her unremarkable life in the shelter of order and system and objectivity. Knew and accepted it. She'd done all the victim assistance and self-help programs; her parents' hard-earned money had likely funded college for Dr. Jackson's kids. Julia accepted that nothing could change the past, and that she had to go on with her life.

She'd done so, but she'd insured every aspect was well controlled, that there would be no surprises. And while it might be dull, it was fulfilling on a number of levels, and most importantly, her life was as safe as she could make it.

As the day went by, Julia lost herself in the intricacies of bifurcation theory and higher order equations, wrote comments and calculated grades, getting up to stretch and move around every hour, until her portable timer went off at exactly four o'clock. She organized and neatly stacked the papers, slipping them in color coded folders, and put them away in her briefcase.

Next, before she prepared an early dinner, she would read her e-mail and make her semiweekly telephone calls to her parents and Marla. She powered up her computer and opened her browser, then her e-mail. She did a quick sweep to prioritize reading order. There was one from Marla, from late Saturday night. That was odd, since they always talked on Sunday.

Julia clicked on the message and read:

Hey Jules, I wanted to let you know I'm going out of town tomorrow. Since I'm off work this week, I de-cided to take a few days and go down to Mexico, maybe meet up with a few friends there. The dog is with me. I'll talk to you when I get back. Love, M.

This couldn't be right. She reread the message. No, something was wrong. For one thing, Marla was rarely im-pulsive. Like Julia, her life was well thought out. A trip to Mexico on the spur of the moment was too impetuous for Marla. Not only that, but she had been planning to paint two rooms in her house next week. She'd already bought the paint and supplies.

Julia read the message a third time. It didn't read right, either. Marla didn't talk or write the way some of the things were phrased. The nickname "Jules" was normal, as was the "M" Marla always signed. But she'd never say "meet up with a few friends," or refer to Bryony as "the dog."

Not only that, but the few times Marla had been away from home, she'd asked Julia or their parents to take care of Bryony. This whole thing was very wrong, very out of character.

Julia picked up the phone on her desk and dialed Marla. Getting no answer, she called her parents' house next. Maybe they would know something.

But her mother was just as baffled. "No . . . Marla didn't mention anything about a trip. She told me she was paint-ing next week. She spent hours finding the colors she wanted. You know she doesn't travel much. And she likes to plan way ahead." She paused, then asked, "You don't think anything's wrong, do you?"

Julia hastened to assure her mother, although her own alarm level was rising. "Oh, I'm sure everything's fine. Maybe she got a last-minute opportunity to go to Mexico and just decided to do something spontaneous."

"Maybe," Mom said doubtfully. "You might check with her friend Rebecca. You know, that British girl? She and Marla appear to be close. She might know something."

"That's a good idea. Let me do that. I'll call you later."

Julia pulled out the personal phone directory she kept in her desk. She never threw out a phone number, not even one given by a passing acquaintance. It was a habit that had been useful on a number of occasions, like now. She looked up Rebecca Smithson's number and dialed.

"Hello," said a brisk British voice.

"Is this Rebecca?"

"Yes. Who's ringing?"

"This is Julia Reynolds. I'm Marla's sister."

"Oh, yes. We met at your family gathering. Quite a lovely group."

"I'm sorry to bother you, but I'm wondering if you know where Marla might have gone."

"Gone? What do you mean?"

"She sent me an e-mail saying she made a last-minute decision to go to Mexico, and might meet some friends down there. I wondered if you knew anything about it."

"What? Miss 'Plans Everything' taking a last-minute trip to Mexico? Well." Rebecca considered a moment. "I'm quite surprised, to be honest. She didn't mention it to me. I'm leaving tomorrow to go there myself, and suggested she go along. She said she was going to paint her house."

A sick feeling settled in Julia's stomach. "Do you think she might try to catch up with you there?"

"It's doubtful. She doesn't know where I'm staying, and I don't think my cellular will work there. No way for her to find me."

Perfect logic, unfortunately. Julia asked, "Anyone else she might be meeting there?"

"Well, I don't know many of her other friends, and she doesn't social much with the blokes at work. But . . . there is this chap she met at the Red Lion on Friday night. He was trying to chat her up."

"Chat her up?"

"Oh, sorry. He was really coming on to her. Asked her to go to dinner with him Saturday night and she agreed."

"She did?"

"Yes. I was chuffed. This chap was bloody gorgeous, and I was pleased she was going to see him again. I wonder if she might be going off with him. I know I'd jump at the chance."

Marla had hardly dated since that night eleven years ago. She wouldn't go to Mexico with a man she'd just met, especially without informing anyone. "What can you tell me about this man?" Julia asked, fear coiling inside her like a snake.

"He was big, over six feet, long blond hair, stunning blue eyes. His name was Luke something or other . . . started with a *P*, I think. Oh, hell, I can't recall it."

"Anyone else there with them?"

"Hmmm. They were sitting at the bar, on the far right side. A young woman was tending. She had that fake red hair."

"You said it was the Red Lion. On Friday night?"

"Right. Happy hour. Listen, is there anything I can do?"

"No." Julia drew a deep breath. She didn't even know what *she* was going to do. "You've been helpful, and I appreciate it. Tell you what—let me give you my home and cell phone numbers. Will you call me if you talk to Marla, or hear anything?"

"Of course I will. And I'll give you my cellular as well."

They exchanged numbers, and Julia said good-bye and hung up. She tried to tell herself everything was all right, that Marla was fine. But the old sick feeling was back, the shaking that started inside and worked its way out like a scream.

Julia was very, *very* afraid that Marla might have gone off with this blond man, a man who could be a criminal . . . a monster. And Julia knew firsthand there were real, live monsters in the world. She hoped she was wrong, and that Marla had really gone with friends to Mexico. That she was safe and having fun.

But what if . . . Julia drew another deep breath, forced herself to calm. She was an intelligent, resourceful woman. She wouldn't let Marla sink into the depths of hell without a fight.

Her first order of business: a visit to the police.

FOUR

MARLA sat at the kitchen table, Bryony cuddled in her lap. Another point in Luke's favor, as he seemed to realize she needed the familiar comfort of the poodle's warm—albeit tense—body. He'd even shown admirable restraint when Bryony went for him the moment she was untied.

Marla didn't understand it. At home, Bry always barked at visitors, but calmed down after the initial contact. Yet she didn't like Luke. Marla hoped it was the odd energy he emanated, and not some inner core of evil only the poodle could sense.

Now Bryony tracked his every move, growling whenever he stepped in their direction. He was fixing breakfast, displaying an easy, practiced skill in the kitchen. A pound of bacon was sizzling in two ancient cast iron skillets, and ten biscuits baked in the oven, while a fresh pot of coffee brewed. Mr. Macho Chef. All he needed was an apron and one of those tall white hats, although he looked really fine in those faded jeans and white T-shirt. The kitchen towel threaded through his belt loop didn't detract in any way from his breathtaking masculinity.

Marla watched in amazement as he cracked an entire dozen eggs into a bowl. "Um, I really don't eat that much," she said. "Even if I am . . ." She glanced down her jeans—relaxed fit—noting how they stretched over her generous thighs.

He paused his mixing. "If you're what?"

Stupid fat genes. "Never mind." She waved a hand at the stove. "Who's going to eat all that food?"

"I expect you to eat some of it. I'll handle the rest." He turned and started removing the bacon from the skillets. "Sentinels have very fast metabolisms. I eat a *lot* of food."

Life was *so* unfair—assuming he was telling the truth, about any of it. "So these Be-lee . . ." Marla stumbled over the word.

"Buh-lee-ins," Luke sounded it out. "What about them?"

"They're really bad, huh?"

"Think Hitler, Ted Bundy, Jeffrey Dahmer."

"They were all Belians?"

Luke drained one of the skillets into a can. "Not all bad people are Belians. But many of them are."

"And they come to Earth why?"

The egg mixture went into the drained skillet, and Luke turned on the burner beneath it. "It's complicated. All of this started in Atlantis."

That again. "So you're saying Atlantis really existed?"

Luke looked at her. "Yes, I am. It came into being over 100,000 years ago."

She mulled that over while he cooked the eggs. She got up to help when he began bringing food to the table, but he waved her back down. "I can do this. Just keep psycho dog in check."

On cue, Bryony growled as he set the bacon on the table. "Hush." Marla gave her a little shake. "If you don't behave, you'll have to go back outside." She set Bry on the floor. "You stay right there." The poodle lay down, keeping an eye on Luke.

Luke put everything on the table, including dishes and silverware—no knife for her, Marla noted. He took the chair opposite her, for which she was grateful. Even from here, she could feel the pull of the energy between them, although it was somewhat muted.

He piled his plate with an outrageous amount of food and dug in. Still suffering a headache and feeling queasy, Marla started with a biscuit. "You were talking about Atlantis."

"Yeah. The first Atlantians were enlightened and peaceful. They worshiped one God, although their term was The One. They were very advanced, in both psychic powers and technology. They could travel through space and time—"

"They did time travel?"

"Sure did. They were very advanced beings."

She tried to get her mind around that. "So what happened to them?"

"First off, they got enmeshed in the Earth. They started out as spiritual beings, but then they took on physical bodies. Physical substance is denser than spiritual substance. They began to forget their connection to the Creator."

That actually made sense, which was kind of scary. She realized Luke was pausing at regular intervals, probably to give her time to absorb what he was saying. That sharp blue gaze was watchful and assessing, that powerful body deceptively relaxed, ready to move if she went ballistic. Which might happen at any time, if this story got any weirder. "Go on," she said.

"The first Atlantians were known as the Children of One, because they worshipped one God. But eventually, the paradise became corrupted. An Atlantian named Belial began gaining power. His followers became known as the Sons of Belial."

"Belians," Marla murmured, making the logical jump.

Luke nodded, approval in his gaze. "The Belians thrived on darkness, power, and blood. They began making human sacrifices to their dark gods. And because the Children of One were peaceful and passive by nature, the Belians easily gained power. They took control of the great crystal that provided all the power for Atlantis. And they turned it into a death ray, to battle their enemies. But that eventually backfired, when misuse of the crystal destroyed Atlantis."

"But according to you, the Atlantians aren't really gone," Marla said, remembering their earlier conversation. "Because they're being reincarnated on Earth again." Not that she believed in reincarnation—or at least hadn't before now.

"Right." Luke got up for more coffee. "The Belians started coming back when technology began to approach what it was on Atlantis. Since they are corrupted souls, they began spreading destruction and terror on the Earth. So the original Atlantians—mainly those who had served in the temple—also began reincarnating to track down the Belians. They—we—are the Sentinels."

The theme music from *The Twilight Zone* started playing in Marla's head. "And you said that they—you—are psychic?"

He slid back into his chair. "To an extent. We use psychic powers to track Belians. I can go to a BCS—Belian crime scene—and pick up the energies that were expended during the crime. I can manipulate those energies to create the Belian's psychic signature. The more I work with the energy, the more bits and pieces of information I get about the Belian's identity. I know it sounds complicated, which it is."

It sounded more crazy than complicated, but Marla kept that opinion to herself. "So, if you're psychic, can you read minds?" Oh dear God, she hoped not. She'd been having some very erotic thoughts about Luke.

He gave her a slow, knowing smile that made her want to sink beneath the table. "No, I can't read actual thoughts. But I can sense feelings and strong emotions or disturbances. Like right now, I know you still have a headache."

How could he know that? "It's getting better," she said, relieved he couldn't perceive her thoughts. "Tell me more about Belians and Sentinels."

"We're both fairly evenly matched in powers and abilities. And we're also both in mortal human bodies, so we can be killed. Fortunately for the Sentinels, there is a small group of humans who also have special abilities. We call them conductors."

And he considered her one of those people. "What kind of abilities?"

"They're able to link with a Sentinel and magnify his or her psychic tracking abilities. While linked, they can make it easier to unravel the Belian's psychic signature. Usually, they have some psychic abilities of their own." He paused, watching her. "Which I'm assuming you have. Tell me about them, Marla."

Her odd quirk was something she had never discussed with anyone. She assumed she had it because the trauma of Julia and her being attacked had done something to her psyche. It occurred to her that maybe it was better if she didn't tell Luke, either. Although she couldn't deny he had nonhuman abilities, she still hadn't ruled out the possibility he might be one or two cards short of a full deck.

"Marla."

She felt that same compulsion to obey that she'd experienced earlier, and realization jolted through her. She shoved back from the table. "You're using your powers to manipulate me." She stood, and Luke followed suit.

"I'm not doing anything that will hurt you. I'm just trying to get your cooperation."

"Just like you did last night, and this morning. I'm well aware you did something to me every time I got upset or tried to fight you."

His gaze was steady. "I merely sent calming energy through you. There was no sense in you panicking and hurting yourself. Although I seemed to be getting the brunt of it."

"You're controlling my thoughts." Another horrifying possibility occurred to her. "You're making me have these . . . feelings for you!"

"No! Nothing like that. Sentinels follow a strict code of honor. We can't harm innocents, and we can't force a conductor to work with us. And we certainly don't use our powers for sexual gain. Your physical responses are the result of the Sentinel/conductor reaction."

Anger flared through her. "A code of honor? One that condones terrorizing me and Bryony and then kidnapping us?" She turned on the wildly barking poodle. "Bryony, shut up!"

"I'll admit I pushed the boundaries with that. But only because you were too inebriated for me to explain everything last night."

"I was not drunk!"

"All right. Tipsy, then."

Her headache was coming back full force, and she felt like screaming. And throwing something, specifically at him. "So I can't trust you, or believe anything you say."

"Shit." He ran a hand through his hair. "Marla, I'm sorry. I've already admitted I mishandled this from the start. But I *really* need your help. Please bear with me a little longer."

"Not unless you promise not to zap me with any more energy."

"That depends. *You* have to promise you won't try to knee the family jewels, bite me, pull a gun on me, or kick me. Or run without at least hearing me out." He glanced down at his ankle, where Bryony had attached herself. "Or sic psycho dog on me."

"Bryony! Stop that!" She darted around the table and pried Bry away from Luke's leg. Straightening, she realized she was mere inches from him and feeling the barrage of energy.

How could he possibly fake a surge of sensation like that? And why did he have to have that wry, heart-twisting sense of humor? She stared into his eyes, telling herself she wouldn't get sucked under. "Do you promise to keep your so-called powers and energies to yourself?"

He reached out, sliding his fingers through her hair and cupping her head. Heat sizzled from her scalp to the tips of her toes and everywhere between. "I promise not to invade your mental and physical privacy, unless your safety or well being is compromised." His fingers slid down, kneaded the knots in her neck and shoulders. She felt warmth shooting into her muscles, and the headache eased.

He dropped his hand and stepped back. The whirlpool of sensation slowed, and she dragged air into her constricted lungs.

"I want to take you somewhere," he said.

"Where?"

"A place where the Belian was staying. I think you'll be able to sense the energy it left behind."

Oh great. Now I can experience evil and darkness. "And then what?"

"Then we'll discuss doing a conduction."

She had no idea what that entailed, but thought of one of her mother's sayings: *In for a penny, in for a pound.* She was already here, wherever that was. And she was pretty much at Luke's mercy, although she was actually beginning to feel safe with him. *Don't forget about me!* her throbbing body screamed. Well, except for that. She might as well see this through.

"All right," she said. "Let's go."

MARLA held on tightly to Luke, the wind rushing past her, a hell of a lot of horsepower rumbling beneath her. She'd never been on a motorcycle before last night, which didn't count because she barely remembered it. But this, this was elemental—wild, free, and, she had to admit—exhilarating. If she hadn't had some serious doubts about the driver and her current situation, she would have enjoyed herself. Still she certainly couldn't complain about what she was holding on to—two hundred pounds of pure, primal male.

When she'd donned the helmet Luke gave her and slid onto the bike behind him, she hadn't known where to put her hands and tentatively gripped his leather jacket. But when he revved the motor to life and wheeled down the gravel road to Highway 36, she found her hands curved around his waist, her fingers digging into some rock-hard abs. And when he took some sharp turns, she found herself pressing against his back. He felt so solid.

Needville sat on the northern edge of Brazos Bend State Park, which incorporated a stretch of the Brazos River, various lakes, and hundreds of moss-draped live oaks. Much of Texas was rural, and this area had its share of small roads and far-spaced homes with dusty prairie stretches between them.

Luke drove to a structure that was basically just a shack. Situated on a deserted stretch of an old FM road, the structure's wooden slat walls were weathered and warped, the tin roof rusted. The yard was barren, more dirt than grass, no bushes or plants of any kind. Yellow crime scene tape flapped across the front of the shack.

He powered down the motorcycle, but Marla felt a residual vibration between her legs and in her rear. She climbed off the bike, unhooked her helmet and let him take it.

"Have the police been here?" she asked, noting the tape.

"Yes. I notified them after I discovered evidence that the Belian had created weapons here." Luke set their helmets on the bike.

"How did you know to look here?"

"I investigated the first crime scene, and I picked up some images of this place. Then I spent hours driving around and checking out all area rentals from the past year, until I got here. I could feel the Belian's energy. The place was deserted, but I found incriminating evidence inside. So after I worked the energy patterns, I notified the authorities."

Marla stared at the shack. It seemed to emit malevolence. "Energy patterns?"

"All living things put off energy. As I explained earlier, a Sentinel can pick up the residual energy a Belian broadcasts. I don't want to give you specific details yet, because I want to see what you can pick up. Come on."

He urged her toward the structure, and apprehension began churning inside her, although she didn't know why. The uneasiness grew stronger with each step closer, like a weight pressing down on her. She stopped, not wanting to go any farther.

Luke slid off his sunglasses, looked at her. "What's wrong?"

"I don't know. Something about that building bothers me."

"Belian energy." Triumph gleamed in his eyes. "You can sense it."

She still wasn't ready to tell him she'd been feeling emotions from those around her, with him being the odd exception, for the past eleven years. Nor did she like him thinking she was a conductor, even if she didn't fully understand what that was. "It just looks creepy."

"It's all right." He took her elbow, guided her forward. "The place is completely deserted. The Belian is long gone."

Then why did she feel panicky as they approached the sagging porch? Why did it seem as if a horrifying darkness was eclipsing the sun? Out of nowhere, blackness descended on her. Surrounded her, a force so evil, it chilled her to the core.

Sensations of intense hatred mingled with visual flashes of a knife and blood, bits and pieces of . . . bodies. *Oh, God!* She struggled against the darkness, but the depravity wrapped around her. Tighter and tighter. Suffocating her, stealing her soul. She tried to scream, but nothing came out. She felt walls closing around her and fought to free herself.

"Marla! Marla, stop!"

She flailed wildly, hit something hard.

"It's me, Luke. You're safe. Nothing here can hurt you. *Marla.* Focus on *me.*"

Light illuminated the darkness and she blinked at the sudden sunshine, stared at the long, masculine fingers holding her upper arms. She managed to gulp in air, but when she tried to speak, a low, keening sound rose from her throat. Through the bloody mental images, she saw Luke's concerned face.

The sense of horror continued to suffocate her. "It's here. It's still here!" she gasped.

"No. It's not."

Yet evil surrounded her. "I can feel it. I can see it . . . the blood, the bodies." Spasms clenched her stomach. She struggled against Luke's grasp. "I'm going to be sick. Let me go!"

He released her, and she staggered a step away before collapsing to her hands and knees and retching violently in the dirt. She was vaguely aware of his solid presence next to her, of his hand rubbing her back. When the heaving finally stopped, she sagged weakly beside him, mortified, but too spent to even apologize. He murmured something, but she couldn't hear through the buzzing in her ears.

She didn't protest when he swept her into his arms and carried her as if she were a small child to the motorcycle. He lowered her to the ground, eased her into a sitting position against the rear tire. Squatting beside her, he gripped her shoulders. "Take a deep breath."

She did, and the buzzing receded.

"Take another breath." He waited until she complied. "You okay now?"

Battling to maintain control, she nodded.

"Can you still feel it?"

Oh, yes. The macabre visions were gone, but she still felt pure, unadulterated evil pressing on her. It felt like the monster emanating that evil knew who she was, and where to find her. "Yes," she whispered, her throat raw. "Like it's watching me."

Luke kept one hand on her shoulder as he reached beneath the top of his shirt and pulled out a silver chain with a pink oval stone attached to it. He closed his fingers over the stone, began chanting in a beautiful language she didn't recognize, at least not intellectually.

But the words and cadence touched her on a visceral level, sent a frission of awareness through her. She felt a surge of . . . *something* . . . like an electrical current or energy flare that surrounded them.

The evil receded, whipping away like it had been touched by fire.

Yet a dark residue lingered inside her, like the awful feeling experienced after a very bad nightmare, or that of a *real*, horrific memory. A renewed wave of nausea rolled through her, and she wrapped her arms around herself, afraid she'd be sick again.

Then warmth whispered through her, a soft touch of reassurance and a glowing light. She somehow knew it was coming from Luke, but she didn't care that he was using his energy on her. She welcomed the light and warmth, reached for it fiercely, desperately and felt the darkness retreat completely.

But she knew, on a soul-deep level, it wasn't gone for good. "What did you just do?"

"I shielded us. That broke your link with the Belian."

"I was linked with that thing?"

"It appears that way."

He shifted back, and she collapsed against the bike, unable to marshal any coherent thoughts. She watched as he dug out a bottle of water and a clean cloth from the bike's rear storage compartment. He wet the cloth, stroked it over her hot face. Too exhausted to protest, she let him.

"Better?" he asked. She managed a nod, and he handed her the water. "This might help."

She rinsed out her mouth, leaning sideways to spit, and then gulped a few swallows. Still squatting, Luke returned his hands to her shoulders. "Are you going to be okay?"

She nodded again, and he settled onto the dirt next to her, stretching out his long legs. "I had no idea you were that sensitive, or I would never have brought you here. And I sure as hell would have shielded us before we went up to that shack. You should have told me, Marla."

Told him what? That she was mentally unbalanced, and had been since the attack on Julia eleven years ago? Being able to feel the emotions of those around her was apparently a side effect of witnessing the assault, and possibly of the concussion she'd suffered when Julia's attacker hit Marla on the head. Shivering despite the moderate temperature, she hunched into her jacket.

Luke made a frustrated sound. "At some point, you're going to have to trust me. And you're going to have to be honest with me. This Belian is dangerous enough without any other surprises broadsiding me."

He wanted to talk about trust? She turned her head and just looked at him, but he got her message loud and clear.

"I am being completely honest with you now, I swear by The One," he said. "I'm telling you everything. No games, Marla, no tricks. What you felt here today is just a taste of what we're dealing with."

That was *so* not what she wanted to hear. The worst of it was that she now believed Luke's wild tale about Belians and Sentinels. She thought she'd experienced real hell eleven years ago. But this, this evil, easily rivaled it.

"Think you're up to the ride back?" he asked. When she nodded, he stood and helped her up, holding on to her until her shaking legs held.

She didn't look at the shack as they put on their helmets and got on the bike. She tried to keep her mind blank, to focus on Luke's solid presence, on the aura of strength and protection that he emanated.

But, like a moth drawn to the flame, she couldn't resist the urge to look back. Darkness hovered around the shack, the remnants of pure evil. And she felt like the fires of hell were touching her soul.

JULIA was at the downtown Houston Police Department on Monday morning. She'd called ahead to make sure Barbara Gray was in. Sergeant Gray, who had been the investigator on Julia's case eleven years ago, was still with the force, and still with the Sex Crimes Unit, which ironically was part of the Homicide Division. Maybe that designation wasn't really so strange, Julia thought, because parts of her had certainly been murdered that night—her naïveté, her faith in humankind, her future.

But her memories were alive and well. Standing in the front waiting area, she felt a disturbing sense of time collapsing on itself, as if her attack had happened only yesterday. The smell of coffee, the sound of ringing telephones and muted voices, the sense and feel of the station, were just as she remembered. A dignified aura of authority and law mingled with the lingering overtones of the grief and fear of victims and their families.

"Julia." Barbara Gray came through a doorway leading to the back. "Good to see you. How have you been?"

She looked pretty much the same—a short, trim woman with sharp blue eyes and straight blond hair that stopped at her jawline. The blond shade was lighter now, the effects of encroaching gray, and there were a few more lines on the investigator's face, but Julia would have known her anywhere.

Julia shook her hand. "I've been doing okay. And you?"

"Good." Barbara's assessing gaze swept over her, taking in the cane. "Glad to see you on your own two feet. You look well."

She didn't add the 'but,' the fact both of them understood all too well—that there was never a complete recovery from what Julia had endured. Ever.

"Come on in here." Barbara led the way to a small interview room with a round table and three chairs. "Have a seat."

Julia set her cane to the side and painstakingly eased herself into a chair. Barbara sat across from her. "I'm guessing this isn't a social call. What can I do for you?"

"I'm here about my sister."

"Oh. It's Marla, right? How is she doing?"

"I think something has happened to her."

Barbara leaned forward, concern etched on her face. "What?"

Julia quickly explained the e-mail, how it sounded wrong, and that Marla would never act so impulsively.

Barbara considered the information. "Maybe her impulsive behavior has to do with this man she met. Sometimes people act out of character when love or lust is involved."

"No," Julia said firmly. "Marla hasn't dated since . . . that night."

"I see." Barbara's gaze was sympathetic. "That's tough."

That was one of the things Julia had appreciated about the officer—her straightforward, honest manner. No lip service or flowery words of comfort, just the truth, tempered by a genuine compassion.

This woman had been Julia's lifeline in a sea of madness, a calming presence in the ER immediately after the attack; a bedrock through the arrest, trial, and sentencing of William Bennett. Julia hadn't even considered going to someone else about her sister.

"I know Marla wouldn't have gone off like this, and certainly not without telling us about it," she said. "It's just not in character for her."

"Have you been to her house yet?"

"Yes. I went last night, after I received the e-mail."

"And?"

"She wasn't there. Neither was her dog, which is another reason to be suspicious. I can't imagine Marla taking Bryony to Mexico. If Marla was going anywhere, she'd have left Bry with me or Mom and Dad."

Barbara frowned. "Was the house in disarray, or anything taken?"

"No." Julia said, and then amended, "Well, maybe some of her toiletries were gone. I didn't see her toothbrush, and her shampoo products were gone from the shower. But still, I know something is wrong."

"Look," Barbara said briskly. "It's really hard to prove there might be . . ." She hesitated, appeared to reconsider her words. ". . . something wrong, as you say, especially when there are no signs to indicate it. And you did get an e-mail."

"I know my sister," Julia insisted. "And I know she would *never* change her plans and go off on a whim, much less without telling her family."

"Then you need to file a missing persons report. Unfortunately, I can't help you with that. You'll have to go to the Missing Persons Unit, at our southeast substation on

McKawa." Barbara rose from her chair. "But I can call them and get you a contact there. And I'll give you directions."

"Thank you." Julia slowly pushed herself up, grasped her cane. "For now, and for . . . then."

Barbara turned at the door. "It's my job. I just wish . . ." Her expression hardened. "I wish I could castrate every rapist out there and then let the bastards bleed to death."

Julia felt the exact same way.

FIVE

LUKE knew he was pushing Marla too fast and too hard. She'd endured some shocks from his bumbled semiabduction and his blatant power display, not to mention learning about the existence of Sentinels and Belians. Then the situation at the shack had gone haywire, possibly putting her at risk, because there was a very real possibility the Belian had picked up on the link.

Damn! Adam had warned him to proceed with caution, but he'd been too focused on a being that thought nothing of killing innocent children to follow correct protocol. And Marla was paying for it.

So in an effort to get things back on track and give her a chance to assimilate everything, he'd backed off for the rest of Sunday. He'd taken her back to the house, encouraged her to take a shower and relax for the rest of the day. They'd sat in the backyard and watched psycho dog's antics. He'd grilled hamburgers on the cheap charcoal grill he'd picked up in Needville, and answered her occasional questions, but he didn't volunteer any more than she asked for.

She'd appeared subdued, probably still feeling the effects

of the Belian link. When she began wilting from fatigue and stress, it was a simple matter to convince her to turn in early, and then put her into a deep, dreamless sleep with a mild mental push.

But this morning, she was fully alert, and not at all malleable. She sat at the kitchen table, her hands wrapped around her travel coffee mug (he still felt the need to hedge his bets, so the top was firmly screwed on it), and watched him cook breakfast. "You did something to make me sleep last night."

He checked the French toast, began flipping it. "Yeah, I did." He met her gaze. "You were exhausted and needed the rest."

Her mouth tightened. "I asked you not to use that woo-woo stuff on me."

He set the spatula down, leaned his hip against the counter. "I only do it when it's necessary."

"*Necessary?* More like abuse of power."

"Deal with it." He couldn't resist grinning at her glare. "And get out some dishes while you're at it."

"Why don't you just levitate them to the table?"

"Didn't we just determine that I only manipulate energy when it's necessary?"

"I think we actually determined you're an egotistical tyrant." She rose and went to the meager silverware collection lined up on a clean towel. "So you're going to let me near the knives now?"

"Just the table knives. If you're real good today, you might get to move on to steak knives."

"Very funny," she muttered.

He appreciated her obvious intelligence and quick wit. And he liked the way she looked—not a true beauty, but attractive, wholesome—with that wild mass of chestnut curls falling to her shoulders and those honey-colored eyes. She was dressed in jeans and an olive green sweater that set off her golden coloring. He also appreciated the fact that she wasn't thin like so many women, that she had full, womanly curves. As a matter of fact, she had a really fine rear end.

The smell of something burning jolted his attention back to the stove, and he quickly started scooping up some over-browned French toast.

"So what's on the agenda today?" Marla asked as she put the plates and silverware on the table. "If you need my help as badly as you say, then let's do whatever it is, so I can get back to my life."

What he needed was to perform a conduction with her. Just thinking about it sent a heated surge through his body, making him instantly hard. He'd worked with a lot of conductors, but this reaction was a first. One thing was certain— he wouldn't have any trouble losing himself in her lush body.

He was actually looking forward to it, despite the psychic drain all Sentinels experienced during a conduction. He was so finely tuned to Marla, so sensitized to her conductor energy, he felt certain their physical union would blow the top of his head off.

"Let's eat first," he said, hoping she didn't notice his aroused state. "Then I'll explain conductions."

Another blast of anticipation shot through him. While Marla might object to getting naked and down and dirty with a virtual stranger, the raw chemistry between them should be enough to convince her.

And it would bring him that much closer to catching the monster capable of murdering innocent children in cold blood.

HE stroked the pale yellow stick of Semtex like it was a lover. In the right hands—*his hands*—shaped by his brilliance and expertise, it would become an avenging weapon. No one could make a better bomb than he could. He'd been the smartest, the best, when he'd earned his physics degree at Cal Tech. No one had ever surpassed him, before or after.

He stroked the Semtex again. Even through his latex gloves he could feel its putty texture, its essence, its destructive *power*. He'd read that it was becoming harder to obtain, that its production and distribution was being tightly controlled by the Czech Republic government. But he was clever and capable, had the funds and had cultivated contacts in Europe. In exchange for small bits of his vast knowledge on bombs and weapons, he could get whatever he needed. Belial was impressed with his resourcefulness.

He slipped on his goggles and got to work. Around him lay the things he needed to create an instrument of retribution: blasting caps, fuses, black powder, flash bulbs, broken glass, nails, and a remote detonator. He never relied on a relay timer to ignite his creations. Besides, he wanted to watch the punishments.

To see the blood. To glory in it.

He already had his next target—a place that dispensed blasphemous information. In a few days, he'd be ready to implement the punishment. This time, even more transgressors would die. Justice, to those who refused to listen to the truth.

Belial would be pleased.

AFTER eating some delicious French toast that Marla was certain would go straight to her hips, she and Luke exchanged their coffee for iced tea, and settled outside in the backyard, in rusted metal patio chairs that had once been green. It was pleasant and not overly humid. Bryony was unusually mellow, and after an initial growl at Luke, settled down at Marla's feet.

She leaned back, inhaled deeply and, for a moment, almost forgot where she was, and why. "Nice morning."

"Yeah, it is."

Luke had a beautiful voice, deep, rich, calming. She met his azure gaze. "I'd like to check in with my family today and let them know I'm okay."

"That can be arranged. I'd prefer you e-mail them."

Sure he would. "As opposed to me calling them and blurting out something to the effect of 'A reincarnated

Atlantian has kidnapped me and is forcing me to help him hunt Belians'?"

He grinned, which somehow made him look both California-surfer wholesome and impossibly sexy at the same time. "Directing what you say on the phone could be a problem. Best to avoid it."

"Anyone ever pointed out you're a control freak?"

"I'm just careful." He drank some tea. "You have to be, when dealing with Belians."

"I'm sure you tell that to all the women you kidnap."

He leaned back, lazy indolence that she suspected could turn lethal in a New York second. "You're the only who's ever resisted me, babe."

Yep. Definitely sexy. She forced herself to remain focused on the current topic. "Speaking of that, why me? I'm assuming you've worked with other conductors. Why couldn't you use one of them?"

His expression turned serious. "I wish it were that easy. First off, there aren't that many conductors that we know of. Second, not every conductor is a good match with every Sentinel. And right now, there aren't any conductors available to work with me. I've already tried that route."

"No dial-a-conductor service, huh?" Marla knew she was being flippant, but it was either that or freak. She could still feel the sense of evil that had nearly suffocated her yesterday, like a nightmare that continued to haunt long into the waking hours.

Luke remained serious. "No, there's not. Besides that, very precise matches, like you and I have, are rare."

The thought of being a precise match—whatever that meant—with Luke sent an unnerving warmth through her. "Great," she muttered, willing her body to calm. "So I'm the cavalry." She thought again about the evil that had touched her yesterday, and the warmth changed to a shiver. "About these conductions, what are they, exactly?"

"A conduction is a meditation ritual, for lack of a better way to describe it, between a Sentinel and a human conductor."

"But aren't you human, too?"

"I have a mortal, human body. But my spiritual makeup is different. A conductor, on the other hand, is always human. And always the opposite sex of the Sentinel."

"Why is that?"

"Because—" He hesitated, an unreadable expression on his face. "It has to do with chakra energies. Have you ever meditated?"

"No. Is it like praying?"

"Not exactly. In prayer, the participants are basically doing the talking, or sending out energy. In mediation, the participants are listening, or receiving energy."

"Okay." She nodded to show she understood so far. "So what is chakra energy?"

"Let's start with the basics. The chakras are spiritual centers in the human body that correlate to both physical areas of the body and a specific color. For example, the fifth chakra corresponds to the thyroid and is represented by blue. The third chakra is the adrenals and yellow. There are seven chakras—four lower and earthbound, and three higher and spirit centered. They run in a straight line up through the body, from the pelvis to the top of the head— except for the seventh chakra, which is in the pituitary, and is lower than the sixth chakra."

"What do they do?"

"Well . . ." He paused, considering. "They act as receptacles for energy. When they are engaged via meditation, energy flows in and upward through them, from bottom to top, then settles into a figure eight pattern, running through them repeatedly."

"What does that energy do?"

"First off, you need to understand that whenever *any-one*—not just a Sentinel or conductor—meditates, these energies flow in and up through the centers. But with a Sentinel/conductor link, they're greatly intensified. They set up a vibration very similar to the vibratory level of Belians, which only operate in the lower earth-based chakras. This creates a tremendous surge of energy that comes up through the lower four chakras and enhances the Belian's psychic signature that the Sentinel has already gotten from the BCS."

"Tell me again—what's a BCS?"

"Sorry. I keep forgetting you're not familiar with these things. BCS is shorthand for Belian crime scene."

Marla was trying to follow him, but it was a lot of unfamiliar information. "You've mentioned that, but this is pretty much Greek to me."

"I know it sounds complicated." Luke set down his glass, shot Bryony a warning glare when she started for it, then returned his attention to Marla. "But it's all about the energy, especially the initial surge in the base chakras."

The way he was looking at her made her uneasy. "And what is that surge, exactly?"

"It goes back to your question about why matched Sentinels and conductors are always the opposite sex. The surge, which originates in the lowest base chakra, the gonads— relating to ovaries in a woman, testicles in a man—creates a powerful burst of sexual energy." He paused, his intense gaze pinning her like a butterfly on a specimen board.

"Most conductions culminate with sexual intercourse, which creates the closest vibratory level to the Belian. When the Sentinel and conductor come together physically, it melds a link between their sixth chakra and third eye and provides the strongest possible magnification of the Belian's psychic signature."

The words *sexual intercourse* shrilled through her mind, sent her thoughts into a whirlwind. "What exactly are you saying?" But she already knew, and her heart began pounding.

Luke slid to the edge of his chair, leaned toward her. "What I'm saying, Marla, is that we will have sex during the conduction."

MARLA stared at Luke, shock etched on her face. The sunlight danced on her hair, revealing red and golden strands mixed in with the rich chestnut curls. She looked none too happy.

"What did you just say?" she asked hoarsely.

Okay, so maybe he should have been less blunt. But it was a little late for diplomacy. "I said that we would have sex during the conduction."

"A conduction involves sex?"

"I just told you that. That's what makes it so effective. As I also said, the sexual surge sets up a vibration that mimics that of the Belian. The actual sex act locks in the pattern and magnifies the third eye link."

She continued to stare at him, as all color leached from her face. "Then I can't help you."

That was a kick in the pants. He knew he wasn't repulsive, knew the power of the attraction between them. "Why not?"

"Because I don't do sex."

"Look, I realize you don't know me very well, and I'm sure you don't fall into bed with every guy you meet. But this is a special situation, and necessary to—"

"*No.*" She pulled back against the chair, her hands gripping the rusted arms. "The answer is *no.*"

She had a haunted look, and he wondered if some bastard had hurt or abused her in some way. That would explain her skittishness at the Red Lion on Friday night. "I'll make it good for you, Marla. I swear I won't hurt you."

"You. Don't. Understand." She drew out each word as if she were unable to breathe. "I don't do sex. Ever."

He stared at her, trying to sort through what she was telling him. "*Ever?*"

Her chest heaved. "That's right."

Something wasn't clicking here. "Ever, as in . . ." He pondered her defensive posture and the path of the conversation. Jolted as the impossible occurred to him. "*Never?*"

"Never." She met his stunned gaze, her eyes challenging. "I've never had sex, and I'm not planning to."

* * *

JULIA went directly to the Missing Persons Unit at the southeast substation. Missing Persons was part of the juvenile division, which seemed odd. But Barbara said more juveniles went missing than any other group of people. Frightening—and sad.

Barbara had spoken with John Cavender, and he came out immediately when Julia asked for him. He was a bear of a man, with a massive frame, and somewhat overweight. He had sandy brown hair and somber hazel eyes. He wore a rumpled navy suit that did nothing for his coloring.

But his gaze was steady, his handshake brief but firm. "I understand you believe your sister has gone missing," he said.

"I know she has."

"Then let's fill out a report." He shifted the folder he had in his hand and indicated a small table in the corner of the waiting area. He pulled out some forms. "What is the missing person's name?"

"Marla Reynolds."

"Physical description?"

Julia answered his questions—and there were a lot— some eye opening and some that would have been insulting if the situation had been different. But she understood that people and situations were complex, and that some motivations weren't logical or ethical, or were emotionally driven. So she tried not to take offense as they waded through numerous questions.

Finally, Investigator Cavender put down his pen and looked at her. "Ms. Reynolds, I have to tell you that it looks like this may be a voluntary absence. Your sister's things and pet are gone—"

"And I've explained she would never have taken the dog into Mexico. Bryony always stays with family if Marla has to go somewhere."

He held up a placating hand. "So you told me. But your sister might have decided to take the dog this time. Some of her personal items are also gone. She's off work this week and she did send you an e-mail." He tapped the printed message that Julia had provided. "Her absence appears to be aboveboard."

"But it's out of character. If you knew Marla, knew our circumstances—" Julia paused. She wasn't going there, not with this man. "We're a very close family, Officer Cavender. Marla would never tell us she was going off through an e-mail."

He nodded patiently. "I understand. We're certainly not going to ignore this, and we'll do some preliminary checks of hospitals and the . . . uh . . . morgue. I don't think there's any need to look at her house, since you say there's nothing suspicious there."

She stiffened as his gaze softened with what appeared to be pity, which she despised. They didn't need pity, they needed action.

"I will do my best, Ms. Reynolds," he said. "But I really don't expect to find anything that will indicate foul play. Hopefully, your sister will return home safe and sound by the end of the week."

"Sure," Julia said, uncharacteristic anger filling her. "That's what we'll hope for, won't we? Well, I won't waste any more of your time." She pushed the chair back and started the laborious process of standing.

He stood and offered a hand, which she shook only because ingrained manners demanded that she do so. "It's not a waste of time, Ms. Reynolds. It's just . . . well, people go missing for a lot of reasons. I hope this is just a case of your sister wanting to enjoy her time off."

Why won't anyone believe me? Julia made her way out of the building, blinking against the bright glare of the sun. Even though she was upset, she knew that Barbara Gray and Investigator Cavender meant well. But there wasn't much they could do, under the circumstances.

Julia would have to continue on her own. She looked at her watch and wondered when the Red Lion Pub opened for business.

* * *

STILL staring at Marla, Luke upgraded that kick in the pants to a gut punch. "You've *never* had sex?"

"I just told you that," she said, throwing his words back at him.

"But—" He ran his hand through his hair, trying to assimilate the shock. "How can that be? You're thirty years old. In this day and time, no one your age is a virgin, unless there's something wr—" *Damn!* Shock was overriding clear thought and tact. He clamped his mouth shut, before he blurted out something really stupid.

Her eyes narrowed to glittering points. "Unless there's something wrong with me?"

"I didn't say that. It's just—" He paused again. There was always the possibility that Marla had been simply waiting for the right man to come along, but he sensed that wasn't it. "I didn't expect this."

"That's very obvious." She jolted up from the chair.

This was going well. Hell, from the start, nothing had gone as planned with Marla. Resisting the strong urge to bang his head against a wall, he tried to marshal whatever good sense remained. "I'm sorry. It's just . . . you're attractive and smart and sexy and . . . I don't understand."

Her hands clenched into fists at her side. "Look, we've already established why you're interested in me, so quit lying to me, all right?"

"But I'm not lying."

"You know what? You're just like every other man who wants something from a woman. Go to hell." She whirled toward the back door.

He couldn't let it go. "Is it a religious thing?"

She halted, laughed harshly. "Oh, *yes*, that's it. I worship at the altar of the goddess of purity and chastity."

"Marla, I'm trying to understand. Do you dislike men?"

She glared at him over her shoulder. "I don't prefer women, if that's what you're thinking."

"Then why?"

Her expression became shuttered. "It's none of your

damned business." She spun and slammed inside the house.

Yeah, this was really going well.

THE bastard! Marla stormed in the house, ready to kick something. She had more sensitivity in her little finger than the big oaf had in his entire body. She welcomed the anger coursing through her, because it was exponentially better than the pain.

She intended to take refuge in the bedroom and hoped Luke would have the decency to leave her alone. But her gaze fell on the laptop sitting on the kitchen table. If she was fast, she could take it into the bedroom and maybe get off an e-mail before he noticed it was missing.

She reached for it, hitting the stack of papers beside it. They slid, some going on the floor, some fanning across the table. Marla picked up the laptop, but the headline blaring from part of a newspaper peeking out of the papers stopped her in her tracks.

School bus explodes, killing twenty-two children. She shoved the page aside, saw beneath it: *Bus explosion not an accident. Evidence of a bomb discovered.* And below that, another newspaper article: *Bomb used in school bus explosion was a sophisticated device.*

Why would Luke be interested in the school bus explosion, unless . . . *he was the bomber.* The laptop slid from her hands, crashing to the floor. She took a step back, panic roaring through her. *She had to get out of here.*

But even as the near hysteria and the urge to flee had her stumbling toward the front of the house, an inner voice rose above the pounding of her heart. *No. That's not right. Luke wouldn't do this.* She'd been around him less than two days, but she already knew he wouldn't harm an innocent person. So why the interest?

Realization hit her like a tidal wave, and she froze, the ramifications tumbling through her mind. She turned, looked at the papers scattered on the table. Luke must be tracking the bomber. *Which meant the bomber was the Belian.* That must be why she'd seen the body parts in that vision from hell at the shack. *Oh, God.*

"Marla? You okay?" Luke's voice came from the back doorway.

That was a short-lived reprieve. She stared at the last article, her vision blurring. "The bomber," she whispered hoarsely. "That's him, isn't it? The Belian."

"Yeah, that's the monster I'm tracking."

It was the whammy that put her over the edge. Pain and fear combined and exploded like a geyser through her chest. Hot tears filled her eyes. *No.* She was *not* going to cry in front of Luke. She spun from the table, intending to head for the sanctuary of the bathroom, but careened into the counter. Stifling a sob, she stumbled the other way.

"Are you crying?" He stepped toward her.

"No. Leave me alone." She headed the other way around the table. Hiccuped back another sob.

"Ah, shit," he muttered, and she suddenly found herself wrapped in powerful arms and pressed against a hard chest. How had he moved so fast? This guy could catch the proverbial speeding bullet.

She tried to shove away, but it was like trying to move a two-ton wall. She settled for balling up her hand and hitting him on the shoulder. He didn't react. "I'm sorry," he murmured, and she sensed his sincerity. "I was out of line, and I'm really sorry."

So was she, because she was about to embarrass herself big time. She felt the tears overflow her eyes, and her body shuddered from repressed sobs.

He sighed, and his hand stroked her hair. "You might not believe this, but I'm normally not this inept. For whatever reason, I haven't been able to do anything right with you."

She caught a breath, managed an indignant "I'm not something to be handled!"

"Don't I know it. Believe me, babe, if you could be handled, we wouldn't be having these missteps. And if I get out of line again, feel free to bite me. Or sic psycho dog on me."

An image of the places where she could sink her teeth on him flashed into her mind. It wasn't helped by the barrage of sexual energy their close proximity swirled into the emotional mix. She was *so* not going there. "I think I'd prefer to knee you somewhere crucial."

"Sorry, but I can't let you do that. I might need those crucial parts in the future."

She couldn't help it—she smiled despite herself. He must have sensed her tension lessening, because his grip eased. "You going to be okay?"

She took a deep breath, felt her control returning. "Yes. I'm sorry I lost it."

"You're entitled." He released her, and she stepped back, scrubbing away her tears.

Unable to look at him, she gestured vaguely toward the hallway. "I need a few moments."

"Sure. Take all the time you need."

She escaped to the bathroom, closed the warped door and leaned against it with a shuddering sigh. She felt fragmented, like she was in a surreal experience—which she was. Lowering the toilet lid, she sank down, buried her face in her hands. This was beyond nightmarish. The Belian was the bomber, the monster who'd blown up an entire busload of innocent children last week.

She was in a position to help track he/she/it—whatever it was—except, freak that she was, she wasn't capable of the basic male/female sexual relations apparently required in a conduction. It seemed that no matter how much time passed, or how far she tried to run, the past—specifically, *that* night—caught up with her.

Funny how one event could impact a life so irrevocably, even eleven years later.

Somehow, she was going to have to overcome it. She wasn't a deeply religious person. After sustaining her own horrendous injuries and then witnessing the assault on Julia, she'd questioned God's existence. Yet how could she explain being at the Red Lion Pub—when she *never* went to bars—the same exact time as Luke? Or taking the seat beside him? Or the apparently precise Sentinel/conductor match between them?

If one believed in things happening for a reason, then she had been divinely guided to the Red Lion Pub and to Luke on Friday night. And if she was supposed to help him track down a monster capable of killing twenty-two innocent children, then she had better get with the program.

Even if the thought of having sex, albeit with a guy as hot as Luke, made her stomach clench and left her nauseous. All she had to do was keep from throwing up until afterward.

She sat there a long time, taking deep, even breaths, telling herself that bringing justice to the Belian was far more important than her traumatized psyche, with its sexual hang-ups.

She went to the sink and splashed cold water on her face. She stared at her reflection in the mirror. With her red-rimmed eyes and her splotchy face and wild hair, she was certainly a candidate for the "least sexy woman on the face of the Earth" award.

But she didn't think that would matter to Luke. He had only one goal: to track a Belian monster, using sex and chakra energies (whatever those were) as his tools.

She was also one of those tools. There was no sense putting it off. She took another deep breath and turned.

Her hand only shook a little as she opened the bathroom door and headed for the kitchen.

SIX

JULIA entered the Red Lion Pub around 2:00 p.m. There was a small crowd, imbibing either business drinks or after-lunch fortification before returning to work. She had to admit the pub was classy looking, with its fireplace, red leather booths, and intimate seating areas. She hadn't been in a bar in eleven years, but some things never changed—like the mingled scents of food, lit cigars, and stale smoke.

She went directly to the bar, which was made of highly polished dark wood, and had a gleaming brass beer tap behind it. A young woman with short, spiky hair that was an artificial purplish red shade was drawing a draft beer. Remembering Rebecca's description of a Friday night bartender with "fake red hair," Julia waited until the bartender loaded two beers onto the tray of a waiting server.

The young woman turned toward her with a questioning glance. "May I help you?" Then she did a double take. "Dr. Reynolds."

Julia stared at the girl, recognizing her as a student, but she didn't recall the name. "You're in my advanced linear algebra class."

The young woman nodded, the silver hoops in her triple-pierced ears catching the light. "You weren't there this morning. We had Richards instead. What a dork." She didn't seem at all concerned that she was insulting a tenured full professor in front of her own instructor. "What can I get for you?"

"I don't want anything." Julia paused, trying to remember the girl's name. She did try to learn her students' names, but she had over a hundred new ones every semester. "Were you working here Friday night?"

The bartender nodded. "Yes. You don't remember me, do you?"

"I know who you are," Julia said. "You're always in class, and you give correct answers. I just have so many students."

"I know. U of H is so freaking big. I'm Miriam White."

"Ah yes, I do know that name. You hurt the class curve with that ninety-six you got on the last exam." Julia looked at Miriam approvingly. She liked to see women do well in what was traditionally a man's field. "Good job."

"Thanks. Uh, what about Friday night?"

"Did you serve a woman with curly shoulder-length hair and eyeglasses? She was sitting next to a blond man."

"Oh, yeah, I remember them. He was killer. He ordered Fat Tire, draft. She had merlot. What about them?"

"I'm trying to find the man. Can you tell me anything about him?"

Miriam stared at her curiously. "Because he's a private investigator?"

Excitement flared. "Is he?" Julia asked.

"Said he was. That's what he told the lady you mentioned." Miriam angled toward a male server standing at the end of the bar. "Be there in a minute." She turned back to Julia. "He could have been jacking her, because he was really coming on to her, but he had that air about him, you know?"

"Like what?"

"Like he was military or police or something."

"Did you happen to hear his name?"

"Luke. Luke Paxton." She glanced at the waiting server again. "Can you give me a minute, Dr. Reynolds? I've got an order."

"That's all right. I have to go. You sure that was the man's name?"

"Oh, yeah, I've got a really good memory for stuff like that, and he paid by credit card. Plus he was"—Miriam fanned herself to demonstrate—"really hot, if you know what I mean."

Julia never gave men a second glance, but she nodded to be polite. "Thanks, Miriam. Keep up the good work in class." She shifted her weight, wincing. She'd walked far more today than she normally did, and her leg was screaming in protest. "Oh—and be careful when you go into the kitchen here. The floor is wet—and quite slippery."

"How'd you know I'm going on break in a few minutes?"

"Just a hunch." Julia wondered why she ever said anything. It only made people think she was even more eccentric. "Just be careful."

"Uh, sure. Will you be at class on Wednesday?"

Julia stared at the name she'd written in her planner. "I don't know. I might have to take care of some other business."

Such as tracking down private investigator Luke Paxton.

LUKE was working on the laptop when Marla left the bathroom. She noticed there was a second laptop beside it. Trying to calm her racing heart, she stepped into the kitchen. "You have two computers?"

He looked up, his gaze assessing. "I always carry an extra. The screen is cracked on the first one."

Because she had knocked it off the table. "I'm sorry. I'll pay for the damage."

"Don't worry about it. I keep warranties on them. How are you doing?"

Try utterly panicked at the thought of having sex with this man. She suddenly wasn't so sure that she could overcome her demons. She gestured toward the open beer beside him. "Got any more of those?"

"In the fridge."

She took one out, used the opener on the counter to pop the top, then slugged back a fourth of the bottle on the spot. Repressing the urge to burp, she waved her beer toward the refrigerator. "We're going to need more."

"More beer?"

"Yes." She pulled out the chair opposite him, slid into it. "I'm thinking about getting stinking drunk."

He stared at her a long, unsettling moment, and she felt as if that laser-sharp gaze was dissecting her soul. "Marla, what is this about?"

She still couldn't tell him. Wasn't even sure she could scrounge up the courage to do what was necessary to track down a mass murderer. God, she was an emotional mess. She drank another large portion of beer, and reverted to the levity that had helped her remain sane thus far. "Are you talking about my virginity, or your reaction to my virginity, or *my* reaction to *your* reaction to my virginity?"

His gaze didn't waver. "All of the above. Talk to me. Tell me what's going on."

The beer was three-fourths gone now, and she was still wound so tight inside, she knew if she cracked open, she'd never be able to hold back the torrent. Control was vital to her. She and Julia were alike in that regard. Keeping total control of their lives had become their new religion since that night.

She shook her head. "No. I don't want to talk about it. Correction—I *won't* talk about it. The reason why I've chosen to refrain from sex has no bearing on this situation."

"Maybe not. But it sure as hell impacts it, and I don't want any more surprises like we had yesterday. I need to know anything and everything that might affect how you react when you help me track the Belian."

She noticed he'd said "when," not "if," so obviously he

thought they were going forward with a conduction and therefore, sex. Since she fully believed him now, had felt the depravity and evilness of the Belian, how could she not try?

"If you're offering to help me overcome my . . . lack of experience, I"—she slugged back the rest of the beer, set the bottle on the table—"might—*would*—be willing to let you."

He blinked, and she could see she'd surprised him. "You would have sex with me?"

If her psyche didn't splinter into a thousand pieces first. She thought of those poor children, of the precious faces in the pictures that had been in the newspapers. "Yes."

"You," he said slowly, "are a continual surprise." Sitting back in his chair, he rubbed the bridge of his nose. "I admire—and appreciate—your determination to help me bring justice to this Belian. But I can't have sex with you now."

She reared back, certain she hadn't heard him right. "But you told me it was crucial in a conduction."

"No. I told you that it made the conduction more effective. But under the circumstances, we won't be engaging in sexual intercourse."

She should be relieved, but instead a surprising wave of anger swept through her. What type of game was he playing? She'd worked up her courage, taken what was a huge step for her—and for nothing. What, she wasn't good enough for his purposes?

She normally kept a tight control over her emotions, but she was stressed and had the better part of a beer inside her, and the past few days had been too much. She glared at him. "First you want to fuck me to catch the bad guy. Now you won't touch me with a ten-foot pole. What the hell is going on, Luke?"

His eyes flared, but she couldn't tell if he was angry or shocked. She'd certainly shocked herself. She rarely used profanity, and until this moment, the "F" word had never been a part of her vocabulary.

Luke sat back in his chair. "Tell me how you really feel, Marla."

Obviously, he had better control over his own emotions—assuming he felt anything—than she did. "Not funny," she muttered.

"No, it's not. But you manage to keep me off balance." He blew out a breath. "Okay. Let me explain something. You and I will not be engaging in conductor sex because Sentinel law forbids intercourse if a conductor—male or female—is a virgin."

"But why? You just told me how crucial it is to the process, how it creates the closest vibration to the Belian, magnifies the signature, and all that other stuff I didn't understand."

He leaned across the table and captured both her hands in his. Immediately, the attraction between them surged. "Feel this? Feel the energy in your blood, the throbbing in your body?" He stared meaningfully at her breasts, which were already painfully swollen.

"Feel the need, Marla? The desire, rising inside you?" His glittering gaze rose to her face. "Multiply that a hundred times over. Imagine that need hammering your body until you can't think of anything but the Sentinel—or any man, for that matter—pounding into you. Imagine it increasing even more, until you think you'll explode if you don't find release.

"Conduction sex is wild. And fast. And hard," he told her. "There's no finesse, no gentleness, just all-out *fucking*—as you so aptly put it. Anyone who's sexually inexperienced could be injured. That's why our law forbids us from doing a sexual conduction with a virgin. I've pushed the boundaries too far as it is. I'm not totally ignoring the law."

He released her so suddenly, it felt as if a breaker had been thrown. The electricity vanished. He leaned back, seemingly relaxed and unaffected, and his gaze swept her again, lingering on her breasts. "Too bad. We would have been good together."

His black-magic voice sent a shiver through her, but she knew there was nothing sexy about her. He was just playing her. "Give me a break." She rose on shaky legs to get another beer.

"Marla," he said, and she realized he was standing next to her. She mentally added stealth to his other abilities.

Ignoring him, she reached across him for the opener. But she was trembling so badly she couldn't get the stupid cap off. He took the bottle from her, flipped off the top with his finger, and handed it back to her.

She took it without looking at him and headed for the back door. She needed distance and oblivion—which would require some serious drinking—and to get her act together before going home.

"Marla, wait."

She felt a hint of compulsion and stopped. "You're doing that woo-woo crap again."

"Look at me."

With a frustrated sound, she turned, looked at him. Her heart did a double take at the approval in his expression. "You are an amazing woman," he said. "I don't know what happened to make you remain celibate, but I suspect it took a lot for you to offer yourself the way you did."

Her anger evaporated in the face of a sobering sadness. "It's not nearly on par with what those children and their families have suffered."

"But you were willing to go to bat for them."

"It didn't help anything. When are you taking me back?"

"What do you mean?" Opening the refrigerator, he got himself another beer.

"Since I can't help you with your conduction, you are taking me home . . . right?"

"No." He removed the cap from the bottle. "We can still do a conduction. We just won't have sex during it."

"But will it work?"

"It will, to some extent. It might not be as effective, but I have a feeling that you and I are going to be an explosive combination, even without the physical culmination."

Of its own accord, her heart rate accelerated. She wet her dry lips. "So, when are we going to do it?"

His deep-sea gaze touched her like a caress. "As soon as you finish that beer."

Her heart leaped into major overdrive, and her senses heightened. She could feel the warmth of Luke's body, even though he was a good three feet away. Could smell the scents of soap and heat and tantalizing earthiness he emanated.

She couldn't decide whether she wanted to guzzle down the beer, or sip it very slowly. One thing was certain: Even though she believed Luke Paxton wouldn't hurt her, he threatened her on a primal level that put every feminine cell in her body on full alert.

As a matter of fact, he scared the hell out of her.

HE slipped the bombs into the backpack. No one would ever suspect what he had inside, especially considering the target. He was too clever to draw attention. Besides, Belial was helping him. He was excited about the mission, felt the stirring in his lower body. But he hated being in the city, hated the crowds and the traffic and the noise and the stinking pollution. This city was smaller and not as bad as Houston. Yet it still bore the signs of society's dysfunction, the foul leavings of sinners.

Belial had insisted that he come here. So he found a cheap hotel north of the city. He'd found the target; visited the building several times and made detailed drawings. He would make several trips to place bombs on each of three floors, and then detonate from a nearby location. Each placement was carefully calculated to generate the greatest damage.

This place that dispensed blasphemous information, claiming it was truth and knowledge, would be defiled. And those who came here to worship that false knowledge would be punished.

Yes, Belial whispered to him. *Yes, you will punish them,*

and then they'll be sorry they didn't listen. I will be very
pleased.

"There will be blood," he said.

Yes, Belial answered. *A lot of blood.*

MARLA sat at the kitchen table, Luke across from her.
Since there was no furniture in the tiny living room, this
was the only inside place where they could sit. She was
completely sober—unfortunately—despite the second beer.
Thoughts of tracking a soulless bomber who murdered children had killed any buzz.

"When we put our hands together in the traditional
form, the chakra energies will initiate." Luke placed his
hands palm up on the table. Taking a deep breath, she followed suit.

"The energies will come fast and hard, and they'll move
upward through you," he continued. "You may feel burning
sensations or pressure, and definitely sexual desire. It will
feel like your body is rocking really hard, but that's just a
sensation caused by the energies. You'll probably see images flashing by. You might see colors, and hear sounds,
too. Don't let it throw you. You don't have to do anything
but hold on, and let the energies flow. Whatever happens,
don't let go of my hands. That will break the link."

Oh, boy, she could hardly wait to do this.

"First we'll set up some protection." Luke tugged the
chain around his neck, pulling the pink stone from beneath
his shirt.

At the shack, Marla had been too disoriented to question him about it, but now she asked, "What is that?"

"It's pink quartz, the same material that makes up the
great Tuaoi stone that was on Atlantis." He cupped the pendant in his hand, leaned forward so she could see it better.
It was a smooth pink oval, with silver wire woven intri-
cately around its outer edges. "It's tuned to the Tuaoi stone,
and to my own vibratory levels. It helps shield me and also
amplifies my psychic abilities."

"But if Atlantis was destroyed thousands of years ago, and this great Ta–Taw–whatever–stone was there, how can your pendant be tuned to it?"

"The Tuaoi stone wasn't destroyed. It's buried deep in the Atlantic Ocean, but it still puts off energy."

"That can't be good. It seems to me that if Belians got hold of the stone, it would—"

"Be disastrous," Luke finished for her. "That's why the Sanctioned keep a close watch on all deep-sea expeditions off the eastern coastline of the U.S., as well as off the Bahamas."

"One more thing to worry about," she muttered.

"Let me do the worrying. All you have to do is be a conduit for me." Folding his fingers over the stone, Luke sat back and closed his eyes. He spoke in that beautiful flowing language again, his voice low and rich.

She felt the movement of the air around them, felt the flow of warmth and even thought the light grew brighter. "That should do it." He dropped the pendant and reached for her. "Take my hands. Your left palm should be facing up and your right palm facing down."

He showed her, turning his left palm up so that it cupped her right palm, and reversing the position with their other hands. Then he tightened his grip, keeping them firmly linked. "Whatever happens," he repeated, "don't let go."

She felt the energy immediately, a stirring deep in her womb. Before she could analyze it, it shot upward into her abdomen in a heated rush. She jolted forward with a gasp.

"It's okay. That's just the first chakra opening."

The burning poured through her abdomen, and dampness pooled between her legs. Need, desire, hot and intense, fired through her. She clamped her legs together, forced back a moan. The pressure moved upward, and her belly button felt like it was bulging outward.

"Second chakra opening," Luke murmured. "Stay with me, Marla."

Just the second one? She gasped again as she experienced a sensation similar to being punched in the rib cage . . . like when William Bennett had hit her when she tried to defend Julia . . . No time to complete that thought as she heard an audible "pop" and felt the burning in her chest. A green haze filled her vision. She struggled to draw a breath, tried to jerk free.

"Whoa! Everything's fine. Just relax and breathe. Take a deep breath. That's right." Luke's low, soothing voice helped keep her from totally losing it. "Third and fourth chakras are open. Hang in there, Marla. We're through the lower levels."

She didn't know if she could survive three more chakras. Her body felt as if it were a stringed puppet being viciously jerked around. And still, she felt the clawing sexual need. Yearned for, *craved* having a man—not just any man, but Luke—inside her. Filling her, pounding her senseless, giving her the release she desperately needed.

Her throat tightened, closing off as the burn flooded it. Her breath was obstructed! She gave a strangled cry.

"No . . . no," Luke said. "Don't fight it. It's okay. Just relax and breathe through it. That's the fifth chakra."

Relax? He was crazy if he thought she could—A blinding starburst of indigo light exploded around her like a flash bulb, and sharp pain speared through the top of her head. She cried out again, gripping Luke's hands like they were lifelines.

"Hold on. Just hold on, Marla. Almost there. That's the sixth chakra, which links to the third eye. I'm starting to see things . . ." His voice trailed off, and she understood why.

Pictures. Stark, disturbing images, flashed through her mind in rapid succession, too fast to really process. Another burst of light, this one violet, and electricity tingled in the middle of her forehead. She struggled, tried to rise, but the energies slammed her back down.

Then they began shooting up and down her spine, rocking her forward and back. Her eyes clenched shut. A color light show started behind her eyelids: red, orange, yellow, green, blue, shades of purple and violet. Flashing and merging together, only to separate and merge again. More images were interspersed between the colors: a blur of hands putting something together with wires and electronic components, a school bus, an awful explosion, smoke, blood . . . So much blood . . . and body parts.

She heard things: children screaming, the appalled murmurs of emergency crews, and a flat-toned voice, soft and asexual, saying, "The unjust, the wicked, shall be punished. Praised be Belial, and praised be the blood." And she heard unearthly howling.

But worse, far worse, were the emotions bombarding her. Fear and terror, horror and disbelief, overwhelming grief. The darkness and depravity of the monster watching. Of its smugness, its utter lack of humanity. It beat at her, not quite as oppressive as it had been at the shack, but still pressing against her. "No!" She struggled hard now, managed to wrench one hand free. "I can't do this!"

"Marla!"

"Oh God, oh God. Luke, let me go. It's touching me again. I can feel it."

He released her. She twisted up and around, knocking the chair over and tangling with it as it went down. She hit the floor hard. He was there before she could push herself up. He lifted the chair off her and shoved it away. "Are you all right?"

She came to her knees and wrapped her arms around herself. "I don't know. Oh God. I saw it. I saw the school bus explode, saw what was left of those children. And I could feel it. I could feel *everything*. The children's terror, their parents' grief, and that—that *thing*. It was gloating over their deaths.

Nausea rolled through her, and she tried to get to her feet. "I feel sick."

He swept her into his arms and stood. "To the bathroom?"

She wanted away from the darkness still swirling around them. "No . . . outside. Please."

In seconds, the sun was bright in her eyes. She lifted her

face to the light, drew in a deep shuddering breath. Blew it out. "God."

"Yeah. I know. It can be bad. How's your stomach?"

She took another breath, felt the churning calm a little. "Better. You can put me down now."

Instead, he strode over to the rusted metal loveseat and sat down, cradling her against him. Surprised, but grateful for the comfort he offered, she curled into him, letting his warmth and scent chase away the stench of evil. She hated being weak, but right now she needed Luke's solid strength.

He settled back, tightening his arms around her. "Just try to give me a little warning if you're going to hurl."

"I think I'll be okay." But she wasn't. She started shaking violently and despite the moderate temperatures, felt chilled to the bone. She tried to will her body to calm. "I-I don't know why I c-can't stop shaking," she managed.

"It's shock. Here." Luke took her hand, brought it up to his chest. "Hold on to this." He pressed the crystal into her hand, wrapped his own hand around hers and the pendant.

She felt power, but it was a calming flow that steadied her. She "saw," on some inner level, the light surrounding them. Again felt Luke's presence around and within her, and the evil being drawn away.

The shaking eased, and her heart began to slow. The sense of darkness receded, although there was still that sick feeling she sometimes got after a nightmare. She sagged against him, wishing this really was a nightmare. But it was worse, far worse, because it was real.

"I don't know if I can do this again," she said, wondering how he could do it on a regular basis.

He rested his cheek against her hair. "You can. I know it's hard, but you're strong, Marla. I don't think you realize how amazing you are."

She felt the loveseat jolt, saw Bryony had jumped up next to them. The dog whined and pressed against them; didn't even growl at Luke. "Look at her. She can sense the evil, too."

"Sure she can. Didn't you hear her howling out here?"

She pushed back to look up at him. "That was her? I heard howling, but didn't realize it was Bryony."

He nodded, his eyes dark and serious. "It was her. She must have tapped into the conduction. Psycho dog is also psychic dog. Who knew?"

That evoked a small laugh. "Well . . . yeah. I didn't know. She always barks at sirens and some motorcycles—those high-pitched ones. But I've never heard her howl before."

The brief moment of levity slipped away, leaving the dark haunting images. Now that her stomach and the shaking had settled, she was left with a killer headache and a still-raging libido. Her breasts were swollen and aching, and her lower body was just as sensitized.

If the hardness pressing against her bottom was any indication, Luke had the same problem in the libido department. Of course, their close proximity to one another wasn't helping matters. She rubbed her forehead.

"Let me work on that." He brushed away her hand, splayed his fingers across her forehead. "Nonchanneled conduction energy usually results in a bad headache, among other things."

Heat tingled from his fingers into her head, and the pain eased. "That feels good," she said, for once having no objection to him using his powers. "Thank you."

"You're welcome. Unfortunately, there's nothing I can do about the other problem. Not without taking care of it the old fashioned way."

She smiled at his wry tone, and resigned herself to her turned-on state. He was probably more uncomfortable than she was. "So it always comes back to sex."

"In this case, yes. But sex as a solution is generally a guy thing, anyway."

And he was definitely a guy. If she was ever ready to explore that realm, he'd be a great candidate. But for now, there were more pressing matters. She stared up at him. "Would the conduction have been stronger if we'd had sex?"

"Yes. The results would definitely have been more intense."

Great. She drew back. "I'd like to get up now."

He let her go, his gaze watchful as she stood and found her balance. Her legs were shaky, her stomach still queasy, but she was functional. She found her way to another chair, sank into it. The physical distance eased the sexual cravings—a little.

"Luke, I don't think I could have handled more intense. It was . . . pretty bad. You saw my reaction."

"It's tough, especially since you could feel the emotions of the victims and their families. It worries me that the shielding didn't seem to block the Belian."

"I think it helped. I didn't feel it quite as strongly as I did yesterday. But I was still able to feel the Belian." Still chilled, she drew her knees up and wrapped her arms around them.

"Marla, I want you to know, and to believe, that I will never let that Belian get near you. It would have to go through me first. And that's not going to happen. It's my job to protect innocents from Belians. I take it very seriously."

He didn't say it, but she suspected he would give his life, if necessary, in the performance of his job. It was a very sobering realization. "I do believe you. It's just that he felt so real, like he was in the room with us."

"*It.* The Belian is an *it*. Don't ever mistake it for a real person. And it's possible that it sensed us. The initial sexual surge is difficult to shield. Then you were able to connect with the Belian, despite what shielding we did have. This is a very powerful Belian we're up against." He studied Marla, his expression thoughtful. "Have you been empathic all your life?"

She didn't want to consider herself empathic at all—just sensitive. Nor did she want to tell him what had triggered that sensitivity. She shook her head. "I don't want to talk about that. I want you to explain exactly what happened during the conduction, and how it will help us catch this monster."

His lips thinned, and she could tell he wasn't happy with her refusal to answer his questions. But he didn't push her. "All right. We'll talk about the conduction, then. Once the sixth chakra opened, it engaged my third eye, which is the psychic center. Your energies acted like a magnifier for the patterns I'd already picked up from the BCS. Our combined energies created the flash of images, which are like clues."

"But I didn't see anything that we didn't already know." Even though what she had seen had been horrifying.

"I did. I saw how it's transporting the bombs, inside a backpack. And I saw an older blue Toyota Tercel. And a map of the state of Texas, which means it's probably on the move."

When he mentioned those things, Marla realized she'd seen very quick flashes of them as well. But she'd been derailed by the other images, while Luke had been able to keep his focus. "Do you think he—it—is driving the blue Toyota?"

"Most likely. But I couldn't get a fix on where it was headed."

"Did you see the license tag?"

"No, but it's possible I will on the next conduction. That's how the process works, with information revealed in layers."

"Oh." Disappointment swept through Marla. "So is there anything we can do?"

"I'm afraid not. All we can do at this point is to wait for it to surface again."

"With another bombing." It was more a statement than a question—she already knew the answer.

Luke nodded, his face grim. "Yes. With another bombing."

SEVEN

THAT evening, Luke waited until Marla fell asleep before
he called Adam. He usually sent e-mail reports, but felt the
situation warranted a phone call. Adam answered on the
second ring. "Hello, Paxton. I've been waiting to hear from
you."

"Hello, Adam."

"Since you're calling rather than communicating through
e-mail, I assume things are not going as planned. Did
Ms. Reynolds refuse to assist you?"

Luke felt a slight twinge of guilt about his methods of
persuasion, shoved them back before Adam could pick up
on them. "No, actually, she is helping me."

"But?"

"There are a few problems. As I mentioned in yesterday's e-mail, Marla is highly empathic. She tapped into the
Belian's emotions at the shack yesterday. Then during our
first conduction today, it happened again. I'm not sure I
can keep her fully shielded."

"Interesting. I would guess a foray into a Belian's psyche would be very upsetting for a human."

"It makes her physically ill." He felt the punch of worry, also shoved that back. He knew better than most the folly of getting emotionally involved with someone. "I'm concerned about possible long-term effects."

"Probably just an immediate biological reaction rather than anything permanent. She should be fine." Adam's rough voice was cool, logical, with the unemotional detachment of a highly evolved Sanctioned. "Would you consider the conduction a success?"

"To an extent, yes. But that's another thing. We didn't consummate the conduction."

"She refused?"

"No. She . . . she's sexually inexperienced. I'm the one who made the decision to keep it nonsexual."

"Inexperienced? As in *no* experience?"

"Yeah. The lady has never had sex, or so she says." Luke thought of Marla's pale, pinched face, of the way her hands had clenched the chair arms when she told him she was a virgin. Of her genuine pain. "I have no reason to believe she's lying."

"Unusual. She's how old?"

"Thirty. I think something happened to her to make her close off from relationships with men. And it doesn't appear to be a sexual preference for women."

"I don't believe she'd be a conductor if it were otherwise. I'm glad to know you're adhering to our laws." Steel warning edged those words, and Adam paused before saying, "Tell me what you learned from the conduction."

"The Belian is making more bombs. It carries them to the crime site in a backpack. I believe it's driving an older model Toyota Tercel, medium blue, maybe ten years old. And it was studying a map of Texas, so I believe it's not staying in this area, that it's on the move. But I saw nothing that would tell me where."

"Unfortunate. Perhaps another conduction would give you more information?"

"I don't think so. We can try, but I think we need to wait a day. I'm not sure Marla could handle another one so soon. She's no good to us if she has a mental break-down."

"Point taken. She is an innocent, and falls under our protection. As it is, events have already been set into motion. I don't think we would be able to stop the next strike, regardless."

That meant he'd had one of his visions—which were never wrong.

And that there would indeed be another bombing. Soon.

TUESDAY *was a good night to detonate,* he thought. There were a lot of people in the building. The University of Texas in Austin had almost 50,000 students, and the library was always busy, especially at night. Even more so with the school semester winding down, and many students completing term papers or studying for exams. All of them were purveyors of blasphemous information. They deserved to be punished.

The blood would be an offering to Belial.

He hoped *she* was watching. He had sensed her earlier today, felt her mind touch his. Not a Sentinel, he was certain. She'd exuded a different energy, and hadn't been strongly shielded. He wanted her to feel his power, to know how clever and strong he was.

Standing in the dark shadows of one of the dorms, he opened his backpack, and pulled out a remote. He looked younger than his years and dressed in jeans and athletic shoes and a Longhorns jacket, he looked like the students who crawled over the campus day and night. No one would suspect him.

He detonated all the devices. There were three on the first floor. Although he didn't have the pleasure of seeing the explosion this time, he saw the implosion of the glass windows from the two bombs, and the flames and smoke from the incendiary device, which he had cleverly placed near the main entrance.

He imagined the flying shards of glass and nails that he

had embedded in the Semtex; the stacks of books collapsing, the screams . . . and the blood.

There were two more incendiary devices, one in each of
the main stairwells; a bomb on the third floor and one on
the fifth floor. All were detonated. Smoke was pulsing out
now; people erupting from the entries, some screaming,
many injured. He knew more were trapped inside.

"Hook 'em, Horns!" he said with a smirk, making the
trademark symbol of longhorns with his right hand. Certainly *she* would appreciate his keen sense of humor.

While he would dearly love to stay and watch the show,
maybe even mingle with the wounded and pretend to be
helping, he knew it was too risky. So he closed his backpack, slung it over his shoulders and strolled to the parking
lot where he'd left his car.

He looked back with satisfaction as he drove away.

Belial was very pleased. And *she* couldn't help but be
impressed with his brilliance.

LUKE was working on his laptop when his cell phone
rang. He snagged the phone, saw the identity of the caller.
He'd already e-mailed his daily report, so this couldn't
be good. "Hey Adam. What's up?"

"There were just some bomb explosions in Austin, at
one of the university libraries."

"Shit. What time?" Luke looked at his watch, noting it
was 9:30 p.m.

"Thirty minutes ago. Marcus heard it on the police
scanner and notified me. It's probably the Belian."

"Yeah. Not too many known bombers in Texas right
now. We'll be on the road within an hour. I'll notify you
when we get there." Luke disconnected and ran his hands
through his hair. *Damn.* He knew in his gut the bomber had
to be the Belian—and it was escalating, going from buses
to buildings.

It was a good thing Adam had Sentinel initiates sta-
tioned around Texas, monitoring police scanners. It had

only been thirty minutes since the explosion. Luke would move faster this time. The Belian would likely hang around a day or two to gloat, and to plan its next course of action. Luke *would* get the son of a bitch.

He powered down his laptop and closed it, already running through a mental checklist of things to do. Striding to the open back door, he swung out the screen.

Marla was sitting on the metal loveseat, one leg tucked beneath her, the other swinging back and forth. She had on her stylish padded brown jacket over jeans and a turtleneck, and was drinking a beer as she stared up at the sky.

She was something else, he thought, with her satiny smooth skin, her large golden eyes, and that mass of chestnut hair. Even the stylized glasses perched on her nose were cute. Bryony, curled next to her, growled at him as he walked over.

She glanced toward him, her expression relaxed. "You ready to get off that computer and come enjoy this beautiful evening?"

She was obviously a little more settled since the conduction yesterday. They'd spent today on the Harley, exploring the Brazos Bend State Park—at the opposite end of the Belian's shack. They'd eaten dinner at Woodburners Barbeque, and bought ice cream at the Kwik Chek to bring back to the house. He'd discovered that when she wasn't under duress, she was warm and laid back, not at all anal like he figured an accountant would be. Unfortunately, relaxation time was over.

"We have to leave."

"Why?" She put her other foot down, scooted to the end of the chair. "What is it?"

"Another bombing."

"Oh, no." She got to her feet. "Where?"

"Austin. One of the campus libraries."

The color drained from her face. "Oh, God. More students."

"Looks that way." A cold, calm sensation came over him, and all emotion was shelved, for now. He was going into Sentinel mode, ready to do battle. "We're heading out as soon as we can pack up."

Marla took a deep breath, and he could almost see her steeling herself. She was a warrior in her own right, although she didn't realize it. "Okay," she said. "Just tell me what you need me to do."

THEY didn't get on the road until and hour and a half later, because Luke made a few phone calls—terse conversations too low-pitched for Marla to understand. Then they had to take Luke's motorcycle to a storage unit. He had a truck, a killer silver Nissan Frontier, parked behind the house, and felt it would be easier to travel in that. After the phone calls, he packed them up efficiently and quickly, and once the motorcycle was stored, they were out, headed north on Highway 36.

Bryony was delegated to the back extended cab area, which made her very unhappy. But she merely growled at Luke as he put her back there. Maybe the poodle had figured out that she would get zapped if she kept up the psycho dog routine. Or maybe she was beginning to accept Luke.

That was the case for Marla. It was strange, but she felt like she'd known him a long time. They'd been together—what day was this?—only three days, but in that time she'd come to trust him. And trusting men did not come easily to her.

Not only did she trust him, she believed his incredible story about Sentinels, Belians, and conductors. Even more disconcerting was the physical attraction she felt toward him. Part of that was simply the Sentinel/conductor link, but even when there was enough physical distance between them, Marla still felt a pull.

She glanced over at him as he drove, calm, steady, and in total control of the truck and everything around them. He had his hair tied back, and his profile was strong, chiseled, perfect, like a mythological god. She could feel his tension, though, could tell he was upset, although the signs were subtle. She suspected he was always cool and collected, even during the most chaotic situations.

She sank back, fatigue pulling at her, and was appalled that she could be sleepy, especially in view of the fact people were lying bloodied and probably dead in Austin.

Luke glanced at her. "Tired?"

"No." She straightened up. "I'm fine." She shouldn't have had that last beer. She'd been drinking way too much lately. But the way her life had gone these past days, she figured she was entitled. Still, the least she could do was stay awake and keep Luke company.

"You're such a liar." He fiddled with the radio dial, found a classic rock station. The notes of an Aerosmith song pounded out. "Why don't you get some sleep? These last few days have been tough."

"They haven't been any easier on you."

"I'm used to it."

"I don't see how you could ever get used to tracking down monsters that mutilate and murder without conscience." She wasn't just thinking about Belians as she spoke. She fervently hoped William Bennett continued to have his parole requests denied, and that he died a miserable death in Huntsville Prison before his insufficient twenty-year sentence played out.

"What I should have said is that I'm used to putting in long hours and going without sleep when necessary. I'm able to keep tracking down Belian monsters, because then I can send their sorry souls to burn on Saturn."

"*Souls?* Those things have souls?"

"Yeah, they do. We all come from the same source, the same Creator. But with free will, we have choices. Belians chose to follow Belial those thousands of years ago, and continue to do so."

"Well, damn," she muttered.

"You've picked up some bad language since you've been around me. I'm guessing you don't generally use some of the words I've heard from you."

"So I'm impressionable. And you're a bad influence. What's this burn on Saturn you mentioned?"

"Sentinels can kill the physical body of a Belian, but we can't destroy the soul, which is basically indestructible. If we just kill the Belian's body, the soul will find another outlet, either by reincarnating into a new body or possessing one that's already on Earth. So we send its soul to Saturn for rehabilitation." He shot her a feral grin. "It's not a pleasant experience."

"Kind of like hell?"

"Very much so."

"Good. Any chance mere mortals who also perform heinous crimes get to do a stint there as well?"

He looked at her again. "Did you have anyone particular in mind?"

She mentally slapped herself for letting thoughts of Bennett continually creep into this situation. He was in the past, and she needed to put it behind her. "There are just a lot of bad people in the world," she said. "And they're not all Belians, are they?"

"No, they're not, thank The One. I don't know if the souls of regular humans do stints on Saturn or not. But I do know one thing: Karmic laws apply to all of us. What goes around comes around, and we're continually being offered opportunities to rise above our imperfect human nature and operate out of our higher spiritual selves. To experience and create grace."

"I guess that's probably good." But a part of her fervently hoped Bennett burned in some sort of hell a long time before he achieved grace.

"It is a good thing. Otherwise, we'd all be in deep shit."

She had to laugh at that, felt the tension inside her ease a little. She managed to stay awake for most of the drive, although they spoke very little.

They reached Austin a little after two in the morning. Marla yawned and stretched her stiff muscles as they headed into the city. "Where are we going now?"

"I want to see if we can drive by the library."

She came fully awake, dread slithering through her, but she knew they had to get a lead on this Belian, and fast. They circled the campus twice, maneuvering through a surprising amount of traffic, despite the hour, and finding the streets onto the campus had been blocked off. There was also a large number of police and officials in the area.

Luke gave up trying. "There's no way we can get in there, unless we park and walk in. With all the people around, we still couldn't get close enough, and we might raise suspicion."

"But won't a delay make it harder to discover anything?"

"The Belian's energy patterns will still be strong." He looked at her. "Remember how clearly you felt it at the shack?"

How could she forget? Just the thought made her stomach clench. "Oh, I remember."

He returned his attention to the road. "It had probably been gone at least a week when you were there, but its psychic signature was still strong. That type of energy is like an oil spill—toxic, slimy, almost impossible to disperse. So the Belian's energy will still be there, near the crime scene.

"Unfortunately, there will be all sorts of other energies there as well, just like you felt during the conduction—the fear and pain of the victims, the shock and grief and anger from onlookers and rescue workers. I'll have to sift through all that to get the Belian's psychic signature."

"It sounds so complex."

"Hey, I'm a complex kind of guy. You can't accuse me of being shallow."

Marla had to smile. Luke had a charming, good old boy sense of humor that she suspected he used to keep an even balance. "You're full of yourself, but I agree you're not shallow."

"You're pretty deep yourself, lady. Got a lot of layers there."

She ignored the not so subtle hint that she was holding out on him. "Where are we going now?"

"Hotel. There's nothing more we can do tonight. We'll eat, sleep. Go after the Belian tomorrow."

They hit an all-night Wendy's on the edge of the campus, then headed south and found a Holiday Inn that would let them take in Bryony. Luke insisted on getting only one room for them. "The chances are very good the Belian is still in the area," he told Marla as they grabbed their stuff from the truck and let Bryony do her thing in the small grassy area behind the hotel. "I want to keep you close."

"How can it know we're here?"

"It's bound to know we'll come after it." He closed the truck door, beeped the lock. "Because you were able to link with it once, it might be able to sense you, especially since you can't shield yourself."

"Oh, now that makes me feel really safe." She shifted the bags of food to one arm, tugged on Bryony's leash.

"I will keep you safe." Steel edged his voice.

She already believed that, but it was reinforced even more when Luke checked the locks on their room door and jammed a special expanding rod from the knob to the floor. Then he reached inside his jacket, removed a lethal looking semiautomatic, and placed it on the nightstand. Leaning down, he undid an ankle holster with a smaller gun and set it beside the first weapon.

Seeing the guns sent a shiver through her, although she wasn't really surprised. "Well, you're prepared."

"I'm always armed." He removed a wicked looking knife from a special sheath on his boot, placed it on the nightstand. "I just kept these out of your sight and reach until you settled down."

"So Belians can be killed?"

"Just like Sentinels can. We have special abilities, and we're stronger and faster than humans, but we are in human bodies. We can definitely be killed."

Deadly serious, Luke reached into his duffel bag and pulled out Marla's cell phone and her Beretta Tomcat. "I want to give these back to you. But I need your word you won't try to call anyone, especially family or friends. You must understand you can't tell anyone about this."

He'd let her send e-mails to Julia and her parents, telling

them she was using an Internet café in Mexico, and that
she and Bryony were fine and having a great time. Apparently he had a number of e-mail accounts and could route
them through other computers, so the e-mails couldn't be
traced.

Marla was grateful for the opportunity to assure her
family, understood now why she couldn't contact them
directly. "I won't call anyone. You have my word on it."

He studied her, then nodded and gave her the phone. He
held up the gun. "And I'd appreciate it if you don't use this
against me."

"You know I won't."

"The chamber is loaded, and it's got a full clip." He
handed it to her, and she double checked the safety, which
was on. "That's a good weapon," he said. "Small, but the
.32 caliber gives it stopping power. Do you know how to
use it?"

"Yes." Marla thought of the hours she'd spent at a gun
range, determined that the William Bennetts of the world
would never again hurt her or her family. "I have a permit
to carry, which I'm sure you saw when you searched my
purse."

He nodded, his gaze pinning her. "Then the question is,
will you use it? Can you shoot without compunction or
hesitation? Do *not* underestimate this Belian, Marla. It's
smarter and stronger than you can comprehend, and con-
tains no trace of humanity. It will kill you in an instant, or
find some way to use you to its advantage. If you're threatened in any way, shoot it."

She ran her fingers over the dark, cold titanium surface
of her gun, chilled to the bone. "How will I know if it's the
Belian?"

He took the gun from her, set it down. Then he took her
icy hands in his warm ones. The immediate sizzle of
awareness sparked between them. "You'll know," he said
quietly. "You'll sense it, if nothing else. Trust your gut.
And you should be prepared to defend yourself against
anyone who threatens you. The law allows you to shoot,

even to kill, if you feel your life is threatened. I want you to remember that."

She nodded, and he dropped her hands and stepped away. "We'd better eat, then get some sleep. Tomorrow will be tough."

"I can hardly wait."

His gaze hardened, the color of his eyes taking on an icy, gray hue. "Neither can I."

SHE'D thought it would be disconcerting sharing a room with Luke, and with the police scanner he turned on. But she was so exhausted, she felt like a zombie as she got through eating and brushing her teeth, and fell into one of the two double beds, with Bryony curling next to her. She slept deeply, awakening only when Luke called her name.

"What time is it?" she asked, staring up at him through bleary eyes.

"It's still early. I've already taken Bryony outside, and I'm going to the hotel's exercise room." He indicated the nightstand. "There's your gun and your cell phone. I programmed my cell number in your phone directory, under 'A-Luke,' so it's the very first number. Don't let anyone but me in, and call me if you hear or see anything suspicious. Otherwise, I'll be back in an hour."

She glanced at the clock radio, saw it was seven. Only four hours of sleep. Not nearly enough. But she found she couldn't go back to sleep. Muttering under her breath about Sentinels with super stamina, she made a pot of coffee and stumbled into the bathroom to shower, taking the gun and cell phone with her.

She was dressed and watching the news updates on the bombing when Luke returned, wearing a pair of sweatpants and a T-shirt stained with sweat. Bryony jumped out of Marla's lap and ran to greet him. The poodle even stood on her hind legs and did a pirouette.

"Would you look at that?" Marla said. "She's decided she likes you."

Luke bent down to pet Bry, scratched her tummy when she rolled onto her back. "She really needed to go out this morning, so I guess she's grateful I took her. Besides, they all come around, sooner or later."

Marla rolled her eyes. "Sure they do."

But when she looked back at the TV, the grisly images quickly sobered her. "They think there were bombs on more than one floor. Some were the type that start fires."

"Incendiary bombs," he said. "Damn."

"The explosions and the fires did a lot of damage. But only eleven people dead," she added, and then felt appalled at her callous-sounding words. "That came out wrong. I didn't mean to imply that was a good thing."

"I know what you meant." Luke's expression was granite. "They're damned lucky more weren't killed. I understand there are dozens injured, some very seriously."

"Yes." Heartsick, she paused to steady her voice. "Almost all of them were students."

"I know. They were just kids. *Damn it*." His voice vibrated with underlying rage, which Marla found reassuring. It made her feel better to know he wasn't an automaton; instead, he was a man who usually had steel clad control of his emotions.

With jerky movements, he pulled some clothes from his duffel. "I'm going to shower. Then we'll track down this bastard."

He was out in ten minutes, dressed only in a pair of jeans. *Holy moly,* Marla thought, trying not to stare openly as he got out a toiletry kit and proceeded to shave at the vanity sink in the alcove. He was stunning, his muscles smooth bulges beneath golden skin—and so much skin. Broad shoulders and back tapered down to a rock hard midriff. And his abs—oh, my—they were sculpted like a work of art.

When she was a little girl, she'd watched her dad shave, but he'd just been her daddy—tall, slender, dignified, and in a long terry cloth robe. Luke was over six feet of pure, rugged male, and displaying a good portion of bare physique. Watching him shave was a far different experience.

She was intrigued, stimulated, flat-out turned on by the man. Not that he appeared to feel anything for her, outside the Atlantian attraction stuff. Why should he? The guy was so sexy, he could snap his fingers and have anyone he wanted, which wouldn't include a dowdy, plump accountant with crazy hair and silly eyeglasses, and no experience in the seduction department.

One of life's ironic twists, she thought. She'd finally found a man with whom she might be able and willing to have sex, and he was forbidden by his so-called laws to do the horizontal mambo with her. So he couldn't touch her, even if he wanted to.

Blowing out a frustrated sigh, she rose to straighten the room and put her gun and phone in her purse. "Are we going to check out?"

"No." He watched her from the mirror. "We'll stay in Austin until we're able to determine if the Belian has moved on. This one seems to jump around."

Marla wondered briefly when she'd be able to return to her life, and if she'd be back at work next week. But it seemed she was in for the duration; she could hardly refuse to help Luke catch the Belian. Yet the whole thing still had a surreal feel to it, and there were times she wondered if she were dreaming.

Luke finished shaving and dressing, arming himself with the two guns and the knife. Then they had breakfast at the hotel restaurant, and Marla watched him put away enough food to feed a third-world army. Apparently nothing, not even death and destruction, dented the Sentinel appetite.

It was ten by the time they reached the perimeter of the University of Texas. They parked on Guadalupe Street and walked east toward the campus. Luke placed his hand on his chest, over the pendant beneath his sweater. He didn't speak out loud, but Marla sensed the energy swirling around them. Shielding was good, even if it didn't appear to be one hundred percent effective with her.

Luke's cell phone rang just as he lowered his hand, and he answered it. "Hello, Adam . . . Yes, we're almost on the campus. Should be there in five or ten minutes . . . Oh, is he? All right, I'll be looking for him . . . You know I will . . . Walk in Light." He closed the phone.

"Who's Adam?" Marla asked.

"He's my boss, for lack of a better word." Luke took her elbow as they cut around one of the barricades.

"You have a boss? There's a Sentinel hierarchy?"

"Sure there is. You don't have to look so surprised. We're well organized. We have to be, to work among humans without drawing attention to ourselves."

"You'll have to tell me about it one of these days." Trying not to be distracted by the electricity humming from Luke's touch, Marla noted there were a lot of students milling around the campus.

She guessed that, short of the university closing for the day, classes would go on as usual. She and Luke were dressed casually in jeans and sweaters, but they were both too old to be pegged as students. She hoped they didn't look too conspicuous.

Tension wound through her as they turned on the street where the library had been. Even a block away, she could smell the smoke, the heavy stench of scorched debris intermingled with horror. The street was closed to through traffic, completely barricaded with eight-foot mesh strung between poles, so that even pedestrians couldn't get close. All she could see were the upper levels of the building, and the blown out windows.

She thought she felt dark tendrils of evil, but she was so on edge, that could be her imagination. Yet the air felt thick and oppressive. Maybe she was picking up residual energies from last night's onlookers.

They were forced to turn on a side street going away from the library. "Damn," Luke muttered. "I'm going to have to come back tonight and climb over one of those fences. I've got to get close enough to get a reading on the Belian's energy."

"Let's circle around the dorm and see if we can get any closer on the other side," Marla suggested.

"Good idea."

They started around, and then realized they could go into the building because it was a huge public dorm, with shops and food courts on the ground level. They walked through the throngs of students, looking for an exit that would bring them closer to the library.

Marla felt a tinge of something dark and heavy, more pronounced than it had been outside. "Do you feel anything?"

"Like what?" Luke put his arm around her, guided her around some people.

She tried to shake the odd sensation, but couldn't. "I don't know. It just feels . . . bad."

He paused a moment. "Yeah, I feel some negativity. You're probably picking up the emotions of the students. They may have lost friends in the explosions. There." He pointed to double glass doors. "That's about the right place."

The doors were bolted, and beyond them, they could see mesh fencing stretched across the sidewalk.

"Let's go out there anyway," Luke said. "We might be able to see something through the fence."

"But the doors are locked." Marla saw the look he slanted toward her. "Oh, right. You're 'Super Sentinel.'"

"Funny." He ran his palm along the bolt, and it clicked back. He glanced around to see if anyone was watching, then opened the door and ushered her through.

"Neat trick—" she started to say, but a swirl of darkness and emotions assaulted her: hatred, gloating, fear, pain, horror; a mental barrage. She gasped, pressed back against the doors.

"Easy now." Luke took her hand. "It should be safe from this distance."

"No!" Her heart was pounding so hard, she could barely think. "Can't you feel it? Oh, God, Luke, surely you can feel it."

"Feel what?" His brow furrowed, then his eyes widened. "By The One. The Belian—"

"Was here," she interjected. She flattened her free hand against the cold glass door behind her, trying to steady herself. Battled to draw air into her constricted chest. "He—it—was standing right here. I can't—I—" Her legs buckled.

"Breathe, damn it! *Breathe!*" Luke said fiercely, grabbing her shoulders and keeping her upright.

But the evil and depravity spun around her, pressing her down, and blackness closed around her.

EIGHT

VERY little rattled Adam Masters. But he was definitely concerned.

He was a Sanctioned—one of the most powerful beings on Earth. Possessing a highly enlightened soul, he'd lived hundreds of lifetimes, several of them serving The One and the high priests in the great Atlantian temple. It was his job in this incarnation to protect innocents and to ensure Belians were caught and dealt karmic justice. His jurisdiction was the state of Texas, which had one of the highest incidences of Belian activity.

He directed the Sentinels under his command with a velvet-clad steel hand. The Law of One was to be embraced, first and foremost, followed by strict adherence to the Sentinel code of honor. For the most part, universal order dominated Adam's domain, and his well-trained Sentinels did their jobs in accordance with the laws. Belians were tracked down like the animals they were, and justice dispensed.

But this one . . . this Belian was the worst Adam had encountered—at least, in this lifetime.

He hung up from talking with Luke, his thoughts grim. Thirteen more dead—two had died this morning—and numerous injuries, not to mention a swathe of destruction and terror. Typical Belian aftermath, only this Belian was particularly deadly. And less predictable, as it was moving to different geographical locations.

Until they could determine the pattern, or get a really clear conduction, it would be nearly impossible to track it. He hoped like hell Luke and Damien would be able to get a solid signature at the Austin bomb site.

Adam turned to his computer to search for unsolved bombings in other parts of the country. He was so engrossed, he didn't hear the door to the outer office open, which was unusual, as his senses were highly tuned.

"Mr. Masters?"

He turned at the sound of the husky, feminine voice, mentally cursing his secretary for leaving the front door unlocked when she went to the post office. He didn't care to deal with walk-ins. Most of his business, such as it was, came from tracking Belians. He only took on occasional outside cases to insure the agency had an appearance of authenticity.

The woman standing in front of his desk was unremarkable. She certainly couldn't be called pretty. Her medium brown hair was cut short around her square face, although not short enough to tame the waviness that appeared to be natural. Her eyes, shielded behind tortoise-frame eyeglasses, were also brown.

She was average height, a little on the voluptuous side. She wore no makeup and was dressed in a simple, russet-colored pantsuit. A flash of insight told him she deliberately downplayed her looks.

"Mr. Masters?" she asked again. "You *are* Adam Masters, the owner of Masters Investigations, aren't you?"

Despite his irritation at being interrupted, despite her utter ordinariness, he felt an intriguing flare of energy from her. "What makes you think that?" he asked.

Her eyes flashed with disdain. "First off, you're inside

an office that has the name Masters Investigations on the outer door. That's one clue. Secondly, you're sitting behind a desk that has"—she leaned forward and tapped the gold nameplate his secretary had insisted he needed—"the name Adam Masters on it. That's a pretty strong indication."

Very few people, if any, ever treated him with disrespect. He found this woman's attitude challenging. He sat back in his seat. "I believe that's sarcasm I hear in your voice. Since I don't think I know you, I can't imagine why you should find offense with me before we've even met."

"And I can't imagine why you would ask a counter question instead of simply telling me whether or not you're Adam Masters."

"Touché." He swiveled his chair forward and stood. "Yes, I am Adam Masters." He extended his hand. "And you are?"

He could tell she didn't want to take his hand, but he continued to hold it out, subtly insisting that she participate in this simple courtesy. It was then he saw the cane, which blended almost perfectly with her pants.

She slowly, reluctantly, moved the cane to her left hand, and raised her right hand to shake his, very firm and brief. She appeared startled for a moment, but not nearly as much as he was, although he didn't show it. He was a master at keeping his expression impassive.

"I'm Julia Reynolds," she said.

Reynolds? He'd just become aware of another woman with that same last name. Another little surprise. And wasn't the universe just full of them today. "Ms. Reynolds. Please, have a seat."

She looked resigned to yet another necessity in this game of . . . what? Bantering? She certainly wanted something from him. She eased herself into one of the two leather chairs facing his desk, rested her cane against the arm. "Hopefully, this won't take up much of your time."

He sat down. "That would be to your benefit, since my going rate is two hundred dollars an hour."

More disdain in her eyes, and something else he hadn't noted at first—high intelligence. "That's up to you if you want to overcharge your clients, Mr. Masters, but I'm not here to hire you. I'm looking for one of your investigators."

Since her last name was Reynolds, he could well guess which one. There were few true coincidences in the world. The universe was more purpose driven than that. "Who might that be?"

"Luke Paxton."

Surprise, surprise. The world was spinning off its axis this morning. "May I inquire why you specifically want Luke Paxton?"

She paused for a moment, probably debating how much to tell him. "I believe he can help me find someone."

"Really. Why don't you tell me about this person who's missing. Perhaps I can help you."

"I don't think you can, Mr. Masters. This is more of a . . . personal matter."

He glanced down at his right hand, flexed it. "If one of my investigators has done something out of line, then I need to know about it." He looked back at her.

Her gaze locked with his. "Believe me, Mr. Masters, if I knew for a fact one of your investigators had done something out of line, I'd make sure you were aware of it. I'd also file a complaint with the Private Security Bureau. But I need to speak directly with Luke Paxton. He might have information that's vital to a dilemma that is, as I said, personal."

Obviously, Marla Reynolds hadn't adequately explained her absence to her family. Unfortunate, but Adam wasn't about to reveal anything that might result in disrupting a well matched Sentinel/conductor team on a tracking mission. "I'm sorry, but Luke is currently on a case, and I'm not at liberty to reveal any of the details, including his location."

Her eyes narrowed, and her aura flared, vivid blue tinged with red. *Here,* he thought, *was a woman of strength, a woman who would fight for what she loved and valued.*

"You need to tell me where he is. It's *very* important that I talk to him."

He shrugged, kept his expression bland. "I've already explained I can't do that. The case Luke is working on is extremely important, and could have dire consequences if it's not resolved."

Energy surged around her as she leaned forward. "*You* know something. You know something about the person I'm looking for, don't you?"

She was intelligent—and astute. "I know only about the case Luke is on, and how crucial it is to the welfare of many. I can't reveal his location until this case is resolved. I wish I could help you."

She stared at him a long moment, and he realized she was so emotionally contained, he couldn't sense her emotions or her thoughts, although he could most definitely feel the energy she radiated.

"I believe you know who I'm looking for," she said, "and where that person is. And that you are deliberately withholding the information from me. That's not a good idea, Mr. Masters."

"You accuse me of not being forthcoming, but *you* have given me *no* information, Ms. Reynolds. Why don't you tell me who you're looking for and the circumstances of that person's disappearance. Then we'll see if I can help you."

"All I need from you is how to contact Luke Paxton. I have no intention of interfering with any of his cases."

"And, without more information on your situation, I can't give you that. I'm sure you can understand I have to protect the privacy of my investigators and their cases. As a matter of fact, the law says I must maintain complete confidentiality."

She gripped the edge of his desk and pushed herself up slowly before grabbing her cane. He sincerely hoped she wouldn't try to use it on him. He had no desire to give her any glimpses of his power. He stood, his gaze meeting her glare.

"I'm very sorry you won't cooperate with me, Mr. Masters. I'm not without resources. I'll find a way to get the information I need, as well as make things unpleasant for you."

"We all do what we must, Ms. Reynolds. I'll await your next move."

She didn't bother with a last retort, merely turned and made her way from his office. Her walk was so slow and labored that he was amazed she had managed to make it into his office without him being aware of her. He wondered what had happened to her leg.

But that wasn't nearly as burning a question as what to do about the startling reaction he'd had to her. He again stared at his right hand. It couldn't be possible. Yet he knew what he'd felt.

He needed to talk to Luke. And to delve deeper into the background of Julia Reynolds.

Today . . . today, he was definitely rattled.

THE first thing Marla heard was an odd ringing in her ears. Then she heard voices, but they sounded distant, disjointed.

"She'll be fine. Just low blood sugar." That was Luke's voice.

What? She tried to open her eyes, but her lids were too heavy. Wisps of light filtered through the gray fog surrounding her. There were more voices buzzing, then Luke said, "Thanks for getting that. You don't need to worry yourselves further. She really will be fine. Thank you for your concern."

Something cool and damp was pressed against her forehead, and then each cheek. She forced her eyes open, saw a blurry shape above her. She blinked, and Luke's face came into focus.

"What happened?" She glanced around, realized she was lying on a bench against a wall.

"You passed out. Went completely horizontal on me." The calmness of his voice belied the worry in his eyes.

"I did?" She tried to sit up, felt a wave of dizziness, and thought better of it. "I've never fainted in my life."

"Yeah, well, that was before you met me."

She looked around him, saw people moving through the cavernous area. "We're in the dorm." It was coming back to her. "The bombing. We went outside to get closer and it was—" Panic flared. "Oh, God."

"Shhh. Be calm." He wiped her face again with what appeared to be a wet paper towel. "It's over, and you're safe."

She struggled onto her elbows. "I want to sit up."

He looked like he wanted to argue, but he helped her upright and sat next to her, supporting her with an arm around her. She leaned her head against his shoulder, waiting until the spinning stopped.

"Well that was fun," she managed. "At least I didn't get sick. . . ." She twisted a little, looked up at Luke. "Did I?"

His jaw tensed. "No. But you passed out. I'm supposed to protect you. But it appears I can't do anything to block your empathic abilities."

She leaned back and took a deep breath, which seemed to help her equilibrium. After a moment, she said, "Maybe you're not supposed to block them. Maybe I need to be able to sense the Belian." But she couldn't say she was happy about how her unusual sensitivity was manifesting.

"All I know is it's frustrating as hell. And you sensed the damned thing before I did. That's not supposed to happen." With a disgusted sound, he ran his hand through his hair. "How are you feeling? Dizzy? Sick?"

"No. I'm a lot better. *Really.*" She looked up into his fierce face. This warrior was concerned—worried—about her. She had to admit she rather liked it.

Luke's phone rang, and with his crystal gaze still on her, he unclipped it from the belt holster. "Paxton. Hey, man. Where are you? . . . We're in that huge dorm right across from the library. Just had a little incident. We have a fix on the Belian, though. Why don't you meet us inside? We're right by the 40 Acres Bakery. Will do."

He replaced the phone. "Reinforcements are coming. We'll just wait for them here, while you get your bearings."

"Who's coming?"

"Another Sentinel, the one who usually works this area. But there's been a lot of Belian activity this year, and both of us have been stretched a little thin. His conductor, who also happens to be his fiancée, is with him."

She tried to get her mind around that information. "So you have territories?"

"In a way. There they are. Must have been close."

She saw a man and a woman walking toward them. The man, tall and formidable, wore a calf-length leather duster, and his long midnight hair was pulled back from his angular face. The woman beside him looked small in comparison.

Luke stood and shook the other man's hand; they each did the shoulder slapping thing. "Damien, man, it's good to see you. Hey, beautiful." He leaned down and kissed the woman's cheek. "I hope you're keeping this guy in line."

She rolled her eyes. "Yeah, right."

Marla liked her already.

"How's Alex?" Luke asked.

The woman smiled proudly. "He's great. Growing in leaps and bounds. Soon he won't be a little boy anymore."

"He's a special kid. Tell him I said hi." Turning, Luke gestured toward Marla. "This is Marla Reynolds. Marla, this is Damien Morgan and Kara Cantrell, although I think Kara's last name will be changing in the not-so-distant future."

Damien was slightly taller than Luke, and not quite as solid. He appeared aloof, very contained, and exuded danger. Marla would have been terrified if she'd met him in a dark alley. But she knew Luke was just as dangerous and his laid-back attitude highly deceptive. Both men were lethal predators.

Kara presented a striking contrast to Damien. She was lovely, with a creamy complexion and luminous gray eyes that complemented her auburn hair. She was about Marla's height, but probably twenty or thirty pounds lighter.

"Hello." Marla managed a smile. She felt like an idiot, sitting there while these three stunning people towered over her, but she didn't trust her legs yet.

"We just had a little fainting episode, and Marla is recovering," Luke explained.

"Would you like me to have a look at you?" Kara asked. "I'm a doctor."

"No, I'm fine. But thank you."

"Marla is empathic, and can pick up the emotions of the Belian we're tracking," Luke said. "A few minutes ago, we stumbled onto where the Belian must have been standing when the bombs went off, and the energy broadsided her."

Kara's eyes widened. "That must be awful."

"It's terrible. And it's happened three times now. This is the only one where I almost passed out."

Damien's pale blue gaze flashed over Marla before he turned to Luke. "Aren't you shielding?"

"Of course I am, but it doesn't appear to block Marla's empathic abilities."

"This is a first," Damien mused, his gaze returning to Marla. She had the uncomfortable feeling he could see through all her protective layers, into the very depths of her soul. "Have you done a conduction yet?" he asked, still watching her.

Knowing what he assumed they'd have done during that, she felt the heat rising to her face. Luke answered before she could. "One conduction. And she picked up the emotions of the Belian and the victims and families."

"I also heard the Belian talking," she added.

Damien's dark eyebrows rose. "You *heard* the Belian?"

Luke whipped toward her. "You didn't tell me about that."

"I'm sorry. It didn't occur to me. I panicked when I felt the emotions and heard that voice. After I calmed down, it never came up."

Kara shot a quick glance from Luke to Marla. "Why don't you tell us now?"

"Well . . ." Marla tried to remember exactly what she'd

heard. "The voice was soft . . . not very masculine, although it didn't sound like a woman, either. It talked about the unjust and the wicked being punished. And then it said something about Belial and blood." She rubbed her head, which had started aching. "I think that's all."

Damien looked at Luke. "I wouldn't take her to any more Belian crime scenes. She's too sensitive, and the Belian might pick up on her."

"Well, hell, yeah. I know I shouldn't have brought her here. But I was worried the Belian might have already tapped her, and I didn't want to leave her alone. Damn!"

"And *she* is a real live person, and sitting right here," Marla said, feeling like a bug under a microscope.

"You tell them." Kara sat down on the bench beside her. "These guys sometimes get carried away with themselves."

Damien gave a little snort. But his gaze, when it rested on Kara, was heated, devouring. Marla could practically feel the temperature around them rising to heat advisory levels. Man. Luke had been telling the truth about the fire between a matched Sentinel and conductor.

"So what's the plan?" Kara asked.

"Luke and I will check out the BCS and work the psychic signature."

"Go for it. I'll sit here with Marla."

The men strode away, both radiating masculinity and power. Marla blew out her breath. "Wow."

"Pretty impressive, aren't they? All Sentinel males are like that—overflowing with testosterone, protectiveness, and pure animal magnetism."

"It's a new experience for me. Luke is the first Sentinel I've met, and I didn't even know they existed until about five days ago."

"No wonder you're a little shaky. It can be very overwhelming."

"I'll say." Marla cleared her throat, wishing she knew this woman better. There was so much she wanted to know.

"So ask." Kara leaned forward, squeezed her hand, compassion and understanding in her gray eyes. "I'm sure you have a lot of questions. I'll be glad to answer what I can."

"I don't even know where to begin. When did you learn you're a conductor?"

"When I met another Sentinel in Birmingham, over nine years ago. The attraction was powerful, but he didn't tell me why until we'd dated a few months."

It hadn't occurred to Marla that Sentinels might fall in love with their conductors. "So you actually had a relationship with him?"

"Yes. Our connection was instantaneous." Kara's expression turned sad. "You're probably too polite to ask, so I'll tell you. He was killed seven years ago. By a Belian."

A chill shot through Marla. Luke had told her Sentinels were mortal, but he seemed so vital and so competent, she hadn't considered he could actually be killed. "How awful. I'm sorry." She returned the hand squeeze. "But now you're with Damien, and I understand you're getting married. Congratulations."

The luminous glow returned to Kara's eyes. "Thank you."

"Is it common for Sentinels to marry conductors?"

Kara shook her head. "No. For the most part, Sentinels are loners, and don't have permanent relationships with anyone. What they do is very dangerous—for them, and for the conductors they work with, and any humans in a Belian's path. But some Sentinels take mates, and some have children, which is how new Sentinels come into Earth."

"I hadn't even considered Sentinels being babies. It's frustrating to know so little."

"You'll learn as you go. A Sentinel can only be born to a couple where at least one of them is a Sentinel. Damien says the Sentinel soul chooses where and when to enter the Earth," Kara explained. "And the woman won't get pregnant unless that's the case. Traditional birth control won't stop a Sentinel pregnancy. I thought I'd better warn you about that."

Not that Marla had anything to worry about in that department. Luke refused to have sex with her during a conduction, and there was no way he'd be interested in her otherwise. She felt a surprising wave of disappointment. Typical humann-nature case of wanting what you couldn't have.

"Most conductors have psychic abilities, or are very sensitive to the energies around them," Kara said. "You obviously have empathic abilities."

"But I wasn't born with them," Marla blurted, and then considered kicking herself. As much as she liked Kara, she wasn't ready to bare her soul about the attack on Julia. "At least, I didn't begin sensing other people's emotions until I was nineteen."

"They were probably there all along, but just dormant. I began dreaming about events before they happened with I was four."

"That must be unsettling."

"It can be." Kara leaned against the wall. "But we can't change the cards we're dealt when we're born. All we can do is decide how to play those cards. Although the universe, or fate, has a way of directing the game."

Marla thought again of how events had lined up to bring her to that bar stool next to Luke. "I believe you're right about that. It's like I was guided to Luke, or him to me."

"Luke's a great guy. You can trust him with your life." Kara opened her purse and pulled out a card case. "Let me give you one of my business cards. I'll write my home and cell numbers on the back. I hope you'll call me if you ever need anything or have any more questions."

"I will. Thank you." Marla saw the men coming their way, their expressions hard and forbidding.

"Okay," Luke said, stopping beside Marla. "We're done here. Time to get to work."

Marla slipped Kara's business card into her purse and stood. "What now?"

"Conduction." Damien took Kara's arm. "We'll each do one, then compare notes. Luke will take it from there."

Another conduction. More grisly scenes and violence and pain and the Belian, not to mention burning sexual need. Marla could hardly wait.

And she wondered if the connection with the Belian, or the fire that had flared between her and Luke at the last conduction would be stronger this time. Because if it was, she'd either throw up or combust.

JULIA sat in her car, a sensible, older model Honda Accord, and tried to slow her pounding heart. She was so angry she was trembling. Adam Masters was one of the most infuriating and arrogant men she'd ever encountered. He was a pompous ass and a sleazeball, very similar to William Bennett's slimy defense lawyer.

"Isn't it true, Ms. Reynolds, that you led Mr. Bennett on? That you went into his store several times a week, and while you were there, you flirted with him?"

"No, that's not true. His office supply store was near my home, and I was working on my doctorate, so I needed supplies for my classes. I did go there a lot but I never—"

"Oh come on, Ms. Reynolds. Didn't you act interested, give him the impression you wanted to go out with him? Sure you did. You thought it was funny to get him excited, didn't you?"

"No!"

Her lawyer had leaped into the fray then. "Objection! Ms. Reynolds isn't the one on trial."

"Sustained." The judge turned to Bennett's lawyer. "Back off, counselor."

Where had that trial memory come from? Julia never allowed herself to think about Bennett and that night, or the months that followed, and now she ruthlessly shoved the memory away. But, she decided, there wasn't any difference between Bennett's lawyer and Adam Masters. Both of them were lowlifes.

That didn't diminish her reaction to Masters, however, or what to do about him. He knew something about Marla, Julia was sure of it. Her anger gave way to fear for her sister's safety and concern that she might have mishandled

Masters. But her instincts had gone on full alert the moment she saw the man.

He'd exuded danger, with his short black hair silvering at the temples, those inscrutable black eyes and the diamond stud in his left ear. His expensively cut designer suit hadn't impressed her—she knew very well that monsters could hide behind a veneer of affluence and civility.

Damn it. She was *not* going there again. She had worked too hard and too long to put the past behind her to let an unpleasant experience dredge it up again.

The encounter with Adam Masters had shaken her up badly, something she hadn't experienced for years in her controlled, planned life. His looks and his odd, raspy voice had raised her hackles, but it was when they shook hands that the full reaction kicked in. She'd felt a startling rush of energy, almost like an electrical shock, and her heart went into overdrive.

It was as if her body recognized him in some primal way. She could only assume it was her survival instincts, honed by nearly dying eleven years ago, warning her of danger. She trusted her intuition more than any physical or social indications to the contrary.

She'd made the instant decision not to trust him, not to give him any more information than necessary. His hedging and evasiveness about Luke Paxton's whereabouts further convinced her that she'd been right. But it hadn't provided any information to help her find Paxton, or her sister.

She wasn't sure what to do now, or if she had any legitimate leverage to use against Adam Masters. But she planned to contact the State of Texas Private Security Bureau. She'd also contact a lawyer and speak with the chief of police of the Corpus Christi Police Department.

One thing was certain—she wasn't going to give up searching for Marla. And since she was convinced Adam Masters knew where Marla might be, she was going to hound him day and night.

NINE

Luke brought Bryony back inside and bolted the door. She headed straight to the small desk and stood on her hind legs to sniff at the sacks of food they'd purchased on the way back to the hotel. "Hey! Get away from there," he said, sending a small burst of energy at the poodle.

She dropped down and shook herself. With an indignant sniff, she trotted over to jump on the bed beside Marla, who was sitting against the headboard with her knees drawn up.

Luke's stomach rumbled, and he looked longingly at the desk. "I don't suppose you want anything to eat first?" he asked, then reconsidered. "No, probably not a good idea."

"Probably not. Until I met you, I hadn't had stomach problems in years. The last time I can remember throwing up was when I was a kid and caught one of those twenty-four-hour viruses. But I seem to get sick around you. What does that tell you, Paxton?"

He heard the nervousness in her voice, understood she was trying to keep things light. A lot of women would have vocalized their fears or complained about having their entire world turned on its end. Marla had done neither, and he respected her for that.

"I have to go and find a conductor who's a smart-ass." He took off his jacket, hung it over a chair. "Listen, before we get started, there's something we need to discuss."

"Can I ask you a question first?"

"Shoot."

"Have you ever been involved with any of your conductors?"

Whoa. What had motivated that question from out of the blue? "As in emotionally involved?" he asked cautiously. "Like dating?"

"Yes." She angled her head, pinned him with those honey-toned eyes. "Like Damien and Kara."

Ah, hell. He took a deep breath, went to sit on the edge of the opposite bed. "No, I've don't get involved. Ever. Not with conductors, or anyone else. Commitment is something many Sentinels avoid."

She dropped her legs to the side, turned toward him. "But if you don't, how can you bring more Sentinels to Earth? Kara said Sentinels are born to couples when at least one of them is a Sentinel. I couldn't imagine you—or Damien, for that matter—fathering a child and walking away."

"Thanks for the vote of confidence. You're right. We cherish and nurture our children and pass along our heritage. As odd as it may sound, a Sentinel pregnancy apparently doesn't occur unless the couple is committed to one another. To the best of my knowledge, I've never fathered a child, and I don't believe I ever will. Many Sentinels keep to themselves. What we do is just too damned dangerous. A lot of us die fighting Belians, and I have to tell you, so do some conductors. It's just safer not to get involved."

"I understand. Some things hurt too much."

The sadness in her voice tugged at his heart, and he knew she was talking about more than whether or not he was capable of a commitment. She had her own secrets that she was unwilling to share.

"You've got that right," he said, and felt the flare of his own grief. One life snuffed out had irreparably altered four other lives, and he would never again submit himself, or anyone else, to that. "Some things do hurt too much."

He leaned forward, willing her to understand. "Marla, don't read anything into what you and I are doing. We have a Sentinel/conductor relationship, nothing more. It can never be anything else."

She stared back at him, all solemn and self-contained. Despite what he'd just said, he wanted to take her in his arms and kiss her until her barriers crumbled, until they both forgot the pain. *Damn.* This was crazy, and so not going to happen. But he needed her too badly to walk away, even if it put her at risk.

He was extremely worried about the threat to her. He and Damien had discussed it at length, and agreed the main concern was ensuring the Belian didn't sense Marla and try to hunt her. There was already enough risk that she could be injured or killed during routine tracking.

"Marla, I can't guarantee that I can shield you from this Belian. You're apparently a very strong empath, and you might also be a transmitter, and therefore transmitting to it. Most humans can't create and maintain the type of psychic shields Sentinels can. Most Belians can also shield themselves, which is why it's so damned hard to track them. It's a mystery as to how you're able to pick up on this one. I know it's well shielded, or I'd have a better fix on it."

Her chest rose and fell, and her fingers clutched the bedspread. "So if you can't shield me, and if I'm transmitting, as you put it, then the Belian could be picking up on me?"

"Yes. It could sense your presence, could realize that you're probing and looking for it."

"So I could lead it straight to you?"

He couldn't believe she was thinking of him instead of her own safety. "I hope that brings it on. Better that it focus on me than murder more innocents. But my point here is that this puts *you* at extra risk. The Belian could focus on you instead. That's a dangerous position for a human to be in."

She looked down, smoothed the bunched-up bedspread. "Are you suggesting we stop the conductions?"

"I wish we could do that, I really do. But I need your help more than ever. I do have to warn you of the danger, and to make it clear that your cooperation is voluntary. I can't force you to do this."

She raised her head, looked him in the eye. "But you still think conductions are necessary to catch this monster?"

"They're the only resource we have right now. I give you my word I will do everything in my power to keep you safe."

"So this is just the disclosure statement and waiver of liability and indemnity?"

He smiled, in spite of the situation. "Yeah. Something like that."

A spark of humor flared in her eyes. "Do I have to sign anything before we begin this conduction?"

He choked back a laugh. "You really are a smart-ass."

"Better to laugh than cry." Her eyes became sober again. "I'm not backing down, Luke. There are a lot of monsters out there, maybe not all of them Belians, but they're there. Someone has to stop them, before they hurt anyone else."

She was speaking of her personal experience again, he was certain of it. She carried a virtual arsenal of weapons in her purse, had some training in self-defense (he had bruises and scars to attest to that).

Something had happened to make her resort to those measures. Maybe she'd trust him enough to confide in him one of these days. Except he'd be long gone. He was real sorry about that. She was one classy lady.

He held out his hand. "Ready?"

"Not really. But I guess we'd better get to it." She slid her feet off the bed, and he saw her toenails were a sexy, pale pink. Her coral-toned turtleneck caressed her generous curves, and her curly hair framed her face in soft disarray. She was all woman, despite her self-enforced celibacy.

He pushed back the wave of nonconduction lust that

slid through him. This would not do. Not only was Marla off limits, but he had to focus on keeping her safe and tracking the Belian.

With a shrill bark, Bryony whipped around into Marla's lap and gave Luke the evil eye. "Hey baby," Marla cooed, stroking the wiry fur. "You want to help?"

Trying to ignore the thought of how it would feel to have Marla stroking him that way, Luke said, "We'd better put her in the bathroom, or she might interfere."

"You're right." Marla rose, cradling Bryony in her arms. "Poor baby. I'm so sorry to do this to you." She put the dog in the bathroom and closed the door, then returned to sit on the edge of the bed opposite Luke. The sound of scratching then an indignant bark came from behind the door.

"I'm afraid I've spoiled her." Marla took off her glasses, placed them on the nightstand. Despite the lines of strain on her face, her eyes were clear and calm. "I'll do my best not to break the link this time, but it's difficult to maintain when I feel and hear the Belian."

"Just try to hold on to my hands until I release you." He held out his right hand. "Give me your left hand, while I do the shielding."

She rubbed her palms on her jeans, and then offered her hand. Her skin was cool and smooth, and he wrapped his fingers around her hand. He held the crystal in his left hand, closed his eyes, focused and chanted the ancient words of supplication, which basically translated to: *Being of Light, surround us in your love and protection. Shield us from all that is not of the Light. Guide us to vision and truth, so that we may serve the Light.*

A near blinding, golden glow burst through his mind, behind his eyelids. He felt the power move through him, and around them.

"Whatever you're doing, I can feel it."

"That's good." He hoped it would offer enough protection. "Give me your other hand now."

She did, and they barely closed the connection before the energies exploded without any prompting from him.

More brilliant light, along with heat, flowed through him. He felt the crystal pulsing with power against his chest, felt his body pitch and sway.

Earth fell away, and he was airborne, flying through a wall of mist—the veil—that separated lifetimes. Sapphire blue water flowed beneath him, surrounding the green beauty of Atlantis. All his lifetimes merged together and stretched before him. Another starburst of light flashed behind his eyes, igniting the seeking.

Then the sexual surge hit, potent and intense. Fingers of fire licked upward through his abdomen. He was instantly hard, his erection straining painfully against his jeans. He felt Marla jolt, heard her gasp. Her arousal created a tantalizing scent that threatened his sanity. He battled the red haze, the powerful urge to tear his clothes off and bury himself inside her lush body.

"First two chakras open," he managed to say, his voice harsh.

"This is fun," she muttered.

He started to smile, but the energy shot up to his midriff, worse than the burn from a hundred sit-ups. Bright yellow flared in his mind then morphed into green as the burn moved into his chest. "Through the four lower chakras," he said. Not that it helped anything; the sexual need was a clawing, living thing, voracious in its hunger and demands. He half expected his jeans to burst open, would have welcomed the relief from the agonizing pressure.

Marla gripped his hands so hard, he could feel her nails scoring his skin, but she was hanging in there. The energy moved to the throat, the blue color that followed soothing a little, but he knew it was just the lull before the fireworks. "Get ready," he murmured.

Sharp pain flashed dead center in his head, along with a blanket of indigo swirls. Marla jerked, almost let go. He tightened his grip. "Easy now. Stay with me, babe."

"I'm trying," she gasped, jumped again. "Oh, God!"

The seventh chakra had just burst open with an audible

pop. Brilliant light poured into his head, along with a thousand megawatt jolt of power. "We're in. Hang on for the ride."

The energy gathered, coiled, and began snaking through the chakras in a figure eight pattern, faster and faster. It whipped his body into a rocking motion, as the brilliant chakra colors flashed in alternating bursts behind his eyelids. A high-pitched howling started up from the bathroom.

And through it all was the burning sexual need, emanating the denser energy closest to the vibratory level of the Belian. He had to fight the ancient, instinctive urge to pin Marla to the bed and pound himself into her until they were both senseless. Had to push aside the primal need in order to focus on the images flashing faster than the blink of an eye.

He could sense her own struggle, felt the racing of her pulse beneath his fingers, heard her labored breathing. And he could feel horror and fear rolling off her in great waves; knew she must be picking up on the Belian. Bryony's howls cranked up to a feverish pitch.

"No," she whispered. "I don't know if I can . . . do . . . this."

He took on the additional strain of trying to strengthen the shield, while balancing the energies and absorbing the images. "Just hang on . . . almost there."

She soldiered on, but he felt her anguish, knew she was barely holding on. It was he who finally broke the link by letting go of her right hand. "Almost done," he said.

He maintained his grip on her other hand as he mentally began releasing the energies, directing them away from his and Marla's bodies, and dispersing them back into the ether. Outside of a sexual climax, this was the safest and best way to release the buildup. The howls in the bathroom stopped, followed by a few whimpers, then silence.

Finally he dropped her other hand and drew back. "We did it."

"God." She collapsed on the bed, drawing her legs up until she was in a ball. "It was awful."

He ignored his still-raging need and moved over to her.

"You're all right. You're safe. It's over." Sitting on the edge of the bed, he smoothed her tangled hair back from her clammy skin, framed her face in his hands. "Open your eyes, Marla. Look at me."

She did, and her pupils were so dilated, her eyes looked black. Her face was colorless. He sent a flood of warming, calming energy into her, concentrated on the darkness lurking in her mind and burned it away with pure light. Tension coiled in her chest, and he directed energy there. "Breathe," he ordered, and she took a shuddering breath.

He ran his hands over her arms. "How's the stomach?"

She sagged against the pillow. "I think it's okay, for now."

"Good to know." He went to work on her headache, placing his hands over her temples, and sending more calming energy into her head.

"That feels much better," she murmured. "Thank you."

But her breasts were still taut beneath the turtleneck. He knew she was wet between her legs, could sense her readiness. He wanted to strip off her jeans; to dip his fingers and tongue into her sweetness; to sate himself in her curvy warmth. He knew instinctively that she would let him, and that he could get lost in her. *Not a good idea.* He stood hastily, intending to put a safe distance between them.

She grabbed his arm, struggled to sit up. "No. Stay here. Please." She came upright, pressed herself against his midriff, her body perilously close to where his jeans tented out. "Please hold me for a minute."

Guessing she'd brushed up against the Belian's mind again, understanding she needed comfort, he resigned himself to the torment for a little longer. Sending a prayer to The One for self-control, he sat on the bed.

She immediately cuddled against him. "It was like a nightmare, only worse," she whispered. "First I felt him, gloating again. Proud of himself, enjoying the destruction. Standing there outside the dorm, watching the smoke and the injured students running out of the building. Luke, it turned him on."

"Yeah, I know. I saw it fondling itself."

She shuddered. "I saw that, too. Now I know I wouldn't like porn movies."

He went for a little levity. "Sure you would. A true porn movie involves gorgeous naked women and well-endowed, handsome studs."

She shook her head against his chest. "You're such a guy."

That was 110 percent true at the moment, as his rock-hard erection was reminding him. He shifted, trying to ease some of the pressure. "What happened next?"

"Then he looked right at me. At least I think he was looking at me. It was like one of those investigative reporting shows where they interview an informant, but blur the face so the person can't be identified. All I could see was a wavering oval where his face would have been."

"*Its* face," he corrected. "I know it looks like a human, but you have to keep reminding yourself that it's not. Damien and I saw a blurred face, too, when we read the crime scene on the campus today. That's typical. Belians can't avoid leaving behind energy patterns, as all living things do, but they can shield the energy to some extent. When a Sentinel visits a BCS, he or she can generally see how the crime happened, but not a clear visual of the Belian."

"Well, doesn't that just suck?"

He wished she hadn't used that particular word—it brought to mind an image that had nothing to do with Belians, and everything to do with her enticing mouth. "Ah, yeah, it does. That's why we have to do conductions. Anything else?"

"Yes." She shuddered again, held on more tightly. "It looked right at me, and it said: *I know you're there, woman. I know you're watching me. You can see how smart and how clever I am, can't you? You admire me. Just wait. There will be more explosions. More blood.* It said it like I should be *impressed* with what it was doing."

Shock barreled through Luke. *Damn it!* This was far worse than he had feared. The Belian had not only locked onto Marla, but it was able to communicate directly with her. A basic psychic link only facilitated awareness of another being at the other end of the link; it didn't include telepathy.

He had never heard of a Belian communicating in such a manner with a conductor or a Sentinel. He didn't know all the ramifications, but he knew it would make it very difficult to keep Marla safe. He had to talk to Adam about this. There had to be some way to teach her how to block mental intrusions from the Belian.

For now he simply asked, "Was that it?"

"That's all I can remember. It was the same voice as before, soft, not very masculine. But not a woman. I'm almost positive it's in a man's body."

"I'm sorry you have to come so close to this evil. Dealing with a Belian is nasty business." *And this Belian was about to discover that dealing with Luke was an extremely ugly experience.*

"You do it on a regular basis," Marla pointed out.

"I'm used to it. You're not, and you didn't ask for this assignment."

"Oh, that's right—you volunteered me."

"Such a smart-ass." He felt the tightness in his chest easing. "Have you always been this way?"

She leaned back to look up at him. "Since middle school. I was frumpy and nerdy and didn't fit in with any of the cliques or groups. I learned that being funny got me some attention and some acceptance. I became the class clown. So now, whenever I'm tense or nervous, I make smart-aleck remarks. Sorry."

"No, that's good. Humor can be good. It's gotten us this far. We did pretty well on the conduction. You didn't break the link, and you haven't thrown up yet. I think we're making progress."

"I guess. I am feeling better now." She moved away from him and leaned against the headboard, but she was still deathly pale, and there were dark circles beneath her eyes. "Thanks for indulging me. What about the images I saw?"

"Let's sort through them." He rose and went to let Bryony out of the bathroom. As he expected, the poodle immediately went to Marla and climbed in her lap. He was concerned that she might still be shaky, and he hoped Bry would offer some comfort.

He sat on the other bed. "I saw a blurred face, but I also saw hands taking the bombs from the backpack, placing them where they wouldn't be seen."

"I saw glimpses of that," Marla said. "Weren't there stairs?"

"Yeah. It put the incendiaries in stairwells, so people would be trapped by the fire. The bastard. I also saw what I believe were remote detonators. Then I saw jeans and athletic shoes. I think we got images from two different events—the first, when the Belial was planting the bombs; the second when it was detonating them. I don't think they were done at the same time."

"Detonators. So that's what those were. They looked like garage door openers." Marla hugged Bryony against her; he noticed her hands were trembling. "It's funny— during the conduction, the images flash so fast, I don't know what they are. But when you mention them, I realize that's what I saw."

"That's how it works. I can store the images like a video that I can play back."

She scratched behind the poodle's ears. "What else was there?"

"The blue Tercel again."

She nodded. "Yes, I saw that. No license plate?"

"Not that I saw. Did you see the atlas? It was open to Texas, and there was a line drawn north along Interstate 35."

Marla leaned over Bryony, got her glasses, and put them on. "I remember a vague image of the map, but not the drawn line."

"I-35 runs through Dallas. I'm thinking this thing is choosing sizable cities. It's easier to avoid discovery, and if you're a bomber, you're going for body count. My guess would be that the next target is in Dallas."

"But you don't know that for sure."

"No. But I don't think this Belian will stay in one place. I'd just hate to go to Dallas and have something else happen here."

"Basically, this means we don't have any clues about the Belian's actual target. We have to wait until there's another explosion."

She'd hit the nail on the head, and he felt the rage building inside him. "I'd say that sums it up."

"So that's it?" she asked, her expression troubled. "There's nothing else we can do right now?"

"Damien and Kara are doing a conduction, too. Let's see what they come up with." He stood and stretched. "Should we flip to see who gets to take a cold shower first?"

Her gaze drifted lower to the bulge in his jeans. "Maybe you should do the honors. That looks painful."

He grinned. She really was entertaining. "You're right about that. You going to be okay?"

She managed a wan smile. "I'm fine. Really."

"I won't be long. Don't eat all the food."

She arched her brows. "Better shower fast."

HE'D been a loner all his life. His parents, supposedly the social match of the century, had hated each other's guts and divorced when he was only three. Neither situation—a child nor a divorce—had affected their oh-so-busy schedules, which were crammed with corporate meetings for his father, and social and charitable events for his mother. There was plenty of money for nannies and tutors and boarding schools, which effectively dealt with the inconvenience of his existence.

His parents had never been affectionate, and his first nanny had been the same woman who'd cared for his father. She was old school, didn't believe in holding babies because it might spoil them. And when children got older, making them sit for hours in the corner, restrained with corded curtain ties, taught them obedience.

By the time the old bitch died when he was five, he had an aversion to being touched by anyone. While some of the successive nannies had tried to be demonstrative, they gave up after he continuously bit and pinched them.

Boarding school took care of that problem and suited him, as it allowed him to keep to himself. He was too smart, too special, to associate with the other boys, far too mature for their asinine pastimes. He was also smarter than his teachers, so he had to educate himself when he wasn't in class.

No one had ever appreciated his brilliance. His grades certainly hadn't reflected his off-the-chart intelligence. But then what could one expect from moronic instructors?

He'd done better at Cal Tech, but again, he'd had to teach himself, because the professors weren't in his league. Not finding anyone worthy of his respect, he'd continued to remain aloof and alone through the passing years.

But now *she* was watching him. He was impressed that she was able to reach out to him, and at the same time, strengthen his own outstanding abilities to the point that he could mentally communicate with her. He could sense her intelligence, her awareness, her warmth. For the first time in his life, he thought he might be able to connect with another person.

He even felt stirrings of desire, which he'd only ever felt when he blew up things. He might actually be able to fuck this woman—and enjoy it.

He intended to track her down and find out.

TEN

ADAM called while Luke was in the shower, taking care of business, something he didn't usually have to do. He preferred the old fashioned way, he thought wryly.

Marla knocked on the bathroom door. "Your cell phone's ringing," she called out. "Do you want me to get it?"

Great timing. "Just let it go," Luke called back. "I'll take care of it when I get out." He knew it would either be Damien or Adam, and that whoever had called, it was important.

He finished showering, dried off, and slipped back into his jeans. Blotting his hair with a smaller towel, he strode into the main room and picked up his cell phone. Marla was on the bed with Bryony, and the food was untouched. Her gaze slid over him like a warm wave. *Shit.* He really didn't want another cold shower.

"Let me return this call, and we'll eat." He turned away so he wouldn't be further affected by her golden gaze. Seeing Adam's number on the phone display, he punched the callback then strode over to part the drapes and stare out at the fading day.

"Hey, Adam. What's up?"

"I wanted to know if you had any results. I assume you did the conduction."

"Yeah, we did." Luke recapped what he and Marla had seen and what she'd heard. "The Belian has not only locked onto her, but it's communicating telepathically with her. Have you ever heard of that happening?"

"No, I haven't. This is a startling development."

"I'd say that's an understatement. There's got to be some way for Marla to shield or block those communications. I want to start working with her on that."

"No, don't do that yet," Adam said slowly. "This might be to our advantage."

Luke didn't like the sound of that. Using Marla as a lure to draw the Belian was far too risky. "It's damn sure not to Marla's advantage. It's downright dangerous." He paused, aware she could hear the conversation, lowered his voice. "What happened to our creed of protecting the innocent?"

"I don't like putting Ms. Reynolds directly in the Belian's path any more than you do. But this thing is killing whole groups of people, *all* of them innocent. If I have to weigh the risk to one person against the lives of many, the choice is clear."

"Like hell!"

"Luke." There was a wealth of warning in Adam's quiet tone. "You'll just have to keep her protected. Things always happen for a reason. We can't ignore this development or miss such an opportunity."

Not for the first time, Luke thought the guy must have ice water instead of blood in his veins. He'd never been totally certain that Adam, or any of the Sanctioned, was truly human.

"Luke? Did you hear what I said?"

He pinched the bridge of his nose. "Yeah. I heard you. It's funny, but Marla basically said the same thing, that maybe the Belian was supposed to sense her."

"Astute. Like her sister."

"Like her . . ." Luke turned to look at Marla. "Sister?"

She came to attention, put aside the newspaper she'd been scanning, and slid to the edge of the bed. He held up his hand in a "wait" gesture.

"Yes. Julia Reynolds paid me a visit this morning. Wanted to know where you were."

"What? How could she know about me? I sent Marla's e-mails for her, bounced them from another computer. There was no mention of me or anything suspicious. Unless—" He looked at Marla again.

She shook her head emphatically. "I did *not* talk to her—or anyone else. I swear it!" She radiated sincerity and, knowing her integrity, Luke believed her.

"Marla didn't tell her sister anything," he told Adam.

"I didn't say she did. I think Ms. Reynolds found out about you and Marla meeting at the pub. She probably talked to someone there, got your name, and did some investigating. A little digging on the Internet, and she could easily learn that your private investigator's license came through the agency."

"That's not good. What did she say?"

"She wouldn't tell me directly that she was looking for Marla. She said she needed to find you for personal reasons. I explained that you were on a crucial case, and I couldn't give her any details or reveal your location. Needless to say, she was not happy about that."

"I'll bet. We don't need her tracking down Marla and stumbling into this mess. Do you want me to have Marla phone her, tell her she's fine, and call off the hunt?"

"No. Not yet."

What was Adam up to? "What do you want us to do, then?"

"Do nothing about Julia Reynolds. I want to talk with her again. I discovered something very interesting when we shook hands."

Coming from Adam, this was a very strange conversation. "What did you discover?"

"Marla's sister is also a conductor. A matched conductor . . . for me."

"What?" To the best of Luke's knowledge, no Sanctioned ever tracked Belians directly, or worked with conductors. They had an entirely different purpose on Earth. "I don't understand."

"Believe me when I tell you I don't, either."

Stranger and stranger. "So what's next?"

"You and Marla need to go to Dallas."

"You must have spoken with Damien."

"Yes. When he and Kara performed their conduction, they saw Dallas circled on a map. They also saw a large cross. I believe the Belian might be targeting a church in Dallas next."

It wasn't surprising that Damien and Kara had culled more specific information than Luke and Marla had. Sexual conductions packed a lot more punch. "There are hundreds of churches in Dallas. They didn't happen to get a fix on which one, did they?"

"No, but it will be a large church," Adam said. "Higher body count. More blood for Belial. That would follow the pattern."

"Yeah, I think you're right. Okay, then Marla and I will head for Dallas." He glanced back at Marla's pale face. "We'll spend the night here, because neither of us has had much sleep."

"Tomorrow will be soon enough. So you'll be in home territory."

Luke thought of all the memories, a lot of them negative. "Yeah. Good old home territory."

"At least you have a base to work from. Let me know when you get there. And don't let Marla contact her sister until I give the go-ahead. Walk in Light." Adam disconnected.

Luke closed the phone, blew out his breath. "That conversation was a kick in the pants."

Marla was immediately up and by his side. "What about my sister?"

"She's fine," he said, addressing what he knew would be her immediate concern. "But . . . it's pretty unbelievable. I don't know what to think."

"About what? *Tell me!*"

At least she had some color back now. And she looked ready to slug him if he didn't talk. "I'm going to explain everything." Except using her as a live lure. He wanted to think on that some more.

He turned toward the desk. "Let's eat, and I'll tell you what Adam said about your sister, and what we know about the Belian."

But he'd keep the implications, which were looking pretty damn grim, to himself.

ADAM hung up the phone. Things were lining up for tracking the Belian. They were gathering more information, and the noose would soon be closing around it, The One willing. Marla's ability to link with it might be an important key. She and Luke would be in Dallas tomorrow, and until they got there and determined the next target, there was nothing more that could be done.

Julia Reynolds, however, was another matter. Something definitely needed to be done about her, and Adam was still considering possibilities. While he'd never admit it to anyone, he'd been totally broadsided when he shook her hand this morning and felt the unmistakable flare of a conductor connection.

While that was a first for him, and unusual enough, it wasn't the kicker. No. That had come from the surge of sexual attraction that accompanied the Sentinel/conductor connection. Adam hadn't felt sexual desire of any kind for lifetimes now—for at least a few hundred years.

Yet that had changed with a single touch that had given him an impressive hard-on. He couldn't remember the last time that had happened, or the last time he hadn't had total control over his body. He certainly couldn't remember what lifetime he'd last had sex.

Sanctioned and High Sanctioned were created to be above matters of the flesh. That was a given for the High Sanctioned; they didn't possess physical bodies, existing in spirit form. But even though the Sanctioned did have human bodies and had to eat to survive, the other physical tendencies and appetites didn't affect them. Their minds and souls were closely connected to the higher spiritual realms, and they led a far more ethereal existence than the Earthbound Sentinels did.

And yet, a single touch from Julia Reynolds had raised a tidal wave of lust in Adam.

Things like that simply didn't happen, unless there was a reason. This situation was definitely part of the universal plan, facilitated by The One. But why? What purpose could possibly be served by a Sanctioned joining with a conductor?

It also brought up another intriguing question that Adam had never considered. Could there be a genetic link between conductors? Until now, it had been believed that conductors were born in a seemingly random pattern; that they were special souls—possibly those of the piteous "things" that had served as slaves to Belial's followers on Atlantis, enduring horrendous abuse—coming back into the Earth to see karmic justice fulfilled.

Conductors were born into every race and every religious and ethnic background, with no evidence of an Earthly pattern. Adam had never heard of more than one conductor born to a family, but then, he'd never investigated such a possibility. Yet here were Marla and Julia Reynolds, sisters who were both conductors. That wasn't a coincidence.

Nor was it an accident that he and Julia were matched. There was a reason, a purpose. There always was. But in the wily and unfathomable ways of the universe, the truth might not be unraveled for many lifetimes, if ever.

He had to trust that events unfolded as they were meant to, although he would certainly begin investigating family members of all known conductors. Knowledge was power, and he'd been given an amazing nugget of information.

But what to do about Julia Reynolds? He had to admit he was looking forward to their next encounter. No one had challenged him like she had for more years than he could remember. She didn't know what he was, or what he was capable of, and he suspected it wouldn't matter if she did. She would go to the mat for her sister. And he had no doubt she would be coming back for round two very soon.

He was looking forward to it.

LUKE got up early the next morning and roused Marla to let her know he was going to work out again. He made sure her gun and phone were in reach before he left. She squinted at the clock. Six freaking o'clock in the morning. Who in their right mind got up that early if they didn't have to?

Actually, she'd gone to bed early last night, pretty soon after eating fast food Luke had reheated by holding his hands over it (which was pretty darned cool). Drained and exhausted, with only four hours sleep the night before that, she hadn't been able to keep her eyes open. She had vague memories of Luke watching the late news and listening to a police scanner, but she'd had no trouble sinking back into sleep.

Now she yawned and fluffed her pillow, planning to get at least another hour's sleep. Beside her, Bryony rolled onto her back with a little doggy groan. Marla snuggled against her and drifted off.

Voices again . . . Must be the police scanner . . .

"What's your name? . . . Can you hear me? . . . What's your name?"

That definitely wasn't a police scanner. Must be a dream.

"I can feel your energy. Tell me your name."

"Marla," she mumbled. Interactive dreaming.

"Mar-lah. A version of Mary, I believe. Where are you, Marla?"

Cold . . . she was so cold. Luke must have turned on the air-conditioning again. She huddled beneath the covers.

"Marla, are you ignoring me?"

It was dark, too, and she suddenly had that sick sensation

in the pit of her stomach, the one she always got when she had a bad dream. But this didn't seem like a nightmare . . .

"Why aren't you answering me?" The voice rose in pitch, fury edging the soft tone.

Okay, this was weird. Time to wake up now. She reached for consciousness, but something was blocking her, sucking her under. More darkness, then a familiar sensation of utter evil . . . *him!* Beside her, Bryony started growling.

"Who is this?" She managed to get her eyes open, but an unseen, depraved force cocooned her.

"You know. You've been watching me. Admiring me."

Oh God, oh God, oh God. Think! Invoking God's name seemed to clear her mind a little bit, although her heart was pounding so hard, she feared it would burst out of her chest. "What is *your* name?" she whispered.

"Come now, there's no hurry. While I like your eagerness, there is plenty of time for us to get to know one another."

"No." She struggled to get the covers off her, becoming even more panicked because she was tangled. *"No!"* She flailed wildly, hurtling off the bed and onto the floor, still embroiled in the covers. Bryony barked frantically.

Kicking the covers free, Marla surged to her feet and grabbed her gun. Chest heaving, she thumbed off the safety and scanned the room. She was shaking so badly, she wasn't sure she could even aim the Beretta. "Go away. *Go away!* Whoever you are, whatever you are, get the hell away from me!"

Nothing. Just the lingering taint of evil. She began praying out loud, desperately, calling on God and every angel and saint she knew to protect her. Bry stopped barking, shifted to intermittent growling.

Finally, pretty sure he—it—*whatever the hell it was*—was gone, Marla sank to the bed. She placed the gun on the nightstand, then wrapped her arms around herself and rocked. Her teeth were chattering and her stomach roiling, both in rhythm with her thundering heart. She forced air into her lungs, telling herself she would *not* throw up.

She wanted Luke. Wanted to feel his solid arms around

her. Wanted to absorb his warmth into her chilled soul, and hear his deep, calm voice tell her she was all right. That she was safe. She started to call him, but stopped herself. She was beginning to need him too much. Becoming dependent on him. Not a good thing.

She wasn't a good bet for a relationship, even if he was willing—which he wasn't. He'd made that quite clear. Besides, who was she kidding? If a man like Luke Paxton ever decided to get serious about someone, it wouldn't be an overweight, plain accountant who worked at a sheet metal manufacturing plant and was more boring than dirt.

Just her wild hair and glasses were enough to put off men who were merely average. And Luke was so far above average, he was like the Sun, while she was Pluto, which wasn't even a planet anymore, having been demoted in 2006. She was just a second-rate ball of ice. And a pathetic one at that.

Luke couldn't be there every time she was scared or threatened. She'd been taking care of herself for years, had learned self-defense moves and how to shoot a gun. Okay, so she hadn't been very effective against Luke, but he had super powers. That didn't count.

She could stand on her own two feet. *Sure, like you did eleven years ago,* an inner voice taunted. Old memories surged forward.

Coming to Julia's defense, she rushed William Bennett. He punched her, breaking her jaw and snapping her head back so hard her teeth went through her lip. Another punch to the side of her head gave her a concussion and put her down. But he wasn't through with her. He kicked her viciously, breaking ribs and rupturing her spleen.

Then he finished beating Julia to a bloodied mess— before he raped her. And Marla could do nothing but lay there . . .

"No!" she screamed, leaping up, fisting her hands. She stared around the room, although she knew she was alone. "I won't let you do this to me. I won't be afraid, and I refuse to dig up old demons. Do you hear me? *You will not win!*"

She picked up a pillow and hurled it against the wall. "Damn it," she muttered, trying to stop shaking. It wasn't fair. Bad enough that she had to deal with a psycho bomber with no conscience, and with whom she was now on a first name basis, a one-sided one at that. But for it to dredge up *that night* was just too much.

She grabbed a towel and went to shower. Hopefully it would help her get warm and calm down. And to regain her composure before Luke got back.

SHE was dressed and packed when he returned to the room. His hair was tied back, and he was all sweaty, which didn't do a thing to diminish his sex appeal.

"Hey," he said. Bryony gave a little whine and scampered over to him, then huddled into a ball at his feet. He squatted down. "Hey, psycho dog. What's wrong?" He scooped Bry up and cradled her against him.

Marla stared at his large hands, so strong, capable of controlling the massive Harley at a flat-out run, yet so gently holding her dog. Something tugged at her heartstrings, but she resolutely ignored it.

"We had a little scare." Discomfited at the way he was looking at her, she ducked her head and turned away. "After you left, I had this really strange dream, or at least I thought it was a dream and—"

He was beside her in an instant, his fingers grasping her chin and lifting her face to his discerning gaze. "Is that what upset you so badly?"

She refused to be needy. "I'm not upset."

His expression hardened. "Don't give me that bull. You look like you've seen a ghost. And I can feel the disrupted energy in the room. What the hell happened while I was gone?"

So much for maintaining her cool, or keeping anything from a Sentinel. Of course she had intended on telling him about the Belian, but he didn't need to know about her emotional vulnerability.

Marla pulled free and stepped back. "The Belian contacted me."

"What?" He stared at her incredulously. *"It called you?"*

"Not on the telephone. It spoke to me in my mind. I was half asleep, and at first, I thought I was dreaming."

His eyes went arctic. "Tell me everything."

She sank to the edge of the bed. Luke sat across from her, his gaze fixed on her face as she told him about the conversation with the Belian.

"Shit," he said when she finished. He ran his hand through his hair, forgetting it was bound. When his fingers tangled with the leather strip, he growled and ripped it off, hurling it across the room. "We have to block this thing, keep it from communicating with you, at least when your defenses are down. I need to tell Adam about this."

Luke had told her about the conversation with Adam; how Julia had approached Adam, and his discovery that she was also a conductor. Adam didn't want Marla talking to Julia yet, so Marla was worried about her sister on top of everything else. "Just who is this Adam Masters?"

"It doesn't matter right now. Why didn't you call me when this happened?"

"I didn't see the need. I managed to break the connection, and I couldn't sense it anymore." She caught herself twisting her hands together, stilled them. "I had my gun. And there was nothing you could have done."

"Maybe not. But I might have been able to get a reading off the energy. And you were upset."

"I didn't think about you checking out the energy. I'm sorry."

"Marla, you should have called me, regardless. You didn't have to deal with this by yourself."

"I'm a big girl, Luke. I've been taking care of myself for a long time. You can't protect me from everything."

"In this instance, you need to defer to me. This is what I do. I'm used to dealing with Belians, and you're not. I don't need you to be a hero. I need you to let me do my job."

Her pent-up fear and the stress of the past few days rose

to the surface. "Oh, and I'm supposed to sit here like a use-less fixture until you need me to do a conduction?"

"No. That's not it, and you know it." He reached out and placed his hand over hers, his eyes warming to a stunning blue. Awareness flowed between them, sending currents of sensation to all the hot spots in her body.

"You've been a huge help already," he said. "And your ability to sense the Belian—hell, to talk to the damned thing—might be the key to bringing it down.

"But I have to know that you're going to keep me in the loop on everything, and that you won't decide to do some-thing on your own. This thing is incredibly dangerous, more so to you, since it's somehow linked to you. You can *not* keep anything from me. Even the smallest bit of infor-mation could be crucial to our success, even our survival. Do you understand?"

He was right, of course. She realized he wasn't pulling a macho routine, despite possessing an abundance of testos-terone and protectiveness. He appeared to respect her and was willing to consider her opinions. But he was the gen-eral heading up this war. He had to be in control, and be aware of everything that happened.

Meaning there would be no way to maintain the emo-tional distance she desperately needed. So she'd just have to bury her feelings deeper. Dig in hard to control her reac-tions. And do her damnedest not to let the Belian, or mem-ories of William Bennett, get to her. She nodded. "Yes, I understand."

"Good. Part of my job is protecting you. I don't want you to get hurt."

"I know that." She freed her hand and stood. "I'm all packed. I hope there's a washing machine where we're go-ing because my clothes are beyond dirty."

"You'll be glad to know there are both a washer and a dryer at my house." He rose and went to his duffle for clothing.

"Your house?"

"Yeah. I'm from Dallas. While we're there, no reason to pay for a hotel when we can stay at the family homestead."

He glanced back at her, must have noticed her surprise. "The house where I grew up. Where my father and sister, and sometimes my brother, still live."

Well, wasn't he just full of surprises. She didn't know anything about his family, but then she hadn't shared anything about her life, either. "Oh, *that* homestead. Where's your mother?"

"She died when I was fifteen."

"I'm sorry." Marla paused, unsure what to say next. "I guess you're pleased to be going home."

"Sure," he said. But he looked bleak as he tore off his T-shirt and headed for the bathroom, taking his cell phone with him.

She heard his voice behind the closed door, and knew he was already conveying the news about her conversation with the Belian to Adam. It was a long time before he stopped talking and turned on the shower.

She listened to the running water, thinking about Luke's words. She knew he'd do his best to keep her safe— physically. But emotionally safe was another matter, and beyond anyone's control. Despite her attempts to remain aloof, her emotions were already engaged.

It would be a letdown when they completed this so-called mission and went their separate ways.

Assuming she survived.

ELEVEN

ADAM Masters didn't have to wait long for his second round with Julia Reynolds.

She made her move at ten the next morning. He heard his secretary's raised voice, and another female voice, and knew the battle was engaged. He strode to his office door, heard Cheryl say, "I'm sorry but Mr. Masters is busy right now. If you'd care to tell me what you need, I'll be glad to make an appointment for you to meet with him."

He waited for the comeback. "I think evasive would be more accurate than busy," came Julia Reynolds's brisk voice. "Especially since there are two cars in your parking lot, not counting mine. And since he is withholding vital information from me. I think it's very telling that he's hiding behind you rather than dealing with me face-to-face. Now please move. This isn't your battle, and I suspect he doesn't pay you enough to deal with me."

Adam did in fact pay Cheryl very well, and she knew that discretion and keeping him from being disturbed were his two ironclad requirements. She'd probably take a caning from Ms. Reynolds before she'd let her into his inner sanctum.

He opened his door before the situation came to blows. Cheryl was standing in front of it, trying to block it with her 110-pound body.

"It's all right, Cheryl. I don't believe having your blood shed on my behalf will be necessary today. Ms. Reynolds, do you always make a habit of bullying anyone who doesn't give you what you want?"

She raked him with her crystal-sharp gaze, one that he suspected put the fear of God in her students. "Do you always engage in verbal sparring to keep from dealing with people?"

"Only with those I find intriguing and capable of engaging in a verbal battle."

She blinked, and he gave himself the first point. He stepped back, swept his arm toward his office. "Please come in."

She looked at Cheryl. "I apologize for my rudeness. I know you were just doing your job, which must be horrendous, considering who you work for. I'm dealing with extenuating circumstances, and I'm sorry you were a casualty."

Cheryl managed a nod. "Sure. I understand." She shot Adam an apologetic look and returned to her desk.

"At least you're somewhat civilized," Adam said, closing the door behind Julia.

"It's not her fault that you're difficult, arrogant, and dishonest." She leaned her weight on her cane.

Today she was wearing a dark brown suit with a double-breasted jacket and etched gold buttons. Her only jewelry was gold hoop earrings. Her hair was pulled back into a tight knot at the base of her neck, making the square angles of her face more prominent.

"Please have a seat. We can both better engage the battle if we're comfortable." He returned to his own leather chair.

She remained standing. "Is that how you look upon this? A battle?"

He steepled his fingers together as he regarded her. "Well, let's see. You've contacted the Private Security Bureau, the Corpus Christi police, attorney Mark Sutter, and filed complaints about me and my agency with each of them. I would say that's an opening volley."

She glared at him, and her fingers tightened on the cane. "Is this a game to you, Mr. Masters? Because I can assure you, it's not to me."

"No, it's not a game. In fact, the case Mr. Paxton is working on is a matter of life and death. Also, it is illegal for me to disclose the details of any case my agency handles, unless the client instructs me to do so, or there is a police investigation or a subpoena. That's the law, Ms. Reynolds. I could lose my operating license if I breached confidentiality."

"And my sister's life could be in jeopardy. What does the law say about that, Mr. Masters?"

"Your sister? You didn't mention her yesterday."

Emotion flashed in her brown eyes. He wondered if she realized just how expressive they were. "You're very aware of the purpose of my visit," she said. "I could tell yesterday that you knew the whereabouts of Marla and refused to tell me."

"What would make you think that?"

"Let's just call it woman's intuition. Also, I know your kind, Mr. Masters."

"Why don't you call me Adam? If we're going to step into the ring, we might as well be on a first name basis. What exactly is my kind, Julia?"

She stiffened, most likely at his use of her first name. "You're a lowlife, arrogant and self serving. You probably don't care about anything other than yourself or getting paid. You like feeling powerful, enjoy withholding information as a way of wielding that power."

He was amused by her perceptions. "I have no doubt that you're intuitive, Julia. But unfortunately, fears and life experiences have a way of filtering and distorting impressions. I would like to think your impression of me is inaccurate, although I have been accused of arrogance, more than once."

She took a step closer. "I don't give a flip about whether or not you're really a jerk. I just want you to tell me where Marla is."

Even with the massive desk between them, he could feel the pull of her energy. His body tingled in response to a surge of pure, raw lust. He reached for his formidable self-control. "And if I don't?"

Resolve hardened her expression. "Then I'll find the leverage to force the information."

She was beginning to look strained, and he wished she would sit down. "Since you've talked to the police, a state agency, and an attorney, you already know that unless there's a crime scene and a criminal investigation, there's no legal way to make me release information on a case. Was there a crime scene, Julia? Any evidence that your sister met up with foul play?"

Her lips compressed into a thin line, and he knew she'd run out of ammunition. "Damn you," she said. "And damn the law. I just want to find to Marla. I want to talk to her and see for myself that she's—" Her voice trembled, and she paused, took a deep breath. The sheen of tears glistened in her eyes.

Ah, there was the real person beneath that tough exterior of bravado and acerbic words. He understood now why she had built such a hardened shell. He'd done a thorough background check, uncovering her double doctorates in math and physics, and the fact that she was a full professor at the University of Houston. Far more revealing was the information on what happened to her eleven years ago.

Steel forged in the fires of hell, he thought.

She gripped her cane, her knuckles turning white. "She's my sister," she said fiercely. "And I deserve—*I need*—to know she's all right. Is that too much to ask?"

He leaned forward, resting his forearms on the desk. "No, it's not," he said quietly, meeting her gaze. "I can tell you that Marla is well and safe. That she made the decision to assist us in a case, of her own free will and a desire to help. I can also ask her to e-mail you on a regular basis."

"She's on a case?" Julia considered. "No, that's not right. She's an accountant, not a private investigator. She would never do that, and certainly not without telling us. And she took the dog with her. She never takes Bryony when she travels."

"She couldn't tell you about it. It turns out she has certain abilities that will help us with this case. And since we don't know how long it will take, perhaps she felt it best to take the dog along."

"No." Julia shook her head in denial. "This is crazy. It makes no sense. I want to talk to her. I want to hear her voice and decide for myself if she's really all right."

Tired of looking up, Adam pushed back his chair and stood. Now he looked down at her. Her eyes widened, but she held her ground. "I'll have her call you," he said. "That's the best I can do. I'm sorry, but I can't tell you anything else."

"I suppose I have your word that she'll phone me?"

He ignored her derisive tone. "You do."

"Great. The word of a scum."

"I'm really not that bad," he said mildly.

"Let me tell you something." She shifted closer, her eyes flashing fire. "If anything happens to my sister, I'm coming after you, privacy laws or not. I will hound you to the ends of the earth. You definitely have my word on that." She turned, nearly stumbling as her leg gave out.

Adam forced himself to remain behind the desk, allowing her to catch herself and regain her balance. He was torn between stopping her and trying to figure out why she was a matched conductor to *him*, and what in the Light to do about it, or simply letting her go and allowing the universe to orchestrate the rest. He decided to let the universe handle it.

She opened the door and started through, then paused. She turned, her gaze now glacial. From fire to ice in a matter of seconds. Fascinating.

"I hope to God you're telling me the truth," she said. "I can only believe that you walked away unscathed from that accident with the red truck so that I could find Marla. Other than that, I wouldn't have cared if you'd suffered painful—no, make that excruciating—injuries."

He stared at her, too stunned to fabricate an intelligent comeback. Another first for him. "How did you know about that?"

She shrugged. "Oh, I don't know. Perhaps the same intuition that tells me you're a lowlife." She turned and walked out, leaving his thoughts whirling.

How could she have known about the accident? Unless she'd been trailing him, but he was certain that wasn't the case. He was always scanning his surroundings, always watching the traffic around him. No one had followed him when he left the office last night, or coming in this morning.

The accident had occurred yesterday on Interstate 37 as he was headed home. There was no way Julia could have been on the busy highway at the exact location and time the red pickup truck had changed lanes without looking, careening into Adam's Mercedes. His car had been totaled, but he'd sustained only minor injuries, which he'd already healed.

So . . . had she seen it in a vision? Perhaps she had precognition or retrocognition. Virtually every conductor possessed some sort of psychic gift. If Julia Reynolds had the ability to see something before it happened, or even see it clearly after the fact . . . then the universe had just thrown him the ball.

"Wait," Adam called, moving quickly around the desk. "We need to talk."

THEY were two hours out of Austin when Luke's cell phone rang. He turned down the Queen song blaring on the radio and snagged his phone. "Hello, Adam."

Marla watched him, already familiar with his features and expressions: the way his firm lips pressed together when he was listening; the furrow that appeared between his brows; the increased tension in his jawline. The dark Ray-Ban sunglasses hiding his eyes enhanced his rugged, bad-boy good looks. Her breath hitched. The man definitely stirred up her libido.

"She's told you she's precognitive? Wow. You think that will help us? . . . You're coming, too? . . . Okay. What?" His mouth quirked into a small grin, so Adam must have said something amusing.

"Oh, yeah? Must run in the family." He cut his gaze toward Marla. "Hardheaded and smart-ass."

"Are you talking about me?" she demanded indignantly.

He flashed a smile that sent her heart racing. "If the shoe fits, babe."

She resisted the urge to punch him, since he was driving eighty miles per hour on Interstate 35. "What are you talking to Adam about?" she demanded.

He ignored her. "She does? Can't say I blame her. That's a lot of information to take in, especially from someone like you . . . Nope, not going to qualify that."

Marla fidgeted in her seat, impatient and anxious. She was certain they were discussing Julia.

"All right," Luke said. "E-mail me your itinerary. I'm giving the phone to Marla now." He held out the cell phone. "Talk to your sister. Adam wants her to come to Dallas to help us. She's giving him a hard time and isn't convinced he's telling the truth. Maybe you can enlighten her."

Stunned, she reached slowly for the phone. "He wants Julia involved in this? Is he planning to do a conduction?" She thought of the brutal rape Julia had endured eleven years ago; how she hadn't dated a man since. "I don't think that's a good idea."

"It's not your call." Luke returned his attention to the road. "It has to be her decision. All I'm asking you to do is tell her the truth, answer her questions about Sentinels and conductors, and then let her decide." He glanced toward her. "*Her choice,* Marla."

"Like I got to choose?" she sniped, off balance from this turn of events.

"You're still here, aren't you? You could have left any time after I explained the situation to you."

His voice was low and calm, and she felt bad for lashing

out at him. Besides, he was right. He'd basically kidnapped her, yet once she'd had the facts, she had willingly remained. But this was Julia. It was different.

She raised the phone to her ear. "Hello?"

"Marla! Is that you?"

"Yes. Oh, Jules, it's so good to hear your voice. Are you all right?"

"Of course I am. It's you I'm worried about. Are you okay? Are you safe?"

"I'm fine. I'm safe, I promise. Where are you?"

"I'm in Corpus Christi, dealing with a very annoying man."

Hearing Julia's brisk, no-nonsense voice loosened the tension in Marla's chest. "What are you doing there?"

"I was looking for Luke Paxton, and his PI license is through this agency in Corpus. I couldn't locate Paxton, but I found his boss. Talk about arrogant. I suspect he's also delusional."

"Actually, he's not delusional, Jules. Has he demonstrated any unusual powers?"

"Just some parlor tricks. Levitating chairs and computers, closing the door when I started to leave. That sort of fake *Ghost Whisperer* stuff."

"Is there really any way he could fake that? You have a doctorate in physics. What do you think?"

"That Newton and Einstein are turning over in their graves."

Vintage Julia. Marla laughed, then sobered. "It's not fake, Jules, it's for real. Has he told you about Sentinels and conductors?"

"That really put the cap on the delusional theory."

"I know it's hard to believe. But it's true. All of it."

There was a moment of silence. "You believe this insane story? Is that why you took off without telling us anything? You just sent that e-mail that didn't sound at all like you, and took Bryony. She is with you, isn't she?"

"Yes, yes, Luke sent that e-mail, and yes."

"Marla, you need to get away from Paxton and come

home. We'll sort through this together, visit Dr. Jackson
and—"

"It's true, Jules, all of it. Let me ask you something. Do
you feel anything strange when you're close to Adam or
when you touch him?"

"Well, there's a bit of a sensation, like static electricity.
But it could be his carpeting or his shoes, or any number of
logical explanations."

"It's not. It's the energy that is created when a Sentinel
and a conductor are in close range of one another. Have
Adam take off his shoes and go outside. Stand on the sidewalk or the ground and then touch him. It will still be there."

"I seriously doubt that. Marla, maybe they've brain-
washed you or drugged you."

"No, they haven't. Listen to me, it's all true." Marla
paused, wondering how to convince Julia. "What about
your unusual tendency, Jules? You know, how you're able
to predict things before they happen. That's not logical and
scientific. How do you explain that?"

"It's just an aberration. Some sort of chemical alteration
that occurred in my brain after—after that night."

"Jules, the monster we're hunting is the one who blew
up that busload of children in Houston, and the university
library in Austin. We believe its next target is in Dallas. It's
not human, and Adam is not lying. I'm going to Dallas
with Luke."

"This is crazy," Julia said, but she sounded shaken.

"Adam won't force you to do anything. If you ask him if
you can leave, he'll have to let you. It's your choice."

"He already told me I was free to go. But then he
pointed out I wouldn't know what was happening with you.
What a jerk."

Marla glanced at Luke. "They can be pretty manipulat-
ing. Listen, you don't have to get involved with this, but
I'm seeing it through. I'll try to call you every day so you'll
know I'm okay. Tell Mom and Dad not to worry, okay?"

"Wait a minute. You really believe this whacked-out
story?"

"I not only believe it, but I've seen firsthand evidence to back it up."

"Oh, this is just great." There was another pause. "Well, then, if you insist on going to Dallas, I'm coming, too."

"It's dangerous, Jules, and . . . difficult." Her sister had no idea how disconcerting or terrifying. "You don't have to do this."

"I'm not leaving you alone with these arrogant nutcases. I'll drive my car back to Houston and fly to Dallas from there. Paxton's boss can find his own way. I'm not going anywhere with him."

Marla wouldn't argue with that plan. She wasn't at all sure she wanted her sister alone with Adam Masters, especially if they were a Sentinel/conductor match. He couldn't begin to comprehend how damaged Julia was, or how a conduction might unbalance her.

"That sounds best, if you insist on doing this," she said. "I'll e-mail you tonight, from an address you can answer. I have my cell phone back, and I'll leave it on, so you can call me, or I'll call you. Is that all right?"

"I guess it will have to do," Julia said grudgingly. "I'll be in Dallas tomorrow, then. And Marla, I love you."

A lump formed in Marla's throat, and her eyes blurred. "I love you, too. Good-bye." She closed the phone, wiped her eyes. "She's coming to Dallas."

"Here." Luke opened the console between them and took out a box of tissues, which he offered to her. "It's good your sister is coming. Adam says she's precognitive."

Marla took some tissues, blew her nose. She was turning into an emotional wreck. "What does that mean?"

"That she can see events before they happen. I gather from your conversation that you were aware of this."

"Yes. She's been that way since—" *Great, Marla, just spill your guts in a weak moment.* "Since her early twenties. Luke, her being in Dallas isn't a good idea. I don't think she can handle this. She's not . . . whole."

He was silent a moment. "We each have a purpose for

being on Earth, and we're not alone in our journey here. We have help, and we're given the abilities we need to do what we came to do. Sometimes you just have to trust in a higher power or the universe, or whatever you want to call it."

He had a point. Maybe it was time to start some heavy-duty praying. Because from what she could see, they desperately needed a miracle.

HE could communicate directly to *her*. *Marla*, an unusual but not unacceptable name. Of course, he was brilliant and had numerous talents, so he wasn't surprised that he could mentally project to another person. But Marla had been able to respond, and he was certain that was a sign she was highly intelligent and special. It was logical that she was superior and therefore meant for him. He deserved nothing less.

He caressed the metal-studded form of his newest creation, the implement of Belial's wrath. He thought of the old, stately structure that would crumble when he detonated this bomb, how the people within—those spreading blasphemous knowledge about a false god—would suffer and pay for their sins. Belial would bathe in their blood. He got hard, thinking about it.

As his arousal increased, his thoughts shifted back to Marla. She would be impressed with this upcoming victory, would know he was unstoppable. She would naturally be attracted to him, as most women were. Holding the bomb in one hand, he reached down to touch himself with the other hand. He couldn't wait to fuck her, to finally have a woman worthy to receive his seed.

Thinking how he would bask in her admiration while he sated himself in her body, he stroked himself harder and faster.

He'd communicate with her again. Very soon.

MARLA hadn't been to Dallas in years, but the view of downtown was much as she remembered it, with its modernistic look created by odd-shaped buildings and walls of steel-encased shimmering glass, grouped around the ball-topped column of Reunion Tower, all spearing upward into the sky. It wasn't much different from Houston, although it was smaller and created a different profile against the sky-line.

It felt strange being here. She'd rarely left the Houston area since that night, and although she had known she was hiding behind self-imposed restrictions, she hadn't realized just how much. A part of her thrilled at seeing the changes to Dallas, and at simply being somewhere new, while another part of her was frightened to be venturing so far from her safety net. Even more unsettling was finally facing the fact she'd let life pass her by, too wounded to really live. She'd missed so many opportunities.

She glanced over at Luke. Way too many opportunities—although she'd never have a shot at someone like him. Still, it was time she stepped out of the shadow of the past. The sobering pall of the past few days settled over her, and she amended her resolve to first getting through this horror.

They drove past the downtown skyline, through moderate early afternoon traffic and to a residential area in north Dallas. This was an older middle-class neighborhood, as evidenced by the larger yards and generous houses, some of them getting a little worn. Luke pulled into the driveway of a two-story house of brick and siding. It was one of the worn houses—with the brown paint peeling on the trim, some damage on the roof, and junk on the porch. The yard was poorly maintained, with grass that needed cutting and shrubs that needed trimming. There were no flowers to soften the desolate look.

"Home, sweet home," Luke said, without emotion. He turned off the ignition and opened his door. "You get Bryony and I'll get the stuff."

Wondering at both the house's shabby appearance and his attitude, Marla snapped the leash on Bry's collar and let her jump down.

Bryony wanted to explore the yard, and Marla finally

had to pick her up and carry her to the house. As she approached, she saw that the glass storm door was badly smudged and the porch siding had dirt and spiderwebs on it.

Luke shook his head and made a sound of frustration as he opened the storm door. "She's just as bad as Beau."

"Who are we talking about?" Marla hefted Bryony more securely beneath her arm and walked into a small foyer. The beige tile floor needed mopping and the small rug was covered with tracked-in leaves.

"Barrie, my little sister, and Beau, my older brother." Luke looked around in disgust. "They never do anything around here. Although Barrie's the only one living here with any regularity."

"Where is Barrie now?"

"She's at work. I called her last night while you were showering. She's a patrol officer for the Richardson Police Department, and she has a swing shift. Doesn't get off until six tonight. Then she has a karate class, so she won't be in until later."

Marla looked into a large, wood-paneled great room with a large stone fireplace at the other end. The room was cluttered with clothing, mail, and a few dishes piled on the coffee table. There was a gun case filled with rifles against one wall. She wondered if a weapons cache was a staple in a Sentinel household. "What about your father?"

"He's rarely here. He travels wherever the Sanctioned need him," Luke said in that flat tone. He stared at the great room a moment. "Dad pretty much lives on the road."

Marla felt his tension, decided to leave it alone. "I see. Okay, where should I take my stuff?"

Before Luke could answer, a huge orange and white striped cat strolled up to rub against Luke's legs. Bryony went ballistic, barking like crazy, and leaped out of Marla's grasp. The cat hissed and ran down the hallway, Bry in hot pursuit.

"Bryony!" Marla started after her, but Luke stretched out his hand, and Bry levitated four feet into the air. She hung there with her leash dangling, her legs skittering back and forth, still barking and trying to catch the cat.

"Wow. I'm impressed." Marla walked into the hallway and retrieved Bryony from suspension. She turned to smile at Luke, wishing she could relieve the sadness she sensed from him. "That's quite a talent, Mr. Paxton."

He flashed his killer grin. "Oh, I have a *many* talents."

I'll just bet you do, she thought, feeling a rush of heat though her body. Geez, her long repressed libido had proclaimed its independence big time. "So is that cat vicious?"

"Naw. Crash is a big baby and a lover. Although he could do some serious damage to Bry if she ever caught him."

"*Crash*? What kind of name is that?"

"That's a 'huge cat who runs into things and knocks them over' name." Luke glanced around again, shaking his head. "While I can't get my siblings to do anything around the house."

"You can't do everything." Keeping a firm grip on Bry, Marla picked up her suitcase. "Where should I put this?"

"I'll take it." Luke got it and her smaller case. "I'm going to put you in Beau's room, although we'll probably have to sterilize it before you can sleep there. All our bedrooms are upstairs."

Marla followed as he led the way, noting the dirt on the stairs and the clutter in the upper hallway. Beau's room wasn't too bad, although it needed a good dusting and vacuuming. The queen bed was neatly made, and the floor and furniture were debris free. There were two tall bookcases filled with books, and a desk and chair along the wall next to them.

"I take it Beau likes to read," she commented.

"Yeah. He was the smart one. Went to college on a full scholarship."

"Didn't you go to college? You said you were in the service, but you didn't mention if you were an officer."

"You have a good memory. I did go to college, but not

on scholarship, although I maintained a 3.5 average. I got a degree in criminal justice then went into the Air Force as an officer. Security Forces. It was a good way to learn about the criminal mind and how to track and defend."

"A 3.5 average sounds pretty smart to me."

He shrugged. "I had to work for it. Beau always breezed through. He was the studious type. I was into sports."

"And girls?" Marla couldn't resist asking. She remembered well the popular athletes from high school, always surrounded by girls.

"Of course. That's the best part about being a jock."

"Now look who's a smart-ass," she muttered.

Luke grinned and turned toward the doorway. "Let's see if there's anything to eat around here."

It turned out the fridge was pretty bare—milk, orange juice, a bag of apples, some leftover pizza and Chinese carry-out. "That brat." Luke closed the door. "Barrie's a fast-food junkie and rarely eats at home. Her idea of a good breakfast is found at the Burger King drive-through."

"Let me guess. She has the high Sentinel metabolism and can eat whatever she wants. She is a Sentinel, isn't she?"

"Yeah, she's a Sentinel. Any child born to a couple where one or both are Sentinels always has the power. And yes, she has a high metabolism."

"That's disgusting."

Laughing, Luke grabbed her arm. "Come on, grumpy. We need to do some grocery shopping, and then we can get down to the Belian hunting business."

"Typical Sentinel. Always thinking about food."

"Always. It's a primary concern."

They went to a Kroger and bought an outrageous amount of food, along with wine and beer. Marla had fun shopping with Luke. His laid-back sense of humor was irresistible, and she found herself laughing a lot, despite the unsettling sexual tension that throbbed between them like an incessant ache. Luke seemed to take it in stride, and she was learning to ignore it, for the most part.

They took the groceries back to the house, unloaded them, had a late lunch, and then went to work.

Four hours later, they sat at the kitchen table, looking at Luke's laptop. A pot of spaghetti sauce simmered on the stove, and the house had been dusted and vacuumed and clean sheets put on the beds. Marla had insisted on helping, despite Luke's protests.

She'd also been doing laundry and had a second load going. Luke had done a surprisingly good job of packing for her before he took her to Needville, probably because he had a sister, but she was still limited in items, and they'd all been dirty.

Now the strains of a Tom Petty song rocked from the stereo in the family room, while the washer hummed in the small utility room off the kitchen. The mouthwatering scent of the spaghetti sauce filled the kitchen. It felt strange doing homey things with Luke. Oddly, he seemed very at ease with the domestic scene, yet it didn't diminish his breathtaking masculinity in any way.

They'd spent the last two hours on the Internet, compiling a comprehensive list of the largest churches in the Dallas area, along with addresses, phone numbers, and service times.

Marla was surprised by how methodical and objective the Sentinel tracking process appeared to be, despite the sexual and mystical overtones of the conduction process. But there were a few things she didn't understand.

"With the Belian getting ready to bomb a church, why aren't you contacting local authorities?" she asked.

Luke sat back in the chair. "We work with the authorities when we have concrete information. In this case, reporting the bomber now would make things worse. We'd be under close scrutiny and questioned about how we got this information. That could slow down the tracking. Homeland Security would raise the advisory system warning in this area to 'High,' and people would panic.

"Every church would want the bomb squads checking

their facility, crackpots would start calling in false bomb threats. The police don't have the resources to check out the majority of bomb threats. They don't usually send their bomb techs unless someone finds something strange or suspicious inside the building in question."

"I didn't know that," Marla said. "I just assumed the police came if you called them."

"They can't, not with the high number of reported bomb threats they get. Take it another step further. If Homeland Security raised the alert level, and news agencies reported a threat, people would stop going to church.

"Not only would the Belian thrive on the fear and the chaos, but it wouldn't halt its plan. It would either wait until things calmed down and the alert level was lowered, or it would go forward anyway. Or maybe set off a diversion bomb, then strike somewhere else."

"I never thought about that."

"Belians are extremely cunning. They're powerful enough to redirect human thoughts and actions, so this one could slip by police, even during a security crackdown. Another possibility would be that the Belian, knowing we've gotten this close to it, would leave and go elsewhere. Then it would be harder to track, and could take a lot more lives before we caught up with it again."

"But still, we're talking about risk to innocent people."

"Believe me, I know. We don't want to lose any more lives, but if we don't catch this thing soon, the casualties will be much worse. As soon as we get a fix on its next target, we will contact the authorities. As a matter of fact, there is a Sentinel among Homeland Security staff. She's been alerted and is being kept up to date."

"Wow. You guys are really organized."

That got a small smile. "You betcha, babe." He started shutting down the laptop. "Tomorrow we'll start visiting some of the churches and see if we can pick up anything."

"But there are so many. How will we cover them all?"

"Adam will be here tomorrow, and Damien and Kara will be here on Saturday. It's possible Adam is calling in other Sentinels, if they're not on crucial trackings. We'll do the best we can."

Marla hated the sense of helplessness she felt; to know such an evil existed and what it was planning, and not be able to do a damned thing about it. At the same time, what Luke said made sense.

His expression became serious. "There is one thing we can do tonight, though. We can try to contact the Belian—through you."

TWELVE

"ME?" But she already knew exactly where this was going.

"Yeah. Adam and I talked about it. We think this un-usual link you have with the Belian might help track it. But any contact needs to be in a controlled environment, not when your defenses are down."

Her heart sped up; she could feel her palms growing damp. "So we're going to do another conduction?"

"No. We need more of the Belian's energy pattern be-fore another conduction would benefit us. We've already worked the energies we have so far." Luke closed the lap-top, moved it aside. "But you seem to have a direct psy-chic link with it, even though I don't believe you're telepathic."

She wiped her palms on her jeans. "Then how am I able to communicate with it?"

"*It* is communicating with you. Remember that both Sentinels and Belians have the same basic powers, includ-ing strong psychic abilities, with two differences. The first is that Sentinels operate out of the three higher chakras, Be-lians from the four lower earth-based chakras. The second difference is that some Sentinels have matched human conductors."

"There are no matched conductors for Belians?"

"Not that we know of."

An ugly possibility halted her breath. "How can you be sure? What if I'm matched with this thing?"

Luke shook his head. "No. From your reaction when you first encountered its energy, it's safe to say there's no mutual attraction."

Relief skittered through her. "Thank God."

"But because you're sensitive to the Belian's emotions, your reaction somehow broadcast to it. It sensed your presence, homed in on your energy and created a psychic path."

A shiver ran through her. "So it has a direct pathway to me."

He placed a reassuring hand on her arm. "Not exactly. You have natural shields that you're not even aware of. You also have as much extra shielding as I can give you. But there is a path, and we might be able to open a link to the Belian. It might unknowingly give you some information that could help us."

He pushed his chair back, angling it so he faced her. "Assuming that you agree to do this."

She moved her chair back as well, tried to calm her racing heart. "Is this the liability waiver thing again? I thought I already signed off on that."

That got a small grin. "You did, smart aleck. But this is different from a conduction. It will bring you in closer contact with the Belian."

She thought again of the victims and their families. "So what do I do after I get this thing on the psychic phone line? I don't know what to say to it."

"Right now, we just want to establish a bond with it. If you make contact, don't give the Belian too much information. Don't tell it where you are, not yet. Don't mention Sentinels. It may not be aware that you're working with us.

"This Belian is probably very smart, as are most Belians—and most successful bombers—and a psychopath.

It will have a huge ego and an over inflated sense of importance. Play on that. Tell it you admire it, that you're impressed with its intelligence. Try to get a name, a location, possible next target, anything that might help."

She drew a deep breath. "What if I screw this up?"

"You won't. We have nothing to lose by trying this." He held out his left hand. "Give me your right hand."

She did, felt the immediate flare of energy. "What are we doing now?"

"Creating a connection between our third eyes. I'll feed you the Belian's energy pattern, which will hopefully open a psychic path on a vibratory level that it will sense. When you feel a link forming with the Belian, just direct your thoughts and questions toward it."

And she'd be hooked up to that thing. "When do I break the link?"

"Any time you feel in danger, or if the Belian tries psychic manipulation, let go of my hand, which will end the conduit. I'll be right here, monitoring the energies. I won't know what the Belian is saying to you, but I should be able to sense anything dangerous."

"This feels like Russian roulette, only with psychic bullets," she muttered.

"With any luck, the Belian will get the loaded chamber." Luke gestured with his free hand, and the music cut off.

He pulled the pink quartz pendant from beneath his shirt and wrapped his fingers around it. In the ensuing silence, she felt an increasing intensity around them. "Ready?" he asked.

She nodded. Immediately, she felt pressure inside her head; saw a photo flash of indigo light. "Third eyes engaging," he murmured.

Darkness rushed at her, depravity and hatred flooding her. It was like being back at the shack, engulfed in the Belian's evil. She gasped, instinctively trying to pull back.

"Stay with me. This is just the residual Belian energy, the psychic footprint."

And he'd been carrying that around inside him? How could he stand it? Still feeling the horrifying onslaught,

Marla battled to draw air into her lungs, to keep her stomach from heaving. She sensed Luke's energy flowing around her, balancing and supporting her.

Drawing on sheer will, she forced herself to flow with the darkness and to open mentally to the Belian. In her mind, she could actually see an energy trail rolling away from her, toward a distant horizon. Then, as if a doorway had opened, she felt the pressure change, sensed she was on a threshold.

And he—*it*—was on the other side. She tried to speak, but managed only a hoarse rasp. "Just direct your thoughts," came Luke's quiet voice. She started to panic when she felt him pulling back. "I'm still here. I'm just shielding my energy so the Belian won't sense me. Talk to it, Marla."

She tried to breathe, tried to think, and then resolutely reached out. *"Hello. Are you there?"*

Silence, punctuated by her erratic heartbeat.

"Hello," she repeated. *"I've been wanting to talk to you again."*

"You," came the odd hissing. *"Mar-lah."*

She resisted the urge to break the link. *"Yes, it's Marla. I—I've been looking for you."*

"Why would you do that?"

She could sense its suspicion. *"Because I find you so interesting. So . . . intelligent."*

"I am much more than you realize. Few can comprehend my brilliance."

She felt the darkness rolling off it in waves. Bile rose in her throat. Taking another breath, she forced it down. *"That's why I like talking to you. What is your name?"*

Ignoring that, it asked, *"Where are you, Marla?"*

She resisted the compulsion behind the question. *"Are you still in Austin? I—I would like to meet you."*

It radiated disapproval. *"I do not like aggressive women. I hope you are not pushy, Marla. I would be most disappointed."*

She could barely think, with the evil stench inundating her, with the fear tearing at her. *"I'm sorry. I'm not normally aggressive. I just—I find you fascinating."*

"Of course you do. Tell me where you are."

"When will I get to see another impressive display of your brilliance?" she hedged.

"You are ignoring my question. Where are you?"

Fear sent adrenaline pounding through her body. *"I— uh, I'm far away."*

"Your answer isn't logical. You don't even know where I am."

"I assume you're still in Austin."

"It is not your place to ask questions. I will tell you what I want you to know. Where are you? Answer me!"

She could sense its growing anger, knew she wouldn't gain any information now. *"I have to go. Someone's here."*

"Is it a man? I do not want you to talk to other men. I will have to punish you, if that is the case."

Fear grew to panic. *"No—no, it's my sister. I'm going now."* She maintained enough presence of mind to add, *"I hope we can talk again soon. Good-bye."*

She pulled her hand free from Luke's, shoved the chair back. Clutching the edges of the chair seat, she drew in great gulping breaths. She could still feel the taint clinging to her.

He leaned forward. "Hey, you okay?"

"Hell, no." Chills wracked her, and she wrapped her arms around herself. "I've never felt anything so awful. Well, actually, there have been a few other things, since I met you."

He reached over and rubbed her arms. His fingers felt so warm, and she was freezing. *To hell with not being needy.* She scrambled from the chair and into his lap, her head hitting his chin.

"Ouch! Hey, take it easy," he said, but he slid his arms around her and gathered her close.

Yes. She settled against him with a sigh, and soaked in his warmth and calmness. She could get used to this, to cuddling with him every time they visited a BCS or did a conduction. He shifted to hold her better, and the chair groaned in protest. Poor chair. Neither of them were lightweights.

"Do you think we'll end up on the floor?" she asked.

"Maybe. Let's move to the couch. Think you can stand?"

Very reluctantly, she nodded. He stood, easing her to her feet, and she felt bereft at the loss of his warmth and touch. But he held her arm as they walked to the sofa. After sitting next to her, he turned his body sideways so he could face her. He kept his hand on her arm, rubbing in a slow, soothing pattern.

"Want to tell me what happened?"

She angled her body toward his. "You didn't hear what I said?"

"No, you weren't talking out loud. I could feel your anxiety and fear, but that was it."

"The contact wasn't successful. The Belian was suspicious and wouldn't give me any information. It kept wanting to know where I was. Then it told me not to see any men, or it would punish me."

Luke's eyes narrowed. "Tell me everything that it said."

So she repeated the conversation as close to verbatim as possible. It didn't make her feel any better; the darkness lingered, like a taint on her soul.

"I still feel the presence of the Belian." A horrifying thought occurred to her, and panic surged. "What if it's possessed me?"

"No, it hasn't." He grasped her chin, tipped her face up. "Look at me, Marla."

He leaned closer, and she stared into his eyes, falling into the blue depths. Warmth and brilliant light swirled through her, chasing away the darkness. "You will never be possessed by a Belian," he said firmly. "You have too much light and love within you. The darkness can't overcome that."

His face was mere inches from hers. She felt the pull of the sexual energy between them; knew from the tension in his body that he felt it, too. Her gaze shifted lower to his firm mouth. A very enticing mouth.

He radiated sensuality and heat, and she wanted desperately to kiss him. She inched closer, her thigh hitting his and shooting electricity through her. She saw the flash of awareness in his eyes. Responding on a primal level, she licked her lips, saw his attention focused on her mouth.

She wasn't sure how . . . it just . . . happened. She found herself stretching upward, sliding her hands along his face, and kissing him.

She felt his jolt of surprise and the sensual rush flowing between them. Felt his slight hesitation and dug in, determined to have this bit of sheer pleasure, no matter how brief. She teased his lips with her tongue, thought for a shattering moment he wouldn't let her in.

But then she sensed his acceptance as his hands slid up to cup her face, his fingers tangling in her hair. He opened his mouth and she welcomed the slide of his tongue against hers. He tasted like coffee and mint. She inhaled his clean, woodsy scent, intoxicated by every sensual detail.

He was a primo kisser, and she soaked up the pleasure. She hadn't kissed anyone in a long time. After Julia's attack, she'd tried the dating scene, along with the good night kisses at the end of the evening. They'd left her cold.

But kissing Luke was like touching fire. It might ultimately burn her, but she didn't care. With a small hum, she leaned into him. That seemed to shake him, and he started to pull away.

Uh-uh. She wasn't finished with him yet. She tightened her hands on his shoulders, tugged him back, and resettled her lips over his. He tried to say something—probably a protest—but she took the opportunity and slid her tongue back into his mouth.

He gave a little groan, and then his tongue joined the dance with hers, slow, thorough, and electrifying. He was light and fire, warming every atom of her body. Lost in sensation, she discovered there were many subtle variations of a kiss—of which Luke was a master—and that the mouth was exquisitely sensitive. It also had a direct link to the rest of her body, which was blazing with need.

Oh, man, why had she waited so long to experience this?

He adjusted his position, allowing her to slide between his legs and come flush against him. His body was hard and hot and she could practically feel the pheromones flowing out of him.

All her body systems were on full, green light *Go!* Here was her chance to experience what Julia's attack had almost destroyed. She grabbed Luke's hand from her hip and placed it over her breast. That got his attention. He freed his mouth. "Marla, we have to stop now. This isn't—"

"Just shut up. I want this, and I'm not going to let your scruples ruin it." She kissed him again before he could protest further, felt a victorious surge when he made a guttural sound, and his fingers curved around her breast.

His thumb rubbed over her nipple, and she thought she might combust right then. He left her mouth to press his lips against her neck, and then to where her sweater dipped down. She knew he was fully in the game now, and sensual shivers raced through her.

"Luke," she gasped, close to melting, all logical thought obliterated.

Her mind might be mush, but she was hyperaware of the sensations, of the feel of him when she slipped her hands beneath his pullover. His skin felt like heated satin over swells of muscles, his nipples small tight nubs. He reciprocated, sliding his hands inside her sweater and teasing her breasts along the edges of her bra.

She was burning between her legs, with a desperate need almost as powerful as that created during a conduction. She could feel Luke's hardness pressing against her, felt the same tension in his body.

This is it, she thought. They were going to dispense with her damned virginity here and now, before Luke came to his senses, and remembered his honorable intentions. *Finally, thank God!* She reached down to stroke him, savored his harsh groan.

This was definitely it.

"Hello? Luke? Are you here?"

The husky feminine voice pierced the sensual fog, and Luke pulled back and lifted his head.

"Luke! I'm home!"

"*Shit!* Barrie's here." He bolted off the couch in a blur of movement, and the cooler air hit Marla like a slap.

It took a few seconds more for the reality of what he'd said to sink in, and she swung up with a gasp. He smoothed down his shirt and ran his fingers through his hair.

Not much to be done about the massive bulge in his pants, she thought as she jerked down her sweater and frantically finger combed her own hair.

"Luke—oh, there you are!" There was a squeal, then a young woman raced around the couch and threw herself at Luke in a graceful, athletic leap. She slammed him so hard, he stumbled back a step. Laughing, she pulled his head down and butted her forehead against his. "Brother! I'm so glad you're here."

"Hey, brat." Pulling back, Luke looked at Marla over Barrie's shoulder, his expression inscrutable. "It's good to see you, too."

"Well you could come home more often, you know. You don't have to be such a stranger."

"I think you just want me here to clean up your mess." He kissed her on the cheek. "But, yes, I missed you."

"You'd better say that." The young woman turned, offered Marla a stunning smile. "Hi. I'm Barrie, the little sister. Don't believe anything this big goof might have told you about me."

Marla returned the smile. "I'm Marla."

Luke's sister was adorable, a petite pixie with straight, silky blond hair cut just beneath her chin, longer in the front. She had the same stunning blue eyes as Luke, but her face was heart shaped and her nose dainty. She was several inches shorter than Marla and tiny, probably no more than 110 pounds soaking wet. She was wearing a traditional karate uniform, loose white cotton pants and a kimono-style top that was tied with an impressive black belt.

"Nice to meet you, Marla. Luke's never brought a conductor home before."

"Maybe because I'm never here," Luke said, scowling at his sister.

"At least you admit it." Barrie turned toward the kitchen. "What'd y'all have for dinner? I'm starving."

"Spaghetti. We ate it all."

She was already in the kitchen; obviously all Sentinels had that supernatural speed. "What a liar. You haven't even cooked the pasta yet. You're building some bad karma, brother."

"And your eating habits are terrible." Luke followed her into the kitchen.

Wanting to give them some privacy, Marla returned to the couch and picked up the TV remote. She channel surfed, settling on *Law & Order*. She tried to focus her attention on Jack McCoy relentlessly prosecuting the bad guys. It was futile; her heart was still racing and her body still throbbing with need. So close. *So unfair!*

She sank back with a sigh, thinking how wonderful kissing Luke had been. She could hear the voices from the kitchen—Barrie's loud and exuberant, and doing most of the talking, and Luke's deep drawl—but not their actual words. The kinship and affection between them was obvious. She and Julia shared that kind of bond. She'd be seeing Julia tomorrow and still hadn't come to terms with that. She wished her sister hadn't gotten involved in this Belian business.

The scents of spaghetti and cooking bread drifted from the kitchen, while Barrie talked virtually nonstop. Marla tried to calm the myriad thoughts bombarding her and focus on the TV.

"Marla," Luke called out. "The food's ready. Come join us."

She went into the kitchen. Barrie was placing plates heaped with spaghetti at three places, and Luke was tossing a salad. Marla wasn't very hungry, which was unusual for her. But her appetite had been repressed ever since she met Luke. She hoped that translated to some lost weight. Feeling like a slow-moving hippo next to Luke's spritelike sister, she got out glasses for iced tea and wine.

During the meal, she picked at her food and sipped wine. She was very aware of Luke's presence next to her, at the head of the table; thought he was somewhat stilted when he spoke to her. He didn't act like a man who'd been about to score, but more like a polite acquaintance.

She sensed a widening chasm between them, and although she knew she shouldn't expect anything from him, it was disappointing. She drank more wine and listened to Luke and Barrie's affectionate verbal sparring while they ate ridiculous amounts of spaghetti and heavily buttered bread.

As if by unspoken agreement, they kept the conversation light through dinner. After her third helping of spaghetti, Barrie pushed her chair back from the table and drew her legs up so that her knees were against her chest. Only a dainty woman could sit like that in a kitchen chair. "Tell me about this Belian you're tracking," she said.

Luke filled her in, starting with the school bus explosion, which was the first known act of the Belian, although there were probably more before that. He told Barrie how he and Marla had met at the Red Lion Pub.

"Marla is an empath," he explained. "She not only feels the energy where the Belian has been, she also feels its emotions and hears its thoughts. She's even communicated with it telepathically."

Barrie's blue eyes widened. "Wow. That's awesome."

"That's not the word I would use," Marla said. "It's pretty unsettling."

"I'll bet." Barrie's eyes were warm with sympathy. "There's no light in a Belian, nothing but darkness and depravity. Brushing up against that would have to be icky."

"That's a good word for it," Marla agreed.

Luke told Barrie everything that had happened up to their arrival in Dallas. "Tomorrow Marla and I will start visiting the largest Dallas area churches and see if we can pick up any traces of the Belian. Adam is flying in from Corpus, and Marla's sister Julia, who's also a conductor, is coming from Houston."

Barrie's eyes got even wider. "Pain-in-the-ass Adam is coming *here*?"

"He is, and you'd be well-advised to show him some respect."

She gave a little snort. "What's he going to do—evaporate me?"

Luke arched his brows. "You never know."

"I can help you track the Belian," she said. "I'll see if I can take a few days leave and canvass some of the churches."

"No, you won't. You're still an initiate, little sister, and you know the rules. You don't fly solo until you complete your training."

"That's only because David—another pain in the ass—is holding me back, insisting we have to work on all this stuff I already know. He's a dinosaur, just as bad as Adam."

"He's also been tracking Belians for over thirty years, and knows exactly what he's doing. You need to listen to him."

Barrie sniffed. "I'm twenty-four years old. By that age, you'd already done lots of conductions. David won't even let me do a full conduction."

Marla wondered if "full" meant a sexual conduction.

"You can't compare yourself to me. Each Sentinel progresses on an individual path. You know that. If David doesn't think you're ready for a full conduction, then you're not."

Barrie's eyes narrowed. "It's a male thing, isn't it? Just because I'm a woman, you and David are being overprotective of me. But I don't need protection. I do happen to know about sex, big brother. I'm not the sweet little prude you think I am."

The expression on Luke's face was priceless—shock and outrage and concern warring with one another. "Meaning what?" He was in major big brother mode.

"None of your business." Barrie slid her legs down and stood. "I'm a grown woman, whether you like it or not. I will be doing full conductions and tracking Belians—on my own—in the very near future. So get over it." She headed for the stairs.

Luke rose from his chair. "Where are you going? This discussion isn't finished."

"Yeah, it is." Barrie sounded like a very feminine Luke. "I'm going to shower and get some sleep. I have a job interview tomorrow with the Dallas Police Department."

"What?" He strode after her. "You are *not* going to work in Dallas. It's too dangerous."

"Oh, please. I'm a Sentinel, for God's sake." She turned and glared at him. "Not only that, I have a black belt and police training. I can take care of myself."

"You're in a mortal body. You can be killed or seriously injured."

"So can you, brother. I'm not talking about this anymore. If I'm not checking out churches tomorrow, then I'll be interviewing. Deal with it."

"Barrie!"

But she was gone, up the stairs in a flash. Luke stared after her. "What the hell did she mean she knows about sex?"

Marla had never seen him this shaken, and she found it endearing that he cared so much for his sister. It was also kind of funny to see him not in total control of a situation.

"I think maybe she was pushing your buttons. You're very protective of her."

"Yeah." He sighed. "I guess I am."

It occurred to her he carried a lot of responsibility on those broad shoulders. "Is your father ever home?"

"Very rarely." He turned, his expression blank. "He's been gone, off and on, since . . . For a very long time." He strode to the table, picked up the empty dishes, and took them to the sink.

Intuitively guessing this was related to his mother's death, Marla twisted around in her chair to look at him. "So you're the surrogate dad?"

He stared down at the sink. "Something like that."

She wanted to go to him, to put her arms around him and ease his worries. But despite the intimacy of two conductions, despite the raw chemistry between them and the fact they'd had their hands all over one another a short while ago, she and Luke didn't have a bona fide relationship.

So she offered words instead. "She's twenty-four years

old, Luke. You can't protect her from everything. And from what you've been telling me, destiny plays a role, too."

"I hate it when my words come back to bite me on the butt." He turned to look at her, and that intent gaze had her body back to flash point instantly. Oh, yes, they had chemistry, all right.

"Marla, what happened between us tonight—it was a mistake. A big one."

She felt a sinking sensation in her belly. "I didn't think so."

He ran his hand through his hair, a sure sign he was perturbed. "This has to stop here and now. We can't do a sexual conduction, and further involvement will only get you hurt. I can't give you commitment. And I'm sure as hell not going to take your innocence, especially knowing you're not the type of woman to indulge in casual sex."

How did he know what type of woman she was? But she knew it wasn't really Luke's sense of honor that was holding him back from jumping her bones. It was *her*. His own kid sister was a knockout, and he could probably have any woman he wanted. She was so ordinary she didn't warrant a second glance. She'd already had this discussion with herself. What had she been thinking?

She hadn't. Her hormones had definitely been rampant, and so had his. That's why he'd caved—the demands of his body had overridden her lack of appeal. She was an idiot.

She clenched her fists until her nails bit into her palms, the pain keeping her on an even keel. "You're right, of course," she said tightly. "I'm sorry that fate matched you with a dud conductor. And I'm sorry about my lack of self-control. How thoughtless of me." She rose and headed for the stairs. "I'll do my best to control myself in the future. Good night."

"Marla, wait. You took that wrong. Marla—"

She ignored him, moving quickly up the stairs. As she turned down the hallway, she heard a thud and a loud "*Shit!*"

It would have been funny if his rejection hadn't stung so badly.

THIRTEEN

───────

It was past midnight when Luke finally headed to bed. He'd had a lot to do—a phone call to Adam, more research on the Internet, his evening meditation, bringing Bryony in for the night and locking a very indignant Crash, along with litter box and food, in his father's bedroom. And—ah, hell, who was he kidding? He'd been reluctant to go upstairs until he knew the coast was clear.

It was ironic. While in the military, he'd been in numerous hellholes and battled terrorists and insurgents. He could track down violent, dangerous Belians and dispatch them with ruthless efficiency. But facing two emotional females stopped him cold. Women were complex and mysterious— and another species, as far as he was concerned.

For the most part, he didn't have too much trouble dealing with women. Most female conductors were in the game for the thrill of the hunt and for the exceptional sex, and had no expectations after the Belian was found and dispensed to Saturn. The other women in Luke's life tended to be worldly and free-spirited, satisfied with an evening of good food and conversation, followed by great recreational sex, with no strings attached. Simple and un-complicated.

But Barrie and Marla were another story. He'd basically raised Barrie, so he had megaprotective feelings toward her. She'd been four when their mother had died. Dad had gone off the deep end, completely withdrawing from everything. Beau had just started his first year at college, so at the age of fifteen, Luke had become both father and mother to Barrie.

That was the reason he'd attended a local college and hadn't gone into the military until he was twenty-five. It had been difficult dealing with adolescence and menstrual cycles and makeup and adolescent boys, but they had managed. She had still been a little girl, even at fourteen, in his mind, when he left.

But she'd grown up while he was in the service and then tracking Belians. She'd developed into a beautiful young woman, and he didn't like the way men looked at her. Didn't like the thought of her having sex with anyone, much less conduction sex.

He knew he was going to have to get over that, as well as the fact that she would be in dangerous situations when she began hunting Belians. But damn, it was just too soon. And if she was already sexually active . . . *hell*, she was twenty-four. What did he expect? But he didn't have to like it.

Then there was Marla, who was an amazing woman. She was warm and compassionate, intelligent, funny, and, unfortunately, sexy as hell. Even without the Sentinel/conductor attraction, he would have found her intriguing. Her wild, sexy hair, her lush body and sensuous mouth, even those funky glasses turned him on. No problem with that, except she was a forever kind of woman. She might not realize it yet, because of her inexperience with men, but it was written all over her.

He'd been determined to keep his distance, but tonight, when she looked at him with those large honeyed eyes and kissed him, he hadn't been able to resist. Big mistake. She'd tasted and felt so good that his body had gone on full alert, a four-alarm blaze.

He'd tried to abort, but when she put his hand on her breast and kissed him again, he'd been lost. All resolve and good sense had disintegrated in the fire that raged between them, and all he'd wanted to do was bury himself inside her sweet warmth.

If Barrie hadn't come home . . . *shit*.

He'd wanted to explain that to Marla, make her understand they needed to maintain emotional and physical distance as much as possible. But, for whatever reason, he always seemed to screw up when it came to her, and he had absolutely no idea why. It was frustrating as hell. So was dealing with Barrie. He couldn't seem to win for losing.

So tonight he did the smart thing and waited until all was quiet before he ventured upstairs. It might be the easy way out, but it maintained the peace. He reached the top of the stairs, Bryony right behind him, and flared out his senses. No music, no sounds of movement, no high levels of energy. They were both asleep.

He went to Beau's bedroom and slowly opened the door. Marla lay on her side, moonlight illuminating part of her face. Her breathing was deep and even. Bryony jumped on the bed and curled into a tight ball behind her knees. Luke stared at her a long moment. She was special, no doubt about it. Sooner or later, the right man would come along, and if the guy had an ounce of sense, he'd snap her up.

For now, her safety and welfare were Luke's responsibility. He didn't want her sleep disturbed tonight, didn't want the Belian touching her while she was defenseless. He and Adam were both in agreement on that. He was hoping that putting her into a very deep sleep would prevent dreams and psychic contact.

He focused, sent the energy and the mental command into Marla's mind, taking her into the deepest possible stage of sleep. As if sensing his touch, she gave a little sigh. Bryony nudged her and whined.

"She's fine," Luke told Bry. "But I think it's best if I don't sleep in here. You watch over her, girl. If you sense anything, pull your psycho dog routine and bark your head off. I'll be here in a blink."

Bryony rested her head on her paws, watching him as if she understood every word. Maybe she did. Luke shook his head. He could communicate with a poodle, but not with his sister or Marla.

One of life's ironies.

HE couldn't find her. He'd been intrigued by her contact earlier today. He'd decided to talk to her some more, but when he tried to reach her, she didn't respond. Maybe she was busy and couldn't "hear" him. Or else she was ignoring him. That thought upset him, and he had to calm himself. She wouldn't do that, he told himself. She was too smart, too special. She admired him too much.

He looked at the beautiful bombs laid out on the table, and gloated over his genius. They were perfect. They would exact punishment against the blasphemous sinners, and very soon. He'd done the initial surveillances today. Tomorrow, he would do a more thorough reconnaissance. Saturday, he'd place the bombs. Then Sunday . . . *kaboom!*

He couldn't wait. He got hard just thinking about it. Not only would Belial be served, but Marla would know that he was not to be trifled with.

He reached for her again, but she wasn't there. He hoped she wasn't ignoring him.

Because then he'd have to punish her.

MARLA woke up groggy. Not even a shower, her usual method for waking up, was able to clear the cobwebs in her mind this morning. She was pretty sure she knew why.

She also knew she was going to have to face the person responsible for her sluggishness. She'd certainly made a fool of herself last night. That was the problem with rash behavior—eventually, you had to face your screwups.

Especially in this case. Her continued cooperation with

Luke was crucial. He'd been totally honest with her from the start. Her feelings were *her* problem. If she could keep her hormones under control and her head clear, she wouldn't keep hitting the wall.

Delaying as much as possible, she made the bed and re-folded her clean clothing. Then she steeled herself and left the room. She saw a flash of dark blue as Barrie, dressed in her police uniform and packing a very impressive gun, headed down the stairs.

Marla followed slowly, reluctant to go down. Hearing Luke's voice, she paused on the landing. He and Barrie were talking below in the foyer. Not wanting to interrupt, Marla sank onto a step and waited. She didn't want to trudge back up the stairs and she wanted to see if they made up. Okay, so she was nosy.

"Got some coffee in the kitchen," Luke was saying.

"I can't—I gotta get going."

"Listen, Barrie, about last night—I'm sorry if I over-reacted."

"You did. You're such a big brother sometimes," she said affectionately. "I'm not trying to be difficult, Luke. But I'm *really* not a little girl anymore. I'm grown up, in case you hadn't noticed. And I'm a Sentinel. I'm ready to go out into the world and do what I was born to do."

"Yeah, I can see you're grown up. You're a beautiful young woman. You need to watch out for all the wolves out there."

"I can take care of myself."

"I know you think you can, brat. And I know I'm a little overprotective."

Barry gave an unladylike snort. "A *little*? Listen, I really want that Dallas police officer position. I could get so much more hands-on experience. Nothing ever happens in Richardson, except for burglaries and petty theft. Working for Dallas would prepare me better for tracking Belians."

"I thought about that last night, and as much as I hate it, you're right. You need to get some solid experience. Just promise me you'll be careful."

"I'm always careful, big bro."

"Yeah, right. Come here, you."

Marla peeked around the corner and saw Luke giving Barrie a big bear hug. His sister was so small she was almost lost in his muscular arms. Marla was glad they were back on track.

"Gotta go," Barrie said, stepping back. "The interview is in an hour, then I'm on duty. Gotta hit the Burger King, too."

"You could get up a little earlier every day and eat a *real* breakfast here."

"Whatever. Hey, think about my offer to help with this Belian, okay?"

"I'll think about it."

"Sure you will. Maybe you'll even give me an answer before next year." She stood on tiptoe, kissed his cheek. "Love you."

"I love you, too, brat."

Barrie breezed out the door, and Luke shut it behind her. "Did you sleep well, Marla?" he asked without turning around.

Busted. She came around the corner and walked down the lower flight of stairs. "I'm sorry. I heard you talking, and I didn't want to interrupt. I'm glad you and Barrie are all right again."

"Me, too." He turned and looked at her, his expression serious. "How about us, Marla? Are we all right?"

Time to get this over with. "We're fine. You were right last night. We—ah—we probably shouldn't have kissed." *And don't forget it, Marla.*

He relaxed a little, which only made her feel worse. "I'm glad we're good," he said. "Come on out to the kitchen. There's fresh coffee and we can whip up some breakfast."

Sentinels and food. She rolled her eyes and followed him. She heard Bryony barking outside in the large fenced-in yard, probably chasing a squirrel. Luke must have let her out. She watched him get out coffee mugs. "You did that woo-woo crap on me last night, didn't you?"

He turned, coffeepot in hand. "Am I going to have to put the top on your cup again?"

She leaned a hip against the door frame. "You might need to hide the knives, too. I hate it when you do that. It makes me fuzzy."

"I know, but I will continue to do it if I think it's necessary. We've talked about this. Adam and I don't want the Belian coming at you when your defenses are down."

She made a face. "I guess if I have to choose between quality time with a Belian and funky sleep, I'll take the sleep. Let's catch this thing fast, okay?"

"I plan on it, babe."

She had to smile at him. He was such a gorgeous charmer. She pulled out a chair from the table and sat down. "That thing scares the living daylights out of me, but I'm much more concerned about it blowing up more innocent people. I'll try to talk to it again, if you think it will help."

His mouth tightened. "I hope we can keep your contact with it to a minimum.

She looked up at him as he set a mug in front of her. "I trust you to protect me, Luke. And I have to trust that a higher power, or the universe, brought us together to catch this thing."

He sat across from her. "You've been paying attention. By the way, you're an amazing woman."

"Not really." She avoided his intense gaze, took a sip of coffee. "So what's on the agenda today?"

"We'll start visiting churches and see if we can pick up any Belian energies. At some point, we'll meet up with Adam and Julia. I've printed out the e-mail with Adam's schedule, and I'm assuming Julia will call you when she arrives. We'll brainstorm with them, see if your sister has any precognitive flashes.

"And then . . ." Luke paused, his expression hardening, his eyes becoming icy. "We're going Belian hunting."

* * *

FRIDAY morning, Julia was the last passenger off the airplane. She didn't want to hold anyone up with her painfully slow gait, so she waited until everyone exited before making her way through the walkway to the terminal.

In the past few days, she'd walked far more than usual, and her leg was aching. Add to that the worry about Marla, and trying to assimilate the crazy story about superhero Sentinels fighting bad guy Belians and psychic human conductors, and she felt totally upended. She hated being out of control.

The tall figure standing just inside the terminal only made her mood worse. She looked past him, kept on walking. He fell into step beside her. "Ignoring me, Julia?"

That harsh voice was extremely annoying. "What are you doing here?"

"Southwest flights from Corpus usually come into Love Field."

She halted, resigned to having to take time to get rid of him. "I meant, what are you doing at my gate? How did you even know what flight I was on?"

He gave her a raised brow look.

"Oh, right, let me guess. You did something illegal to find out my flight number. I should report you to the authorities."

"It would just be a waste of their time and taxpayer money."

God, he was arrogant. She moved around him. "Don't you have better things to do, like following cheating husbands or something?"

He walked beside her. "I've already explained to you, Julia. The agency exists to track Belians."

"Oh, yes, that delusional dribble. Why don't you go bug someone at *Ripley's Believe it or Not*, or maybe the *National Enquirer*? I'm sure they'd be fascinated." She tried to speed up the pace, her leg protesting.

"How would I explain to them the unique energy between a Sentinel and a conductor?" He slid his hand over her upper arm, halting her steps. "How, exactly, would I show them this, Julia?"

It felt like an electrical current was flowing from his hand into her arm, then dispersing into a wave of startling warmth targeting her chest and lower body. At the time Julia had been attacked, she'd been twenty-five and sexually active with a steady boyfriend.

Although since then she'd been seemingly frigid and the boyfriend long gone, she still remembered what that heated rush of desire felt like; the breathless sensation coiling with a thrilling tension. And she felt it now, a one-two punch that sent her staggering.

"Let go of me!"

He released her, and the electricity receded, although her body still throbbed with sensation. "There is no logical explanation for this attraction between us," he said. "At least not in physical terms."

"You've got something on you," she insisted. "Something that's creating a current when you touch me."

"Tell me how. There would have to be a closed electrical circuit to create a current, which you probably wouldn't feel. Unless of course, we're creating a magnetic field between us, and you're the other part of the loop."

So the man knew something about electricity—and unfortunately, he was right. "I don't care what the explanation is. You go create all the magnetic fields you want. I'm here to see my sister, and my plans don't include you."

"The situation your sister is involved in does indeed include me." He matched his gait to her faltering one. "Don't you think you should rest for a minute?"

Her leg was burning, and she knew he was right—again—but that only made her more determined to put some distance between them. "I only have to get to the rental car agency. I'm not an invalid. You can just go on about your business."

Her leg chose that moment to spasm, and she lurched forward with a gasp, her cane the only thing that kept her from hitting the floor.

"Stubborn woman," Adam muttered. He swept her off her feet and into his arms, no easy feat since she certainly wasn't a lightweight. Yet he didn't appear at all strained.

Stunned, she struggled to get free, heedless of the pain. "Put me down!"

"I plan to, in a minute. Stop fighting me." His arms felt like bands of steel around her as he carried her to a nearby seat and lowered her into it.

Her leg was drawn up, the muscles knotted and the pain so intense she could barely think. Gritting her teeth, she reached blindly toward the leg, but Adam beat her to it. Kneeling before her, he took her leg in his large warm hands, pushed up her pants leg, and began kneading it. It hurt so badly, she couldn't keep back a groan.

"Easy. Just give it a moment."

A curious, tingling warmth began spreading through the screaming muscles. It wasn't the same sexually charged energy as before, but soothing and calming. Almost immediately, the muscles relaxed and her foot stopped cramping. The pain receded as the warmth spread up into her thigh, and she managed to draw a full breath. Adam kept massaging the leg. She stared at his bent head, at the thick dark hair faintly streaked with white, and at the long, elegant fingers rubbing her calf.

The pain was completely gone now, and she leaned back with a sigh. She hadn't had an episode this bad in years. She'd also never gotten relief this fast. It had always taken two Vicodin, moist heat, and an hour of intense pain before the leg settled down. But he'd calmed it in less than a minute. How?

Adam looked up at her. "I tapped into healing Earth energy and directed it into your leg," he said, as if he'd read her mind. "Otherwise, you'd still be in agony. I can reverse it, if you'd like further proof."

"No," she said quickly. "That won't be necessary."

His well formed mouth quirked at the corner. "You don't believe I eased the pain, but you don't want to test your theory."

She stared into his midnight eyes, thought she saw tiny starbursts of light. Man, she must be more tired than she realized. "You can let go of my leg now."

"Not even a thank-you. Well, then." He rose gracefully, dusted off his expensive charcoal slacks.

He straightened his suit coat and walked over to retrieve her cane off the floor. He returned and took the chair beside her, propping the cane on the other side, where she couldn't reach it. "It would be best to let your leg rest a few minutes."

"My leg and I can rest just fine without you. May I have my cane?"

"When I think you're ready to stand, I'll give it to you. Until then, I will keep it over here, in the interest of self-preservation."

Frustration roared through her. "This is ridiculous. Give me my cane and go away. Otherwise, I'll call security."

"Julia." His tone was implacable. "I am here for two reasons. The first is to help track down a being that is more evil than you can comprehend. The second is because of you."

"I don't—" Her voice froze midsentence. She stopped, tried to speak again. But her vocal cords were so constricted, she could barely whisper. *What the—?*

"You'll have your voice back in a minute. But first, you will listen to me. I know I've thrown a lot of information at you. I also know you're brilliant and logical, and what I've told you goes against known science. And I know you're worried about your sister, and you want to see her."

Finally, they agreed on something. She tried to talk, to no avail. She rubbed her throat, panic flaring.

Adam appeared oblivious to her distress. "I suggest we agree to a truce for now. We'll go see Marla, and maybe she can put some of your doubts to rest."

Or maybe Julia could get Marla away from these crazies and somewhere safe. She nodded, tried to agree and allay his suspicions, but the words came out as a harsh croak.

"Try it now," Adam said.

"What—" She cleared her throat. "What just happened?"

"I'd like to think you'd accept my ability to keep you from talking as further proof that I really am a Sanctioned. But I'm not overly optimistic."

Still dazed, she could only stare as he stood and offered his hand. "I think we can make it to my car now."

"I already have a reservation for a rental car," she said, ignoring his hand. "I can find my own way around Dallas."

"It would be much simpler if we rode together, I think."

And that much harder for her to get Marla away from these guys. But she was learning that opposing him openly didn't have a high success rate.

"I might want to do some sightseeing and shopping while I'm here. I need my own car." She struggled to stand and he took a firm grip on her arm and pulled her up.

Her leg tried to give and she instinctively reached out, locking her hand around his free hand. As soon as their hands connected, she felt a flare of energy, and then a scene flashed into her mind, at a location she didn't recognize.

What she saw next sent her reeling. Stumbling back in shock, she hit the seat behind her and fell sideways. She barely felt Adam's arms come around her and jerk her upright. She was too caught up in the event unfolding in her mind to be aware of anything else.

As quickly as the images appeared, they faded into gray. For a moment, she saw nothing but the void. Then edges of color seeped back, and her vision cleared. The next thing she saw was Adam Masters hovering over her.

He watched her, his eyes so black, she couldn't tell where his pupils began and ended. "You had a precognitive vision, didn't you?"

She'd never experienced anything quite like this before. "I don't know."

"Tell me what you saw, Julia."

She stared at him, fear beginning to take root. Fear that he might really be telling the truth about who he was . . . and that the horror of what she had just seen might actually come true.

FOURTEEN

MARLA was beginning to discover just how extensive Luke's powers were. They'd been to five sizable churches this morning. The churches had administrative offices that were open, and it was easy enough to walk in. But it wasn't quite as easy to roam the building or the grounds without being approached and questioned.

But Luke could redirect the thoughts of anyone who questioned them. He could convince a questioner that he and Marla were there legitimately, or make the person forget they'd been there at all. It was both amazing and unsettling. No wonder she slept so deeply when he willed her to.

They not only went inside the churches, but they walked the grounds as well, on the chance the Belian had been doing advance surveillance. Neither of them picked up any energy traces indicating it had been there.

The process was slow and tiring—at least for Marla. Sitting in Luke's truck, she slipped her shoes off and wiggled her toes. Luke checked off the church they'd just visited and consulted his Mapsco.

"It's going to take too long, isn't it?" she asked, thinking about the beautiful sanctuaries they'd seen, the wonderful stained glass windows, and the people who would be attending services there. "It will strike again before we can find it."

"I hope not." Luke shook his head. "But there are hundreds of churches in Dallas. Plus the Belian might not necessarily pick the largest. He could go for a medium-sized church, or for a church where the pastor is well known, or any number of variables. We just have to keep looking."

Marla groaned inwardly. "Where to next?"

"We'll stay in north Dallas. The next church is only a few miles away." Luke started the truck just as his phone rang. He retrieved it from his leather jacket. "Hey, Adam . . . She's with you? . . . Oh, I see. Don't say I didn't warn you."

Marla knew he was talking about Julia. She wondered what the warning had been about—the stubbornness of Reynolds women, or Julia's emotional frailty, which she'd tried to explain to Luke without telling him about the attack.

"Don't do that yet. Maybe Marla will have better luck with her."

That answered that. Adam must have run up against Julia's ultrastubborn streak.

"We've checked out five churches, but no luck so far," Luke was saying. "I thought I'd wait for you before we went to that monster church in Plano. That would be a prime target . . . Okay. Where should we join up?"

He listened a moment, looked at his watch. "It's almost noon. Why don't we meet at a restaurant? I'm sure the ladies are hungry and I can always eat." He grinned. "Yeah, I know. There's a Carrabba's Italian Grill right off the Tollway, just south of Frankford. Should take you about twenty-five or thirty minutes from Love Field. We can eat and discuss our plans, then head north on the Tollway. It's just a few minutes from there to the church . . . All right. Walk in Light."

He closed the phone, glanced at Marla. "Julia is with Adam, and I don't think he's too happy with her right now."

"Is she okay?" Marla tried to keep the worry out of her voice, but didn't succeed very well.

"Of course she is. Adam would never mistreat an innocent woman. But I don't think he's ever been challenged like this, either. Apparently, your sister is giving him a hard time."

"I wonder why. Maybe because she doesn't like overbearing, arrogant men telling her what to do."

"How do you know that Adam is overbearing or arrogant?"

"Call it an educated guess. He's a Sentinel, isn't he?"

"I resent that." But Luke was smiling as he said it. He knew very well he could be a poster boy for macho men everywhere. "Actually, Adam is a Sanctioned."

"You've mentioned that word before. What is it?"

"He's a step above Sentinels. He's in a human body, but he's more powerful. He doesn't do conductions and normally doesn't track Belians. He supervises the Sentinels in his area, coordinates their locations and activities."

"So he's the big boss."

"Well, I guess you could say he's my boss, in a way. But he's not at the top. Above him are the High Sanctioned—who don't have physical bodies—and above them, The One, whom most people refer to as God."

She guessed it wasn't surprising that there would be a celestial hierarchy, but it was still mind boggling. A week ago, she hadn't even met Luke, couldn't have imagined this secret world.

They reached Carrabba's before Adam and Julia did. It was peak lunchtime and the restaurant was crowded, with a waiting list. Since the April day was balmy and the sun was shining, they elected to wait outside. A short while later, a big black Mercedes rolled into the lot and parked in one of the few available spots at the far end. The vehicle's tinted windows prevented them from seeing inside, but Luke came to attention before the car was fully stopped.

The passenger door swung open, and Marla saw her sister slowly pulling herself out. She headed for the car. A tall, dark-haired man got out of the driver's side and walked around to Julia. Marla got there in time to hear him say, "I don't suppose you'd allow me to assist you."

"I've got it," came Julia's testy reply.

Knowing how important it was to her sister to maintain her independence and dignity, Marla didn't offer help, either. As soon as Julia stood on the pavement, she closed the distance and hugged her tightly. "Jules, it's so good to see you."

Julia hugged her back, and they simply held on for a moment. "You scared the daylights out of me," she told Marla. "But I'm glad you're all right."

"I'm fine." Even though it appeared the world was going to hell and back. Marla pulled back and smiled at Julia, who looked tired and strained. "I'm sorry I had you worried. I have a lot to tell you."

"I'll bet you do. But it can't be any wilder that what I've already heard."

"I wouldn't count on it." Linking her arm with her sister's, Marla turned her toward Luke. "Julia, this is Luke Paxton. Luke, this is my sister, Julia."

"It's nice to meet you," Luke said.

Julia studied him. If she was impressed by his size and looks, she didn't give any indication. "I should take my cane to you for getting my sister involved in this."

"Wait a minute—" Marla started to say.

"I understand," Luke interjected. "If it were my sister, I'd do more than that. But I give you my word that I'm doing everything in my power to keep her safe."

"I'm holding you to it."

Rolling her eyes, Marla turned toward Adam, who'd been quietly taking everything in. He was Luke's height, but had a leaner, more elegant build. His black hair was cut short, and his features were sharp, autocratic. His eyes were like bottomless black pools. His life force was so vital she could feel it across the five or six feet separating them.

"Marla." His voice had a strange rasp, like he was permanently hoarse.

He stepped forward, held out his hand. It could have been the simple courtesy of a handshake, but she instinctively sensed it was more. Shaking his hand would allow him access to her personal energy, to her being. Yet to refuse would be rude, and there was no sense in alienating him.

Resigned, she placed her hand in his, startled by the jolt of energy, even though she'd expected it. Luke radiated power, but this man *was* power. It flowed through him like blood pumping through a heart, a powerful life force. It was almost overwhelming.

Thankfully, he wasn't projecting any emotions, or she probably would have passed out, like she had with the Belian. He held on a moment longer and she felt certain he could see into the depths of her soul, could read her innermost thoughts. It was not a warm and fuzzy contact.

He dropped her hand, and she thought she saw approval in his eyes. "It is my pleasure to meet you."

"Um . . . thank you." She resisted the urge to rub her tingling hand.

Adam looked past her. "Luke."

"Adam." Luke stepped forward and the men shook hands, then Luke dipped his head in a sign of deference and respect.

Julia tugged Marla farther away. "What is going on here? Who are these guys—really?"

"Exactly what they say they are." Marla wondered how she'd be able to convince Julia. "We need to talk."

"Maybe you can persuade your sister to tell me about the vision she had at the airport," Adam said, "since she refused to discuss it with me."

Julia's expression hardened. "You don't have any idea what happened at the airport."

Adam ignored her, his disconcerting gaze on Marla. "I believe what she saw had something to do with the Belian because she had the vision after we linked hands. I spent yesterday afternoon in Austin, at the library crime scene, and absorbed the Belian's signature. She probably tapped into that." He took a step closer, his harsh voice deceptively soft. "I will retrieve it, if I have to. But better if it's given voluntarily."

Whoa. Julia might be oblivious to this man's power and his implied threat, but Marla certainly wasn't. "I don't care who, or what, you are. You leave my sister alone."

"I will do what I have to," Adam said.

Great. She tightened her grip on Julia's arm and moved them toward the restaurant. "Let's find a place to talk, Jules." She glanced at the men over her shoulder. "*Alone.* You guys get us a table, and we'll be there in awhile."

There was still a wait for a table, but there were some seats at the bar. Perfect, Marla thought, even though it was a struggle for Julia to hoist herself on a stool. At least they could drink.

She ordered them each a margarita. Then she leaned close so she could keep her voice low and told Julia everything, from meeting Luke at the Red Lion Pub, him taking her and Bryony to Needville, the events there, the trip to Austin and the events there, and the trip to Dallas.

The only things she left out were Luke's personal family situation and her foolish infatuation with him. From time to time, she glanced over to the table where Luke and Adam sat, deep in their own conversation, yet keeping a watchful eye on Julia and her.

"It's all true, Jules, I swear," she finished.

"Oh, that's great." Julia downed the rest of her drink. "I so don't want to hear this." She squeezed Marla's hand. "And I don't like you getting close to this Belian thing."

Marla finished her own drink, thought longingly of ordering another one, but nixed the idea. "So do you believe now?"

Julia stared at her glass. "Believe? That's a word I associate with God, not that I'm sure there is one. I've certainly never associated it with reincarnated Atlantians with superpowers."

"But there are many unexplained things in the world," Marla said. "What about my ability to feel people's emotions and your ability to see things before they happen? Those things aren't considered normal."

Julia sighed, shook her head. She stared off into space.

"What I saw at the airport today supports what you've told me."

"So you *did* see something. Why didn't you tell Adam?"

"Because he's an arrogant bastard, and I don't like him. I also refuse to jump when he tells me to."

"Good for you—until he decides to put the whammy on you. I'm not sure you understand how much power these guys wield."

Julia waved a dismissive hand. "I don't cave to power. I'm not afraid of many things anymore. I've already died once." She noted Marla's surprised expression. "I never told you, did I? At one point after the attack, they pronounced me dead. I saw the tunnel and the light at the end, just like you read about. I went through that tunnel. I felt wonderful—weightless, flying, free. And I felt loved, like the light was unfolding and reaching for me. Then suddenly, I was jerked back. I didn't want to go, not back to the horror and the pain. Guess we can't always have what we want, huh?"

Marla's eyes filled with tears. She swiped at them, then leaned forward to give Julia a fierce hug. "I got what I wanted," she whispered. "I got my big sister, and I'm *so* glad you didn't go into that light, Jules." She drew back, dabbed at her eyes. "Maybe we both survived so that we could come to this time and place and fight this evil."

"I don't know." Julia cast a glance toward the men. "Maybe I'm supposed to take Adam Masters down a notch or two."

Marla found herself smiling. "That applies to all men. So tell me, what did you see today? Was it a vision?"

"Yes. And like Adam said, it occurred when I was trying to stand and grabbed his hand. It came on like a video clip. I saw a church. One second it was sitting there, the next it was exploding. The stained glass windows blew away, and there was smoke and some flames." She clutched her glass stem, and then shoved it forward. "Bartender! I'll have another margarita."

"I need one, too," Marla told the man behind the bar and

turned to Julia. "Do you think you saw that because we suspect the next target will be a church?"

"The thing is," Julia said slowly, "you told me about the school bus, and you told me about the library. But you didn't mention a church, Marla. You just said you were going to Dallas. No one mentioned a church until Adam and I were in the rental car, and he told me. If he's right about me drawing on the Belian energy he absorbed, then what I saw is linked directly to that thing."

She took the margarita the bartender handed her and drank a healthy swallow. "Yes," she said. "Now I believe."

THEY were all in the Mercedes. After they'd discussed Julia's vision, Adam thought that for the time being, they should check the churches together. He pointed out Marla might feel something at one of the churches, and Julia might see something, and both could be equally important. They drove north on the Tollway to check out the largest church in the area.

The Baptist church was a huge modern structure, situated on acres of beautifully landscaped land. As they pulled into visitors parking, Julia shook her head. "No. This isn't it. This is not the church I saw in the vision. The building that exploded was smaller. It was older and more traditional in style. It did have an unusual front that bowed out, but it wasn't contemporary."

"All right," Adam said. "Why don't we do a quick walk around while we're here, in case the Belian might also be scoping out this one?"

So they did, but it wasn't quick. The place was huge. Julia was flagging and didn't even snap at Adam when he made her sit and rest. Marla and Luke got through most of the place, which even had bookstores and restaurants, and a huge amphitheater-style sanctuary, but neither sensed anything.

"That was something," Marla commented as they drove away. "They obviously have a lot of members."

"But it doesn't appear to be a Belian target," Adam said.

"Julia, you're certain you'd recognize the church in your vision if you saw it?"

"Yes. The image is very vivid in my mind."

"All right then. We won't do any more walking through churches for now. Instead, we'll drive by as many as we can to get a visual. After it gets dark, we'll go online and look at the ones that have websites and hopefully photos."

They drove past churches until it was too dark to see clearly, and they were tired and hungry—except for Adam, who ate very little, and seemed to never tire. They got take-out Chinese, and went to Luke's house.

There, they ate and used both Luke and Adam's laptops. But Julia didn't see the church from her vision. "That doesn't mean anything," Luke said, "because there are still dozens of churches we haven't looked at."

"He's right," Adam said. "We'll start again tomorrow. Damien and Kara will be here in the afternoon, so we'll utilize them as well."

"Hey! I'm home!" Barrie called out from the foyer. "The Dallas PD interview went really—" She halted as soon as she came around the corner and saw them. "Oh, you're not alone."

Adam stood. "Barrie."

Her eyes were wide and she had an "oh, shit" expression, but she lowered her head respectfully. "Sir."

He held out his hand. "Come here to me."

She flashed a look at Luke, whose expression was neutral. Wiping her hand on her uniform pants, she walked to Adam and placed it in his. They stared at each other several moments. Marla could have sworn she saw energy sparking around them.

Adam nodded, released her hand. "We will talk while I'm here."

Barrie stepped back. "Okay. I mean, yes, sir." She headed into the kitchen. "Any food left?"

Adam shook his head, his mouth tilting up at the corners, and Marla felt the tension easing. "I'm ready to call it a night. Julia, shall we go?"

"I'll be very happy to see my room at the hotel, even if it's way too hoity-toity for me." Julia pushed up to her feet and gave Adam a challenging look. "And you're not paying for it."

He shrugged, and Marla suspected he would win that battle. He had probably already paid for their suites. She went to Julia and gave her a hug. "I'm so glad you're here," she murmured. "But be careful, okay?" She leaned close to whisper, "*No conductions!*"

"Trust me, I wasn't planning on it." Julia picked up her cane. "Good night, everyone."

After they left, Marla started toward the stairs, Bryony on her heels. "I'm exhausted. I'm going to bed." Halfway there, she turned to took at Luke.

He closed the distance between them, and her heart stuttered. He had taken the tie off his hair, and it looked like golden silk against his shoulders. He stopped a foot away, but didn't touch her. Not that he needed to; he was close enough that the energy hummed between them.

"You'll sleep well tonight. I'll see to it," he said. "But if anything happens, I'll be right across the hall. I expect you to get me. Okay?"

"Sure." She really wasn't hero material. She was terrified of further contact with the Belial, especially when she was asleep and might say the wrong thing. For once, she would welcome the woo-woo stuff. "Good night, Luke." She was aware of his gaze on her as she went up the stairs.

She didn't know what was emotionally worse—dealing with the Belian, or with her growing infatuation with Luke.

HE was very satisfied with the day's accomplishments. He'd been successful, but then he never failed. They thought they could outsmart him, but they had no idea who they were up against. Oh, yes, he knew they were looking for him. He'd felt the power of a sexual conduction on Wednesday. Stupid Sentinels. They were no match for him. He was far too clever.

The only person worthy of his attention was Marla. No one else had ever been able to breach his shields. Her touch had been like fire chasing away the darkness. She wasn't involved in the conduction he'd felt—that had been another female. A good thing, because if his Marla was fucking someone else, or involved with Sentinels, he'd have to punish her. All sinners had to be punished. And Belial demanded blood.

But he didn't think that was the case with Marla. Hadn't she reached out to him on her own? She admired him, wanted to see him. While he didn't approve of her being so forward, he could be forgiving, as long as she learned the error of her ways and deferred to him in all things. He sat on the bed in his cheap hotel room, looked at his tools and materials precisely lined up on the Formica table. She would be very impressed with his latest diversion tactics.

And those cursed Sentinels would be surprised at what was coming.

FIFTEEN

IT was a grim group that met at Luke's early Saturday morning to come up with a game plan. Barrie, insistent on helping with the tracking, was closeted with Adam in the back den. Marla, Julia, and Luke drank a second cup of coffee as they looked at churches on the laptop.

Marla wasn't at all happy that Julia had been drawn further into the Sentinel world. She was afraid the next step would be a conduction, and feared Julia's psyche was still too fragile to handle it.

But Adam was calling the shots. Marla knew Luke would defer to him, and she was certainly no match for Adam. Besides, she had to admit that any new information, no matter how bad, was better than none.

"I don't see the church," Julia said as picture after picture flashed on the screen.

"Then we'll have to drive by the ones that aren't online." Luke looked up as the den door opened and Barrie walked out, followed by Adam.

Barrie looked subdued; Adam had that effect on people. He had his usual enigmatic expression, so Marla had no idea what had transpired during their meeting. He strode over to Luke. "I've agreed to let Barrie assist us, on the condition that she works with me."

"That sounds reasonable." Luke looked at Barrie. "I think it's safe to say you'll follow Adam's instructions."

It was also probably safe to say that disobeying Adam could have dire consequences, but there was no need to state the obvious. A brief rebellious expression crossed Barrie's face, but she said, "Of course. When are we leaving?"

"Now." Luke powered down the laptop and stood. "Julia didn't see the church on the Internet," he told Adam. "The only thing we can do is drive by as many as possible."

"Agreed. But I think we should split up. Julia described the church to me in great detail. Barrie and I will take part of the list and check those churches. If we see anything that looks like the description, I'll call you."

"All right." Luke picked up his leather jacket. "Let's go, ladies."

The day was cool and overcast with gray clouds that fit the bleak mood. Marla shivered, grateful for her heavy sweater. They chose churches in central and northern Dallas, because they were older, like the one in Julia's visions. Even after yesterday, Marla still couldn't believe how many churches Dallas had. So many of them, yet people continued to be immoral and cruel to one another. It was sad.

They looked at churches for two hours, and it was now late morning. They were in one of the old-money sections of Dallas, and turned on a narrow street. Sitting in the front with Luke, Julia went rigid. "That's it!" she said, pointing. "That's the church I saw!"

Marla's heart sped up, and she studied the building as Luke called Adam. It was a stately dark brick structure, with an interesting bow front, just as Julia had described. A huge arched window crowned the square windows in the bowed section, and farther back, a squared turret probably held bells.

Luke snapped his phone shut. "Okay, we're going to check it out, but from the outside. If the Belian was here, we should be able to tell. I don't want either of you going in. There may already be bombs planted."

"I think that's a good plan," Marla said. She'd seen firsthand the carnage this Belian's bombs could inflict. She got out behind Julia. "Since I can sense the Belian, why don't I take one side, and you take another?" she said to Luke.

He considered. "The Belian could be nearby, but you'll probably know if that's the case. Got your cell phone?"

"Yes." Marla dug it out.

"Call me on my phone, and we'll maintain contact as we go around the building."

"Agreed." Dialing his number, Marla went to the right side of the building, Julia moving slowly behind her. She waited until Luke answered and said, "Can we do heavy breathing now?"

"Smart-ass." But there was a trace of humor in his voice. "Be careful."

"You, too." Her nerves jittering, she walked alongside the church.

She'd only gone a few steps when she felt it. Dark, insidious, a lingering presence of depravity. Her chest tightened and her legs went weak. She pressed a hand against the brick to keep her balance. "Luke. It's been here."

"Yeah, it's been on this side, too. I need to spend a minute and work the energy."

She was battling to push back the darkness and the ensuing panic. She *had* to learn to cope with the residual Belian energy and emotions, or she was no good to anyone.

"Marla? You okay?" Luke asked.

She forced herself to speak coherently. "I'm getting there."

"You need me to come around?"

"No." She drew a deep breath, imagined light infiltrating the darkness. "I think I'm on top of it now."

"That's my girl."

Julia caught up with her. "What is it? You look like you've seen a ghost."

Marla turned the phone away from her mouth. "The Belian was here. Can't you feel it?"

Julia looked around. "I don't know. It might be a little colder over here, but I'm not sure."

"Don't worry about it." Marla spoke into the phone. "What do you want us to do?"

"There's really nothing you can do. Go back to the truck. I'll check that side when I'm finished here."

She could feel the darkness still pressing on her, despite her efforts. "Fine by me. Do you want to maintain contact?"

"Yeah. No telling where that thing might be."

Holding the phone against her ear, she motioned to Julia to start back and they moved slowly toward the front of the church. "There's something bothering me," Julia said. "Something I must have seen in the vision, but can't remember."

"Keep looking around. It might come to you."

They reached the front lawn and walked toward the truck, Julia scanning the area. "Oh, God," she said suddenly.

"What is it?"

"Tell me what's going on," Luke said in Marla's ear.

"I don't know yet." She watched Julia staring at a man riding a lawn mower around the church sign.

"That man," Julia said. "He was in the vision yesterday. He was wearing the same straw hat and blue jumpsuit. And he was going down the left side of the church. Just as he reached the end past the church, the church exploded." She turned toward the parking lot. "And that van! That gold van was parked in the first handicapped slot, like it is now. This was the exact scene I saw."

As she said that, the man drove the lawnmower to the lawn on the left side and started cutting the grass there. "Not good, Luke," Marla said into the phone. "Julia thinks we're at the point in her vision where the church is going to explode. Like right now!"

"Get away from there! Get across the street and as far away as you can."

"There are people in the church." Horror swept through Marla at the realization.

"Marla, I said get away fro—"

She didn't wait for him to finish. She shoved the phone at Julia. "Keep talking to Luke. See if he wants you to call the police. I'm going inside to warn everyone."

"No, you can't!" Julia tried to grab her, but Marla side stepped.

"I have to. You can't help, because you're too slow. Just go. Get away. Please."

"Don't do this, Marla. For God's sake, don't go in there!"

But Marla knew with absolute certainty it was something she had to do. "I don't have time to argue, Jules. I'm going." She pressed the phone into her sister's hand.

Julia's face crumpled. "I love you."

"I love you, too. Go!" She turned and ran toward the church.

"The explosion will be in the front, in the bowed out area," Julia yelled after her. "Tell everyone to go out the back."

"Sure," Marla muttered. "Piece of cake." A part of her was terrified, yet it all seemed surreal, as if she were standing outside herself and watching. As if another part of herself, one with a strength she'd never known she possessed, was taking over and doing what had to be done. There was no time to be afraid.

She raced into the foyer, glanced through double wooden doors. The front of the church was indeed the sanctuary, and appeared to be deserted. "If anyone's in here, get out! There could be a bomb!" she shouted.

She whirled and headed down a corridor toward what appeared to be offices. She saw two ladies coming toward her and yelled. "There might be a bomb! Get out!" She flashed past their startled faces, and kept yelling. "There might be a bomb in the building. Go out the back way!"

She kept shouting her warning. She saw about a dozen people, and while they all looked shocked, no one tried to stop her. Ahead on her left, she saw one of those fire alarm boxes. She ran to it and yanked the handle. The loud wail of an alarm blared through the hallway. "Everyone get out!" she shouted, her voice now hoarse.

She turned to go on, but hard arms came around her from behind. "You're getting out of here *now*," Luke said, his tone brooking no argument.

"Then you're coming, too."

"Out," he ordered, pointing toward the rear of the building and giving her a shove. His phone rang, and he snapped it open. "Yeah, Julia." He grabbed Marla's arm and started hustling her down the hall. "Shit."

He swept her off her feet and ran like a demon was after them—which in a way, it was. She wrapped her arms around his neck and held on tight, amazed by his super speed. They reached the rear double doors, and Luke slammed against the release bar just as she heard an explosion. Then they were flying through the air, hitting the ground with a bone-jarring thud.

He immediately rolled on top of her. His weight pressed her into the ground and she could barely breathe. She heard another explosion. She also heard sirens in the distance.

Luke rolled off her. "We've got to get out of here. We don't want to be questioned by the police, or for anyone to take a picture of us. Think you can get up?"

"I don't know." She pulled up on all fours, groaned. She felt much like she had when Bennett beat her, but since she could move, she took that as a sign there were no broken bones.

Before she could struggle to her feet, Luke picked her up again and traveled rapidly around the church. He was limping, but still moved faster than a normal human. Marla gasped when they reached the front of the building and she saw the blown-out windows of the church front and the smoke.

She gapped at it, too shocked and stunned to process it all, as Luke took her across the street to where Julia waited by the truck. He opened his door, flipped the seat and slid her into the back. She tried not to groan as her bruised body protested.

"Get in," he told Julia as he slid inside. "There's nothing more we can do here. We have to leave." He reached over and helped Julia in, then started the truck. He was pulling away before her door was fully closed.

He didn't speak until they were a few blocks away and stopped at a traffic light. "Damn it!" He pounded the steering wheel with his fist. He flipped open his phone—Marla was surprised he still had it—tried to dial, without success.

He threw it down. "That one's toast." He looked at Julia. "Have you got a phone? Good. Call Adam for me." He recited the number.

Marla sank back, hurting all over, and sick to her soul. She still couldn't believe what had happened. She watched Julia hand her cell phone to Luke. She thought of the burning structure they'd left, a beautiful old church destroyed, and prayed fervently no one had been seriously injured.

Worst of all, the Belian was still out there.

MARLA barely remembered the drive back to Luke's. Everything was a blur, except for the image of the smoldering church, and the lingering taint of evil. By the time they reached the house, she was numb and cold. She stumbled getting out of the truck. As she grabbed the door frame to steady herself, she saw her sweater arm was ripped and blood was oozing through. "I'm bleeding."

"Yeah, you are. In several places," Luke informed her.

She took a step, winced as her body protested. It felt like she was one big bruise. With her body stiffening up, she suspected she'd feel even worse tomorrow. She gripped Luke's arm so she wouldn't fall flat on her face.

Julia followed them inside. She lowered herself to the couch and set her cane to the side. With a groan, Marla sank down beside her.

Luke's expression was fierce as he shrugged out of his

ruined leather jacket, snagged a portable phone, and
punched in a number. He looked as bad as Marla felt—cuts
on his face and hands and his hair a tangled mess. "Hey
Adam. Still at the scene? Yeah, you won't have much
longer. Okay. See you back here."

He tossed the phone on the coffee table. "I'll be right
back." He went down the hall to the bathroom.

Julia gave Marla her severe professor look. "You're an
idiot. And you took ten years off my life today."

"I'm sorry. I think I took years off my own life." Marla
gripped Julia's hand. "But Jules, I couldn't stand by and let
this monster take more lives. I just . . . couldn't."

"I agree with your sister," Luke said, returning with first
aid supplies. He pushed the coffee table back far enough so
that he could ease in front of Marla and sit on the table. His
hard gaze pinned her like a bug to a board. "What the hell
did you think you were doing, going into a building that
was about to explode?"

She could see the anger in his eyes, feel it simmering
just beneath his controlled facade, but she was beyond caring. "What do you think I was doing?"

His lips thinned. He wet a cotton ball with hydrogen
peroxide. "Something incredibly stupid. It was gutsy, I'll
give you that, but it was rash and foolish. I told you to go
back to the truck, and you ignored my order."

Her own anger flared. "I don't take orders from you."

His gaze turned arctic. "You'd better start, babe. If you
ever pull a stunt like that again, you will be *very* sorry."

That really steamed her. "I'm not afraid of you!"

He took her chin in an iron grip, forcing her to stare into
his icy eyes. "Then you're not very smart. *Listen to me*. I'm
the one who's supposed to take the risks."

She jerked her chin away. "Oh, better you get blown up
than me?"

"It's my job to protect innocents. Besides, I'm faster
and stronger. I have a better chance of surviving a blast
than you do." He took her arm and pushed her sweater

back. She winced when he began blotting the main cut. "Be still," he ordered.

The pain distracted her momentarily, but when he stopped with the peroxide and studied the cleaned cut, she found her voice. "What about you? You're in a mortal body, and you can be killed. You told me that yourself."

He reached for the antibiotic cream. "Oh, I can be killed. But that goes with the territory. I'm a Sentinel. I was born to do this. If you can't follow orders, I'll leave your fine ass behind."

Marla started to snipe back, but Julia intervened. "What did Adam say?" she asked, giving Marla's hand a warning squeeze.

"He and Barrie went by the church. He wanted to see if he could pick up anything before the area is completely cordoned off. He said it's a madhouse there."

"You think?" Julia shook her head sadly. "I hope everyone got out of the church. And I hope to God I never see anything like that again." She shot Marla a sharp glance. "And that my sister lets the professionals handle things from here."

"Oh, she will." Luke gave Marla another long look. "I'll make sure of it."

Arrogant Sentinel. Glaring at him, she grabbed the hydrogen peroxide, wishing it was iodine. "It's *my* turn to doctor you."

THEY spent the afternoon in what Marla thought of as a war council. Adam and Barrie returned to the house, and Damien and Kara arrived from Austin. A police scanner was on, as was the television, and all developments were monitored.

Two people were dead, one of the ministers and a maintenance man. Tragic, but far better than Marla had feared. It was good to know her dash into the church had saved lives, and made it well worth the lectures, and the stated dire consequences should she disobey orders again, that she received. Apparently Sentinels were immovable when it came to the safety of the humans in their charge, and could get pretty heavy handed. But she'd do it again in a heartbeat.

She looked around the kitchen table, where everyone had gathered. The four Sentinels, or actually three Sentinels and a Sanctioned, formed a ring of intimidating power. Barrie, although untried, appeared as focused and resolute as the others.

The energy humming through the room made Marla's skin tingle. Kara, a seasoned conductor, seemed unaffected. Julia also appeared undaunted, but then she had literally faced down death. But Marla felt like a lightweight next to these commanding personalities.

"I wasn't able to pick up much energy at the BCS," Luke said. "I'd just started working it when Julia realized the church was about to blow." He looked her way. "I'm very grateful for your attention to details. And that you told me when the mower reached the end of the church. Otherwise, Marla and I might not be here."

Julia's hand tightened around her coffee mug. "In the years that I've had this ability, or curse, or whatever you want to call it, I've only seen relatively minor future occurrences—someone falling, losing a job"—she shot a quick glance toward Adam—"a car accident. At least, they were relatively minor when compared to a church blowing up."

"Unfortunately, death and destruction go with Belian territory," Kara said.

"Yes," Adam agreed. "But today's blast doesn't make sense. I think it's a reasonable assumption that the bombs either went off early, or the Belian was alerted to our presence and set off the explosions ahead of time. More likely it planned to detonate on Sunday, when the building would have been full of people."

"I agree," Damian said. "Unless this explosion was a planned diversion, and there's a bigger target—or targets."

"I wouldn't put it past the bastard," Luke said. "But we don't know that for a fact."

"And we don't have much to work with," Adam said. "Barrie and I were able to pick up Belian energy from a donut shop across the street from the church. It either did surveillance or detonated from there—assuming the blast wasn't accidental."

"Are you saying he could have been watching us, and set off the bombs because he realized we had found the target?" Marla asked.

"It's a possibility."

A chill swept through her. "So *we* could be responsible for the blast today."

"Wrong," Luke said fiercely. "The Belian is totally responsible for those bombs, for their detonation, and for the loss of lives. And it will pay."

"Quite a paradox," Julia mused. "Did my vision show what was already fated to happen, or did we create the situation by acting on the vision?"

"So did your actions become the catalyst that fulfilled the prophecy? It's another version of the question, 'Which came first—the chicken or the egg?' and a universal mystery," Adam told her. "I choose to believe that things happen for a reason, and pretty much unfold the way they are intended to manifest."

His steady gaze went around the table. "No sense second guessing ourselves. What we have to do is finish this thing here and now. Luke, you and Marla see if she can link with the Belian again and find out anything about what happened today."

So she had the honor of coming into close contact with the monster. Marla punched down rising panic. She'd survived William Bennett—she would survive this.

"Barrie, since you absorbed some of the Belian's energy today, see if you can work on a signature and do a deep meditation. Be sure you're fully shielded."

Excitement flashed in Barrie's eyes. "Yes, sir!"

"Damien, check out the area around the church. See if

you can get close to that donut shop and the church grounds and pick up anything. Then you and Kara work with the energy. If you can't get close enough, use what you picked up in Austin.

"I'll continue to work the energy from my end. I want to be notified immediately if there are any new developments. Keep your scanners on through the night, and meet back here at eight tomorrow morning. Are we all clear on what we're doing?"

Everyone responded in the affirmative.

"All right, then. Walk in Light." Adam's midnight gaze went to Julia. "Shall we go? Tomorrow will be a long day."

Marla remained in her chair as everyone else rose and prepared to go their separate ways. She was exhausted, her body ached, and she longed for a long soak in the bathtub.

But first, she and Luke had a Belian to contact.

HE was furious. He had never failed—*never*! Today wasn't his fault. *No.* It was those cursed Sentinels. How had they gotten so close to him? He was too careful, too smart. He'd been fooling them for years. It was a test, that's what it was. Belial was challenging him.

He would show them. Everyone would know that he was the best. He couldn't be stopped.

That calmed him a little, until he thought again about what had happened today. Then the rage almost consumed him. He rampaged through the hotel room, kicking over furniture and stabbing two pillows into shreds.

After that, he cut himself, to prove he was still strong. The pain was good, calming. It was punishment for allowing them to get so close; it was a distraction from the inner rage and the pounding in his head. He longed for a live body to sink his six-inch hunting knife into. The screaming, the fear and the blood, the stench of death, would make him feel better.

He stared at the blood oozing from his arms and at the tufts of foam and fabric scattered across the bed, forced himself to take a deep breath. How had they found the church? He'd just finished planting the bombs an hour earlier, and was enjoying a crème-filled donut, along with the view of the church, from the donut shop across the street.

He'd taken the detonators with him, like he always did, so he could slip his hand into his pack and feel them while he envisioned the upcoming explosion and let the anticipation excite him.

He'd seen the silver truck pull into the church parking lot, hadn't thought much of it. But when the man and two women got out, he thought he felt a glimmer of the power. That had gotten his attention, and he'd watched the three people intently. He didn't feel anything else, but he kept a watchful eye. Unfortunately, the truck was parked in such a way that he couldn't see the license plate.

When the man went down one side of the church, and the two women, one moving slowly with a cane, went down the other side, he knew something was definitely wrong. He stood and moved to the plate-glass window, holding his backpack. They couldn't possibly know.

But then the man stopped at the exact spot where he himself had studied the building foundation and planned the best place to weaken the structure with a blast. He'd felt another flare of the power then, knew without a doubt the blond man was a Sentinel.

Before he could react, the two women returned to the front parking lot. The one with the cane pointed at the riding mower on the church lawn. He'd stepped outside then, trying to hear them. The other woman had run inside the church. As she flung open the main door, he heard her shout something about a bomb.

They knew! But how? He had paced the sidewalk, one hand in his backpack, as he debated his options. When the blond man—the cursed Sentinel spawn of The One—ran inside, he knew what he would do. He would detonate now. He hated having his plans disrupted, but he was flexible and could think fast on his feet.

The church explosion would send the Sentinel and the

woman to the fires of Belial. It would still be a clear warning to the blasphemous messengers, would strike terror in all those who persisted in believing.

They didn't know that he already had bombs planted at another target. He'd let the fear rampage, and then wait until things calmed down and the fools began returning to their routines, like mindless sheep. Then he'd strike.

So he had detonated the bombs, feeling the rush of sexual excitement that always accompanied detonation. But he hadn't allowed himself release, because he hadn't carried out the plan exactly. When he saw the Sentinel spawn come from the back of the church, carrying the brown-haired woman, a wave of fury rolled through him.

How dare they escape! Sirens wailed in the distance as the man and women climbed into the silver truck. The authorities were arriving way too quickly. He stepped forward, intending to cross the street and get the license plate of their vehicle. But a fire truck came roaring down the street, sirens and lights flashing.

Damnation! He stepped back as the fire truck blocked his line of vision. When he could see around it, the silver truck was gone.

Thinking about it now, in the trashed hotel room, renewed rage filled him. They would pay. Every single one of them. After he blew up the next target, he would track them down like dogs. They would suffer slow, torturous deaths, until finally their cursed souls were dispatched to Belial.

JULIA walked stiffly down the carpeted hallway, well aware of Adam Masters behind her. Not that she could hear him. He was one of those ultrastealth types who moved without any whisper of sound, just another irritating part of his devious persona. But she could feel him, feel the heat he radiated, and that damned energy that hummed between them whenever they were in close proximity.

Maybe it was the hellish day behind them, or her utter

fatigue and aching body, but the energy grated on her even more tonight. "Do you have to walk so close?" she snapped over her shoulder. "And since you appear to have more money than God, couldn't you have gotten rooms—oh, excuse me, suites large enough for ten people—closer to the elevators?"

"I did the best I could on a day's notice. I'd be happy to carry you if the walk is too much of a hardship."

"Your condescending attitude doesn't become you, but then none of your obnoxious traits do."

"Ah, Julia, that's what I like about you. No games, just brutal honesty. Well, here we are." He stopped beside a door.

"No, here *you* are. In case you've forgotten, my suite is the next one, and I will continue to keep the connecting door bolted."

"As is your privilege," he said in that smooth way that made her see red. "But we are not quite through for the evening."

"Oh, I think we are. Good night."

"Wait." His hand shot out, clamped over her arm. "We need to do one more thing."

She didn't like the sound of that. Nor did she like the ramped-up energy surge his touch engendered. She turned, stared into his black-as-sin eyes. "We are *not* doing a conduction—not tonight, not ever."

"Not even to stop the Belian?"

Demon memories rushed at her—William Bennett's twisted, hateful face as he rammed himself into her. No man had touched her in any intimate manner since that night. The very thought of it sent tremors of panic through her.

"I would do almost anything to stop this monster. But I—I don't think . . . don't know if I could do a conduction." She clenched her free hand, hating her cowardice and her inability to overcome the past. Hating the fact that even after eleven years and numerous therapy sessions, her wounds were still raw.

Adam's expression seemed to soften, or maybe it was an illusion of the dim hallway lighting. "I wasn't suggesting a conduction. We're going to do something less . . . engaging." Keeping his grip on her arm, he waved his free hand over the magnetic lock, and the green light flashed. No key card for him.

"Show off," Julia muttered. She made a mental note to push a chest in front of the door connecting their suites.

"I just prefer expediency." He opened the door and stepped back. "After you. I have a bottle of merlot, your preferred choice of drink, I believe."

"This isn't a social event." She stepped into the plush sitting room with a gold brocade sofa and two matching wingback chairs, along with an elegant table and straight back chairs.

He closed the door behind them. "No, it's not. It's a matter of life and death."

"Oh, really? Thanks for the news alert."

"If the situation were different, I would find you highly entertaining."

"And I'd find myself as far away from you as humanly possible."

"I'm well aware of your feelings about me." He slipped off his suit coat and draped it neatly over the couch arm. "Let's get to the heart of the matter. Tonight, I want to do a third eye link with you. That's apparently what happened at the airport yesterday. When you took my hand, you tapped into the Belian's psychic signature, which I had absorbed. That energy gave you a precognitive vision. I want to try a third eye link again, in the hopes you might see something else that will help us track this thing."

"That's all that's required? Holding hands?"

He stepped in front of her, his gaze probing. "The only touch that will occur between us will be the linking of hands and energies. I assume you can handle that."

Julia turned and went to sit in the nearest chair. She didn't like this man, didn't like touching him. She certainly didn't like visions of death and destruction, or the sick feeling she always had after a mental flash. But she hated monsters who victimized innocent people even more.

"All right, but I want to know the difference between a conduction and a third eye link."

"I would expect nothing less from a woman of your intelligence." Adam pulled the other wingchair around to face her, and seated himself. "First, let me explain that the third eye is linked to the sixth chakra and facilitates psychic vision. You know a Belian leaves behind energy patterns and Sentinels form those into a psychic signature.

"You also know that during a conduction, the signature provides information about the Belian. During that process, the third eye energies of both the Sentinel and the conductor merge, greatly amplifying the psychic abilities of both parties. That point can only be reached by energies coming up through the base chakras and facilitating a sexual surge.

"In a simple third eye link, only the Sentinel's third eye is involved. The Sentinel becomes a conduit so that the conductor can tap into the energies the Sentinel has absorbed and sometimes see what the Sentinel saw at the BCS. In your case, however, I'm hoping that when you link to my third eye, rather than seeing what I saw in Austin and at the church today, instead you'll have a precognitive vision, like you did at the airport yesterday."

"So you're telling me that you think the Belian energy pattern stored in your so-called third eye will act as a springboard to trigger one of my visions—hopefully one about the Belian."

"Precisely. That's all you have to do, Julia. Take my hand and see what happens."

He held out his left hand. "Are you willing to do that?"

She could hardly refuse, although she knew touching him would stir unwelcome sexual desires. She rested her cane against the side of the chair, and slowly raised her right hand and placed it in his.

SIXTEEN

LUKE awoke, instantly alert. All Sentinels trained themselves to sleep lightly and wake quickly. He glanced at the clock, noting it was 1:34 a.m. He'd been asleep about two hours. Wondering what had awakened him, he listened intently and heard rustling in the hallway.

He rolled out of bed, palming his gun and walking silently to the door, which he'd left open so he could monitor Marla. He paused at the side of the doorway, flared out his senses. He heard movement, then a sniffling sound; sensed familiar energies in the hallway. He looked around the doorframe, saw a figure on the floor, huddled against the wall.

"Marla?" He lowered the gun and crouched beside her. "What are you doing out here?"

She raised her head. "I'm sorry. I didn't mean to disturb you. Well, actually, I was going to wake you and tell you, but I was trying to, um, get it together." A small sob escaped her. "Damn it! I'm such a mess. I'm trying not to be needy, really—"

"Marla," he interrupted to stop the outpouring. She

sounded a little on the hysterical side. "What's wrong?" He laid the gun down and reached for her.

She was wrapped in the comforter from Beau's bed, and she was shivering. "The B-Belian," she said. "It woke me up."

That wasn't good. They had aborted their attempt for Marla to link with the Belian earlier in the evening, when all she encountered was waves of fury and no coherent communication from it. After that, Luke had made sure she slipped into the deepest possible sleep state to avoid unplanned contact.

"Tell me what happened." He started to pull her to him, heard a low growl. There was a movement beneath the comforter. "Bryony in there?" he asked, lifting a fold of the comforter and getting another growl from the dark form pressed against her.

"Out of there, you." He picked up the dog and set her on the floor. Then he scooped up Marla and carried her to his bed. She would be sleeping with him for the duration. There was no help for it; he couldn't leave her alone if the Belian could reach her despite protective measures.

He sat her on the bed. "Why don't you ditch the comforter and get under the covers. I'll be right back, and we'll get you warmed up."

He got a protesting Bryony, put her in Beau's room and closed the door. He retrieved the gun from the hall and placed it back on the nightstand, and then slid under the covers beside Marla. "Come here." He drew her cold body close, steeling himself against the surge of Sentinel/conductor chemistry. "Jesus, your feet are freezing!"

"I'm sorry. I don't know why I'm so cold. I hate to get you up like this."

He was up all right, he thought wryly, his body responding to a karmic link that went back thousands of years. The feel of Marla pressed against his bare skin—even a shivering, distraught Marla—turned him on. He was wearing only a pair of boxers and she was in an oversized nightshirt. He probably should have put on more clothing before climbing into bed with her.

He was a big boy, he could handle it. He settled her against him, smoothed her hair back. "You're supposed to get me if anything happens. Belian contact is way up there on the scale. Tell me what happened."

"I was sound asleep—you probably did the woo-woo crap on me. Then, it was like the first time the Belian contacted me in the hotel room. I heard a voice calling me, thought I was dreaming. I should have realized it was the Belian, should have known what was going on. Especially since it's happened before."

"Marla, you were in a deep sleep. Clear and logical thought are not present in that state."

She sighed, her breath warm against his chest. "I know. I'm just so terrified I'll say the wrong thing, give it information that it can use against you."

"You can't worry about that. Worry about the things you can control. What did the Belian say?"

"Some of it's hazy. Let's see . . . it called my name. Told me it was not my place to contact it, like I tried to do earlier tonight. It said when I saw what it was getting ready to do, I would realize it was superior to me, that I must defer to it. And it demanded to know where I was. It was so full of hate and anger. When it began threatening me, I freaked and broke it off. Maybe I shouldn't have done that."

Anger began burning inside him at the thought of Marla being terrorized and threatened, but he kept his voice calm. "You did exactly the right thing. First off, you shouldn't try to talk to the Belian without me there. Second, if you're not getting any useful information and if it's threatening you, you cut the link. Then if I'm not around at the time, you find me immediately. Got it?"

She nodded against his chest. "I was coming to tell you about it. But I was so upset, I thought if I could just calm myself first . . . I'm sorry."

She was a trooper. He knew she'd been flying solo for a long time and admired her independence, but she had to let him handle things. "Don't wait to tell me stuff. Let me help you get calm and sort through things. That way, we don't lose any time."

"I know. You keep telling me that. I understand why you're angry with me, especially after today."

She didn't know the half of it. It wasn't anger, but absolute terror he'd felt when he realized she'd gone into that church. He could see her being blown to bits, couldn't bear to think about never again seeing those warm honey eyes and those lush lips quirking into a mischievous smile. He'd never moved so fast in his life as he had going into that church after her.

"I'm not angry, Marla, but you scared a few lifetimes off me. If you ever pull a stunt like you did today, I'll have to forgo my vow to never hit a woman and put you over my knee."

"Really?" She raised her face toward his. There was enough moonlight coming through the window that he could clearly see her features. "Sounds kinky."

"You're just as bratty as Barrie, you know that?"

He felt her tension easing a little. "I wish I was as cute," she said.

"I like you just the way you are." He meant it. She was soft, curvy and lush, all woman. And she always smelled good enough to eat. His body stirred at the thought. Okay, best not to go there. As if sensing his thoughts, Marla curled closer into him. The breath hissed from his lungs.

"Luke?"

"Yeah?"

"I want you to make love to me."

That put all systems at full alert. His heart began pounding and his dick swelled to painfully hard proportions. "What the hell are you talking about? We've already discussed this." Shock made his voice harsher than he intended, but maybe that was a good thing.

She pushed herself upright, stared down at him. Her hair was a riotous mass of curls around her face. "You told me we couldn't have conduction sex. Is there anything in the Sentinel code about screwing just for the pleasure of it?"

Damn. He didn't want to lie to her, but didn't want to lead her on, either. "Well, not exactly, but—"

"Good. I don't want to die a virgin."

He sat up, the covers falling to his waist. Her gaze dropped to his bare chest. He should have put on more clothes. He ran his hand through his hair. "First off, you're not going to die. Second, I'm fairly certain—make that 100 percent positive—that after you find the right man, you will no longer be a virgin."

"I *have* found the right man."

He started to protest, but she placed her fingers over his lips. "Wait. Hear me out. I . . . I had a horrendous experience when I was nineteen. Julia and I were attacked by a man who'd been stalking her. We were both seriously injured. And I watched, unable to do anything, while he—" her voice broke. "He . . . raped Julia."

Luke took her hand from his mouth. "I know."

Her eyes flared wide. "*You know?* How long have you known? You've never said a word."

"After Adam met Julia and realized she was also a matched conductor, he ran a full background check on both of you. To be honest, I should have already done that. We usually check out conductors pretty thoroughly before we work with them." He rubbed his thumb over her hand. She had the softest skin. "I figured if you wanted to talk about it, you'd tell me."

She drew in a shuddering breath. "Then you should understand. After that night, I was dead inside, at least sexually. I tried to date, tried to find men that attracted me. But every time I had an opportunity, I felt nothing."

"It just takes time—"

"It's been eleven years, damn it! *Eleven years.* I'm thirty, as you pointed out. I'm a freak. No—make that a *virgin* freak."

He hated the pain in her voice. He slid his hands over her shoulders. "Listen to me, Marla. You are not a freak. You are a beautiful and intelligent woman, and—"

"Oh, give me a break," she muttered. "You've told me

that Sentinels and conductors do get killed, so you can't guarantee that the Belian won't win this war. You've just told me that when I find the right man, I'll be able to overcome my hang-ups and have sex. I *have* found the right man. *You.* When I'm around you, I'm turned on. I feel sexual desire. In other words, I want to jump your bones."

Oh, man, this was not going well. His body was humming and all too willing to take care of her little problem; to ignore every decent and honorable inclination he might have. But beyond initiating her into the sensual realm, he had absolutely nothing to offer her. He wouldn't be like his father. He would never put himself in a position where love could hurt him or others.

"Marla, the desire you feel is just a result of the attraction between a Sentinel and a conductor. You know that. That's *all* it is. It would be wrong for me to take advantage of it. We're *not* doing this."

She stared at him, her eyes huge and dark. "Fine, then." She swung off the bed, picked up the comforter from the floor.

"Where are you going?"

"Back to my own bed." She marched toward the door.

He went after her. "No, you're not. You're sleeping with me until the Belian is caught."

She turned, freezing him with her glare. "No. I do have some pride, even if it's not apparent right now. I'm not going to sleep with a man who finds me so repulsive he won't have sex with me."

Shock speared through him. *"What?"*

"Oh, please. Cut the act." She started out the door. "I know I'm no beauty. It's obvious you can't bring yourself to fuck me."

He grabbed her arm. "Whoa! Hold on a minute. What the hell are you talking about?"

Her shoulders sagged and she turned slowly. "I keep doing it. I keep thinking maybe you're as affected by the attraction as I am. You know what? I'm a fool. I should never have said anything."

"You think I don't want you?" He stared at her in total disbelief.

"Just look at me." She waved a hand down her body. "I'm— Oh, just forget I said anything. Okay?"

"You think I don't want you." He still couldn't believe it. He was trying *hard*—key word here—to do the right thing and to ignore the fact that he wanted nothing more than to bury himself deep inside her. And she thought he found her repulsive. "You are so wrong, babe."

He pulled her close and placed her hand over his raging hard-on. "What does *that* feel like to you? Does that feel like a lack of attraction?"

Her gaze locked with his, and she curled her fingers around him. He couldn't stop the groan that escaped. Maybe he shouldn't have been so hands on. *Big*—key word again—mistake.

Her gaze dropped lower, and she stroked him through the fabric. Her tongue darted out to wet her lips. She might be innocent, but she was a natural. "Luke." Her voice was low, husky, filled with need.

Desire raged through him, his entire body throbbing with its own need. And right now, he couldn't seem to convince himself that he should maintain as much distance as possible from Marla.

God help him, but he was about to do something he was *really* going to regret.

SHE couldn't believe she was standing here, stroking Luke's sizable erection. What had she been thinking? She wet her lips again. Now what? Feeling her face flush, she forced herself to meet his gaze. The heat in his eyes took her breath away. "I—I— Are we going to do something?" she stammered.

He removed her hand from his penis and raised it to his mouth. "Yeah, babe, I think we are," he murmured before running his tongue over her palm. He pulled her to him, wrapping one arm around her and pressing her against him. She could feel the hard length of him against her abdomen.

With his free hand he took her chin and tilted her face up to kiss her. No subtlety here; it was a full-blown assault of his tongue against hers. She tangled her hands in his hair and gave as good as she got, and it was good. They were both breathless when he drew back.

"Let's get this straight," he said raggedly. "I'm attracted as hell to you. I've wanted you from the moment I met you. I'm going to fuck you until you scream. That clear enough for you?"

As clear as the fact her heart was trying to burst from her chest. His raw gutter language triggered a rush of wetness between her legs. The breath left her lungs like air from a punctured balloon. "Oh," was all she managed.

His glittering gaze never leaving her, he gestured with his hand. The door swung shut; she heard the lock click. Another hand wave and the bathroom light flashed on, throwing a square of illumination into the bedroom. More light than she would have liked; she felt awkward exposing her less than perfect body and would have preferred the cover of darkness.

"Um, isn't it a little bright in here?"

He leaned down to nuzzle her neck and murmured, "If we're going to do this, we're going all in."

All in, then.

His hand slid down over her belly, brushing tantalizingly close to ground zero, and grasped the edges of her nightshirt, pulling it up her thigh in a slow tease. He brought his other hand around, tugged her shirt higher over her belly and midriff.

She held on to his shoulders to steady herself and hoped he wouldn't be turned off when he saw all of her. "So we're going for full disclosure?"

He rolled the shirt above her breasts, his full attention on her body. "Oh, yeah."

The air felt cool on her bare skin, and her nipples hardened. He cupped one breast, leaned down and licked the nipple. Her legs went weak, and only her grip on his shoulders kept her from sliding to the floor in a boneless heap. He slipped one arm around her, drew the nipple into his mouth. Fire shot through her, like a lightning strike spiking different directions. She dropped her head back with a groan.

He pulled back and straightened. "Raise your arms." His voice was low and guttural. She lifted her arms, and he pulled off the shirt. She was completely exposed and felt vulnerable, but then his hands were sliding over her body, slow and sure.

"God, you're beautiful," he murmured, the sincerity in his voice sending a heated glow through her.

"So are you." She started her own explorations, awed by the contrast of rock solid muscles and smooth warm skin. "But you're not fully disclosed yet." She tugged at the tented boxers, but he stopped her.

"Uh-uh. You already got to touch. My turn."

Her protest was cut off by his mouth taking possession of hers and totally distracting her. The man could kiss. And move incredibly fast. In the blink of an eye, he had her flat on the bed and was spreading her legs and staring at her like a fox eyeing a rabbit.

Then he was kissing her and touching her more. Despite his obvious arousal, he didn't rush. He returned to her breast, swirling his tongue over the nipple before taking it into his mouth while he caressed the other breast.

Pure sensation flowed like molten lava through her veins and headed due south. She arched against his mouth, and he made a low sound in the back of his throat. The electricity sparked between them, tingling along her skin.

Then he moved his attention to the other breast. Her body was engulfed in flames now. She twisted against him, trying to touch him in return, but he was evasive. He ruthlessly used her body against her, keeping her in such sensory overload, she couldn't think straight.

Finally raising his head, he swept his hand down her body. He paused when he touched the scar where her ruptured spleen had been removed eleven years ago. Leaning down, he kissed it gently. His action touched her deep inside, a balm to her soul.

Without comment, he continued the downward sweep over her body. He stroked his fingers over her belly and her thighs, down and back up, trailing them through the brown curls but not quite touching where she desperately needed him to. "You're so soft. So womanly," he murmured, repeating the motion.

She was wet and aching between her legs. "Luke!"

"What?" he asked innocently, teasing her mercilessly with another near-strike sweep over her abdomen.

She clamped her hand over his wrist, tried unsuccessfully to move it down. "God, Luke, please! Touch me."

"Oh, is that what you want?" He slid his hand between her legs. "Like this?"

More electricity shot through her and she almost jolted off the bed. "About time!" she managed to gasp.

He laughed softly and stroked her, and she moaned. Slipping a finger inside her, he kissed her breast, murmured, "You sure you're ready for this?"

She groaned, arched against him. "I was ready an hour ago."

"So impatient. Haven't you ever heard that good things come to those who wait?" He slipped in a second finger, started a devastating rhythm. He knew exactly what he was doing, and she was helpless to stop him.

She began unraveling. "Luke!"

"Go for it, babe. I've got you." He stroked harder, pressed his thumb against the sensitized nub, and sent her into total meltdown.

It was a tsunami wave of pure pleasure. She was so lost in the sensation of her first social orgasm all she could do was ride the wave. When reason returned, she found herself breathless and cradled in Luke's arms.

She should be embarrassed, sprawled nude in a pool of light, having just come apart from his expert touch. Talk about exposed. But all she could think was that she wanted more. She slid her fingers inside the waistband of his boxers and jerked them down, freeing his swollen penis.

"I want these off—now!" she said fiercely.

He complied this time and then she had him in her hand and decided payback was in order. It was another new sensory experience for her as she explored his impressive length. He was big, he was turned on, and he was all hers. She caressed and teased until suddenly she was on her back, and he was settling between her legs.

"Playtime's over," he growled, nipping her lower lip and then ravishing her mouth. He stroked her to ensure her readiness and fitted himself against her. She felt real pressure then, realized this first time wouldn't be easy, given his size and her virginal state, but she didn't care. She pushed upward, felt the burn, couldn't control the involuntary gasp.

"Whoa! Slow down." He slid his fingers through her hair, cradled her face.

A sudden floating sensation warned her he was up to something, but before she could object, things got fuzzy and surreal. She was drifting in a dream state, unable to move or think coherently. There was pressure between her legs, but it didn't seem real, and it wasn't painful.

Then the mental fog cleared a little, and she saw Luke above her. He moved, and she felt him inside her. He pulled back, slid in, creating an amazing friction. She was still a little punchy and a lot confused.

"What happened to the grand entry?" she demanded.

He grinned, leaned down and ran his tongue along her ear. "We skipped that part. We're going straight for the good stuff." He stroked again, and she forgot about the logistics.

"Oh, yes," she moaned. "Do that some more."

He laughed and slid in deep, and she arched up to meet him. It was good—no, more that good—it was incredible. It was Luke. It was physical, it was emotional; it was an intense, primal act between a man and a woman.

She gloried in it. She stared up at him, taking in the

lines of his face, made harsh by need and passion. She met his thrusts, her body completely in sync with the rhythm of his. When it became too intense, sucking her into a maelstrom of sensation, she closed her eyes.

She and Luke were totally attuned to one another, linked mentally and physically. When she exploded this time, he was right there with her, his deep groan reverberating through her.

As they both shuddered and then collapsed together, gasping for breath, she was shaken by the startling realization that sex, with the right person, was far more than a mere physical act. It was a spiritual experience, and an act of love, transcending Earth and time.

At least on her part. She had no illusions that it had been anything but just sex for Luke.

It was going to hurt big time when they went their separate ways. But for now, she basked in the afterglow of fantastic sex, and celebrated the demise of her virginity.

SHE woke slowly from a deep and dreamless sleep. She was groggy and disoriented, but a relentless voice kept calling her. Surely it wasn't . . . *the Belian*. That got her attention and brought her more quickly to a conscious state.

"Marla, wake up. I know you're tired, but I need you to wake up."

She blinked her eyes open, stared up at Luke in confusion. "Luke? What's going on?"

He was sitting on the edge of the bed, and he was nude. "We have to get out earlier than planned. Here, try to sit up."

"But . . . why?" She pushed up with his assistance, her mind muddled. It was still dark outside, with the light in the room coming from a nearby lamp. She looked around her, at the navy sheets and comforter. This wasn't her bed . . . wait. Last night she and Luke—Her gaze whipped down to her bare body. The sheet was pooled around her hips and her breasts were just waving in the breeze, so to speak.

"Oh." She grabbed the sheet, yanked it up over her chest. "I—I'm having a little trouble functioning."

She looked back at Luke, gorgeous in all that bare skin, and saw he was holding his cell phone. His startling blue gaze was steady and focused on her. "You're having trouble because you've only had a few hours sleep and I put you into a deeper sleep level after we . . . settled in for the night."

"Oh. Yes. That." Her gaze dropped to his morning erection, then jolted back up to his face.

He shrugged. "It has a mind of its own. Sorry to wake you, but Adam called a few minutes ago. There's a new development, and we have to get moving. Everyone will be here in about thirty minutes. I'm going to take a quick shower. You need to get ready as fast as you can. You functional yet?"

"I think so." She swung her legs over the edge of the bed, keeping the sheet against her body. Even with last night vivid in her mind, she just couldn't bring herself to parade naked in front of Luke.

"Okay." He rose and headed for the bathroom. "Meet us downstairs when you're ready."

He had a great butt. She watched until the bathroom door closed behind him before she stood and started looking for her nightshirt, which she found in the corner where he'd tossed it last night. The memories of last night were coming back to her. The soreness in her lower body was further proof she wasn't imagining anything. It had been . . . incredible.

But she didn't have time to think about it now. Something had obviously happened with the Belian. Marla looked around for a clock, found one next to the lamp. 5:00 a.m. It couldn't be good if Adam was rousing them that early. She hurriedly slipped on her nightshirt—inside out, she realized—and went to take a shower in the other bathroom.

Everyone was there when Marla came downstairs forty minutes later. Luke, Adam, Damien, and Barrie were standing in the den in powwow formation, serious and forbidding.

She came into the den and saw Kara and Julia were at the kitchen table, working on Luke's laptop. Marla could feel the tension in both rooms.

She opted to talk to Kara and Julia, rather than interrupt the powwow. "Good morning," she said, entering the kitchen. "What's going on?"

Julia looked up from the laptop, and Marla was dismayed to see how tired and haggard she appeared. "I had another vision last night."

Marla went over to give her a hug. "You look awful. What did you see?"

"Gee, thanks for the compliment." Julia leaned back in the chair. "I saw another church explosion, which apparently means the Belian already has another target. Adam thinks he—it—may have chosen multiple targets, even before yesterday."

"Damn it," Marla said, then looked askance at Kara. "Sorry for the profanity."

"Oh, no offense taken. I said more than that when Damien told me." Kara shook her head. "This is the worst Belian I've ever helped track. It's killing whole groups of people."

"Adam and I were up most of the night, looking at churches online," Julia said. "He also talked to his contacts at Homeland Security and the Dallas police, and we passed the church description along to them. Since today is Sunday, and people will be going to services, they're debating how much to warn the general public."

"Why the hell wouldn't they warn people?" Marla demanded. "There's a good possibility this thing will blow up another church today."

"Our concern exactly," came Adam's voice from behind her. She turned to see him standing in the entryway. He was in full business attire, in a severe black suit, white dress shirt and jewel-toned striped tie. She wondered if he ever wore jeans.

"We'd like to try to find the church before we put out a public alert. We have to balance the safety of the members of one church against the Belian escaping and continuing its bombing spree elsewhere. Our police contacts are canvassing the local officers for a list of all white churches in the area, which will be passed along to me."

Marla turned to Julia. "It's white?"

"What I saw was. An old white church, with huge arched stained glass windows."

"Great. That could be any number of churches." Marla looked back at Adam.

He was staring at her thoughtfully. "We're leaving right now to check all of them." He turned to the others, who had gathered near the kitchen. "We're going in four units: Luke and Marla, Barrie by herself, Damien and Kara, Julia and me. Take your digital cameras. Stop at every church on your list, take a picture to send to my computer, and then do a quick walk around. If there's no Belian energy, move on to the next church. Be quick about it. Check in with me every thirty minutes."

"And if there's no sign of the Belian?" Julia asked.

"Then police patrols will be posted at every white church in the area, and will turn away anyone who attempts to attend services. It will be done as unobtrusively as possible. They'll tell people it's a gas leak or some other building problem."

Marla breathed a sigh of relief. Hopefully no one would die in a bomb blast today.

"If we don't find the church by eight o'clock, the police will move in to warn people away. Let's get going," Adam said. "Luke, a few other things."

The way he kept looking at Marla, she had a sinking feeling he knew exactly what had happened between her and Luke last night. But when he faced them, he said, "If the Belian was watching the church that blew up yesterday, and I'm certain that it was, then there's a good possibility it will recognize you and Marla, as well as your truck. Since Barrie's in uniform, she'll take her police squad car, so I want you to use her personal car. And I'd like a private word with you, Luke."

"Okay." Luke looked at Marla. "Give us a minute?"

"My purse is upstairs. I'll go get it." As she started up, Adam and Luke began talking in low voices. She looked back to see Adam gesturing with one hand and Luke's jaw tensing. She'd bet the farm they were talking about her.

She was tempted to go back down and tell Adam what she and Luke did on their own time wasn't his damned business and not only that, it had been *her* idea. But she knew this wasn't the time and place. It wasn't about Luke and her right now. It was about a monster with no conscience—one that was planning to kill more innocent people. She turned and went up the stairs.

It was pretty cold at 6:00 a.m. in April in Dallas. Barrie's car was a cute light blue Volkswagen Eos convertible, but of course they didn't put the top down. They took coffee with them, which Marla sipped as they drove to the first church on the list. She still felt blurry and out of it. Luke, on the other hand, seemed fully alert and ready for anything.

They didn't talk much, which was fine with Marla. She wasn't functional enough to discuss what had happened last night. Even if she'd been at the top of her game, she wouldn't know what to say. She had never taken After Sex Etiquette 101. Was it appropriate to say something like, "Thank you for screwing my brains out last night. Let's do it again soon"?

And if she didn't say anything, then what would Luke think? That she was ungrateful or hadn't enjoyed it? At the same time, she didn't want him thinking she was needy and expected a repeat performance, either. For all she knew, he might be considering the sex a done deal, mission accomplished. He had rid her of her virginity as requested.

Another unpleasant possibility occurred to her. Maybe, since he knew about the attack eleven years ago, it had simply been a mercy fuck. Her heart twisted at that thought, but she'd known going in that Luke didn't want involvement.

No regrets, she told herself firmly. Besides, it was time to focus on stopping this Belian creep. So she pushed away thoughts of mind-blowing sex with Luke and turned her attention to their first church.

It was strange walking around a church in the early morning, with the sun just starting to come up over the horizon. Marla kept expecting local police patrols to stop and question them, but she knew Luke could probably handle mere human police.

They settled into a routine. Luke would do the walk around while she'd take a picture of the church, return to the car, and plug the camera into the laptop to send the photo to Adam. She also made the progress calls every thirty minutes, while Luke was either driving or checking out a church. So far, there'd been no energy traces from the Belian. Unfortunately, Dallas appeared to have a huge number of white churches.

The sun was fully up, and it was rapidly approaching the deadline time to bring in the police, when Luke's cell phone rang. He'd just gotten back in the car from checking another church and he opened his phone.

"Yes, Adam. You found it? Give me the address and we'll be right there." He disconnected, looked at Marla. "Barrie located it, believe it or not." Pride reverberated in his voice.

Despite the circumstances, Marla smiled at him. "Of course I believe it. She *is* a Sentinel, and she seems very smart and very conscientious. She'll do great when she's on her own."

Worry replaced the warm glow in Luke's eyes as he wheeled the Eos around. "I hope so."

"I know so, big bro."

He shook his head, but he grinned back at her.

It took them ten minutes to get to the church. It was only a few miles from the first church, in the same old-money area of Dallas. Shaped like a giant arch, with the doorways and windows repeating the shape, it was a huge, stately, beautiful building that was almost one hundred years old.

There were various vehicles already on the scene: Adam, Damien, and Barrie's vehicles, two Dallas PD squad cars and two vans that had "Dallas Criminal Intelligence Unit" written on them. "The Dallas Terrorism Squad falls under the DCIU," Luke explained.

"Are they basically the bomb squad?"

"Yes." He parked and got out. "Stay here until I find out what Adam wants us to do." He leaned down and gave her his no-nonsense look. "You don't want to cross me on this, Marla."

"I'm not going anywhere. I promise."

He gave her another look, closed the door and walked over to where Adam was talking with three uniformed officers. Obviously, the Sentinels were working with the local authorities in this instance.

Luke talked with Adam and the police for a few moments, then returned to the car. "Adam, Damien, Barrie, and I are going to do an outside walk around and try to pick up the Belian's energy. Since we know its using remote detonation and might still be in the vicinity, we'll also check the area before anyone goes into the church. Adam wants you, Kara, and Julia to get into the Mercedes, drive it a few blocks down, and wait for us."

Marla wanted to argue. She hated the thought of Luke being near the church and it possibly exploding. But at the same time, she accepted that he didn't need her help this time, and that he and the other Sentinels could work better knowing their human counterparts were out of harm's way. So she slid out of the car and closed the door. Luke was already walking away.

As she went to join Julia and Kara, Marla offered a prayer for the Sentinels and the police, all working perilously close to a time bomb—literally.

SEVENTEEN

HE couldn't believe it. He fucking couldn't believe it. They had found his target. How? How could they have known? Someone was helping them. Someone who somehow knew his actions . . . Marla? Could it be? No. He'd been smart and clever with her. She didn't even know where he was.

Still, he would find her and make sure. No one was going to stop him. Belial would see to that. But the rage vibrated inside him as he watched the people milling around the church, watched those he was certain were Sentinels. They radiated the power. Damn them to the fires of Belial! His fury was so strong, he was shaking. He wanted to kill someone.

Too bad he'd already dispatched the stupid old lady who owned this house. It had been ridiculously easy. As soon as she'd seen him, she'd opened the door like he was a long lost son. His knife had taken the smile off her face, though. Belial had been pleased with the blood.

So he had a house right across the street from his target, and he could see everything. He'd planned to wait until the eleven o'clock service, when they had the highest attendance. Then he was going to blow the worthless fools to the skies and watch the activities from the safety of the house. No one would even think to look for him here. It had been brilliant, perfect. And they had ruined it!

With a howl of fury, he whirled and grabbed up the detonator he'd placed on the antique side table. He'd show them. Walking back to the window, he fingered the remote. The anticipation of detonating made him hard, his cock pressing painfully against his pants. But he wouldn't be allowed release this time, either. No, his plan hadn't been executed perfectly. Belial would not be pleased.

He set off the bombs.

MARLA dragged into Beau's bedroom and threw herself facedown on the bed. God, what a day! She'd witnessed another explosion, and wasn't she the lucky one? Fortunately, no one had died in the explosion, because the police hadn't yet entered the church.

They'd just started a search of the immediate neighborhood to try to determine if the Belian was in the vicinity when the blasts had blown out the front windows of that grand old church. The sanctuary had been destroyed. Some of the officers had suffered cuts and contusions, but nothing fatal. If there had been people inside . . . Marla shuddered at the thought.

The explosions had triggered a massive manhunt, which had led to the discovery of the poor old lady in the house across the street, after Adam sensed the Belian energy around the home. Her throat had been cut, and her breasts and abdomen slashed numerous times.

There had been no sign of the Belian, not a single scrap of metal or wire, although the forensics crew had taken samples from the home, hoping to find fibers or DNA or anything that would lead them to the guy.

Marla didn't hold much hope for the scientific approach, but Luke said they'd gotten some strong energy patterns from the house. She was glad she hadn't gone inside; she didn't think she could have dealt with the Belian's killing energy as he massacred that helpless woman. Just the thought made her sick.

She lay on the bed, utterly exhausted, and actually wished Luke would come and zap some woo-woo mojo on her, so she could forget about the past few days and the murdered grandmother. She hadn't felt truly safe since Bennett's attack on Julia, but this was even worse. There was a superhuman being on the loose that had no conscience and thrived on violence and death. And she had touched it on an ethereal level. She didn't even want to think about it.

She rested a few minutes, trying to get up enough energy to either go downstairs and join in the war council in progress or take a long hot bath. She felt dirty from the smoke and from the negative and horrified energies of the police and onlookers, and from the discovery that a helpless old woman had been murdered, not to mention the knowledge that the Belian had been nearby while she and Kara and Julia were sitting in Adam's Mercedes. But she wasn't sure anything could wash away the stain.

"Hey," Luke said.

She rolled over and saw him standing in the doorway. "Hey. Have the joint chiefs of staff disbanded?"

He came in and sat on the edge of the bed. "You're so entertaining."

Bryony, who'd become his constant companion, trotted behind him and jumped on the bed. Marla sat up and stroked the poodle. "Can't help it. This has been one the best days ever—*not*." She sighed. "I am so tired. I'm sure you are, too."

He rubbed the bridge of his nose. "We all are. I've never seen Sentinels come together like this to hunt a Belian, and the damned thing is still eluding us."

"Where is everyone?"

"They're leaving. We each have our assignments, and we need to eat and rest and regroup. Julia said to tell you she'll see you tomorrow. She didn't want to disturb you, especially if you were sleeping."

The thought of Julia brought up another concern. "When Adam gave out these so-called assignments, did he mention a conduction with Julia? Because if he did—"

"He didn't." Luke interjected. "He's far more powerful than Damian or me, and he can accomplish as much with a simple third eye link as we can in several conductions. Besides, he's well aware of Julia's past experience and wouldn't do anything harmful to her."

"He was willing to let a church blow up without warning anyone, because he didn't want the Belian getting away," Marla pointed out, referring to the first church.

"You know that's not entirely true. We had no idea where the church might be, and we couldn't just set off a panic. We hoped we had until today to find it. The Belian jumped the gun on that one. Believe me when I tell you that protecting innocents is a primary goal."

"I'm not sure what I believe anymore." She rolled her head and shoulders, hoping to ease the tension. "I'm sorry. I'm not fit company tonight."

"Understandable. We're all on edge." Luke watched her a moment. "There's something you and I need to do."

Her stomach did its clenching routine. Like Pavlov's dog, she'd become conditioned, responding to thoughts of the Belian with physical distress. Good thing she hadn't eaten in hours. "Great," she muttered. "I get to talk to psycho bomber."

"That's not our assignment."

"It's not?"

"No. We believe the Belian is out of control. The rage and hatred are driving it now, and you probably wouldn't get any useful information at this point. Plus the danger to you would be greater."

Relief swept through her. "Oh, darn. I was so looking forward to exposing myself to depravity and evil."

"Yeah, I'll bet." Laughter flashed in Luke's eyes; then his gaze turned serious. "We're going to do a conduction instead."

She had mixed emotions about that. Chakra energies and

the sexual barrage were darned uncomfortable. But maybe they'd get some solid information. "I can hardly wait."

"Marla, Adam wants us to do a full conduction."

Surprise and fatigue were dulling her thought processes, and it took a moment for her to realize his full meaning. "We're doing a *sexual* conduction?"

"Yes. Unless you refuse."

She hadn't considered that possibility, not even after doing the horizontal mamba with Luke. Not that she'd had much time since then to think about anything other than the horrors perpetuated by the Belian. "So Adam knows about last night. He knew when he saw me this morning, didn't he?"

"Yeah. He can read auras and energies around people."

"Gee, that's comforting. I hope you told him that what happened between us was none of his damned business."

"The Sentinels and conductors operating in Adam's region are very much his business. I told him I accepted full responsibility for last night."

That really irritated her. She came to her knees and stabbed a finger against his chest. "Listen Mr. Macho Hero, what we did was *my* idea. I can take responsibility for my own actions, thank you very much." Bryony, thinking they were playing, shoved between them with a playful growl.

Luke picked up the dog and put her on the floor. "Stay!" he ordered. Then to Marla, "I *am* responsible. I should have had more control."

Back to that again. He obviously regretted what had happened, which hurt more than she wanted to admit. "And I suppose that makes me a bimbo who doesn't know her own mind."

He swept his hand through his hair, his expression frustrated. "Damn it, Marla, you know that's not the case. But we shouldn't ha—"

"It's done, okay?" she snapped, furious and upset. "And I, for one, don't regret it. So quit the noble crap. When are we going to do the conduction?"

Staring at her, he heaved out a breath. "Although you're

no longer a virgin, you're still not experienced. And I'm sure you're sore after last night. The sex during a conduction can be rough. You'd don't have to do it."

More likely *he* didn't want to do it, and hoped she'd opt out. But right now, she was willing to do whatever it took to bring the Belian to justice. Beyond that, she was just selfish enough that she wanted to experience every ounce of passion that she could with Luke. She didn't know if she'd ever have the same sexual desire with any other man. When this was over, Luke would walk away. But for now, he was here. She intended to savor every sensual moment with him.

"I've already signed the waiver of liability and indemnity," she said, keeping her voice even. "If a full conduction will help find the Belian, then I'm in. Let's do it."

AFTER his shower, Luke didn't bother to get dressed. He'd soon be getting horizontal with Marla, so why go to the trouble? He hung up his towel and went to smooth the rumpled bed covers. With his heightened sense of smell, he readily picked up the comingled scents of sex and Marla, and his body tightened in response. By The One, she was sexy, and she didn't even realize it. That in itself was a powerful aphrodisiac.

There was an intense pull between them, and he knew it superseded the normal Sentinel/conductor attraction. She was smart, courageous, and funny. He'd never realized how much humor added to a personality. He'd laughed more with Marla than he'd laughed in years—maybe since his mother died.

Yet he knew they had no future. They were both scarred from different life events. Hopefully, Marla would overcome her personal demons and find the love and security she deserved. But that was not his destiny. Sentinels were generally loners by nature, partly because what they did was so damned dangerous. Luke firmly believed that remaining distant from others would insure less pain and suffering all the way around.

He went to his closet and pulled out one of the indigo candles he kept stocked on the top shelf. He set it on the special holder by the bed and lit it. The scents of frankincense and ginger drifted through the air. The energies from the color and the fragrances would enhance the conduction and create a stronger sexual surge, which was why the candles weren't used for nonsexual conductions.

That done, he slid beneath the covers and waited for Marla. She'd probably be surprised to find him nude and in bed, but there really wasn't any other way to start a full conduction, since the energies rose so quickly and the surge was raw and wild.

While he waited, he entered a light meditative state to center himself. The soft knock pulled him back to the here and now. "Come in."

Marla opened the door, her eyes widening when she saw him in the bed. "Uh, are you ready?"

"Always. Come on in."

She walked in, adorable in the same nightshirt she'd worn last night. Her hair was in its usual riotous curls, and her glasses had slipped down her nose. She stood there, chewing her bottom lip. That sexy unconscious gesture sent the blood spiraling downward. He was already hard and she hadn't even gotten close enough to engage the Sentinel/conductor energies.

"Close the door, please."

She did as he asked, then turned slowly. She was nervous, which was not surprising. He might have taken her innocence last night, but that didn't make her sexually experienced. She had an innate purity that radiated from her. It was probably one of the things that had drawn the Belian to her.

He patted the mattress. "Come over here."

She walked to the bed. He raised the cover for her, and she slid beneath it. Her closeness and her fresh soapy scent sent the energies racing through him. He suspected they were about to have a killer conduction. He scooted closer, rested his hand on her hip. He sensed her heart pounding.

"Nervous?" he asked.

"Not at all."

"Liar."

"If you knew the answer, why did you ask? And do you always start full conductions naked?"

"There's my Marla. The answer is yes. For a sexual conduction, it's always easiest to 'assume the position,' so to speak. It gets wild pretty quickly. Got anything on under that shirt?"

"No."

Knowing Marla was naked beneath the nightshirt brought the vivid memory of how smooth and supple her skin was, how she'd felt beneath him last night, but he forced it away. He could let her keep the shirt on, but after last night's intimacy, that seemed absurd.

"Why don't you just slip that off while I shield." He wrapped his hand around his crystal, drew in energy and circled it around them.

"I can feel that," she said as she pulled off the shirt.

"Good." He dropped the pendant and eased her against him.

She was warm and soft and delectable. For a crazy moment, he wished they didn't have to do a conduction, that he could simply taste and touch her as he wanted to. Resolutely, he brought his focus back to the matter at hand. He touched her lightly, his fingers sliding over the resilient flesh of her thigh, and coming to rest on her hip. He heard the quick intake of her breath.

His body was already thrumming with need, his cock painfully hard, and they hadn't even joined hands. He reached down and tugged off her glasses. She stared up at him, her gaze trusting and accepting. She was turning him inside out.

He cleared his throat. "We'll start by joining our hands like we've done before. Your right to my left, and my right to your left. The chakra energies will come fast and strong, followed by the sexual surge. The energies will flow through all seven chakras as before, and you'll feel pressure, possibly hear sounds, and see images. You don't have to worry about anything but maintaining the link. Just don't let go of my hands."

She nodded. "What about the sex?"

"Is that all you ever think about?" he teased, trying to ease the tension down a notch or two.

A small grin turned up the corners of her generous mouth. "Actually, I thought that was the guy's job."

"Then I'm batting a thousand." He placed her glasses on the nightstand, took her right hand in his left, and felt a jolt of chemistry. "We'll both know when it's time to join our bodies. No instruction manual needed. Ready?"

She took a deep breath. "Yes."

He took her other hand and the connection was instant. It was like grabbing a lightning bolt. Electricity leaped in a wild arc and the energies initiated spontaneously. They burst upward, snapping the first two chakras wide open and he literally saw flashes of red and orange. The sexual surge hit like a tidal wave, and Marla gasped.

"Easy," he murmured. "Just hang on."

The energy was a roaring inferno now, pounding through the adrenals and the thymus as the next two chakras burst open. Sexual need permeated every cell of his body. Joining with Marla became a necessity for survival, a response to a primitive instinct ingrained in man since the beginning of time.

She thrashed against him, her fingers digging into his arms. "Luke!"

He rolled over her as blue blanketed his mind; fifth chakra open. She spread her legs and arched up to meet his thrust. She was wet and more than ready as he slid into her heat. The sixth chakra exploded open with a burst of indigo.

God, she was tight, like a fist wrapping around him. He groaned, struggling to maintain. But he couldn't control the frantic need to thrust hard and deep. "Am I hurting you?" he asked raggedly, pounding into her even as he spoke.

"No." She pulled her legs farther back, taking him impossibly deep. "Don't stop."

As if he could. They moved together in a mating frenzy more compelling than the moon's pull on the tides. The seventh chakra ripped open with a dazzling starburst of violet light. Superspeed images flashed in his mind, battling for precedence over the throes of the most incredible conduction sex he'd ever had.

He automatically committed the images to memory. His conscious focus was on the climax crashing over him like an avalanche. He was aware of Marla crying out, of her internal spasms triggering his own release, igniting wave after wave of pleasure.

He gave himself up to the sensation, felt another climax grip her. He savored her hoarse cries, the aftershocks that shook them both and seemed to go on and on.

Finally, it was over, the reverberations receding like a wave on the beach, leaving tingling warmth and a feeling of utter satiation. Beneath him, Marla went limp, rolling her head against the pillow. "Oh, my God."

"You can say that again."

"Oh, my God."

"Smart-ass." He eased out of her, another twinge of sensation shooting through his cock. He couldn't believe there was any life left in it. He collapsed onto his back beside her. "But that *was* pretty amazing."

"Amazing doesn't begin to describe it. You could market conduction sex. A lot of conductors would pay for it."

Amused, he shifted to his side. "Would you?"

"Hell, yes." She turned her head to look at him. Her eyes had darkened to deep amber; her pupils were dilated, and an enticing orgasm-induced flush spread across her chest.

He hadn't even kissed her, or done any foreplay—not that any was necessary when the sexual surge was rolling in. He couldn't resist running his fingers over the curves of her breasts. Her nipples tightened into tempting pink points.

"How much?" he murmured.

Her breath caught. "How much . . . what?"

He smiled, enjoying her exquisite responsiveness, teased

one nipple lightly. "How much would you pay for conduction sex?"

"Just name your price." Her voice was low, breathy. She reached up, sliding her hand behind his neck and tugging him down.

He knew he shouldn't indulge in after-sex play, knew they should get on with analyzing the images and keep everything on a Sentinel/conductor basis. But her mouth was so lush, the glow in her eyes so appealing. He leaned down, touched his lips to hers—

The cell phone ringing jarred them out of the moment. Torn between regret and relief, Luke sat up. He told himself firmly it should be relief. He sure as hell shouldn't be lingering with Marla like this. He retrieved the phone from the nightstand. "Yeah?"

"You done, big bro?" Barrie asked. "It shouldn't have taken too long."

He shook his hair back. "I'm surrounded by disrespectful females."

"You get what you deserve. Besides, you answered the phone, so I'm assuming you've completed your assignment. I figured it was safer to call than come upstairs and ask."

"Yeah, it's a done deal." And he felt damned uncomfortable talking to his little sister about a sexual conduction, especially where Marla was concerned. "How'd the meditation go?"

"I got some vivid images. This thing is really scary, Luke."

"Tell me about it. What are you doing now?"

"I'm at Angelo's, picking up some pizzas. I was starving and figured you and Marla would be hungry, so I ordered three extra large, along with some salads. You can pay me back."

"We'll have to negotiate that. I should get something for pain and suffering."

"You wish."

"I *know*, brat. Get some of their bread and marinara sauce while you're there."

"Already ordered, along with some cheesecake."

"You might just turn out all right."

She laughed, and then her voice turned sober. "I thought we could discuss our results while we eat. I'd like to bounce what I saw off of you and Marla."

Luke glanced over at Marla. She had pulled up the covers and was half asleep. The dark circles beneath her eyes attested to the stress of the past few days, not to mention lack of sleep. They needed to discuss the images before calling it a night, and maybe that would be easier over food and camaraderie. Plus he sensed Barrie's concern about doing well on her first solo run.

"Sure," he said. "That's a good idea. We'll join you downstairs and go over everything."

"Great. I should be back there in twenty minutes. Bye."

Luke closed the phone, watched Marla's breathing deepen. He hated to disturb her, but they had pressing concerns. He started to waken her, but she suddenly jerked.

"No," she whispered. "No!"

He felt it then. Belian energy, emanating from her.

"YOU." The voice hissed in her mind. *"You fucking whore!"*

She felt overwhelming rage, directed at her. It took her a moment to process what was happening. *"Why are you mad at me?"* she projected, struggling to keep her wits about her. *"I've been waiting to talk to you."*

"You bitch. Did you think I wouldn't sense you and that cursed Sentinel doing a conduction? I could feel the surge all right, could tell you two were fucking like wild animals."

How could the Belian have known that? Unless she had somehow projected to him. *"I don't know what you're talking about."*

"You're a lying whore! You told them, didn't you? Somehow you knew my targets, and you told them. You'll pay for that, bitch."

"No! No, I didn't tell anyone anything. I had no idea

*where you planned to hit next. I—I thought you were still in
Austin, remember?"*

*"You're lying. I don't know how you knew, but it doesn't
matter. I'll find you, Marla. And I'll make you sorry you
ever crossed me. I'll find your Sentinel lover, too. I'll dismember both of you, very slowly so you can feel every agonizing slice of the knife. Then I'll drink your blood."*

Oh, God. This thing would be stalking her, like Bennett
had stalked Julia. Terror, like a sharp sword, pierced through
the shock. *"You're wrong. You don't know what you're talking about."*

*"I know your energy pattern, Marla. I know what you
feel like. And I know exactly what you just did."*

She felt it start to withdraw, and knew she had to try to
get information from it. *"Wait! What are you going to do
next?"*

*"As if I'd tell you. Not that it matters. I'm too smart, too
far ahead of you and those Sentinels. You'll never catch me."*

Intuition told her to strike at its pride. *"We will. Look
how close we came to you yesterday and today."*

It howled in fury, flaring out utter depravity. *"Only
because I allowed you to!"* it screamed. *"I am in control
here. I'm brilliant. You can't touch to me. More will be
punished—many more—before I leave Dallas. And none
of you will be able to stop me."*

The contact was making her nauseous, and she was
trembling. But she held on, trying desperately to shake up
the Belian. *"So you're going to blow up another church?
You're awfully predictable."*

*"I know what you're doing and it won't work. You won't
know my next target until it explodes. After that, I'll find you,
bitch, and I'll dispatch your worthless soul to the fires of
Belial."* Then it was gone, leaving behind the taint of evil.

It was coming after her. Terror permeated her soul. The
darkness pressed down on her, and she couldn't breathe.
Her lungs and throat seemed paralyzed; she was choking.
She bolted up, making an awful gasping sound as she tried
to suck in air.

"Marla!" Strong hands grabbed her, but she struggled wildly. "Whoa! Stop fighting me. Calm down."

Horrific rasping sounds came from her constricted throat; she still couldn't breathe. Luke's hand slid over her chest and rested over the center, and the pressure inside eased. His hand moved to her throat. Heat flowed there, and air suddenly rushed into her lungs. Chest still heaving, she sank back and looked at Luke's concerned face.

"I— He— It—" She paused to take in more air.

"I know, babe. Come here." He pulled her against him and held her tightly.

She clung to him as if he were a lifeline, which perhaps he was. She didn't care that they were naked and bare skin to bare skin. There was nothing sexual in his touch; she couldn't even feel the usual Sentinel/conductor chemistry.

All she could think was that he was the only thing standing between her and the monster now tracking her.

MARLA sat at the kitchen table, watching Barrie and Luke knock back some of the best smelling pizza she'd ever encountered. Despite the fact she'd eaten very little the past few days, her stomach was too queasy for anything more than the crackers and ginger ale Barrie had gotten for her.

Marla stared longingly at the moisture-misted longneck beers the two Sentinels were also enjoying. She sure wouldn't mind a drunken oblivion, but knew she'd pay if she hoisted anything nonbland on her stomach right now. It was so damned unfair. She so deserved primo pizza and alcohol.

Bryony pirouetted between the chairs watching hopefully for any falling food. Crash crouched on the arm of the den sofa, ears back and tail twitching, as he glared at the poodle. It was an uneasy truce, and Bry had some deep scratches across her nose to attest to her participation in the war. Crash didn't have any apparent war wounds, but then he'd soundly won every skirmish.

"I slipped into the meditative state faster than I ever

have," Barrie was saying. "It was like a vortex formed and just sucked me down."

Luke nodded. "If you've worked enough Belian energy to create a strong psychic signature, it will do that. The PS enhances the chakra energies."

"I got some clear images," Barrie said. "That BCS across the street from the church was bad."

Marla was glad she hadn't experienced those particular images. "I saw the form of a man dressed like a minister, but not his face," she commented.

"Yeah. The bastard. It dressed like a minister so that poor old lady would open the door to it." Barrie's voice simmered with anger. "She had the sweetest smile, but her expression sure changed when he pulled out that knife."

"That's enough, Barrie," Luke said sharply.

"Oh. I'm sorry." Barrie shot Marla an apologetic look. "I guess it's heavy on my mind."

Marla shuddered and pulled Luke's heavy velour robe tighter around her. Even with her nightshirt, a pair of his sweatpants and his robe, both of which were way too big, she still couldn't get warm. "Why didn't I see that?"

"It's the actual crime scene. A Sentinel can see the entire event play out, like a movie, only it's blurry and jerky, because the Belian is shielded. The visual images and energies are filtered through the Sentinel's psyche, so the conductor usually sees only snippets of images linked to the Belian," Luke explained.

"Thank God for that," Marla said. "I could feel the Belian's emotions, though. But I don't know if it was when he was . . . killing that poor woman, or detonating the bombs. Whichever it was, he enjoyed it. He—it—was excited. I've never felt such evil, not even when—" Vivid images of Bennett pinning a battered, bleeding Julia to the floor resurrected to join the horror of the Belian murdering an innocent old woman. She drew up her knees and huddled into herself.

Luke leaned over to squeeze her arm. "Hey, you okay?"

She knew he'd been watching her closely since the conduction. Probably thought she might come apart, which was a distinct possibility. It was taking a major effort to hold things together. "I'm fine. Sorry. I'm getting off track."

"It's all right." He dropped his hand. "Let's focus on the details that might help us catch this thing. We know the Belian dressed like a student when it was on the university campus, and we know it dressed like a minister to gain entry to the old lady's house. That might also be how it got the bombs into the churches.

"We know it drives a blue Toyota Tercel. We know it's very intelligent. It would have to be, to be able to put together effective bombs, which takes knowledge and skill. After reading the initial police reports from the crime scenes, we know it used military explosives, so it has military or terrorist contacts, and plenty of funds."

"Could it be a terrorist from another country?" Marla asked.

Luke shrugged. "It's possible, but all Belians are terrorists, when you consider their goal is to murder, mutilate, and cause fear and chaos. Anyone with enough intelligence and resources can create bombs. So let's discuss what we saw tonight."

"I saw a lot of big buildings in downtown Dallas," Barrie said.

Marla nodded. "I saw buildings, too. I saw the Reunion Tower with the ball at the top, and the huge green glass hotel next to it."

"The Hyatt Regency," Luke supplied. "What else did you see?"

"That really tall building, the one that's also green glass. I think it's lighted at night."

"I know the building, but not the name." Luke opened his laptop and powered it up. "Anything else?"

"The commuter train on streets going between big buildings. I'm pretty sure it was downtown. I'm just not very familiar with Dallas."

"That's the DART light rail, and it does go through much of downtown." Luke typed, studied the screen. "That huge green giant is Bank of America Plaza. It's got a lot of floors and a lot of glass. Barrie, did you see the same buildings?"

"No. I saw the Pegasus building and the big library."

Luke's expression hardened. "Great. I saw the main federal court house and Dallas City Hall. That means the Belian could be checking out multiple targets."

"I saw other things, too," Marla said. "I saw a table with large bricks that looked like yellow clay, and wires, and metal parts, and those boxes that look like garage door openers."

"Me, too," Barrie said. "The table was small and cheap looking and it appeared it might be in a hotel room."

"I also saw that. Bomb materials. The yellow bricks are Semtex, which is the military explosive I mentioned. The Belian is definitely making more bombs." Luke ran his hand through his hair. "It sure looks like its next target is somewhere downtown. *Damn it.* There are a lot of people going through there, and it's a lot of area for us to cover."

He shoved back from the table. "I'm going to call Adam."

"Adam the Great," Barrie muttered.

Luke gave her a look and walked toward the den's sliding glass doors as he opened his cell phone. He stepped outside, and Bryony trotted out after him.

"You don't like Adam?" Marla asked, concern for Julia niggling at her.

"It's not that," Barrie took her eighth piece of pizza—not that Marla was counting, or anything. "He's brilliant, he's dedicated to The One, and he works harder than anyone I know. He's just unyielding, arrogant, and a control freak. He wants to know when we go to the bathroom." She rolled her eyes. "And his attitude toward women is archaic."

She must have seen Marla's flare of alarm, because she waved her hand and shook her head. "No, don't misread that. Adam would *never* mistreat a woman, unless she was a Belian. You don't have to worry about your sister with him. She's as safe as she can possibly be.

"It's just that these guys claim to be enlightened, but let me tell you, they're way too protective of the women in their lives. I've been ready to go on my own for months, but Adam won't let me. I'm positive it's because I'm a female. David, my mentor, is just as bad. And so is Luke, but then he's been looking out for me since our mother died from a brain aneurysm when I was four."

"So was your mother a conductor or a Sentinel?" Marla asked, curiosity overriding tact.

"No, she was an ordinary human. It's very unusual for a Sentinel to bond with a human who's not a conductor. But she and my father were apparently crazy for each other. He stopped working with conductors right after he met her, and tracked solo after that. They were so bonded, my father went off the deep end when she died."

Marla remembered what Luke had said about his father. "So your dad was gone most of the time?"

A shadow of sadness crossed Barrie's face. "You could say he was gone all the time, because even when he was home, he wasn't here, not really. He'd spend all his time holed up in his office or out practicing his martial arts or shooting. He might as well have died with my mother. Luke raised me." She grinned. "He can do great ponytails and braids."

Marla was intrigued with the image of Luke fixing a little girl's hair. "I'd like to have seen that."

"He was great, both as a big brother and a surrogate father. He gave up a lot of his personal life to take care of me, made a lot of sacrifices." Barrie sighed. "Unfortunately the basic genetics of being a male Sentinel make him overly protective when it comes to me. He's got to let me fly sometime."

"Looks like you might be testing those wings be pretty soon," Marla said. "We've got to stop this Belian."

"Yeah. Don't tell Luke, but this thing scares the you know what out of me." Barrie took a swig of her beer. "But I think only a fool would have no fear going against these monsters."

"I agree with you." Marla glanced up as Luke came back inside, followed by Bryony, his now constant side-kick. Crash arched and hissed as Bry pranced by the couch.

Luke came into the kitchen. "Everyone saw different buildings in downtown Dallas. Adam wants us all here at eight tomorrow morning."

"Oh, he's going to let us sleep in," Barrie sniped.

Luke ignored that. "Then we'll probably gear up and head downtown. And Barrie, Adam is calling in David. He doesn't want you working alone."

"I'm not going to argue about that, bro. This is one time when I'll be glad to have David at my back."

"Good for you, brat. That shows maturity." He ruffled her silky hair, stepping back quickly when she swung at him. "Hey, pretty good reflexes."

She glared at him. "*Great* reflexes, and don't you forget it. I can kick your ass, bro."

"We'll have to see about that, after we deal with the current crisis."

"You've got an ass-kicking date. I'm eating the cheese-cake." She pulled a foam container from the Angelo's bag.

"You'd better leave me some, or that date may become immediate." Luke looked at Marla. "You doing okay? You're still looking pretty washed out."

She felt completely drained and exhausted, but wasn't sure she wanted to foray into sleep, where she was apparently more vulnerable to the Belian. "I'm fine," she lied.

"Sure you are." He leaned over and started wrestling with Barrie for the container. "We'll go to bed as soon as the cheesecake is taken care of. Want some?"

Marla eyed it longingly. "I'd better not." She took a sip of ginger ale. She should be ten pounds lighter by the time they caught the Belian. If they could catch it.

And if it didn't find her first.

EIGHTEEN

THE shrill beeping cut through the mental fog, rousing Marla from a deep, and thankfully dreamless sleep. She blinked her eyes open, trying to orient herself. She was in Luke's bed, and he was rolling over to knock off the alarm. The movement pulled the covers away from him, exposing a broad, strong back. He was wearing boxers, so she didn't get to see his fine butt.

Even so, the view managed to keep her distracted for a moment. But thoughts of the Belian quickly rolled in, followed by a soul-deep dread and the now familiar queasiness. *Kind of like morning sickness,* she thought, only she guessed it was Belian sickness.

Luke looked over, saw she was awake. "You don't have to get up yet. I'm going to work out before I shower. You can sleep another hour. You probably need it."

She knew she wouldn't be able to sleep, especially without him there. It would be too easy for the Belian to link with her. "I think I'll get up." She stretched, feeling sore all over. She'd never realized marathon sex involved so many muscles.

His gaze went to her chest, and she realized her stretching was pulling the nightshirt taut over her breasts. Good. Let him look. He quickly shifted his gaze back to her face. "You okay this morning?"

He looked great, even with his hair mussed. She was certain she sported a major bed head and raccoon eyes, since she'd been too tired to wash her face last night. She shoved her hair out of her face. "Never better." But the shadow of the Belian was there, like an unpleasant hangover that wouldn't go away.

Turning onto his side, he studied her a moment. "Yeah, that must be why you're whiter than these walls."

The fears rushed at her, new ones mingled with those from the past. "I'm so scared, Luke." Admitting it out loud made it that much worse, made it real. Her chest tightened until she could barely breathe. Blindly, she reached for his hand, needing the reassurance of his touch.

He wrapped his hand around hers. He was so warm, so alive. "The Belian will have to go through me to get to you. I won't let that happen, Marla."

She felt a small loosening of the fear gripping her. "That's good to know," she said. "Thank you."

"It's my job." His simple declaration reflected the heart of the man, what he was—a hero, in the truest sense.

"You're always taking care of people," she said softly. "First Barrie, then the innocents you put your life on the line for. Now me."

A small grin teased his lips. "You've been the biggest challenge of my career."

"Good," she said, the teasing washing away some of the darkness. "I wouldn't want to be too . . . easy."

His lips twitched. "No danger of that, babe."

She stared into his stunning blue eyes, felt their beckoning allure. Felt the air around them intensify with growing sexual tension; heard Luke's intake of breath. It was the most natural thing in the world to reach over and hook her arm around his neck. To lean forward as he shifted toward her, to flow into the kiss.

They were familiar with each other now, and their mouths meshed together perfectly. Their bodies were also primed for one another. The electricity sparked faster than a lightning bolt, slamming heat and need through every cell in a single second. And just like that, Marla was wet and ready. She twisted, pressing against his erection.

He broke off the kiss. "God, Marla—"

"Shut up and touch me." To illustrate what she meant, she slipped her hand inside his boxers—that front opening sure came in handy—and wrapped her fingers around him.

His breath hissed out, and she kissed him again. She could practically feel his scruples crumble with the increased pounding of his heart against her chest. With the way he shifted back so he could slide up her nightshirt and cup her breast. She ran her free hand over his chest and his flat hard nipples, then started to tug at his boxers.

She got distracted from that, however, when his hand slid over her belly and headed south. *Yeah, I'm way too easy,* she thought, as she spread her legs shamelessly, inviting his touch. His fingers found her burning, wet.

He groaned as she resumed stroking him. "Babe, what am I going to do with you?"

She could think of a lot of things he could do, but here, now, with the Belian's taint hanging over them, she wanted this chance to give back to him. To make love to him, to show him what she couldn't say.

She placed her palms against his chest and pushed. He moved enough for her to sit up. She shoved him again, forcing him onto his back. Leaning down, she ran her fingers along the extremely tented front of his boxers as she kissed his chest. "The real question," she murmured, "is what am *I* going to do with *you*?"

She pulled the boxers down far enough to free his penis. It was impressive, like the rest of him. She took it in her hand and stroked, then leaned down to tease with her mouth. She had no idea what she was doing, but from the guttural sounds he was making, she guessed she was doing all right.

"You're killing me," he groaned.

She looked up, saw his eyes were glazed. "I would hate for you to suffer needlessly on my account."

"God, you're a smart-ass." He made one of his superfast moves, pulling her up and onto her back.

He settled over her and leaned down to nip her lower lip. She felt him probing between her legs and rebelled.

"No." She shoved against him. "This one is going to be *my* way."

He let her push him onto his back, and she straddled him. She wasn't sure exactly how things worked in this position, but she wanted to experience every nuance of lovemaking. Oddly, she didn't feel awkward at all; she felt completely at ease with Luke, even in this intimate situation.

He watched her, his heated, liquid gaze singeing her as she slid over him, taking him in slowly. He was big, and he filled her almost to the point of pain, but it quickly became pleasure. Already, the fever was swamping her, the need to move until her body found a release, driving her.

She wanted it fast and hard, but Luke slowed things down, grasping her hips and controlling the pace. He set the rhythm, guiding her over him with languid, prolonged strokes. From his strained expression, she knew he was holding back for her sake.

As they moved in an intimate, erotic dance, she looked down into his glowing blue eyes, and she was lost. Lost in him, lost in what he made her feel. Everything melted into a blur of bodies and movement.

Her heightened senses made her exquisitely aware of the sounds of their bodies separating and coming together and of their labored breathing; of the earthy, masculine scent of Luke; of the incredible friction of him inside her. His hands on her, the sex words he murmured to her in that black-magic voice.

The pressure was building, building, until she couldn't focus on anything but the instinctive need for release. They hurtled over the edge together, the explosion like a brilliant starburst in a midnight sky.

Fire and light vibrated through her, and she didn't know where sensation ended and reality started. And for a few moments, it simply didn't matter.

They lay there in the aftermath; tangled together, heartbeat to heartbeat, neither speaking. But eventually, they had to return to the real world. All too soon, Luke looked over at the clock. "The others will be here soon. We'd better get up and going."

She sighed against his chest, feeling utterly boneless. "You're not going to get your workout this morning."

"Oh, I got a fair amount of exercise." His tone was light, but as he tipped her chin up, forcing her to look at him, his gaze was troubled. "Marla, this was great—hell, it was fantastic. I just . . . I don't seem to have any control where you're concerned. But this isn't . . . *shit*. I'm making this worse. I don't want to lead you on about us."

Pain speared through her. *You knew this,* she told herself. "It's okay. I understand," she managed to say. "You've given me something very special, memories I will always treasure." Then, because it hurt so much, she went for levity. "Or maybe I should say you've taken something very special. At least I'm not a damned virgin anymore."

He cupped her face. "You are going to light up the universe for a very lucky man one of these days."

She didn't think any other man would ever measure up to Luke—or inspire what she felt for him. She was in love with him. It was going to hurt big time when this was over and they went their separate ways. Then she would return to her solitary life.

Reynolds women didn't give their hearts lightly. Luke would probably be the only man Marla would ever love. Fate was a bitch.

But she also had her pride. So she looked straight at him and said, "Damn right I am. But right now, we have a job to do." She slid from the bed, mustering all the dignity she could, considering she was totally naked, with the early morning sun streaming into the room.

She looked back at Luke. "Let's go kick some Belian ass."

* * *

"UNFORTUNATELY, we don't have much to go on." Adam looked around the group. They were all squeezed in at the kitchen table, drinking coffee—the two dozen breakfast sandwiches Barrie had picked up at Burger King long gone—and doing the war council routine.

"It appears the Belian has been moving around the downtown area, either scoping out targets, or to confuse and divert us, or both." Adam's cool gaze moved to Marla. "It believes Marla has been able to see its next targets and that she has betrayed it. It knows she's a conductor and is working with us. We won't encourage any more links between her and this thing."

Thank God for that, Marla thought. But she still had to worry about the Belian contacting her when her defenses were down. As if sensing her anxiety, Luke reached over and placed a reassuring hand on her back.

"We will canvass downtown and see if we can find any pockets of Belian energy and try to get a fix on its next moves," Adam continued.

"What about you, Julia?" Damien asked. "You're obviously a strong precog, and you were right on with the first two targets. Any feel for the next one?"

Julia, who looked pale and tired, shook her head. "No. Last night I saw several buildings, but no explosions in any of them."

"And what she saw doesn't match with what the rest of you saw," Adam said. "That's why I think the Belian hasn't picked a specific target, at least not as of last night. Or if it has, then it hasn't finalized its plans or set the bombs yet."

"Well, that's one good thing," Barrie said.

She was sitting next to David Harris, a nice looking man with medium brown hair and striking green eyes. He was obviously older than Luke and Damien, and Luke had said he'd been tracking Belians over thirty years, but he still possessed a youthful vitality. He radiated the power and danger that was apparently inherent in all Sentinels. Even Barrie had the aura; her petite frame and china-doll looks just camouflaged it better.

"We might have a little more time," Luke commented. "But not long. We know it has already made more bombs."

Adam nodded. "Yes, which means what time we have will be brief. So we'll work downtown in teams, like we did yesterday." He pulled a stack of papers from his briefcase and started handing them out. "Here are maps of the area. We'll divide it up, so we can cover as much territory as possible."

They spent the next thirty minutes plotting out four routes and assigning them to the teams. Once again, Marla was struck by the odd mix of methodology and psychic seeing. It was, she supposed, the result of highly spiritual beings operating out of physical mortal bodies.

"I think we've got most of the area covered. While we're working, we'll use the radio phones." Adam gestured to the new phones everyone now had.

They'd already spent some time checking preprogrammed phone numbers and the radio contact menu. They were a smart tool, Marla conceded. With a down arrow in the menu and the push of a button, she could talk to any of the group immediately, without waiting for a number to dial and someone to answer.

Adam pushed back his chair and stood. "All of you check your weapons. Be sure they're fully loaded and you have spare ammunition. Keep them where you can access them quickly." He watched as everyone pulled out their guns. "God bless Texas, where every citizen can carry concealed."

It was a veritable arsenal, Marla thought, staring at the bad-ass weapons the Sentinels produced—two guns for each of them, and no baby calibers in the lot. There wasn't anything less than a .38, and it went up from there. Plus each Sentinel sported at least one knife, and she understood they all held a minimum of a level one black belt in martial arts. They were definitely well armed.

The conductors weren't too shabby, either. The delicate Kara carried an impressive gun, a nice Beretta semiautomatic, a little larger than Marla's Tomcat. Julia also had a

Tomcat. She and Marla went faithfully to the gun range once a month and both were decent shots.

"We're a freaking bunch of Boy Scouts," Julia commented. "All prepared."

Kara smiled. "You get used to it after awhile."

"Not planning to. It's not on my syllabus," Julia replied. "I'll be glad to forget all of this and return to Houston, hopefully very soon. Assuming I still have a job."

Marla could relate. Earlier this morning, it had been tough explaining to her boss that she needed an indeterminate amount of time off. She'd used a family emergency as an excuse, but hadn't provided any details. It was a good thing she'd been there five years and her work record was solid; otherwise she'd have been job hunting when she returned. Her existence in Houston seemed like a lifetime ago. Hard to believe it had only been ten days since she sat next to Luke in the Red Lion Pub, irrevocably altering her life.

"We'll take two cars," Adam said. "Julia, Barrie, and David, you're with me. Luke, you and Marla go with Damien and Kara." He looked around one more time, deadly serious. "Walk in Light."

The hunt was on.

IT was a nasty day, sunless and gray, and with a light drizzle that dropped the temperature and made things considerably less pleasant. Huddled in her jacket, Marla strolled along Commerce Street, grateful for the cheap umbrella they'd stopped and bought on the way downtown.

With the bad weather, many office workers weren't venturing out for lunch, which cut down on the congestion. There were quite a few construction sites in the area, but very few workmen. Even the number of street people aimlessly wandering about appeared low.

The Sentinel teams were working a grid pattern, first heading east to west on the streets with the most buildings they'd visualized: Young, Jackson, Commerce, and Main. Then they'd work the south/north cross streets.

Marla and Luke were doing opposite sides of Commerce, remaining parallel to one another as they walked, keeping their senses open for Belian energy. She was on the north side of the street, which provided a little more protection from the wind, but not much. It was cold and damp and generally miserable.

Thoughts of the Belian and its ugly words and threats had her wound tight inside. But memories of lovemaking with Luke this morning and seeing him right across the street helped keep her grounded.

There was no doubt in her mind that it had been more than just sex, for both of them. Luke might not want involvement, but she knew he cared for her. It was in the glow in his eyes when he looked at her, in how he touched her, and stroked inside her, and held her afterward.

She might not be experienced, and she might not be able to pick up shielded Sentinel emotions very clearly, but she could feel warmth and affection from him. He cared, damn it, even if he would never act on it—and even if she was too proud to grovel. Love couldn't be forced.

Enough, she told herself. She needed to focus on the most urgent matter at hand, the Belian. Glancing ahead to the right, she saw a Dallas landmark and every woman's secret fantasy shopping place—Neiman Marcus. She knew it was the original store and took up the entire end of the block fronting Ervay Street, with entrances on both Commerce and Main. She stopped at the traffic light, glanced over at Luke, who looked back at her.

She tucked her umbrella against her shoulder and slid her right hand into her coat pocket, felt the cold reassurance of her Tomcat. Her radio phone was in her left hand, with the mode set for Luke's phone. The light turned green, and she crossed and walked alongside the grand old department store. When this was over, she would treat herself to a shopping spree here.

She strolled along, surprised at how few people were out, although it was past lunchtime and there was more construction than businesses along this stretch. Then she felt it—faint tendrils of a dark ugliness, snaking toward her. It was growing stronger, fouler, starting to creep inside her.

She raised the phone, depressed the radio button, and spoke into the speaker. "Luke, I feel something. It's been here. The energy is growing stronger with every step. It's—" She halted as she was broadsided by an overwhelming wave of depravity and evil. *What the—?*

Realization twisted through her with a terrifying jolt as she realized she wasn't feeling residual energy, but . . . She looked at the man walking toward her just as he jolted in recognition and his gaze locked on her.

She stared back at the Belian.

JULIA and Adam were working Main Street. Actually, he was working it and she was in the Roma Express restaurant right across the street from Neiman Marcus, acting as main dispatch for messages and information among the teams. She couldn't walk the distances, and the wet weather made her leg ache more than usual. She hated being so useless, but accepted that sitting it out was better than bogging down the investigation.

So she waited for Adam to swing back by, sipping bottled water and absently rubbing her leg. She had an extremely active mind, but trying to work through events of the past few days was an overload right now.

Deciding to make some notes for her next linear algebra exam, she set her purse on the table and rummaged through it for the small spiral notebook she carried. As she pulled it out, a photo fell from it. She picked it up, saw it was a picture taken of her and Marla at the last family Christmas get together. She started to slide it back in when the gray void dropped around her so suddenly, the picture fell from her fingers.

The vision that flashed in her mind was vivid—and terrifying. She was struggling to her feet and reaching for her cane before the images were fully faded. She had to get to Marla, fast. She moved as rapidly as she could, fumbling for the radio phone as she left the restaurant.

Panic edging her on, she pushed the talk button and continued across the street toward Neiman Marcus. "Adam, come quickly! Commerce Street side of Neiman Marcus. Marla's in trouble."

She yanked open the fancy glass door via the huge stylized metal *N*. Her vision had been coming out of the store onto Commerce Street, so she figured going through it was probably her fastest route.

Adam's voice came though the speaker. "I'm on my way. You stay right where you are. Do not attempt to get to Marla. Do you hear me? Julia?"

She slid the phone into her coat pocket and increased her pace, ignoring her screaming leg. She'd been present in her vision, and somehow knew she had to be there. Besides, her sister was in grave danger. No way was she going to wait it out.

Fear, bone chilling, breath stopping, wrapped around her. *Marla*. Dear God, she hoped she got there in time.

"You!" he said.

Marla took a step back.

He was a little above average height, greyhound slender. He had dark brown hair and brown eyes, and wore a black trench coat over an expensive navy suit. He carried an open black umbrella in one hand and a large handled case, the kind a salesman might use, in the other.

He radiated malevolence so intense, she couldn't believe the few people moving around them could be so unaffected. Recognition filled his soulless eyes. "Marla," he crooned.

Nausea rose swiftly, and she battled to keep her wits about her. "I'm afraid you have mistaken me for someone else." She took another step back.

In a burst of speed, he closed the distance, dropping the umbrella and case to grab her arms. "Oh, no, Marla. I'd know your energy anywhere. I knew I'd find you."

Oh, God. His essence was pure evil, his emotions a

cauldron of hatred and madness threatening to suck her into an inescapable nightmare. "No!" She tried to jerk free, discovering he had the same inhuman strength as a Sentinel.

With a feral sound, he twisted her arm painfully. "You can't escape me. I have to punish you."

She couldn't reach her gun; his hold was too strong. *Think, Marla, think!* She opened her mouth to scream, found her vocal cords frozen. Tried to jolt back, found her body becoming sluggish and uncoordinated. *No!*

His eyes glittered cruelly. "You see Marla, there's no escape from me. I am too powerful, too clever. I'll have to put my other plans on hold—temporarily—while I administer your punishment."

No, no, no! Her mind screamed denial, her body stumbling toward him when he gave a vicious wrench. She fell against him, trying to cringe away. He shook her like she was a rag doll. Then he slung her against the building and stared at her with a satisfied sneer. *Why wasn't anyone coming to her aid?*

"I'm going to enjoy this. I—" His head suddenly snapped to the side, and his breath hissed out. He turned, shoving her so hard, she tumbled to the sidewalk.

She looked up to see Luke charging them, gun in hand. The Belian whirled and made a gesture. Luke's arm jerked sideways, the shot going wild. The Belian leaped at him, and Marla saw the flash of a knife plunging into Luke's right side. She screamed.

Luke punched the Belian in the face with his left fist. The Belian fell back, but then charged, ramming his head into Luke's abdomen. Luke slammed against the concrete wall. The Belian stabbed him again.

Luke's gun fell to the ground. Blood stained his leather jacket; his right arm hung limp. The Belian raised the knife, but Luke punched him again, sent him sprawling. Then he pulled out his second gun with his left hand. In a light-speed move, the Belian rolled and leaped to his feet. He tore a cement trash can from its base and hurled it against Luke before he could fire the gun.

To Marla's shock, he went down. "Luke!" she tried to scream, but it came out like a hoarse croak. She tried to move, but her body was still like rubber. She looked around frantically. "Help!" she called out, her voice a harsh rasp. "Someone, please help us!"

But the few people around appeared unwilling to get involved. Some had cell phones out; she guessed they were calling 911, but knew help would be way too late. Luke shoved the trash can away and was struggling to get up. The entire right side of his coat was now a dark stain.

The Belian stalked toward him, gripping the knife. *Luke!* Marla managed to stand, still sluggish but once again in control of her body. Adrenaline and desperation propelled her forward, gave her the strength to charge the Belian. She leaped on his back, wrapping her arms around his neck and jerking him backward. He stumbled, caught off guard by surprise and her weight, which probably equaled his.

He sliced his knife across her arm. She cried out, her grip loosening. In an instant, he grabbed her other arm and wrenched her sideways and in front of him. His hold across her chest was like an iron band. Luke was on his feet now, but halted when the Belian whipped the knife across her throat. "Try it Sentinel, and your bitch conductor dies."

Marla clawed at the arm across her chest and tried to buck free, until she felt the blade of the knife press against her throat, felt pain and the warm flow of blood.

"You will be still," the Belian hissed, or I will cut deeper and deeper until you choke on your own blood, you whore."

She stilled, horror dulling her wits. *What now?* Luke took a staggering step toward them, but stopped when the Belian cut a little deeper, and Marla gasped. "Not another step, Sentinel. I will slit her throat from ear to ear if you do."

Luke stood there, deathly pale, rage and determination burning in his eyes. He was still bleeding, and the stain on his coat spread; she could see he was growing weaker. She had to do something, but what?

Where were the others? *Please, God,* she prayed, *send help—and fast.*

NINETEEN

HER heart hammering from fear and exertion, Julia finally made it through the store. Gasping, she pushed through the heavy glass door, stepped onto the sidewalk fronting Commerce Street. Hearing raised voices, she looked right—and froze in horror.

About twenty feet away, a man in a black trench coat stood with his back to her. There was a woman in front of him, struggling. He made a jerky motion, and she stopped moving. Julia could see the wild mass of chestnut curls and the brown jacket, and knew then he had Marla. Just like her vision had shown. Sensing the evil radiating from the man, she knew who—or what—it was.

The light mist coated her glasses, making it harder to see. She switched her cane to her left hand, started to reach for her gun. But she couldn't shoot him without shooting Marla. As she eased closer, she saw Luke standing on the other side of the Belian, pale, shaky, and bleeding heavily. No help there.

She heard the Belian say, "Not another step, Sentinel. I will slit her throat from ear to ear if you do."

The past rushed at her. *"Don't resist me, Julia, or I'll kill you,"* William Bennett said as he rammed himself into her. *Not that she could have fought at that point—he'd beaten her too badly . . .*

Feeling a sense of déjà vu and hopelessness, she wondered if history was destined to repeat itself, only reversing the roles this time, with Marla the victim and Julia the observer.

No! she thought fiercely. *It is not going to happen again.* But what could she do? She couldn't use her gun, and she had no other weapons. Wait . . .

She looked down at her cane. It had been her grandfather's, and it was solid oak. Hefting it in her hand, she eased closer to the Belian.

"IT'S not her you want, it's me." Luke's voice was strong despite the fact he was swaying on his feet. "Let her go, and you can do whatever you want to me. I won't fight you."

He took a step closer. With a furious shriek, the Belian whipped his hand out and down, and blinding pain ripped through Marla's thigh. She almost blacked out, barely managed to hang on to consciousness. Then she felt the knife return to her throat.

"Back off, Sentinel, or I'll stab her again."

Luke stood still, his hands up in a gesture of surrender. "You can't have us both. The minute you kill her, it's over. You have to choose one of us."

His gaze shifted suddenly beyond the Belian, but quickly swung back. If Marla hadn't been focusing so desperately on him, she might not have noticed the quick movement, the brief flare of his eyes. Something was going on behind the Belian.

"You're wrong." The Belian moved backward, dragging her with him. She tried to dig in her heels. He jerked her with a snarl, and she felt the burn of the knife. She stopped resisting.

The Belian pressed his foot against the business case on

the sidewalk, dragged it closer. "I have bombs. I can blow up this city. And I still have your whore." Another slash of the knife laid open a cut on her other thigh, and she cried out, despite her resolve not to. *God, it hurt.*

"See?" he gloated. "I can cut her again and again. I can slice her up right in front of you, and there's not a damned thing you can do about it."

Feeling encroaching hysteria, Marla fought not to lose it totally. She couldn't fall apart—she had to remain clear-headed until she found an opening to do something. She kept her focus on Luke. He was her anchor in this madness.

Again, his gaze shifted, and then he looked at the Belian. "Better watch your step with her. She's a biter, aren't you Marla?"

A biter? What—? A burst of insight through her panicked mind told her he wanted her to distract the Belian.

"I am not amused," the Belian hissed. "Get on the ground, facedown, Sentinel. Now!" He moved the knife in another lightning slash, this one to her left arm.

She didn't hesitate, didn't let the pain distract her. She grabbed his knife arm with both hands, twisted down, and bit his wrist as hard as she could. He yelped. She heard a loud thwack, felt a blow against her leg. The leg gave out and she stumbled. Oddly enough, so did the Belian.

Things happened really fast then. The Belian collapsed on top of her, taking them both down on the hard cement. She felt the cold blade of the knife pressing against her cheek; tried to heave the Belian off her.

He was screaming obscenities and threats, and she felt his arm shifting, his hand tightening on the knife. Not in this lifetime. She was squirming into a position to bite him again, when suddenly, he was jerked off her. Gun shots exploded over her head.

Dazed, she tried to move toward Luke, but pain screamed through her stabbed leg. She twisted and saw the Belian in a heap a few feet away. She angled back around. Standing over her, Luke lowered his left arm, a gun in his hand.

He looked down at her, his skin ashen. "You . . . okay?"

"Yes," she said hoarsely.

"Good." He collapsed to his knees, swaying. Then he sagged against the building.

"Luke!" She tried to reach him, slipping in the blood and rain. She couldn't get her legs to work, but she scrabbled close enough to take his hand. Felt a faint squeeze.

Then Adam was there, kneeling beside him. "Good job. We'll take it from here."

Luke closed his eyes and went completely limp. *"Luke!"* Marla screamed it this time, trying to sit up. "Luke, hold on!"

"Be still. You're injured." Adam pushed her back down. "Kara's here now. We'll take care of him. It will be all right."

Marla kept her grip on Luke's hand, refusing to let go, trying to send her own energy through their link, willing him to live. But he just lay there, still and gray.

"Marla!" Julia stepped into her field of vision. "Thank God you're . . ." She choked on a sob.

She was alive. Marla really felt the pain then, oblivion trying to claim her, but she fought it. Her sister was here, and Luke would be okay. He had to be. There was no other option.

JULIA dropped awkwardly to her knees, her leg screaming in protest. She slid her arms around Marla. The cut at her throat appeared shallow, but she was bleeding heavily from several wounds. "I'm here, Marla, I'm here." She heard sirens growing louder; down the block, she saw Barrie and David running toward them.

Marla looked up at her through pain-glazed eyes. "Luke," she whispered. "Don't let him die." Her gaze returned to his still form.

Kara was kneeling beside him, applying pressure to his upper chest, while Adam worked on the larger side wound. Light glowed around his hands. Damien was standing behind them, his steel gaze fixed on the Belian as he intoned something in a strange, beautiful language.

"They're doing everything they can for him," Julia said. "It's all right. I've got you." She rested her check against her sister's hair, her tears mingling with the rain. "I've got you."

She was swept back into another memory . . . *William Bennett had stumbled off into the night, leaving Julia a battered, bloody mess. Marla, seriously injured with a ruptured spleen, broken bones, and a concussion, still somehow managed to inch her way over to Julia. She collapsed beside her, throwing an arm around her. "It's okay, Jules," she mumbled through a broken jaw. "It's all right. I've got you."*

Full circle, Julia thought, watching the ambulance roar up Commerce Street. *Full circle.*

THEY kept Marla in Parkland Hospital overnight for observation and to transfuse her with a unit of blood. Luke was sent to the critical care unit. He had a collapsed lung, his liver had been nicked and he'd lost a lot of blood, but he would recover. Barrie was watching over him. Damien and Kara had already returned to their home in Zorro.

Marla had Julia, her guardian angel, and the most amazing woman she knew. She'd learned that Julia's precognition had guided her to come out of Neiman Marcus behind the Belian. She'd brought it down with her cane, swinging at its knees, a weak point for every human body. Then she'd gotten out of Luke's way.

Luke, despite his injuries, had lifted the Belian off Marla, flung it to the ground, and shot it. After that, while Adam and Kara stabilized Luke, Damien had performed some sort of Belian expulsion, sending the Belian's soul to Saturn for "rehabilitation."

All of that was a blur for Marla. She did remember Julia being present throughout her treatment, which included too many stitches to count. And Julia had been there through questioning by the Dallas police. Adam had also been there for that. He was handling the police and media and any loose ends that might raise suspicious questions.

Julia spent the night in a chair next to Marla's bed, and they both looked pretty frightening when Marla was finally released midmorning. She'd have to see a doctor in Houston to be sure she didn't have permanent damage from the knife wounds inflicted by the Belian, and she faced physical therapy. She'd also need some sessions with Dr. Jackson, since she had a new episode of post-traumatic stress to work through. And wasn't that great?

Because of the stab wound in her thigh, she would be using crutches for the next few weeks. The floor nurse wanted to put her in a wheel chair for the traditional discharge ride to the main entrance, but Marla evaded her and escaped on a back elevator.

She wanted to see Luke before she and Julia returned to Houston. Thankfully, his condition was no longer critical, and he'd been moved to regular room. Marla heard Barrie talking before she reached his doorway.

But when she peeked into the room, her gaze went straight to Luke. It was a shock to see him laid up in a hospital bed, with tubes and IVs running into him, although Adam had told her Sentinels healed very quickly. A lump formed in her throat. She'd come so close to losing him.

He was propped up in the bed, wearing the de rigueur hospital gown. His hair was loose around his face, and his eyes were half-closed. On the table beside him, there was a small bouquet of flowers, with a connected Mylar balloon proclaiming "*It's a Boy!*" in bright blue letters. Marla guessed that must have been the current special in the gift shop, or evidence of Barrie's quirky sense of humor.

"My favorite part was seeing that black soul whip off to Saturn," Barrie was saying.

"Hopefully without you getting rushed to the hospital afterward," Luke said wryly. "Let's not forget that common hazard."

"I *know* that." Barrie's voice had an "oh, please" tone.

Suddenly sensing Marla's presence, Luke turned his head. Their gazes met, held. And she wished things could be different. Wished she could be the woman to convince him to take a chance, wished they had a future.

Perched in the only chair, Barrie looked around. "Hey, Marla. Look at you. You're up and about."

Marla hobbled into the room. "I had real motivation. Nurse Ratched is after me."

Barrie looked confused. "Who?"

"Doesn't matter." Marla stared at Luke.

"Uh, I'll just leave you two alone." Barrie stood. "Time for another snack anyway. I'll bring you something, too, bro. Be back soon."

"Sure," Luke said, his gaze never wavering from Marla.

As Barrie left, Marla swung over to the bed on her crutches. Every movement pulled painfully on stitches and bruised muscles, but she didn't care. Luke was her sole focus. "Hey, you," she said.

"Hey, yourself."

He looked better than he had yesterday, which wasn't saying much. He was still pale, his eyes were dark with fatigue and probably pain. She wanted to climb into the bed with him and hold him close. Like that was a good idea.

"Nice crutches," he said.

"They're the latest fashion edition. They come with an assortment of color coordinated accessories."

His grin was like a burst of sunlight in her heart. She balanced herself, then reached out and took his hand, careful to avoid the IV. "Thank you for charging to my rescue—even though it put you here."

His expression turned serious. "It's my job."

"It's a crappy job, if you ask me. I hope you at least have benefits." Her attempt at humor didn't loosen the knot inside. "I thought I'd lost you when he stabbed you."

"*It*—not he." He squeezed her hand. "I wasn't worried about me. I thought it was going to kill you on the spot."

"Yeah." She managed a shaky smile. "Me, too."

"You were amazing, Marla. You kept your wits about

you, and you probably saved my life when you jumped on the Belian's back—although it was another foolish stunt."

"It might have been foolish, but you still owe me big time for it."

That got another smile. "Yeah, I do. And who'd have thought your biting talent would have come in so handy?" Humor gleamed in his eyes. "You were clearheaded enough to take my hint. That, and Julia's precognition, and a damned good swing with her cane, are what saved us."

"My big sister really came to the rescue, didn't she? She's always looked after me."

"She can be on my team anytime."

They lapsed into silence, staring at each other. She drank in the sight of him, his amazingly blue eyes, his clean, noble features, and wealth of blond hair. She knew their time had run out. She needed to get on with her life—and without Luke. Besides, if she hung around too long, she might end up begging, and she'd hate that.

"Well," she finally said. "I've been discharged from the hospital. Julia and I are flying home tomorrow, and I just wanted to tell you—" She couldn't bring herself to say the actual words, even though this was the end for them. She knew how Luke felt about involvement; knew that caring wasn't even close to love.

Leaning over, she kissed him lightly. She savored the feel of him, tried to store the memory. It would have to last a lifetime. She started to draw back, but he pulled her against him in a hug. She hugged him back, holding on tightly and wishing she didn't ever have to let go. Then he released her, and she felt the finality.

She was mortified at the sudden tears that filled her eyes and tried to blink them away. She righted herself, took a deep breath. "I love you," she said.

Shock flashed in his eyes. "Marla—"

She pressed her fingers against his lips. "No. Don't say anything. Take those words and know that someone really cares about you. Maybe it will get you through rough times."

He watched her as she fumbled with the crutches and took a step back. "Marla . . . I wish—" He gave a small shake of his head. "I hope you'll start living life again. Get out and have fun. Find yourself a great guy who can fully appreciate you."

"Sure," she said, keeping her tone light, although her heart felt like it was shattering. "I'll do that. You take care, okay?"

He looked like he wanted to say more, but he simply nodded. "You, too. Have a safe trip back."

She stared at him a moment longer. *Good-bye, Luke.*

Then, before she did something really embarrassing, like breaking down and sobbing, she turned and maneuvered her way into the corridor and toward the elevator. She was able to hold back more tears until she was alone in the elevator.

Maybe the heartache would distract her from the posttraumatic stress disorder. She'd already been there, done that, anyway. But of the two, the pain she now felt in her heart was far, far worse.

JULIA groaned when she saw Adam standing at the departure gate for their Southwest flight to Houston. "What are you doing here?" She glanced back at the security barricades, then at him. "And how did you get through security without a ticket?"

He gave her his arched brow "how-do-you-think?" look, and she muttered, "Never mind. I don't want to know. Then I'd be an accomplice."

"I told you I'd take you to the airport."

"And I told you we didn't need a ride. The hotel shuttle was just fine."

"Even though you and Marla had to climb steps to get inside? She has a lot of stitches."

Julia felt a surge of guilt. In her haste to get away from Adam's annoying presence, she hadn't considered Marla's condition until she saw her struggling to get into the van. Then she'd felt terrible.

Marla stepped into the fray, pinning Adam with an icy look. "For the record, I did just fine getting in and out of the van." She glanced from him to Julia. "But I need to sit down now. Jules, I'll be waiting over there." She turned and moved away.

Adam's midnight gaze bored into Julia's eyes. "Are you running from me?"

"Don't be ridiculous."

His gaze shifted to the ugly metal cane she'd gotten from the hospital medical supply, since she'd broken the other one on the Belian. He looked back at her. "I know what happened to you eleven years ago."

It was a jolt to her system, but she shouldn't have been surprised. "So? That's not a secret."

"It's why you're hiding from the world."

"Oh, so you're a psychoanalyst now? I already have a very good one—who's actually qualified."

He took a step closer, tall and intimidating in an expensively tailored black pin-striped suit. She caught the whiff of a tantalizing, masculine fragrance, felt the pull of sensual energy. "We're not through, Julia."

"Oh, yes, we—" Her words were cut off by his hand grasping her chin and his lips coming down on hers.

The airport fell away as a wave of desire rushed up like flood waters. Fire and need sparked inside her. Her body went into a wild free fall. He didn't use his tongue, but that didn't diminish the impact of his lips molding against hers, of the savage surge of lust spreading like a flame through her.

She could not—*would not*—allow this. She broke free, brought her hand up to slap him, but he caught her wrist in a lightning-fast move. She glared at him, willing her heart and breathing to slow. "Go to hell."

He stared back, seemingly unaffected. "I hate to disappoint you, but that's not very likely."

"And isn't that too bad." She wrenched her arm free, refrained from touching her tingling lips. "Look, I helped you track down a monster, while I watched my sister get carved up. I've made my contribution, and I'm done. I'm going back to my life. I hope to God I never see you again."

"Liar." But he stepped back.

She straightened her jacket, turned and walked away.

"Julia." Even the way he said her name in that harsh voice of his affected her. She stopped and looked at him over her shoulder. He stood there, darkly handsome, his ebony eyes mesmerizing. "Our paths *will* cross again."

She told herself she was imagining the strange glow in his eyes. "I don't think so."

"Walk in Light," he said quietly.

Grateful to hear their flight being called, she turned without another word. She focused on helping Marla—who tactfully didn't mention what had just happened—stand and get to the boarding area. She didn't look back, although she was sorely tempted.

Once on the plane, she breathed a sigh of relief, told herself it was merely fatigue, not letdown, she was feeling. She was through with Adam Masters, and her life would thankfully return to normal.

Normal, controlled, and predictable.

TWENTY

THE call came in on Marla's private line at work. She picked it up. "Marla Reynolds."

"Hello, Marla," said a raspy voice. "It's Adam Masters."

As if she wouldn't recognize that odd voice anywhere. She could only think of one reason he might be calling, and panic swept through her. "What's wrong? Did something happen to Luke?"

"No, he's fine. I'm calling about another matter."

She wondered if that might be Julia. "What is it?"

"Your condition."

Oh, God. Her hand trembled. Grasping the receiver firmly, she forced herself to speak calmly. "I don't know what you're talking about."

"Don't play games with me, Marla."

He knew, but how? He was one scary guy. "Why don't you just keep your nose out of my business?"

"All Sentinels born in Texas *are* my business. How are you feeling?"

Sick as a dog. She broke off another small piece of cracker, toyed with it. For the past month, she'd divided most of her time between missing Luke so badly it was a physical ache, and hugging the toilet. Unfortunately, because of her condition, she hadn't been able to drown her sorrows with alcohol.

"Marla, ignoring me won't do any good, and it's not advisable."

Adam was forcing her to face what she'd been avoiding. It had only been four days ago that she'd accepted the possibility and done the home test, then gone to the drugstore to buy two more kits. Every one of the damned things had been positive.

"How are you feeling?" he persisted.

She sighed. "Pretty queasy. I have a doctor's appointment next week. Adam, please don't tell Luke, not yet. I'm not ready for him to know."

He was silent a moment. "Let's see how things go. I want you to call me after you see your doctor. Here's my number."

Marla wrote it down and promised to call. As she hung up, she felt tears welling in her eyes, another side effect of her condition. She'd been overly emotional for days. It was so damned unfair that Adam had to know and was butting into her life.

What if he'd already told Luke? That would make matters far worse. While she didn't intend to hide her pregnancy from him, or keep him from his child, she wanted—*needed*—to be stronger before she faced him. And she certainly didn't want him to feel obligated to her. She couldn't stand that. She still had her pride, even if her heart was in shreds.

No, she wasn't ready to talk to Luke yet.

DÉJÀ VU, Luke thought as he channeled energy to turn the dead bolt. Marla hadn't returned his calls, and she wasn't responding to the doorbell or his knocking. On the other side of the door, Bryony was in a barking frenzy.

He stepped into the foyer. "Hello! Marla! Are you here? It's Luke." No response, except for Bryony's yapping.

"Hey girl." He leaned down, his hand out to pet her, but she skittered backward, acting like she'd never seen him before.

The beeping down the hallway reminded him of the security system. He headed to the hall closet to deactivate it, flaring out his senses as he went. No human energy in the house. Just psycho dog, who at this moment was attached to his ankle, being dragged along.

Heck of a deal. The dog must have the memory of a gnat. Hadn't it been only been eight weeks since Bry had been following him around the house, doing that pirouette thing on her hind legs to get his attention?

Actually, it seemed a lot longer than eight weeks since he'd last seen Marla. More like an eternity, as much as he hated to admit it. He still couldn't believe he was here. He didn't need any distractions in his life right now. He had just regained his full strength, was dealing with the fact Barrie was about to go out on her own as a Sentinel, and there were signs of a Belian wreaking havoc in the Panhandle. A lot of stuff going on.

But he couldn't focus on any of it, because one female had him turned inside out. He couldn't get thoughts of Marla out of his mind. If he didn't exert an iron will to concentrate on something else, he'd find himself thinking about her wild hair and sexy mouth; about that lush body and how good it felt to be inside her. It was frustrating as hell.

It was more than lust. He missed her wit, her smile, her laughter, and the way she made him feel. Even so, he couldn't explain the pull that had him picking up the phone to call her—despite his resolve to remain alone—or traveling to Houston when he couldn't reach her.

He told himself he just wanted to see how she was doing, to make sure she had recovered and wasn't suffering any lingering effects from her contact with the Belian. *Yeah, right.* He was full of it. He missed the hell out of her. He wasn't sure what he was going to do about it—probably in major denial mode—but he wanted to see her.

So he'd wait until she got home. He pried Bryony off his ankle—good thing he was wearing his boots—and threatened to zap her if she didn't behave. She took refuge under the couch, while he made himself at home, settling on the couch, turning on the TV, and finding the Houston Astros baseball game. But he had trouble concentrating on the game, kept looking at his watch. Where was she?

Finally, he heard the garage door opening, and he turned off the TV. Bryony scampered out from beneath the couch and made a beeline for the kitchen, her little frou-frou tail wagging. Guessing that Marla would come in through the kitchen, Luke sat back and waited. Anticipation tingled through him.

He heard her voice first, the soft Texas drawl doing ridiculous things to his body. "Hey baby," she cooed to Bry. "What have you been doing? Mama missed you. Oh, your food dish is empty. Poor baby!"

She walked out of the kitchen, Bryony tucked in one arm, her purse in the other hand. "Let me reset the alarm and then I'll feed—" she froze when she saw Luke.

"Hello, Marla." He rose from the couch.

With a little squeak, she dropped Bry, who hit the floor with a yelp. "Luke! You scared the daylights out of me! What are you doing here?"

"Waiting for you."

Her purse dropped from her other hand as she stared at him. He was gratified by the joyful and welcoming expression that flashed on her face. For a moment, her eyes softened and warmed. He started forward, needing to touch her.

But her expression quickly changed to one of disgust. "Oh, isn't this just great?" she said sarcastically.

He slowed his steps. "Well, yeah. It's good to see you—"

She drew back, her body language practically screaming *don't touch me*. "He told you, didn't he?"

"*Who* told me *what*?"

"*Damn it!*" Her fists clenched by her sides. "That sorry son of a bitch!"

This wasn't going exactly as he had planned. "Who are you talking about?"

Her eyes narrowed. "Cut the crap."

This was strange. Her foul language, her tension, her words—nothing made sense. He studied her, for the first time noticing the circles beneath her eyes and the porcelain paleness of her skin. She had on a cream-colored top over jeans that hadn't been that loose before.

"You've lost weight," he said sharply, closing the distance between them. He brushed the curls back from her face, took her chin in his hand, that simple touch sending a current through him. She felt unusually warm. "Are you sick? You look terrible."

"Gee, thanks a lot!" She knocked his hand away. "What are you doing here?"

Something was wrong. "I wanted to see how you're doing."

"I'm just great. Never been better. And you?"

He sensed not just sarcasm underlying her words, but also nervousness. "I've missed you. I wanted to see you."

Pain flashed in her eyes. "Oh." She walked around him, bent to pick up her purse. She stumbled a little, and he moved quickly to grab her arm and help her catch her balance.

"Have you been drinking?" he asked.

"Of course not! Why would you say such a thing?" She gave him an indignant look. "I'm just . . . tired. And my leg is still a little weak."

He wasn't sure he believed that. She was acting oddly, and he knew her propensity to drink when she was upset. He leaned closer and sniffed. *Crackers?*

"Stop it!" She punched him on the arm. "What do you really want, Luke?"

"I want to know what the hell is going on."

Her shoulders sagged and she turned and went to sit on the couch, dropping her purse onto the end table. Bryony jumped in her lap. She patted the dog absently then rubbed her forehead as if it ached.

He watched her, utterly perplexed. He knew he'd hurt her, but he'd thought it best at the time. He'd convinced himself that he couldn't make a life with anyone, couldn't do to any kids what his dad had done to them. So he'd pushed Marla away. But he hadn't been able to stop thinking about her, had begun to realize he didn't want to live without her. Maybe she'd moved on with her life and didn't want anything to do with him.

Not that he could blame her; her experiences with him had been pretty horrendous. Not many conductors had the pleasure of communing directly with a Belian, coming close to dying in a bomb blast, losing their virginity and then going straight into conduction sex, or almost having their throat cut, not to mention enduring numerous knife wounds. He'd definitely put her through the ringer.

And yet, in the hospital, she'd looked at him, her heart in her eyes, and told him she loved him. Those words had been haunting him ever since. He knew she'd never say them lightly.

He went over and sat next to her, ignoring Bryony's growl. "You didn't return my calls."

She turned her head, appearing genuinely surprised. "What?"

"I called both your cell and home phones and left messages."

"Oh." Her brow furrowed. "My cell phone was broken when I hit the sidewalk in Dallas. You know, when . . . the Belian fell on top of me, after Julia hit it with her cane. I just didn't—" She paused, and her breath hitched. "I haven't replaced it yet. I've been using my mom's. And the other phone—I guess I haven't been checking messages. I don't use it much, don't get many calls." Her hand slid to her stomach, pressed against it.

He took her other hand. "Talk to me, Marla. Tell me what's been going on. Who's the son of a bitch you mentioned?"

She looked at him, her eyes dark pools of distress. "You haven't talked to Adam?"

What did Adam have to do with this? "I e-mail or talk to Adam almost every day. Why do you ask?"

"You really don't know, do you?" she murmured. Her complexion had taken on a sickly cast.

Alarmed by her appearance, he tried to keep it low key. "I guess not. Why don't you enlighten me?"

"I—This is . . ." She freed her hand from his and raised it to her mouth. "Not a good time. *Oh, no.*" She lurched to her feet and sprinted into the hallway.

"Where are you going? Marla!" He stood, concerned and baffled. She always managed to keep him upended. He followed, heard her retching in the bathroom. He strode to the door, found it locked, and quickly dealt with it.

Marla was on her knees, hunched over the toilet. Despite her awful pallor, she managed a glare. "Damn it! I locked that door. Could I please have some privacy here?"

He stepped toward her. "You *are* sick. I'm taking you to a doctor."

"No." She held up a hand. "I've already been to the doctor."

"What did he say was wrong?" He opened the wall cabinet, looking for a washcloth. He heard her close the lid and flush the toilet.

"She said my . . . stomach problem would pass in time."

"You had a lot of trouble with that while we were hunting down the Belian." He perused the neat stacks of towels. "Did she give you anything for—" He froze as his gaze landed on a box on the shelf above the towels. A home pregnancy kit.

It took a moment to sink in, the sight of that kit stunning him like a gut punch. Home. Pregnancy. Kit. As in *pregnancy*. He felt as if he'd just touched the live end of a high-voltage wire.

He spun around to find Marla on her feet. "*You're pregnant.* That's why you're throwing up."

Her eyes flared and she grabbed the edge of the vanity. But she lifted her chin and said, "There's a news flash for you."

His thoughts were whirling. "This changes everything."

She stiffened as if he'd slapped her. "No, it doesn't." She shoved past him, got a cup off the counter, and rinsed out her mouth. Setting the cup down, she looked at him. "Go away, Luke."

"Like hell!"

She simply turned and left the bathroom. He followed. "We need to talk. We have to make some decisions."

She whirled on him. "I already told you, this doesn't change anything. It changes *nothing*, do you hear me?"

The shrillness of her voice must have alarmed Bryony, because she rushed Luke, attacking his leg and gnawing at his boot.

"You made your choice," Marla said fiercely. "You made it very clear that you didn't want a commitment, that you didn't want—" More pain flashed in her eyes. "Me."

He felt a sinking feeling, because he could see how she might think that, but she was wrong. "That's not exactly true, and you know it."

"I know we went our separate ways. And I know a one-sided relationship is doomed for failure. Not even a baby can save it." Her expression resolute, she pointed to the front door. "I want you to go now."

"I'm not leaving with this up in the air."

"We'll talk about it, I promise. Just not tonight, okay?" Sudden tears filled her eyes and she swiped at them. "Damn it! Why do I have to get emotional now?"

Luke reached for her, but she backed up, shaking her head. "*Go away.* This is my house, and I'm telling you to leave. I need to be alone."

He ran his hand through his hair, so shaken up and frustrated, he wanted to break something. He knew with a fierce, primitive urgency that Marla was *his*. She carried his child—a Sentinel child—and she belonged to him. And she loved him—information she'd freely volunteered.

He was not going to let his stupidity drive a wedge between them. And he damn sure wasn't going to give her the chance to entrench herself and throw up barriers.

As far as he was concerned, this was war. He was a tactical expert. All he needed was a chance to make Marla see reason. To do that, he'd have to resort to drastic measures.

"Sorry about this, babe," he said, right before he zapped her with a burst of energy.

THE sound of a dog barking outside and the bright light on her face roused Marla. With a groan, she rolled to her stomach and pulled the pillow over her head. She'd slept so well, the best sleep she'd had in weeks. She didn't want to wake up yet . . . *wait*. What time was it? *What day was it?*

Panic racing through her, she flipped over, looking for the clock. She stared around the room, confused and disoriented. Curtainless casement windows, dingy plaster walls . . . This wasn't her bedroom. She saw her glasses on a scarred imitation-pine fiberboard nightstand, snatched them up and put them on.

Squinting against the bright sunlight streaming in, she took in the holes in the wall, the double bed with navy sheets. This was the house in Needville. *Damn him!*

She rolled out of the bed, turned toward the doorway, and there he was. He leaned against the doorframe, dressed in faded jeans that molded every inch of his muscled thighs, and a black T-shirt stretched across that magnificent chest. His hair was loose, a silk blond curtain around the face of a god.

Her mouth went dry and her heart went into overdrive even as she planned his slow, painful death. "I've downgraded Adam from son of a bitch to jerk status. You've just been promoted to his former position," she told him.

His azure gaze drifted over her like a caress. She realized she was in one of her nightshirts, the same one she'd worn in Dallas, as a matter of fact. "I'm sorry, babe. You left me no choice."

"There's always a choice." She looked around the room for something to throw at him—besides herself. He was way too tempting, and she was weak where he was concerned. "We could have talked things out in Houston."

"Tried that. You weren't particularly cooperative."

"I wasn't trying to be uncooperative. I just wasn't ready to talk to you yet, that's all." Her voice broke at the end. She felt those damn tears pooling in her eyes, wanted to stomp her feet and scream and give in to a hormone-driven tantrum. Being pregnant had definite disadvantages.

He was there in a flash of the speeding bullet routine, cradling her against him. "Hey, it's okay. Don't cry, baby. I didn't do this to hurt you. Hell, I already did that in Dallas. I'm sorry. I just want a chance for us to work things out."

The way he said "baby" and the tenderness in his touch practically had her melting. She had missed him so much. She had to forcibly hang on to what was left of her pride, to remind herself she wouldn't accept his pity. But it was pretty darned hard to do that in close range to him, with all that sexual energy pulsing around them.

"Stop it, Luke." She pushed away from him. "Do *not* touch me. If we talk—assuming I don't kill you first—I want it with the kitchen table between us. No Sentinel/conductor energy affecting my brain." She poked her finger against his chest and glared at him. "And no more zapping me, or all deals are off."

He stepped back. "All right. Negotiations in the kitchen."

Shaking her head, she went to the bathroom first, noting the absence of potential weapons. Grateful that her stomach was calm for now, she did her business and went to the kitchen.

Luke was just screwing the top onto the travel mug, which he offered to her. "Here you go."

"Uh, I'm off the caffeine right now."

"I know. I researched the latest medical information on pregnancy on the Internet last night. This is herbal tea, with peppermint to calm your stomach."

Oh, that was so sweet. She noted the top on the mug, looked over to the counter. The knives were gone. "I see you're taking precautions against me becoming violent."

"Seemed the safest course of action, all things considered."

She repressed a smile. She was such a sucker for this guy. She turned toward the table and saw a package of saltines sitting there. She felt the tears again, pushed them back. She glanced at Luke. "Thank you."

"You're welcome. Hey, if you have any special needs—hormonal or otherwise—during this blessed time, I'm here to serve."

The look in his eyes, coupled with memories of their entwined bodies, sent a shockwave of heat through her. "And you think *I'm* a smart-ass," she muttered, trying to ignore her stirring libido.

"I know you are." He indicated a chair. "So let's talk."

They settled across the table from each other, like two negotiators on a business merger. It seemed strange after the intimacies they'd shared, but Marla wanted it that way.

Luke leaned forward, his expression turning serious. "So how are you doing? Is everything going okay with the pregnancy?"

His concern touched her. "I'm fine. The doctor said everything looks normal and is progressing well. The morning sickness isn't unusual." She allowed herself a moment of anticipation and said, "The baby is due January 6."

Luke's face practically glowed. "A New Year's baby. That's great."

She drew a deep breath, cut to the heart of the matter. "I refuse to be an obligation to you."

He sighed. "Marla, I know I told you I didn't want a permanent relationship with anyone. But when you went away, I missed you like crazy. That's why I came to Houston, because I wanted to see if there was some way we could make this work. I did that before I knew anything about the baby."

"You really didn't know?"

"No, I swear. Otherwise, I'd have come sooner."

Hope bloomed inside her. She wanted to believe him,

she really did, and he *had* looked genuinely shocked when he saw the pregnancy kit in her bathroom. But it was still hard to accept, knowing he'd never wanted any permanent relationships. And something else nagged at her.

Luke rose and came around the table. He pulled her chair back and tugged her up. She tried to sidestep him. "Hey! I said no touching."

"Just hear me out here." Framing her face with his hands, he stared down at her, his eyes warm and open. "I love you, Marla, and I want to marry you."

His hand slid down to rest intimately over her abdomen. "I'm thrilled about the baby, and I swear I'll do my best to be a good husband and father. But I would *not* be saying these things if I didn't mean them." He bent closer, his lips hovering over hers. "Say yes, babe. Marry me."

Her heart was doing somersaults, and her body was thrumming from his nearness. But she had to be absolutely certain. She put a hand on his chest, pushed him back. "What's Adam's phone number?"

He looked utterly confused. "What?"

"I want to talk to Adam before I give you an answer."

He scowled. "What the hell does Adam have to do with anything?"

"Are you jealous?"

"No. Maybe."

Oh, she liked that. "Just give me his number."

Frowning, he unclipped his cell phone, flipped it open, and scrolled to an entry. "Here."

She took the phone, jerked her head toward the back door. "Go outside while I talk to him."

He started to argue then seemed to think better of it. Muttering under his breath, he strode to the door. As he went out, she saw Bryony tied up in the backyard. Man, she was so scattered, she'd forgotten about her dog. Luke had a way of doing that to her.

She punched the number and put the phone to her ear. "Yes Luke," came Adam's harsh voice.

"This is Marla."

There was a brief pause then he said, "What have you done with Luke?" He actually sounded suspicious.

"What, you think I could do him in?"

"Knowing you and your sister, I think anything is possible. I assume you're with Luke."

"He's outside right now. I have two questions for you."

"What are they?"

"Did you tell Luke about the baby?"

He didn't hesitate. "I did not. I would have eventually, but I was hoping you would do it. We really do respect our conductors and try to honor their needs and wishes whenever possible."

She believed him, and her heart lightened. "All right. Next question: Is there anything in your code of honor or laws that requires a Sentinel to marry a conductor who gets pregnant?"

"Absolutely not. The One has given us the gift of free will, and we must honor the choices conductors and Sentinels make. Our code demands that we care for the conductor and the child, and that we ensure the child has a mentor and is trained as a Sentinel. That's as far as it goes."

A rush of relief swept through her. Maybe Luke really did love her. "Thank you, Adam."

"I expect an invitation to the wedding."

The call clicked off and she stared at the phone in shock. Adam was a scary guy, all right. She walked to the open back door, looked through the rotting screen. Luke was playing with Bryony, chasing the poodle around the yard, then letting Bry chase him. She was yipping and having a blast.

Marla's heart melted. Here was a gorgeous man and an incredible lover who would protect her with his life, and who even played with her dog. He'd be a great father, too. And he loved her. What more could a girl want?

Luke looked her way, and their gazes locked. He rose from wrestling with Bry, taking a moment to put her back on the rope. Then he turned and started toward Marla, his gaze never wavering. For such a big man, he moved with surprising grace, his body fluid and powerful. Her heart resumed somersaults as he approached her.

He opened the screen door. From the look in his eyes, she felt certain he already knew her answer. He could read her too well, could sense her feelings, often before she even knew them. He leaned against the door frame. "So did you and Adam come to any earth-shattering decisions?"

Her body responded to his nearness, desire throbbing and pooling in all the usual hot spots. "Maybe. But I'm not through with the negotiations."

His gaze became heated and predatory. He *really* could read her. She was going to have to work on that. "Is that so?" He moved closer, his body almost touching hers. "Anything I can do to help things along?"

She was already lost, in his heat and vitality, in the light, possessive skim of his hands over her hips. "I'll let you know," she murmured, stretching up until their lips were separated only by a few air molecules.

"I can hardly wait." He leaned down and teased his mouth against hers.

She kissed him with all the love in her heart, sliding her fingers in his hair as her tongue mated with his. Still kissing, they stumbled into the kitchen, the door swinging shut behind them. They crashed against the table, and cups went flying.

Luke lifted her and sat her on the table. She opened her legs and he stepped between them, pressing her against his seriously hard lower body as he devoured her mouth. Reaching behind him, she grabbed hold of his very fine ass.

Finally breaking off the kiss, he rested his forehead against hers, his breathing ragged. "How am I doing?"

She caressed his rear. "Not bad."

"Not bad?" he asked in male outrage. "Babe, I'll show you *bad*."

Just so long as he did it *very* soon. She glanced at the table. "You know, we've never done it in the kitchen."

He laughed, low and sexy. "Sweetheart, you definitely have a kinky bent. And while I aim to please, I don't think this table is up to what I have in mind." He ran his hands under the nightshirt, stroking her thighs. "I think we need to continue the negotiations in the bedroom."

She yanked up his T-shirt, ran her tongue over a nipple. "Okay."

He laughed again, although his voice showed signs of strain. "You're easy, you know that?"

"Ask me if I care," she muttered as he swept her up and carried her to the bed. Then she didn't think about anything else for a long, long time.

THEY were lying in a tangle of sheets, the sunlight glowing around them. Luke was propped next to Marla's abdomen, where he'd been kissing and stroking her belly, and talking to the baby. Marla was sleepy and relaxed, but then three mind-blowing orgasms could do that to a girl.

She and Luke had teased and laughed and loved, but they hadn't yet discussed any final decisions. He looked totally complacent right now; he was practically glowing with masculine smugness. Time to shake things up a bit.

She sat up and stretched. His appreciative gaze swept over her breasts. "The sex has been great," she said casually, "but it doesn't change anything."

That wiped the Cheshire cat grin off his face. His eyes narrowed, and she could practically see him going into warrior mode. He sat up, sweeping back his gorgeous mane of hair. "This isn't just about sex," he said. "You know that."

"Not on your part, maybe."

"What the hell are you talking about?"

She was definitely enjoying this. "It means that great sex isn't going to influence my decision about you."

"You love me, babe. You told me so in the hospital. I know you weren't lying." He gave her a calculating look. "As a matter of fact, I know you haven't faked *anything*."

Oh man, was it getting warm in here, or what? Must be

the baby hormone thing again. "I might have changed my mind."

His gaze went arctic. "Oh, yeah? Well, let me explain something. We have enough supplies in this house to sustain a year-long siege. We can just stay here until you unchange your mind."

He really was cute when he was in full macho mode. "You want me to stop loving you?"

His brows drew together. "What?"

"What I was trying to tell you was that I don't love you just for the great sex. I love you for a lot of other reasons. And yes, I'll marry you."

The incredulous expression on his face was priceless. "You brat." He lunged and rolled her beneath him. "I should—" He paused, shook his head. "Hell, I have no idea what to do with you."

Laughing, Marla wrapped her arms around his neck. "Just love me back, *babe*."

His gaze turned tender. "I already do. But I can tell that living with you is going to be a challenge."

"Count on it." She drew him down for a kiss.

When they came up for air, he said, "Adam will want to come to the wedding."

"I know. He already told me." She considered a minute. "Julia's sure going to be pissed about that."

Outside, Bryony started barking, probably at a squirrel. Everything in Marla's life had fallen into place. She had her dog, her man, and a baby on the way. She could finally let go of the past and face the future.

And how wonderful was that?

Turn the page for a sneak peek at
Julia and Adam's story
in book three of
Catherine Spangler's Sentinel series:

TOUCHED BY LIGHT

Coming soon from Berkley Sensation!

JULIA slugged back the rest of her bourbon and managed to set the glass back on its paper coaster, despite the Herculean urge to hurl it against the wall.

"Can I get you another one, Dr. Reynolds?" Miriam, who happened to be both the bartender and one of the top students in Julia's number theory course at the University of Houston, took the empty glass.

Miriam's hair was styled into stiff spikes, the color du jour alternating sections of green, red, and blond. The heavy eye makeup accentuating her green eyes, and one pierced eyebrow and multiple silver rings in each ear added to her distinct style. Julia just wasn't hip enough to know if it was Goth or punk, or whatever the current look was.

Not that Julia was familiar with any of the latest trends. She'd buried herself in teaching, with a strong minor in the art of becoming a hermit in twelve short years. She certainly wasn't a spokesperson for the stylish and fashionable.

"Yes, I want another one," she told Miriam. "Make it straight up." No melting ice diluting this drink. Maybe then the bourbon would deaden the pain.

"Sure." Miriam started to leave, hesitated. "Are you okay, Dr. Reynolds? You seem . . . upset."

Upset? Julia battled back the hysterical urge to laugh. Try *terrified . . . panicked . . . barely holding on to her sanity.* What would Miriam think if her staid, unemotional math professor suddenly lost it in the middle of the Red Lion Pub? Could make for an interesting time.

Get a grip, Julia told herself. She drew a deep breath, managed to shake her head. "I'm fine, Miriam. Just enjoying a few drinks."

Miriam's disbelief was clearly etched on her face, but she turned and walked off behind the polished, dark-wood bar. Julia blew out her breath, raised a shaking hand to her throbbing temple.

"You're such a liar, Julia," came a voice from behind her.

Her head snapped up, and adrenaline shot through her like neutrons in a particle analyzer. God, she knew—*and hated*—that odd, rasping voice. Her body went rigid, while her heart decided she must be running a three-minute mile and went into frenetic overdrive.

No! Not now. She fixed her gaze on the gleaming brass beer tap behind the bar. Willed that voice to be the result of her overstressed state. Although she knew her current luck was on the crappy side of negative one. "Go away," she said.

He didn't reply, but she felt the air shift as he settled onto the bar stool beside her. Felt that disconcerting energy buzz that always arced between them, felt the spike in her normally dead-as-dirt libido. Felt the beckoning warmth emanating from his body, in direct opposition to the power and danger he radiated.

She refused to look at him. If she couldn't see him, he wasn't really there, right? But that didn't convince her clamoring senses, which had gone on full alert. His scent drifted to her—expensive, woodsy, totally male. That damned electricity continued bombarding her. Her nipples hardened and she grew wet between her legs. *Damn him.*

"I said go away," she snapped. "Does it work better if I say it three times? Go away, go away, go away. Go. Away!"

"That's six times now, actually. And no, you can't will me away. Besides, I came all the way from Corpus just to see you."

Her shoulders slumped. "Great. Exactly what I needed today."

"I take it you've had a tough day."

"It just got worse," she muttered.

Miriam returned then, before Julia could bring herself to look at Adam. The young woman set the drink down, her gaze going to him, her expression surprised. He was quite striking, and since the bar wasn't crowded, there was no reason for him to be sitting beside Julia. She was dowdy and ordinary, not in high demand as a flirtation partner.

"Can I get you something?" Miriam asked.

"I'll take your top-shelf scotch, straight up."

Miriam nodded and left. Julia clutched her drink, considered slamming it down in one gulp.

"It would be nice if you would look at me." His rough voice washed through her like a nuclear shockwave.

She turned her head, glared into cool, midnight eyes. "What are you doing here, Adam?"

He stared back, calm, intelligent, as always, and—as she well knew—utterly ruthless. His ebony hair was short, meticulously combed back from his high forehead. His features were harsh, aristocratic, with the exception of a surprisingly sensual mouth. The black Italian suit was a perfect foil for his ultra-conservative and autocratic persona, while the single diamond glittering in his left ear seemed incongruous.

"I need your help, Julia."

This man had the ability to make her crazy, to evoke emotional responses that ran the gauntlet from sexually aroused to enraged. He threatened her on levels she didn't even want to acknowledge, especially after today's developments.

"And *I* need a new identity and a new life in another country," she retorted. "Sorry, but you'll have to find assistance for your woo-woo endeavors elsewhere. I'm currently occupied with other matters."

She took a gulp of her drink, almost choked as the burn spread down her throat. "And how did you know I was here anyway?" She returned her glare to him. "Playing stalker? Isn't that beneath you?"

"Ah, Julia, you're as blunt and entertaining as ever. I'm not stalking you, merely keeping track of you."

Tracking, stalking—basically the same thing. She'd already been there, done that, twelve years ago. "Listen psycho-Sentinel, what I do with my life and my time is none of your damned business. Go away and leave me alone."

His expression remained neutral. That was another thing she despised about him—his utter lack of emotional reaction. But then, he wasn't really human. "Actually, I'm a Sanctioned, as I have previously explained. And you *are* my business, Julia. I'm responsible for every Sentinel and conductor in Texas."

"News flash—I am *not* a conductor. Not in thought or deed. Already been there, done that. I helped you track down a crazed bomber and watched my sister get sliced up by that bastard. I'm done. And if I correctly understand the Sentinel code of honor, you can't force me to help you. So go back to your cave."

"I'm not leaving, Julia. Like I said, I need your help."

To hell with that. He could sit there all afternoon and watch her get soused, for all she cared. Miriam returned with Adam's drink and Julia took the opportunity to finish hers. "I'll take another."

"Not unless I'm driving you home," Adam said.

His arrogance upped her inner rage level. "The odds of that happening are about the same as solving Fermat's Last Theorem."

His ebony brows arched. "Hasn't that been done?" He sipped his scotch, his fingers around the glass long and elegant.

The man just had to be brilliant as well as annoying. "It's still being debated, and it's taken well over three hundred years to get this close. You are *so* not driving me home."

"Then we'll settle the tab," he told Miriam.

She hesitated, glanced to Julia for confirmation. Not a problem. There were hundreds of bars in the Houston area, and any that were sans Adam Masters would do for Julia's purposes. Better that she was closer to home, anyway. Then she could call a cab if she needed to.

She nodded at Miriam. "It's all right. Be sure you pad the total a few times over. He can afford it."

She fumbled for her cane, glad Adam had sat on her left side and hadn't thought to confiscate it. It was a good thing for him that using the cane to get as far away from him as possible was a higher priority than smacking his hard head with it. She slid off the bar stool, balancing her weight on her good leg, as Adam handed Miriam a fifty-dollar bill and told her to keep the change.

He moved to block Julia as she started toward the door. "We're not done here."

"We'll have to agree to disagree on that one." She started around him.

He didn't touch her—they both knew that often had undesirable repercussions. But his next words stopped her cold. "I know William Bennett will be released from Huntsville Prison in two days."

So did she; that cold, impersonal call earlier this afternoon had dropped the bombshell. And wasn't the Texas Department of Criminal Justice considerate to inform victims when their tormentors were let loose, not to mention its annoying habit of releasing violent prisoners simply because of overcrowding.

She swayed on her feet, pounded by an emotional barrage. *"I've been waiting for you, Julia." The man stepped from the kitchen of her home in Kingwood. He moved toward her, an ordinary looking man with a monster's soul. "Why did you disobey me, Julia?"* . . .

She was *not* going there. Yet it took a major effort to push back the memories, to pull together her scattered psyche and deal with Adam. She went for levity. "You really know how to make a girl feel safe and secure, you know that?"

His eyes were cold pools of black menace. "I *will* keep you safe. You can count on it."

From psycho-Sentinel to macho-Sentinel—make that macho-Sanctioned. She couldn't deal with any of those options right now. "It's not your problem." She turned and made her way out, cursing the fact her bad leg made her about as fast as a giant Galapagos tortoise on a slow day.

"The hell it isn't," he muttered.

Although he moved silently, she was acutely aware of him following her. Her entire body tingled, and she could feel the hairs on the back of her neck rising. He'd told her the reaction was caused by an electromagnetic current that formed between matched Sentinels and conductors and an ensuing sexual surge through the chakras. She'd told him that was a bunch of crap, with no scientific basis whatsoever. Even though she now knew better.

There was no denying the heart-pounding, visceral reaction she always had when he touched her. And when he'd kissed her at the Dallas/Ft. Worth airport . . . Surely her reactions had to be exacerbated by the fact that she'd been celibate for twelve years. Deprivation could do strange things to people.

So could desperation. As she reached her car and fumbled inside her purse for her keys, Adam was far too close for comfort. She didn't need this—didn't need his unsettling presence. Especially not after that cataclysmic phone call.

She didn't find her keys, but she did find the grip of her trusty Beretta Tomcat. Taking that as a stamp of approval from fate, she slid it out unobtrusively.

"Julia, we must talk," Adam said. "I have a situation that is extremely serious." Then he touched her, damn him, gripping her shoulder. She felt the sparks down to her toes.

"I have a better idea." She turned, shrugging free of his hand and sidling a few steps away, keeping the gun behind her. He started after her, but froze when she swung out the Beretta and aimed it at his chest.

"Back off, Adam." She clicked off the safety.

"Isn't that a little childish?" he asked, not appearing the least concerned.

Actually, it was probably incredibly stupid; she knew that with his thoughts alone he could control her body like it was a marionette. But she was beyond caring. She dropped the gun due south toward a crucial target. "Maybe I'll shoot lower."

Adam shrugged. "That's not much of a threat to a man who hasn't had sex in a few hundred years."

"*What?*" Startled, Julia found herself momentarily distracted. All the Sentinel men she'd met had been ultramasculine, overflowing with testosterone and machismo. Adam was so intense and so forceful, he certainly fit the mold.

Besides, if she wasn't mistaken, that was a sizable erection her gun was aimed at.

"Sure could have fooled me," she said.

"Yeah," he said dryly. "Me, too."